LONG
TIME
GONE

Also by J. A. Jance

J. A. Jance

WILLIAM MORROW

An Imprint of HarperCollinsPublishers

LONG TIME GONE

HarperCollins books may be purchased for educational, business, or sales promotional use. For information please write: Special Markets Department, HarperCollins Publishers, 10 East 53rd Street, New York, NY 10022.

FIRST EDITION

Designed by Cassandra J. Pappas

Printed on acid-free paper

Library of Congress Cataloging-in-Publication Data

Jance, Judith A.
    Long time gone / J. A. Jance.—1st ed.
      p. cm.
    ISBN 0-688-13824-1 (acid-free paper)
    1. Beaumont, J. P. (Fictitious character)—Fiction.   2. Police—Washington (State)—Seattle—Fiction.   3. Seattle (Wash.)—Fiction.   I. Title.

PS3560.A44L66 2005
813'.54—dc22   2004062811

05   06   07   08   09   WBC/RRD   10 9 8 7 6 5 4 3 2 1

To the General and his dedicated crew,
who made writing this book not only interesting but possible

PROLOGUE

BY STANDING ON the tips of her toes on a kitchen chair, five year-old Bonnie could just see out over the sill of the window in the tiny daylight basement apartment where she lived with her parents. The sun had finally burned through the low gray clouds, and now splashes of sunlight cast a crazy-quilt pattern across the rain-dampened grass of the yard and the cracked concrete of the crumbling sidewalk and driveway. Sunlit spring afternoons were rare in western Washington, and Bonnie longed to be outside, but she didn't dare, not with Mama and Daddy gone.

When they went away on those long Saturday afternoons, they'd tell her that she'd better stay inside and be good until they got home, or else . . . Bonnie knew what "or else" meant. If they found Bonnie had been outside while they were off drinking beer and smoking cigarettes, Daddy would take off his belt and light into her. Or Mama would go outside and cut a switch from the weeping willow tree and use that on Bonnie's bare legs or the thin, raggedy panties that covered her equally thin behind.

The outside door was unlocked. Bonnie could have gone up the stairs and let herself out if she had wanted to. She would have loved to run barefoot through the grass, chasing the butterflies that drifted in and out of Mimi's garden, or to play a solitary game of hopscotch on the smooth surface of her neighbor's driveway. But she didn't. No matter how well she tried to hide what she had done, Mama always seemed to know exactly when Bonnie was telling fibs.

So Bonnie stayed where she was, watching and waiting, sometimes shifting her weight from side to side and holding on to the windowsill to help keep her balance. Then something interesting happened. A big car came creeping up Mimi's driveway. Her driveway was far nicer than theirs. It was smooth and clean with no gaping cracks where grass and weeds and dandelions squeezed through.

The car stopped a few feet from Bonnie's window perch. It looked new and shiny, and it was red. Not fire-engine red, but a funny kind of red Bonnie had never seen before. She watched as a man got out, a big man wearing the kind of dress-up clothing Daddy never wore, not even on holy days when Mama made him go to church. The man slammed the car door shut. He hurried over to the steps and pounded on the back door. After a while, Bonnie's friend Mimi opened the door and stepped out onto the porch and stood with her back to the screen door.

During the week when Mimi went to work, she wore dresses and heels and had her hair pulled into a bun at the back of her neck. Today, though, her long dark hair was in a ponytail, which made her look much younger. She wore light green pedal pushers with a matching top along with white sandals. Even from where she stood, Bonnie could see the bright red polish that Mimi wore on her toenails. Mimi had even offered to paint Bonnie's toenails once, but Daddy had said, "No. Absolutely not." And Mama had said Bonnie was too young for nail polish. So all Bonnie could do was look at Mimi's brightly colored toes and wait to grow up.

Since Saturday was housecleaning day, Mimi wore a flowery full-length apron. As she talked to the man on her porch, Mimi crossed her arms under the bottom of the apron as though her arms were cold and covering them with the cloth of her apron might help warm them.

Bonnie couldn't hear any of the conversation, but from the bright red splotches of color on her friend's cheeks Bonnie knew that Mimi was angry. So was the man. He waved his arms. His face turned red. And every time he stopped talking, all Mimi did was shake her head. Whatever the man wanted, Mimi's answer was no.

One of the car doors opened and another woman stepped out. This one looked familiar. Bonnie thought she might have seen the woman before, coming to the house with a vase of flowers or maybe a covered dish for supper. Bonnie had seen Mimi's mother occasionally. The woman was old and sick. Sometimes she was in a wheelchair, but mostly she stayed in bed. Mimi worked in an office all day. The rest of the time she was at home taking care of her mother.

As the second woman walked toward the porch, she opened her purse, reached inside, and pulled something out. Only when the sun glinted off the blade did Bonnie realize it was a knife. That seemed odd. Most of the women Bonnie knew used their purses to carry lipstick and hankies and compacts and change purses. Never a knife.

Why a knife? What was going on?

The woman stepped up onto the porch beside the man. She looked angry, too. Bonnie wondered what was wrong. Why were those two people yelling at Mimi? Bonnie didn't have to hear the words to know they were saying mean and nasty things. At last Mimi turned and started to go inside. That's when the man reached out and grabbed her. Catching her by the arm, he pulled her off the back porch.

Bonnie watched in horror as Mimi fell all the way to the sidewalk, where she lay still for a moment, as though the force of the fall had knocked the wind out of her. Bonnie knew how that felt. The same thing had happened to her once when she had fallen out of the apple tree.

Then, instead of helping Mimi up, the man dropped on top of her, with his knee in her stomach. There was a brief struggle. The man seemed to be hitting her. The woman was standing in the way, so Bonnie couldn't see everything that happened. She wanted to scream out at him, "Stop! Stop! You're hurting her." But her voice froze in her throat. The words wouldn't come.

At last the woman reached down and helped the man up. The two of them stood there for a moment, looking down at Mimi. Even from where she was standing, Bonnie could see that the man's hands were bloody. So was his shirt. After a moment, the man and woman hurried into the house, closing the door behind them and leaving Mimi lying on the sidewalk.

For a time Bonnie didn't move. She didn't know what to do. She might have run upstairs and told their landlady, but Mrs. Ridder was a cranky old woman. Mama had made it clear that she didn't like children and that Bonnie was never, under any circumstances, to go upstairs and bother her. But still, Bonnie couldn't just stand there and do nothing. At last she jumped down from the chair, ran up the stairs, and hurried out the door.

If the afternoon sun was warm on her body, Bonnie didn't feel it. She raced across their driveway and the narrow strip of grass that separated her backyard from Mimi's. A few feet away, she stopped and stared in horror. There was blood—bright red blood—everywhere. Mimi's flowery apron was drenched in it. Blood spilled onto the cement driveway and pooled beneath her. The handle of a kitchen knife that looked just like Mama's stuck out of her stomach.

"Mimi," Bonnie gasped when she was finally able to speak. "Are you okay?"

Slowly Mimi turned her head and looked at Bonnie. Her eyes searched aimlessly. It was as though she were seeing Bonnie from a very long distance away and was having trouble finding where to look. Mimi opened her mouth and tried to speak, but at first no words came out.

"Please," Mimi began finally, but she couldn't go on. Her lips moved, but Bonnie couldn't hear what she was saying. The horrified child dropped to her knees, hoping to lean near enough to hear and to understand what was needed. Mimi reached out, but instead of taking Bonnie's hand, she pushed her away. "Go," she whispered urgently. "Please go!"

Just then the back door opened. The woman hurried out onto the porch. "Who the hell are you, you little shit?" she demanded, staring down at Bonnie. "What the hell are you doing here?"

Bonnie struggled to her feet and dodged backward just as the woman lunged toward her. Fortunately the woman's high-heeled shoe caught on the edge of the driveway and sank into the muddy grass. It was enough to allow Bonnie to scramble out of the way.

"You come back here!" the woman ordered.

But Bonnie saw the blood—Mimi's blood—on the woman's hands. Bonnie shook her head and kept backing up.

Just then Mimi made a strange, gurgling sound. The woman looked down at her briefly. Then she glanced at Mimi's back door and again at Bonnie, who was still backing across the yard as fast as her short little legs would carry her.

"You'd better get the hell out of here then," the woman snarled. "And if you say a word about this to anyone, he'll do the same thing to you, understand?"

At that, Bonnie turned and fled. She ran as fast as she could, past the door into the apartment and around to the back of the house, where she ducked into her favorite hiding place, a small passage between a crumbling toolshed and an overgrown hedge. She crouched there in the mud gasping for breath while her heart thumped wildly in her chest. She cried for a while, but then, afraid the man and woman might be looking for her and hear her sobs, she fell quiet and listened—for what seemed like a long, long time. At last she heard the sound of car doors slamming. Moments later, the big red car nosed slowly past the front of the house. Only then did Bonnie creep out of her hiding place.

She tiptoed around the end of the house, back to the side yards and to the place where she had seen Mimi lying in a pool of her own blood. Mimi was gone, and so was the blood. The sidewalk at the bottom of the porch was wet, as though someone had hosed it off.

For a few moments, Bonnie stood staring at Mimi's back door, wondering if Mimi was inside and if she was okay. But Bonnie didn't go up the steps and knock on the door. It was getting late. Her parents would be home soon. She didn't want them to find her outside.

She hurried back into the downstairs apartment. Once she was inside, she looked down and saw that her dress was splattered with mud and blood. Mimi's blood. If Mama saw that, she'd want to know how it got there. Next would come the switch or the belt. Bonnie was convinced that if she told anyone what had happened—even Mama and Daddy—she was sure the man who had hurt Mimi would find out about it and come looking for her.

So Bonnie took her dress off. She washed her hands and face and knees, and then she changed into a clean dress. She rolled up the ruined one as small as she could make it. She was standing in the kitchen looking for a place to hide it when she heard the sound of her parents' car pulling up outside. Desperate, she shoved the dress as far as she could into the space between the back of the refrigerator and the wall.

Seconds later, Mama and Daddy came in the door. They were laughing and smiling and having a good time. Daddy came over, picked Bonnie up, and swung her around the room.

"There you are," he said. "Have you been a good girl?"

"Yes, Daddy," she told him. "I've been a very good girl."

He put her back down on the floor and pulled a Tootsie Roll out of his shirt pocket. "That's for being good then," he said.

Tootsie Rolls were by far Bonnie's favorite candy. Instead of tearing the paper off and biting into it, she held the paper-wrapped candy in her hand and stared at it.

"What do you say?" Mama asked.

"Thank you," Bonnie murmured.

"Well," Daddy asked. "Are you going to eat it or not?"

So she did. Under her parents' watchful eyes, Bonnie unwrapped the candy and managed to choke down that Tootsie Roll. It was the last one she ever ate. From then on, the very idea of that soft, chewy chocolate reminded her of something that was too awful to think about or remember.

Over the years Bonnie forgot all about her friend Mimi lying there in the spreading pool of her own blood, but she never forgot that the very act of biting into a Tootsie Roll had the power to make her physically ill.

CHAPTER 1

ANYONE WHO IS dumb enough to live on one side of Lake Washington and work on the other is automatically doomed to spend lots of time stuck in bridge traffic. Such was the case one January morning as I headed for my job as an investigator for the Washington State Attorney's Special Homicide Investigation Team, known fondly to all of us who work there by that unfortunate moniker, the SHIT squad.

I live in Belltown Terrace, a condo at the upper end of Second Avenue in downtown Seattle. My office is sixteen miles away in a south Bellevue neighborhood called Eastgate. That morning's commute was hampered by two separate phenomena, both of which were related to a mid-January blast of arctic air that had come swooping down on western Washington from the Gulf of Alaska. The first traffic hazard was black ice, which had turned most of the minor side streets into skating rinks. Unfortunately, I'm a world-class procrastinator, and the winter weather had snuck up on me while my Porsche 928 was still decked out in summer-performance tires.

The other major traffic hazard was mountains—not driving over them, but seeing them. For nine months of the year, the mountains around Seattle are mostly invisible. Hidden by cloud cover, they sit there minding their own business, but when the "mountains are out," as we say around here, and Mount Rainier emerges in all its snow-clad splendor, trouble is bound to follow. Unwary drivers, entranced by the unaccustomed view, slam into the fenders of the cars in front of them, and traffic comes to a dead stop. The frigid air had left the snow-capped mountains vividly beautiful against a clear blue sky. As a result, I-90 was littered with pieces of scattered sheet metal, chrome-trim pieces, and speeding tow trucks.

Between ice- and gawker-related accidents, my normal twenty-minute commute had turned into an hour-long endurance test. Adding insult to injury was the fact that this was my first morning back at work after a weeklong stay in Hawaii.

You'll notice I said stay, not vacation, because it wasn't. I was there as father of the groom. Anyone who's been down that road knows it's no cakewalk.

The wedding had come up suddenly when Scott telephoned the day after Christmas to say that he and Cherisse were giving up their long-planned, no-holds-barred, late-summer extravaganza of a wedding in favor of a hastily arranged and low-key affair that would take place on a private beach near Waikiki the second week in January. As plans for the summer wedding had burgeoned out of control, I had been less than thrilled about the way things were going. A low-attendance affair that would consist of bride and groom, best people, and an assortment of parental units was much more to my liking.

I did wonder briefly if a misstep in birth-control planning had accounted for this sudden change in plans. That certainly had been the case when I had masterminded my daughter's hasty marriage to her husband, Jeremy. Now, several years and 1.6 kids later, Kelly and Jeremy were doing just fine, and I had no doubt Scott and Cherisse would do the same. So I rented a tux, booked my hotel room and plane tickets, and was on my way. I didn't find out that I was wrong about the unwed pregnancy bit until after I checked into my hotel room outside Honolulu.

I had just finished stowing my luggage when Dave Livingston stopped by my room to give me the real story.

Dave, by the way, is my first wife's second husband and her official widower. He's also Scott's stepfather and a hell of a nice guy. Right after Karen died, Dave and I both made an extra effort to get along—for the kids' sake. It may have been a phony act to begin with, but over time it's turned real enough. As far as parental units go, Dave and I are all Scott Beaumont has. Dave had flown in from L.A. the night before and had eaten dinner with Cherisse's folks, Helene and Pierre Madrigal, who had arrived on a flight from France the previous day.

There are a number of things I didn't learn about Dave Livingston until the occasion of Scott's wedding. For one thing, he speaks French. I have no idea why an accountant from Southern California would be, or would even need to be, fluent in French, but he was and is. In the course of that initial dinner he had sussed out that Pierre, age fifty-seven, had recently been diagnosed with a recurrence of prostate cancer. He and his wife had decided to postpone his next round of treatment until after the wedding. This bit of bad news no doubt accounted for the sudden change in wedding plans, and rightly so. In my opinion, postponing cancer treatment for any reason is never a good idea. Scott and Cherisse were obviously concerned that by summertime his condition might have deteriorated to the point where traveling to their wedding would be impossible.

And so I found myself in the middle of a wedding event that was complicated by a family health crisis and confounded by limited communication skills. Unlike Dave, I am *not* fluent in French. My daughter had thoughtfully sent along a French/English phrase book that she thought might be useful. Unfortunately the usual tourist-focused contents made zero mention of PSA counts or prostate difficulties, so I couldn't have talked to Pierre about his situation even if I had wanted.

Dave and Pierre got along famously. In the course of the next several days, the two of them carried on lively breakfast-time conversations in lightning-speed French in which they discussed bits of information both of them had gleaned from that morning's *Wall Street Journal,* so obviously Pierre's grasp of English was far better than he was willing to let on. Meanwhile, Helene and I sipped our respective cups of coffee and smiled sincerely but wordlessly back and forth across the table. Come to think of it, idiotically might be a better way of putting it. As far as I could tell, Helene's English was as nonexistent as my French.

Thinking the wedding would be a good excuse to use up some of my use-it-or-lose-it SHIT-squad vacation time, I had agreed to come to Hawaii five days before the actual wedding. That turned out to be a big mistake because I'm not much good at taking vacations. Never have been. It's one of the criticisms Karen used to level at me both before and after we divorced. And my shrink—the one Seattle PD sent me to see after my partner Sue Danielson was gunned down—told me pretty much the same thing.

"It's one of the main reasons so many retired cops end up blowing their brains out, Detective Beaumont," Dr. Katherine Majors had said during one of my departmentally decreed counseling sessions designed to fix cops whose partners have been killed in the line of duty. "They never manage to separate themselves from their jobs. Once they stop working, they lose their identity and, as a consequence, their whole reason for living."

Okay, so I admit Dr. Majors was probably dead-on as far as I'm concerned. No doubt that explains why I went looking for the attorney general's investigative job before the ink had finished drying on my letter of resignation from Seattle PD. It also explains why the five days leading up to the wedding were unbearable. Dave, the FOTB (father of the bride), and the best man all played golf. I don't play golf. They also went deep-sea fishing. I don't like boats—big or small—so fishing was out of the question. The MOTB (mother of the bride), Cherisse, and her maid of honor were up to their eyeballs in last-minute arrangements with flowers, dresses, hairdos, and other essential pre-wedding preparations. Those left me cold as well. So, as co-FOTG, I had spent the days leading up to the wedding enjoying the bikini-clad scenery on the beach but generally feeling like the proverbial fifth wheel.

The wedding itself was a lovely affair. We gathered on a moonlit beach with the sand around us studded with flickering tiki lamps. Cherisse was tall and slender and lovely in her long white dress. Scott was tall and handsome in his tux. They were perfect together. The ceremony was read first in English and then in French. Dave sniffled unabashedly into his hankie all the way through the ceremony. When it came time for the "till death do us part" part, Helene reached over and leaned against Pierre's shoulder. That small gesture was enough to put a lump in my throat. Nobody was talking about the elephant in the living room, but it was there as big as life.

"I just wish Karen could have been here to see it," Dave told me later on that night after the multicourse wedding supper. "She would have loved it."

We were at an outdoor hotel bar where Dave was drinking Scotch and I wasn't, and I knew he was right. Karen had loved weddings. God knows she dragged me to enough of them over the years.

Some people might think it odd to find the two forlorn men who had shared their lives with Karen Beaumont Livingston sitting together consoling each other. It sounds, in fact, like lyrics from some pathetic country-western song, but the truth is, we were both coming from the same place. When someone dies, other people have to learn to go on with their lives. Weddings happen and babies are born and even the joyful events hurt because the people who are gone aren't there to witness them.

Once the busy merry-go-round of wedding festivities ended and the kids went off to have fun with their best people, Dave and I had fallen to earth like a pair of balloons with all the helium let out. Dave was grieving for Karen and so was I, but I was thinking about my second wife's death as well. Losing Anne Corley on our wedding day had left me in an emotional black hole from which I had yet to fully emerge. So while Scott and Cherisse were looking hopefully toward what the future might hold and Helene and Pierre spent the long shank of the evening dreading the future, Dave and I were mired in the regretful past. Bearing that in mind, I think the four of us deserve a lot of collective credit for not having rained on the kids' parade.

Two days later, as I pulled into my assigned space in the SHIT squad's parking garage, that balmy evening's worth of quiet conversation seemed eons away—eons and more than fifty degrees.

Unit B, my unit, is the Special Homicide Investigation Team's Seattle area office. It consists of four investigators, our commander, Harry Ignatius Ball, who, for perverse reasons of his own, prefers to be called Harry I. Ball, and our office manager, Barbara Galvin. Unit C works out of Spokane. Everybody else works out of the attorney general's office down in Olympia. Unit B's newest investigator is Melissa Soames, an easygoing, forty-something, blue-eyed blonde who prefers to be called Mel. She and I ended up checking in at Barbara's desk at the same time.

"Looks like it's our lucky day," she said.

"Why's that?" I asked.

"Coming down from North Bend, Harry ended up on the wrong side of a twenty-car pileup east of Issaquah," she told me. "That means we won't be doing our morning briefing anytime soon. Hallelujah! So how was the wedding?"

"Fine," I said.

Barbara Galvin and Mel exchanged looks. Mel rolled her eyes. "Men!" she exclaimed, and stalked off to her office.

"What's wrong with fine?" I demanded.

"Never mind," Barbara said with a sigh. She handed me a stack of papers. "Here's some reading material to hold you until Harry shows up."

I took the pile of memos and updates and retreated into my office. In most buildings it would have been a cubicle. It wasn't much larger than a cubicle, but whoever used the building before we took it over had gone to the trouble of creating tiny separate offices with walls that went all the way from floor to ceiling, thus allowing all of us a bit more privacy than we would have had otherwise, and that's a good thing. It means that when I'm at my desk, I don't have to hear Barbara Galvin's phone calls to her son or her new country music. It also means I don't have to listen in on Mel's steady diet of twenty-four-hour talk radio.

Reading steadily and in reverse order, I was about to start on Wednesday's first memo when my phone rang. "Someone's here to see you," Barbara Galvin announced. "His name is Frederick MacKinzie. He says he doesn't have an appointment, but he's waiting downstairs for you to come sign him in."

Frederick MacKinzie. The name sounded familiar, but I couldn't place it. "Who would bother making an appointment to see me?" I returned. "I'll go get him."

I rode the elevator downstairs. The man waiting by the check-in desk was good-looking, medium build, about my age. He wore nice-fitting slacks, a brushed camel sports coat, and carried a leather brief-case. My first guess pinned him as an attorney.

I held out my hand. "J. P. Beaumont," I told him. I signed for him and handed him a visitor's pass. "I hope you're in a visitor's parking spot. Otherwise they tow within twenty minutes."

"I am," he said.

We stepped into the elevator. "Jonas Piedmont Beaumont," he said quietly, filling in the unwritten names indicated by my visible initials.

That one stopped me. Not many people know my full name. It's not something I announce in polite or impolite company. Surprise must have registered on my face.

"You don't remember me, do you?" he went on.

"No," I said apologetically. "Sorry, I don't believe I do."

The elevator stopped and we stepped into the corridor.

"That's all right," he said. "I've changed quite a bit since you saw me last. We went to school together—Ballard High School. I worked for the school paper and the yearbook. When you were on the basket-ball court, I was on the sidelines with a camera taking pictures for *The Talisman* and *The Shingle*."

And then it hit me. "My God!" I exclaimed. "Freddy Mac! I never would have recognized you in a million years. How the hell are you and what have you been up to?"

And it was true. The Frederick MacKinzie I had known in high school was a pudgy, pasty-faced kid, with thick glasses and a mop of unruly red hair. Now the hair was combed down and neatly styled. It was a far more muted red than I remembered, so it was possible that the new Fred was actually dipping in the dye. Freddy of old had been smart but anything but cool. This one had cool down pat.

I ushered him down the hall and offered him a seat in my tiny office.

"I haven't been up to much," he said. Reaching into his pocket, he pulled out a business card and handed it over. "Frederick W. MacKinzie," it said. "Hypnotherapist."

"Got married in college, got divorced three years later," he explained, answering my unasked question. "Then I went back to our tenth class reunion and ran into Debby Drysdale. Remember her?"

Debby I remembered. If Ballard High School had had an "It" girl, Debby Drysdale would have been a contender. She was cute and smart. Head of the cheerleading squad. Homecoming queen our sophomore year and prom queen when we were seniors. I couldn't imagine Debby Drysdale giving nerdy Freddy Mac the time of day. Once again, Fred must have read my mind.

"She was a bit out of my league in high school," he admitted ruefully. "In fact, I don't think we ever exchanged a single word."

"I thought she married Tom . . . What's his name again? I seem to remember he was a real jock."

"Gustavson," Fred supplied with a nod. "And yes, Tom was a jock—an all-state jock and a big-time jerk. Went off to college, got involved in drugs, and burned out his brain on LSD. Committed suicide the night of their eighth wedding anniversary."

"Nice guy," I said.

Fred nodded. "As I said, Deb and I met up again at our tenth class reunion. We were both single. She was looking for someone steady in her life, and I turned out to be the lucky guy. We've been married going on thirty years now. How about you?"

"Divorced once and widowed once," I told him. "Other than that I'm doing fine."

"Kids?" he asked.

"Two. Both married. One grandchild and another on the way."

"Deb and I never had any kids," Fred said with a shrug. "For a long time my whole life was my job—property development. Then, about eight years ago, I had a wake-up-call heart attack. The doc told me to change my life. Lose weight and lose my job or lose my life. So I went to see a hypnotherapist. He helped me so much that now I am one."

As Fred spoke, he opened his briefcase and pulled out a frayed copy of the Ballard High School yearbook, *The Shingle*. Please don't ask me why it's called that. I have no idea.

He opened the book to a page marked with a slip of paper. He passed the yearbook over to me, tapping one picture in particular with his finger. "Remember her?" he asked.

I looked down and saw the picture of a girl—a girl with downcast eyes hidden behind thick glasses, no smile, and a sorrowful expression on her face.

"Doesn't ring a bell," I said.

Fred closed the yearbook, returned it to the briefcase, and closed the lid. "I'm not surprised. Bonnie Jean Dunleavy was two years behind us when we were in school, but she's a friend of mine—a friend and a patient. She's also the reason I'm here."

Glancing first at the open door, Fred looked back at me. "Do you mind?" he asked. With that he reached over and pushed the door shut. "It's about a murder," he said. "One we believe happened many years ago. I'm hoping you can tell me whether or not it really happened. This is a new experience for me—uncovering a crime like this from someone's past—and I need to be really sure it's the truth and not some little kid's horrific fantasy."

"Look," I said, "I'm not a regular homicide detective anymore. I work for the Washington State Attorney General's office. I only work cases I'm told to work, and I doubt Ross Connors would look kindly on my going out and chasing after some cold-case homicide that may or may not have happened."

"It's all right," Fred assured me easily. "Somebody's already squared it with Ross Connors. I'm sure it'll be fine."

It sure as hell wasn't fine with me. Ross Connors, the Washington State attorney general, happens to be my boss. He's also a very political animal. The last thing I needed was to go messing around in a murder investigation that was connected to one of Ross's cronies or to some big-time political contributor. Either one had almost limitless potential for career suicide.

"Bonnie Jean was in town for a conference over the weekend," Fred continued. "She stayed over last night on the slim chance that I might be able to set up a meeting with you today. This morning, in fact," he added. "Whenever you can get away."

Talk about more nerve than a bad tooth! I was floored. Right about then I would have been happy for the return of the old pudgy Freddy Mac rather than his grown-up pushy and very cool counterpart.

"Hang on," I said. "I'll have to check with my boss."

I left Fred sitting there beside my desk and went in search of Harry I. Ball. I more than half hoped he was still stuck in traffic. No such luck. He was talking on the phone when I popped my head into his office. "What is it?" he demanded, covering the mouthpiece.

"I've got this guy in my office . . ."

"I know, I know," he grumbled. "The hypnotist guy. Word came down from on high about that. It's your case, now get the hell out and do whatever needs to be done." With that he waved me away.

I returned to my office with my worst-case-scenario suspicions fully confirmed. Whoever was pulling Ross Connors's string had influence out the kazoo.

CHAPTER 2

WHEN I RETURNED to my office, Fred let me know that my surprise luncheon meeting—a surprise to me anyway—was scheduled at
Equus, the upscale restaurant in downtown Bellevue's Hyatt Hotel.
To get there from my Eastgate office, I had two choices. Get on I-90
and I-405 or stay on surface streets. With the cross-lake freeway may-
hem still fresh in mind, I opted for the surface streets and that decision turned out to be on the money. I later learned that a garbage
truck had jackknifed at Southeast Eighth, blocking all northbound
lanes on 405.

I may not have known about the garbage truck at the time, but I
did notice that traffic on Bellevue Way was bumper-to-bumper and
slow as mud. It gave me plenty of time to anticipate my upcoming
meeting with Bonnie Jean Dunleavy. I had no doubt she would have
changed over the years every bit as much as Freddy Mac. I expected
that LASIK surgery would have corrected her vision problems and so
she would have ditched the glasses. And if she had hooked up with one
of the movers and shakers in state government, she'd probably be

wearing a size 3 dress and dripping in diamonds. I have a natural aversion to women like that.

I pulled into the Hyatt's entry drive and was glad to see it had been thoroughly sanded. I always worry when I hand over the keys to my 928 to a valet parking attendant. Anne Corley gave me my first Porsche, and I wouldn't have one now if it hadn't been for her. For the valet car jockeys it's just another high-powered car. For me the 928 is pretty much the only memento I have to remember Anne. I watched until my Guards' Red baby disappeared around the corner of the building, then I went inside.

Midmorning is an odd time to show up at hotel restaurants. Breakfast service is generally over. The waitstaff, setting up for lunch, can be less than hospitable. I looked around for Freddy. He had left my office a good ten minutes before I had, so I expected him to be there first. That wasn't the case. The restaurant's sole diner was a woman sitting near the fireplace in the far corner of the room. As I walked in her direction, she stood and beckoned me toward her.

One glance made it clear that Bonnie Jean Dunleavy was definitely no fashion plate. I had expected designer duds. Instead, she wore a plain white blouse and a simple gray skirt topped by a matching gray cardigan. Instead of killer high heels, she was comfortably shod in Birkenstocks and heavy black stockings. And she wasn't dripping in diamonds, either. Her only visible piece of jewelry was a gold crucifix that hung on a thin gold chain around her neck. She still wore glasses. The lenses were even thicker now than they had been in high school, but the once popular cat's-eye style had given way to a simple wire frame. What set her apart from the girl in Freddy Mac's yearbook was the expression on her face.

In high school Bonnie Jean Dunleavy had looked as though she carried the weight of the world on her shoulders. Her eyes had seemed haunted somehow. The corners of her lips had turned down. This woman was totally at ease with herself. She approached me with a relaxed smile, an air of breezy confidence, and a hand outstretched in greeting. Something had worried Bonnie Jean as a teenager, but it no longer seemed to trouble her as an adult.

"Hello, Mr. Beaumont," she said. "I don't believe we officially ever met back in high school. After all, you were a senior when I was a lowly sophomore, but I certainly remember seeing you back then, and I'd still know you anywhere. It's so good of you to come."

She led me back to the table. I glanced over my shoulder at the entrance. "Fred will be here eventually," she said. "He called a few minutes ago. He's stuck in some kind of traffic tie-up on the freeway. Can I get you something, coffee or tea? It's a little too early to order lunch."

"Coffee would be fine," I said.

She waved down a waiter and I ordered coffee. As soon as the waiter had left, she sat up straight, folded her hands on the edge of the table, and studied my face. "How much did Fred tell you?" she asked.

"Not much," I admitted, probably sounding as grumpy as I felt. I've never liked being jerked around like a puppet by the whim of some invisible puppeteer.

"Did he mention that I'm not Bonnie Jean Dunleavy anymore?"

"No," I said. "As a matter of fact, he didn't."

"That's all right," she said. "He made it clear that if you were going to know about any of this, it would have to come from me directly. He didn't want to run the risk of violating my privacy. My name is Sister Mary Katherine now. I joined a convent—the Order of Saint Benedict—right out of high school. Now I'm mother superior of a small convent over on Whidbey Island."

"He made no mention of that, either," I said.

"It's a long story," she said. "Are you sure you have time?"

I thought about Harry waving me out of his office. "I'm at your disposal," I told her.

"My folks married young. Daddy was eighteen and Mama was six-teen when they eloped. They left their disapproving families behind in Pennsylvania and came west. Neither of them had a high school diploma. In fact, I didn't realize until after my father died that he had never learned to read. With benefit of hindsight, I suppose he was dyslexic, but I doubt people knew much about dyslexia back then. My mother covered for him as best she could, but he moved from one me-nial job to another and finally ended up working as a mechanic. By the time I graduated from eighth grade, I must have attended twenty dif-ferent schools. That meant I was always behind academically, and the older I got, the further I fell behind."

"It must have been tough," I offered.

She nodded. "It was. Everybody thought I was stupid. Eventually I thought so, too. The summer before my freshman year, we were living in Seattle. My mother was working as a maid at one of the motels on Aurora, and my dad had a temporary summertime job working for a logging company over near Randle.

"I'm not sure how Mother did it, but somehow she wangled a scholarship for me to attend a weeklong CYO camp outside Leaven-worth. We'd never had enough money for me to go to camp before, and I was thrilled. My parents' fifteenth wedding anniversary was on Saturday while I was away at camp. My mother drove all the way to Randle by herself so she and my dad could celebrate. They planned to have a picnic lunch up on Mount Rainier, but they never made it. On their way there they were hit head-on by a runaway logging truck that came careening around a sharp curve. They both died instantly."

She told the story with only a trace of sadness, with the poise that comes from having adjusted to a long-ago tragedy, but hearing about the deaths of Bonnie Jean Dunleavy's parents certainly explained the sad expression that had been captured so clearly in her high school yearbook photo.

"Because I was away at camp, I had no idea what had happened. Mother and I, and occasionally my father, attended Christ the King Church up on Phinney Ridge. The priest there, Father Mark, had taken an interest in us, and he was the one who had made it possible for me to attend camp. When word of the accident reached him, Father Mark came all the way to Leavenworth to tell me what had happened and to bring me back home. Realizing no one would be there at our apartment to take care of me, Father Mark had one of the camp counselors, Maribeth Hogan, leave camp to come be with me. She was there through the funeral and stayed for the remainder of the summer. Not surprisingly, we've been friends ever since."

"You were lucky to have people like that in your life," I said.

"More than lucky," she replied. "As I said earlier, my parents came from Pennsylvania. They were pretty much estranged from both sides of their families. None of the relatives from back there bothered to come out for the funerals, but when the logging truck's brakes were found to be faulty and it looked like there would be a sizable insurance settlement, those very same relatives—my father's mother and my mother's two brothers—descended on Seattle like a swarm of locusts, all of them bent on going to court to be declared my legal guardian. Father Mark came to see me and asked if I wanted to live with any of those relatives. I told him I didn't even know them. The last thing I wanted to do was go all the way across the country to live in a strange place called Pittsburgh where I knew no one. Fortunately, Father Mark listened to me. I also think he suspected that my relatives were far more interested in laying hands on the insurance money than they were in looking after my welfare. He got in touch with Catholic Family Services. They placed me in a foster home in Ballard.

"Adelaide Rodgers, my foster mother, had entered a convent as a young woman but had been forced to drop out after only two years. Her mother had taken sick, and she'd had to go back home to help look after her younger brothers and sisters. These days you hear lots of horror stories about what goes on in foster homes, but Adelaide was wonderful. She was a loving, pious woman who went to Mass every Sunday and who lived her faith every single day. She believed in living frugally. She worked as a teller in a bank, but she sewed all her own clothing, and she taught me to do the same.

"Adelaide never used a dime of my insurance settlement. She said it was a nest egg for me to use when I was ready to go to college. She invested my money right along with her own. Over the years my nest egg grew to surprising proportions, and so did hers. Adelaide never officially adopted me. I don't think it was possible for single women to adopt in those days, but as far as she was concerned, I was her daughter. When she died a number of years ago, she left me a small fortune and a farm she had inherited up on Double Bluff Road on Whidbey Island. She left me the property and the money but with an important request. She asked that I use both the property and the money to found a convent in her mother's memory—which I did. It's called the Convent of Saint Benedict."

"Double Bluff Road. Isn't there a country club somewhere around there?" I asked. "I think I went there for a conference once."

Sister Mary Katherine—I had to teach myself to think of her as Sister Mary Katherine and not Bonnie Jean—smiled and nodded. "Useless Bay Country Club," she said. "They're neighbors of ours. We like to think of ourselves as the Useful Useless Bay Country Club."

A nun cracking jokes and referring to her convent as a country club? That came as a bit of a surprise. "How did you go from Ballard High School to Mother Superior?" I asked.

"As I said, because I changed schools so much, I was way behind academically by the time I reached high school. Even with Adelaide's nightly tutoring sessions, college prep courses were far beyond my abilities, but I was a star in Miss Breckenridge's home ec classes."

Miss Lola Breckenridge—I hadn't thought of her in years. Even now it seems ironic that the woman in charge of Ballard's home ec department had been an old maid. She was a tall, bony, yet imposing creature who dressed impeccably in designer-style fashions that she sewed herself. And she was tough. Boys who got crosswise with Miss Breckenridge in study hall or the cafeteria soon wished they hadn't. A word from her to some misbehaving boy's coach would have even star athletes benched for that week's game.

"Home ec was great. Because of what I had learned from Adelaide, I could sew circles around the other girls. Miss Breckenridge even let me come in before and after school to use the machines. Next to Adelaide, Miss Breckenridge was the best thing that ever happened to me. I may not have been able to make sense of algebra or geometry, but if I could sew well, I knew I'd be able to support myself."

"That's what my mother did," I put in. The admission surprised me. "She was a seamstress and a single mother. That's how she supported us the whole time I was growing up."

Sister Mary Katherine looked thoughtful. "That's interesting," she said.

Just then Freddy Mac came hurrying up to the table. "Sorry I'm so late," he said, taking a seat. "Traffic on the freeway was horrendous. By the time I realized there was an accident at Southeast Eighth, I couldn't get off. I had to wait it out. What have I missed?"

"Nothing much," Sister Mary Katherine said. "I've been filling Mr. Beaumont in on some of my background."

"Beau," I interjected.

She smiled. "And I was just getting to you, Fred," she added. "By the time I was a sophomore, Adelaide was worried that I was focusing all my energies on home ec. She wanted me to try my hand at something else. That's how I wound up following Fred here around while he tried to teach me how to be a photographer. Despite his very capable mentoring, I never made the grade in the photojournalism arena, but he and I became good friends. We still are."

The waitstaff, which had made itself scarce while there were just two of us, began hovering the moment the third member of our party showed up. They refilled coffee cups and took food orders. As soon as they disappeared once again, Sister Mary Katherine resumed her story.

"By the time I was a junior in high school, I knew I wanted to be a nun. With my sewing abilities, joining the Benedictine order was a natural."

That one stumped me, and Sister Mary Katherine must have realized it. "How much do you know about the Catholic Church?"

"What I don't know fills volumes," I told her.

"Traditionally Benedictine nuns serve the church by sewing—making altar cloths and vestments for priests. That's what we do up on Whidbey, too. Saint Benedict's is a small convent. Twelve nuns and two lay sisters. We sew and we pray. For much of the day and night we live in self-imposed silence so we can spend our time with our hearts and minds focused on God rather than chatting endlessly about the weather. And that brings me to why we're here."

I have to admit I had been wondering. Nothing in Sister Mary Katherine's story hinted at any wrongdoing, and she certainly didn't strike me as a potential murderess.

"We're supposed to maintain certain hours of silence," she continued. "About a year ago I broke the silence by waking up screaming in the middle of the night. As I said, Saint Benedict's is small. Having the mother superior roust everyone out of bed by screaming her head off was unsettling. I knew I'd had a nightmare, a terrible nightmare, but I couldn't remember any of it. I had no idea what the dream was about. Eventually everyone returned to their own rooms, and we all went back to sleep. A few weeks later it happened again—exactly the same way. It's gone on like that for months now. I started avoiding going to sleep at night because I was afraid of having the dream and disturbing everyone else, but having a sleep-deprived mother superior is almost as bad for a convent as having one who wakes everybody up screaming like a banshee.

"One of my younger nuns, Sister Therese, was a psychology major in college. She suggested that perhaps the reason I couldn't remember the dream was that it had its origins in some terribly traumatic event in my past. Whatever had happened was so horrific that I had suppressed it, but now it was attempting to surface again via the dream. Sister Therese also suggested that I consider using hypnosis. She thought that remembering what the dream was about might make it go away." Sister Mary Katherine looked at Fred, who beamed back at her. "Fortunately for me, I had a good friend who just happened to be a hypnotherapist."

Our food came then. Fred and I both tucked into steak sandwiches. Sister Mary Katherine had a Caesar salad, which made me wonder if it was possible Benedictine nuns were also semi-vegans.

"So you went to see him?" I asked.

"Not right away," she replied. "People tell me I'm stubborn, and I guess it's true. I assumed the nightmare had to have something to do with the deaths of my parents. Being orphaned at such a young age was pretty much the defining moment of my life. It seemed reasonable to me that if that's what it was, I could do what needed to be done on my own. If I thought about what happened to them long enough and hard enough—if I meditated and prayed about it—the nightmare would eventually reveal itself. But that didn't happen, and unfortunately the screaming didn't stop, either. Finally the sisters staged a small revolt. The entire convent signed a petition asking me to do something about it. And I did. Three weeks ago I came to Seattle and had my first official appointment with Fred. I think it worked because the trust I felt for him back in high school makes it easy for me to trust him now."

"And?" I asked.

Sister Mary Katherine put down her fork and peered at me through those thick lenses of hers. "The nightmare isn't about my parents," she said. "According to what I told Fred while I was under hypnosis, sometime when I was very young, I may have witnessed a murder."

A chill ran down my back. "You actually saw it happen?"

"I believe so, but we're not sure. Under hypnosis I seem to remember looking out through a window and seeing a man murder the woman who lived next door to me." She turned to Fred. "Did you bring the tapes?" she asked.

Nodding, Fred reached into his briefcase and pulled out three separate videotapes. "I often tape sessions so I can go back through them and look for things I might have missed the first time—facial expressions, nervous tics, that sort of thing," he explained. "In cases of repressed memories, I usually do several sessions. Bringing painful memories to the surface is a lot like peeling an onion. Often more substantial details are recalled with each subsequent session."

"When Fred told me about this, my first thought was that I'd made the whole thing up, that it was nothing but a childhood fantasy," Mary Katherine resumed. "If I had really seen such an awful thing—a man and a woman stabbing someone to death—how was it possible for me to have forgotten it completely?"

"Man and woman?" I repeated. "So there were two of them?"

"Yes. And the dead woman's name was Mimi."

"No last name?" I asked.

Sister Mary Katherine shook her head. "No, just Mimi."

I took my notebook out of my pocket and wrote down that one name: Mimi.

"Whereabouts did she live?"

"That's the thing. I have no idea," Mary Katherine answered. "We moved around so much when I was little that I really don't know, but I'm assuming it was somewhere here in Washington."

"It's still possible that you did make it up," I suggested mildly.

"Perhaps," Mary Katherine said, "but I don't think so. When Adelaide died and I was going through her things, I found several boxes with my name on them. They contained the few paltry belongings I brought with me when I came to live with Adelaide. Catholic Family Services had attached a complete inventory sheet. Inside one of the boxes, I found this."

Mary Katherine reached into a briefcase-size purse and extracted a slim book, which she passed over to me. It was a much-read volume of Watty Piper's classic children's book, *The Little Engine That Could*. That book had been a particular favorite of mine when I was a child. It was a story my mother read to me over and over, and this copy, with its tattered but familiar dust jacket, came from that same era.

"Look inside," Sister Mary Katherine said.

On the inside cover I found an inscription written in fading blue ink. "For Bonnie, Merry Christmas. Love, Mimi."

"I got rid of most of the rest of the things, but I kept the book and a few photos. I always wondered who Mimi was. I thought maybe she was some friend or relative of my parents. Clearly we had been close once, or she wouldn't have given me such an expensive gift. And I thought it was odd that I never heard from her after my parents died. As soon as Fred told me what I had said under hypnosis, I knew why. Mimi was dead long before my parents died. So I asked Fred to see if he could find any record of a woman named Mimi being stabbed to death. I wanted to know whether or not the people who did it were ever caught and punished. I felt I owed her that much."

I glanced at Fred. "Any luck?" I asked.

He shook his head. "I guess I'm better at being a hypnotherapist than I am at being a detective. That's your job, not mine."

"And how exactly did this particular case get to be my job?" I asked.

"That's my fault," Sister Mary Katherine said at once. "Fred was the one who knew you worked in that new investigative unit in the attorney general's office."

I made a mental note not to call us the SHIT squad in the good sister's presence.

"Before Father Mark retired from Christ the King, he had a young assistant priest named Father Andrew who moved up into the diocese office years ago. Father Andrew is now the new archbishop's right-hand man. He was a huge help to me personally when I was starting Saint Benedict's and needed to cut through mounds of red tape."

She stopped talking as if she had said enough, but I still didn't get it.

Obligingly, Freddy Mac clued me in. "Years ago, Father Andrew Carter and Ross Connors played football together at O'Dea High School."

Click. In that one sentence, my worst suspicions were confirmed. With those kinds of high-placed connections, this was indeed a case with almost unlimited potential for disaster. Bearing that in mind, I decided it was time to treat it that way. I hauled out my notebook and began asking questions and taking notes.

CHAPTER 3

By THE TIME I LEFT THE HYATT, it was early afternoon, but traffic was already a mess. Make that *still* a mess. Unit B has a conference room with a VCR, but when I called into the office to see if I could use it, Barbara told me the room was booked.

"All right then," I told her. "Tell Harry I need to spend the next several hours reviewing videotapes, and I'm going home to do it."

"Absolutely," Barbara said. "No sense sitting around the office waiting for rush hour."

Barbara Galvin is a good twenty-five years younger than I am, but that doesn't keep her from mother-henning anybody who gets near her, me included.

"And the DJ on KMPS just said it's going to get worse," she added. "They're expecting more black ice tonight and maybe even the *s*-word for tomorrow."

The *s*-word is wintertime Seattlespeak for snow. I'm sure the people who live in Buffalo, New York, and other places where it *really* snows would find it hilarious that two or three inches of white stuff can bring this whole region to a grinding halt, but that's the way it is. And if it's more than three inches? Then we can look forward to days of downed trees and power outages.

With that cheery prospect in mind, I headed back across Lake Washington. By three o'clock I was settled into my recliner with the first of Sister Mary Katherine's videos playing on the VCR. It was a lot like viewing tapes done in cop-shop interview rooms everywhere—only this was shot with higher-quality equipment, so it had better sound and better resolution.

When the first interview started, before Fred MacKinzie put Mary Katherine under, she sounded just as she had earlier that day at lunch. That first session was a fishing expedition as Fred carefully led her back through her years as a nun, through high school, her years with Adelaide Rodgers, and back to that fateful day at camp when she first learned of her parents' tragic deaths. I think Fred and Sister Mary Katherine both expected to find the answer to her mysterious recurring nightmare lurking in the details surrounding that accident, but her answers remained lucid and unforced, with no resistance to Fred's probing questions.

It was only then that Fred switched tacks. "Tell me," he said quietly, "about the first thing you remember."

"No!"

Her instantaneous and flat-out refusal brought Fred MacKinzie to full attention. It had the same galvanizing effect on me.

"Why not?" he asked.

"Because I don't want to."

I noticed a subtle sudden change in the mother superior's voice. It seemed younger somehow. Her words were now being delivered in the singsong staccato of a small child.

Fred remained smoothly reassuring. "How old are you?" he asked.

"I don't know."

"What's your name?"

"Bonnie Jean Dunleavy."

"Have you started school yet, Bonnie Jean?"

"I don't think so."

If she's not in school then, that makes her four or five years old, I wrote. *Either 1949 or '50.*

"What are you wearing?" Fred asked.

Homicide detectives do the same thing with suspects. They ask indirect questions, thus creating a fabric of story. If the suspect tells lies, those spur-of-the-moment fibs will fall apart later under more detailed questioning. Here Fred's indirect questions—ones that weren't related to the troubling memory itself—allowed Mary Katherine to answer. But even this cautious, roundabout approach caused visible agitation. During earlier questioning Mary Katherine's hands had rested at ease in her lap. Now, as Fred MacKinzie moved closer to dangerous territory, her hands moved fitfully about. Sometimes she tugged anxiously at the hem of her skirt or the sleeve of her sweater. Sometimes she covered her eyes as if shielding herself from something too awful to face.

"A sundress," she answered at last. This time she closed her eyes rather than shielding them. I wondered if shutting out her view of Freddy Mac's office made it possible for her to see the dress she had worn so long ago. "A bright blue sundress with yellow sunflowers on it."

I scribbled into my notebook: *Time of year is summer. Where?*

"What are you doing?" Fred asked.

"I'm standing on a chair by the sink, looking out the window."

"What are you looking for?"

"My parents' car."

"So they're not there with you?"

"No."

"Is anyone else there, a babysitter? A friend, perhaps?"

"No. I'm alone."

"Alone and looking out the window?"

"Yes."

"What do you see?"

Her eyes remained shut. "The sun is shining," she said slowly. "I want to go outside and play, but I can't."

"Why not?"

"Because Mama and Daddy won't let me. I have to stay inside and wait until they come home."

"Where are they?"

Sister Mary Katherine shrugged. "I don't know," she said. "Just out."

"What can you see through that window?"

"Grass. And two driveways, ours and hers."

"Whose driveway?" Freddy asked.

"I don't know." As Sister Mary Katherine delivered her answer, her body shifted uneasily in her chair. She squirmed in her seat like a little kid who has waited far too long to head for a rest room.

"Can you tell me your neighbor's name?" Fred asked.

"No. I can't talk about her at all." Slumping in the chair, Sister Mary Katherine seemed close to tears. "Don't you understand?" she pleaded. "I'm not allowed to talk about her. Ever. If I do, something bad will happen. Someone will hurt me."

I jotted down: *Who's going to hurt her?*

Fred was following the same track. "Who will hurt you, Bonnie Jean? Your father?"

"No, not my father!" she said forcefully.

Clearly the current line of questioning was so upsetting that Fred backed away from it for a time. "Tell me about your house," he suggested.

"It's an apartment in a basement. It's cold here even when the sun is shining."

"Who lives upstairs?"

"A lady who's old and sick. Mama looks after her, and she lets us stay here."

"Do you know the lady's name?"

"No, but I know she doesn't like kids. That's why I have to stay inside when Mama and Daddy are gone. So I don't bother her. She might make us move out."

"Tell me about her house," Fred said.

"It's old and big and it's made out of brick."

"So it's a nice house, then?"

"I guess."

"And are there other children living nearby?"

"I don't know."

So she's not in school yet. If she were, she'd know the other kids in the neighborhood.

"Your mama looks after the lady upstairs. What does your daddy do?"

"He works."

"What does he do?"

"I dunno."

"Does he dress up when he goes to work?"

"No. And he comes home all dirty. He has to shower before we can eat dinner."

"Let's go back to the window for a moment. What time of day is it?"

"Afternoon, I think."

"And if you could go outside, what would you do?"

"Watch ants or play jacks or hopscotch or hide in my secret hiding place."

"Where's that?"

35

"Around behind the shed."

"Who do you play jacks with?"

In answer, Mary Katherine twisted her hands and shook her head.

"The person you can't talk about?"

Mary Katherine nodded.

We're talking about a playmate then, I scribble into my notebook. *But she just said she didn't know any other children.*

"How old is this person you play jacks with?" Fred asked. "About the same age as you?"

Sister Mary Katherine shook her head.

"Older or younger?" Fred asked.

"Older."

"How much older?" Fred persisted.

I swear, the guy could have been a cop. Right down the line, he was asking the same questions I would have asked had I been there.

Mary Katherine shrugged. "I dunno."

There was a long silence after that, as though Fred himself wasn't quite sure where to turn next. Finally he said, "Bonnie Jean, do you ever play pretend?"

"Sometimes."

"What's your favorite game of pretend?"

"I pretend I'm a horse, running through the tall grass."

"Would you play a game of pretend with me right now?"

"I guess."

"Okay, so let's go back to that chair beside the window—the one you were standing on a little while ago."

Once again Sister Mary Katherine squirmed in her seat. "Please," she said. "Don't make me go back there."

"You won't," Fred assured her. "We'll pretend there's a camera instead of you standing on that chair. A movie camera. If the camera tells us what you see outside the window, the camera might get in trouble, but you won't. Do you think that would work?"

"I'm not sure."

"Let's try it. If it gets too scary, we'll stop, okay?"

"Okay."

"Tell me about the chair. You said you were standing on it. How does that work?"

"I pushed it up to the front of the sink."

"The kitchen sink?"

"Yes. And then I climbed up on it."

"The chair or the sink?"

"The chair. I had to lean across the sink to see out. I had to hold on to the windowsill to keep from falling."

"All right. Now we're going to put a camera up there in exactly the same spot where you were. You won't even have to be there. Okay?"

"Okay." Sister Mary Katherine's voice was little more than a whisper.

"Now you tell me. Is the camera in the same spot you were?"

"Yes."

"What does the camera see?"

"A car."

"Where?"

"Coming up the driveway."

"Your driveway?"

"No. Hers."

Need her to describe the car, I write. *Make, model, year.*

"What does the camera see next?"

"The car stops and a man gets out."

"A passenger or the driver?"

"Driver."

"Do you know this man? Is he someone you've seen before?"

Sister Mary Katherine shrugged. "Maybe," she said.

"What does he do?"

"He walks away from the car. He goes up to Mimi's back porch and knocks on the door."

Mimi! I jot down. *The name from the inscription in the book.*

"What happens then?"

"She comes to the door. The camera can't hear what the man's saying, but it can see that he's angry. He's yelling at her."

"And then?"

At that point, Sister Mary Katherine dissolved into frantic tears. "I can't," she said. "I don't want to see anymore. Don't make me watch. Please."

Dismayed and relieved, I listened as Fred MacKinzie walked Sister Mary Katherine away from the edge of Bonnie Jean Dunleavy's cliff of remembrance. He had been so close. I was frustrated that he hadn't gone ahead, but the exhaustion and strain on Mary Katherine's face when she emerged from the trance told me Fred had done the right thing. He'd managed to come up with a few nuggets of information. In situations like this, something is better than nothing.

"How are you feeling?" he asked Sister Mary Katherine.

"Okay," she said. "But tired, very tired. Did you learn anything?"

"Maybe," he said. "Do you remember someone named Mimi?"

"Not right off the bat. You think my nightmare may have something to do with a person named Mimi?"

Fred nodded.

"Did I mention her last name?"

"No."

Suddenly Mary Katherine's face brightened. "Wait a minute. Now I do remember. There was a Mimi in my life. She gave me a book once—as a Christmas gift when I was just a little girl. I still have it."

"Where is it?"

"On Whidbey. Why?"

"Let's take a look at it. Maybe there'll be a clue in it that will tell us where it came from."

"Are we going to look at the tape now? Maybe if we look at it, it'll trigger some additional memory for me."

"No," Fred said. "Not right now. The memories you're recalling under hypnosis seem to be totally devoid of contamination from the present. I think it's best to keep it that way. If you remember spontaneously, then that's another thing. It may mean that you're coming to terms with your hidden nightmare without the need of another hypnotic trance, but seeing the tape of our session might precipitate your remembering something before your mind is ready to process it. Does that make sense?"

Mary Katherine nodded. I had to agree, but not for the same reason. If the little girl had been an eyewitness to a murder, it was important to keep those memories separate from her present reality until we had mined them for all possible details.

"What do we do next?"

"We should schedule another session for next week," Fred said. "We need to give you time in between. Can you come back then?"

"If we're going to get to the bottom of this, I suppose I'll have to," Sister Mary Katherine said. "What day works best for you?"

Not interested in the appointment-making process, I punched "rewind" and prepared to watch the tape again. Before I could, however, the phone rang.

"Mr. Beaumont?"

I recognized the distinctive drawl that belonged to Jerome Grimes, Belltown Terrace's most recent doorman.

"It's me, Jerome. What can I do for you?"

"I got a guy down here by the name of Ron Peters. He's wondering if it's all right for him to come up and see you."

Belltown Terrace seems to run through doormen and resident managers with disturbing regularity. Had Jerome been a long-term employee, he might have remembered a time when Ron, his wife, Amy, and their three kids had all called Belltown Terrace home. I keep trying to tell the condo board that we need to pay our staff better so they'll stay on longer. So far that idea has gone over with all the grace of a pregnant pole-vaulter.

It takes a while for the building's elevators to climb twenty-five stories from the lobby to my penthouse condo. I wouldn't be living here or driving a Porsche if it hadn't been for Anne Corley. That's what makes it so tough. Her brief appearance in my life left me far better off financially and way worse off emotionally. I guess you could say Anne was, and is, both a blessing and a curse in my life.

I left the door to my unit open and went out into the hallway to wait for Ron to emerge from the elevator. Actually, I was a little surprised that he would drop by without calling first. Years ago a work-related accident left him a paraplegic. Getting himself in and out of his wheelchair and the chair in and out of his Camry isn't an easy task.

Eventually the elevator doors opened to reveal him sitting inside. As soon as I saw his face, I knew something was wrong.

"It's Rosemary," he said at once. "She's dead."

Rosemary was Ron's ex-wife. She had been gone from Ron's life long before I ever met him. One night while he was working the graveyard shift at Seattle PD, Rosemary had split the scene, taking their two young daughters, Tracy and Heather, along for the ride. The three of them had ended up living on some far-out, pot-growing commune in the wilds of eastern Oregon. With the help of Ralph Ames, my friend and attorney, Ron eventually managed to extricate the girls from their wayward mother's indifferent care, leaving her in a sort of drug-induced free fall. The last I remembered hearing about Rosemary Peters had been several years earlier. She had been headed into treatment and was trying to get her life in order.

"I'm so sorry, Ron," I said, and meant it. "What happened? Did she OD?"

Ron shook his head. "She was murdered," he said. "Somebody shot her." Grasping the wheels of his chair, he pushed away from the elevators and headed for my unit. I followed him inside and closed the door.

"When?" I asked, sounding like a newspaper reporter looking for those elusive four Ws. "Where?"

"Sometime over the weekend," he said. "Down in Tacoma. They found her body by the water yesterday. It took until today for them to identify her. Two Tacoma homicide detectives came by the office a little while ago to let me know. Oh, God, Beau. What the hell am I going to tell the girls?"

The girls. Heather and Tracy. They're fifteen and seventeen now, but whenever I hear their names without having them right there in front of me, I always picture them the way they were the first day I saw them. Once Ralph Ames had enlisted in Ron's custody battle, I watched from the sidelines while the attorney worked what I would later come to realize was his customary magic. First Ralph managed to convince a judge to grant Ron full custody of the two girls. Court order in hand, Ralph had flown down to Pendleton, Oregon, and personally retrieved Heather and Tracy from the commune where they had been living.

Ron and I were waiting at the airport when their flight landed at Sea-Tac. Ralph came off the Jetway leading Tracy with one hand and packing Heather on his other hip. I had first met Ralph when he showed up in Seattle as Anne's attorney, and he's the kind of guy you love to hate. No matter what, his trousers are always properly creased, his hair is always neatly in place, and his ties are usually spotless. Not that day, though. For the first and only time in my life I saw him looking frazzled and disheveled. Single-handedly looking after the girls had taken its toll on both him and his clothing. His expensive yellow tie was marred by a long dark dribble of chocolate, but with Heather nestled up under his chin, he seemed totally unconcerned about the unsightly, and no doubt permanent, stain.

Heather and Tracy wormed their way into my heart that day, just as they had into Ralph's. And that was permanent, too, all these years later.

"You just come straight out and tell them," I advised Ron. "They're sensible, smart girls. You and Amy have done a great job raising them. They'll be able to handle the news."

I sat down in the recliner so Ron and I would be on the same level. He looked totally distraught—more so than I would have expected given the fact that he and Rosemary had been divorced for the better part of fourteen years.

"Look," I said. "I know what it's like when an ex-spouse dies. I've been there, remember? Divorces are all about the bad times, but when somebody dies, the good times resurface. They come back to bite you in the butt when you least expect it."

"The divorce wasn't exactly over," Ron said bleakly.

"What do you mean?" I demanded. "Wasn't I the best man when you and Amy got married?"

"Rosemary was trying to regain custody," he answered. "Of Heather. Tracy's close enough to her eighteenth birthday that it's not really an issue for her, but Rosemary claimed that since I've had Heather all to myself for so long, she wanted some time with her as well."

"When did all this come about?" I asked. "The last I heard, Rosemary was just out of jail and was going into a drug-treatment facility. Was she clean and sober then?"

"That's all a matter of opinion," he replied. "Whenever she got involved in something, she always went overboard. While she was in treatment, she hooked up with this religious group, and she dove into that the same way she dove into drugs. It's called Bread of Life Mission. They operate soup kitchens for the down-and-out all over the country. Rosemary ended up managing one for them. It's down near the Tacoma Dome, corner of Fifth and Puyallup. She lived in an apartment over the storefront."

I thought of the nice home on Queen Anne Hill in which Ron and Amy Peters were raising their three children—Tracy, Heather, and Jared Beaumont Peters—a cute little guy who happens to be my namesake and who's already charming the socks off the little girls in his kindergarten class.

"Surely Rosemary didn't expect Heather to go live there, did she?" I demanded.

"As a matter of fact she did," Ron replied. "In a run-down building that backs up to the railroad tracks and with drug-using bums lined up outside day and night."

"Sounds like the perfect place to raise a precocious, headstrong teenager," I said. "If you want her to turn into a druggie, too, that is."

"That's exactly what I told Rosemary on Friday," Ron said. "And I told her I'd see her in hell first."

"Probably not the best choice of words," I said. "Especially in light of what's happened. What did she do?"

"Called her lawyer, evidently. He's the one who sicced the Tacoma cops on me. He told them I had threatened her. I didn't, Beau. I swear. It was strictly a figure of speech. Rosemary's been so big on hellfire and damnation lately that I thought I'd put the situation into terms she'd understand."

"So what happened?"

"Two Tacoma homicide dicks turned up at my office down at Internal Affairs about three this afternoon. They claimed they were coming to notify next of kin, but I wasn't born yesterday. I did that job long enough to know the drill. They notified me, all right. Then they asked as many questions as they thought they could get away with without having to read me my rights. You know where all this is going, don't you?" he asked.

Unfortunately I did. "Straight to the SHIT squad, right?"

Ron nodded. "I wanted to give you a heads-up, Beau. I owe you that much."

"Believe me, Ron. You don't owe me a thing."

"Thanks," he said. "I needed a place to vent. Now I'd best get home. I have to tell the girls what happened—before someone else does."

For some time after Ron left, I sat and wrestled with the uncomfortable knowledge that one of my best friends was about to come under the scrutiny of my colleagues at the Special Homicide Investigation Team.

A year earlier Tacoma's chief of police had run off the rails. He had used a gun to murder his estranged wife and had then taken his own life while their horrified young children observed the carnage from a few yards away. Subsequent investigations had revealed that for years Tacoma PD had either ignored or covered up reports of domestic violence at the chief's house. Had those reports been handled differently, a terrible family tragedy might well have been avoided. The city of Tacoma hasn't exactly stood up and accepted responsibility for the mishandling of the case, but I personally have no doubt the city's coffers will be greatly depleted by the wrongful death suit that's been filed on behalf of the dead woman's survivors.

Police-related domestic violence has long been one of law enforcement's dirty little secrets. When cops are involved in such incidents— as either perpetrator or victim—we tend to turn a blind eye. That had certainly been the case with my dead partner, Sue Danielson. She had gone to great lengths to conceal her former husband's violent nature and the recurring bouts of domestic violence that had preceded her divorce. I've often wondered what would have happened had she reported it. Would he still have managed to kill her? I don't know.

But when Sue died, she was just a cop—an ordinary foot soldier— and hardly anybody noticed. Besides, she was the victim, not the perp. When a police chief is the one pulling the trigger, though, everybody pays attention—even the state legislature. They got busy down in the state capitol and have been drafting a slew of new laws that will require uniform policies and procedures for reported cases of police-related domestic violence. And if one of those cases results in a fatality, it's automatically kicked upstairs to the attorney general's office, where his Special Homicide Investigation Team becomes the lead investigating agency.

Ron and I were close friends. That meant I wouldn't be one of the investigators working the case, but I'd still be part of the investigation. I'd be one of the witnesses my colleagues would be questioning, and the fact that Ron had come straight from the next-of-kin notification to talk to me wouldn't look good for either one of us.

Now instead of one disaster-bound case, I was dealing with two.

It was enough to make me wonder why I'd even bothered to come back home from Hawaii. Bored as I was, I should have known when I was well off and stayed there.

CHAPTER 4

FOR SOME STRANGE REASON, after that, my heart wasn't into ana-
lyzing Fred MacKinzie's taped interviews. Instead, I called Lars
Jenssen—my stepgrandfather and AA sponsor—at Queen Anne Gardens, the assisted-living facility where he and my grandmother, Beverly, have taken up residence.

"Hey, Lars," I said, once he'd adjusted his hearing aid so he could
talk on the phone. "It's Monday. Want me to come pick you up and
bring you down the hill for the meeting?"

On Monday nights Lars and I usually grab a bite to eat and then attend the AA meeting that's held at the old Rendezvous Restaurant on
Second Avenue. And since Lars no longer drives (he's ninety-three, so
that's a good thing!), I pick him up and drop him off. Lars has been sober
for so long that I'm not sure he actually needs to go to meetings anymore, but he gets a kick out of being the oldest guy there—in terms of
age rather than sobriety. As for Beverly? She let me know once that she
appreciates having him out from underfoot occasionally, too. That
way she can spend time hanging out with some of the other "girls."

But on this particular evening, Lars turned me down. "No," he said. "I t'ink I'll stay home tonight." His Norwegian accent tends to be thicker on the telephone than it is in person. "The missus isn't feeling too good. I need to stick around and keep an eye on her."

Beverly Piedmont Jenssen is a sprightly ninety-one. "Nothing serious, I hope," I said.

"Oh, no. She's yust a bit under the weather."

Lars, a retired fisherman, loves his fish—baked, deep-fried, grilled, sautéed, stewed, and chowdered. On Monday nights when he's out with me, we usually stop off at Ivar's for clams. I can take fish or leave it. And on this occasion, leave it is what I did, opting for Mexican food instead, something Lars won't eat.

Pulling on a leather jacket, I braved the weather and hoofed it up Second to Mama's Mexican Kitchen. The after-dinner meeting was short. Only about eight guys showed up, all of them regulars. The people in attendance were far more interested in talking about the weather than they were in the Big Book or the drunkalogue, and rightfully so. By the time we came back out onto the street, it was snowing. And sticking.

Back at Belltown Terrace, the night doorman was among the missing, so I buzzed myself into the building with the keypad. Then I went upstairs and turned on the gas log. I checked the phone for messages, hoping to hear how things were going for Ron at home. All evening long I had been wondering how Heather and Tracy had handled the disturbing news of their mother's murder, but my light wasn't blinking. There was no message from them, and none from Harry I. Ball, either.

I wondered briefly if I should call Harry at home and tell him what had happened, but I got over it. Harry would find out about the case through regular channels soon enough.

You're better off letting the wheels of bureaucracy grind away at their own pace on this one, I told myself. *No sense borrowing trouble.*

And trouble was coming. As soon as news of Rosemary Peters's death hit the media, I'd be in it up to my eyeballs. For one thing, the fact that Ron and I were former partners was a long-established fact. Unearthing our friendship wouldn't be difficult for anybody. I hated to think what someone like Maxwell Cole, an old fraternity brother and my longtime nemesis, who was a columnist down at the *Seattle Post-Intelligencer*, would make of the fact that Ron had stopped by my condo to tell me about his former wife's death before he went home to tell his two daughters. With a little imagination combined with journalistic license, Max would probably turn that visit, along with my presence on the Special Homicide Investigation Team, into the second coming of *Conspiracy Theory*.

After a several-hours-long hiatus, I forced myself to return to the VCR. I watched all three of the Sister Mary Katherine tapes in order. Carefully, in a nonthreatening fashion, Fred encouraged her to delve more deeply into the forgotten memories of that awful day that had clearly become pivotal in Bonnie Jean Dunleavy's childhood. It was a fascinating and eerie process. By the time the third tape ended, I felt as though I had been standing on the kitchen chair beside that traumatized and frightened little girl as she witnessed a vicious stabbing and murder. If I hadn't been convinced beforehand, the clincher would have come during that last tape when Bonnie Jean revealed that when she had returned from her hiding place, she had discovered the body was gone and the blood washed away.

With my notebook open and a pencil handy, I went through the tapes again, jotting down questions and comments as I watched.

How much hand-eye coordination does it take to play jacks or hopscotch? BJ has to be five or maybe six. Doubt kids younger than that could do either. So we're talking about 1950 or, at the very latest, 1951.

She's evidently not in school. It could be because it's summertime (sunny) or that she isn't going to school yet. If they were living in Washington State, when did schools around here start offering half-day kindergarten? Need to check school records to see if I can find her listed.

Need to take a look at the photos she still has, the ones in the boxes her foster mother kept for her.

Need details about the perpetrators' vehicle. What make and model?

Need to check old DMV and driver's license records for possible addresses on her parents.

What happened after the murder? There must have been an investigation. Did detectives ever take a statement from Bonnie Jean? If not, why not?

It was interesting to realize that I was treating this as an unsolved case simply because it was unresolved from Sister Mary Katherine's point of view. More than half a century had passed since the murder. It was likely that the two people responsible for Mimi's death had long since been brought to justice. Hopefully they had paid for their vicious crime either through execution or by serving long prison stays. Verification of that would, I hoped, put a stop to Sister Mary Katherine's haunting nightmares. And, with any kind of luck, it would also short-circuit my own potential problem with the attorney general and the archbishop's right-hand man.

I was so involved in watching the videos and taking notes that I completely lost track of time. Since my body was still functioning on Honolulu time, I was astonished to realize it was close to midnight. I was on my way to bed when the phone rang. I picked up, expecting the caller to be Ron Peters. Instead, it was his daughter Tracy.

"Uncle Beau?" she asked. "I'm downstairs. Can I come up?"

I buzzed her into the building. Despite the long elevator ride, when she greeted me, her light brown hair and her purple-and-gold Franklin High School jogging suit were both dotted with not quite melted snowflakes. Her eyes were bright and her cheeks flushed.

"Tracy!" I exclaimed. "Come in. What on earth are you doing here?"

Overheated and still out of breath, she stripped off the damp jacket and dropped cross-legged onto the window seat. "You heard what happened?" she asked.

"Your dad stopped by and told me on his way home," I said. "I'm sorry, Tracy, so very sorry."

"I'm not," she returned hotly. "Sorry, I mean. She never was much of a mother."

By any standard, this was an unarguably true statement. Still, it was a hurtful admission for a teenager to have to make, and there were tears in Tracy's eyes as she said it.

"Your mother was a troubled woman," I countered, trying to make the poor girl feel better. "I'm sure she did the best she could."

"Her best was pretty damned lame."

While Tracy leaned back against the window, I hovered uncertainly near the front door. Now the hurt and anger in Tracy's voice prodded me into action. "Can I get you something?" I asked. "A soda, maybe, or hot chocolate?"

"Hot chocolate would be nice. I remember how, when we were kids and came upstairs to visit, you always had marshmallows to put in our hot chocolate. Big ones, too. Not those puny little ones that taste like cardboard."

"I remember all right," I said. "But no marshmallows today. Sorry. When you and Heather stopped dropping by on a regular basis, that last bag of marshmallows turned to solid rock. If I had known you were coming . . ."

A few minutes later, when I returned from the kitchen, Tracy was staring outside at the falling snow. It was coming down steadily—the flakes as big as feathers whirling in the city lights. I handed her a mug of hot chocolate and then sat down beside her.

"Do your folks know you're here?"

"No."

"How did you get out without their knowing about it?" I asked.

"Through a door in the furnace room," she answered. Tracy glanced up at me through lowered eyelashes. Catching what must have been a clear flash of disapproval on my face, she bristled. "Heather's always sneaking in and out that way and getting away with it. Why shouldn't I? After all, I'm older than she is."

Sneaking in and out of the house hadn't been part of my teenage years. I doubt it was for many kids back then. For one thing, my mother would have killed me. But things are different now. My own kids had straightened me out on that score while they were still in junior high.

"Heather sneaks out, too?" I asked.

"All the time," she answered. "To see Dillon."

"Who's he?"

"Her boyfriend—Dillon. He's a jerk. Mom and Dad don't like him either. Since they won't let her hang out with him, he comes by when they're at work, or else she sneaks out to see him late at night, after they're asleep."

I wondered if Tracy was telling me this with the expectation that I wouldn't tell her father. Or was she hoping I would?

"You said you needed to talk," I told her. "What about?"

Suddenly Tracy's tears began to flow. "Why did Rosemary have to try to get custody of Heather?" Tracy wailed. "Heather didn't want to go. Why would she? Her friends are here. If she'd had to go live in Tacoma, she wouldn't have known anybody. It would have been awful for her. Why did she have to go and spoil everything?"

I was struck as much by Tracy's blaming the victim as I was to hear her referring to her biological mother by her first name, rather than calling her "Mother" or "Mom." I certainly shared Tracy's sentiments about Heather's being plucked out of her comfortable home and settled situation in the Seattle school district in order to be dragged off to the wilds of Tacoma, but since it was now clear that Heather wouldn't be making that move, how could everything be spoiled? Besides, with Rosemary Peters dead, I somehow felt obliged to defend the poor woman.

"I've never been a mother," I told Tracy, "so I certainly don't know everything that went on in Rosemary Peters's life. I've been a father, though. I'll be the first to admit that when my kids were little, I wasn't much of a dad. I had a lot of the same difficulties your mother had."

Tracy looked at me. "You did drugs?" she asked.

"My drug of choice was alcohol," I told her. "I was into booze bigtime. For years after Karen and I got divorced and while I was still drinking, Scott and Kelly didn't have much to do with me. I don't blame them. And you shouldn't blame your mother either. Once she ditched the drugs, she probably realized what she had been missing all those years and simply wanted to reestablish a relationship with you two girls. It's understandable that she'd like to get to know her daughters again. She was hoping to make up for lost time."

My answer didn't have much of a beneficial effect. Tracy turned away from me and stared out the window, saying nothing.

"Look," I said. "What's happened to your family is terrible. Your mother was never a responsible parent, and that's too bad—for you and, even more so, for her. But having even a bad parent murdered is an incredible tragedy. It's not something that goes away. It stays with you forever. When something like this happens, it comes completely out of the blue. It's so unexpected that it hits you in all kinds of ways. Many of these reactions won't make sense. Your mother essentially abandoned you to drugs, so maybe you think you shouldn't feel anything right now, but you're hurting anyway. And part of you is mad as hell at your mother for dying. That's a standard reaction, too. It's like she's abandoned you all over again. That's how grief works, Tracy. You're alive and she's dead. You're operating in a storm of warring emotions. Anger is only one of them."

Tracy took a ragged breath. "I'm scared, too," she whispered.

"Scared of what?" I asked. "That the same thing will happen to you? That your mother's killer will come looking for you?"

"No," Tracy said, shaking her head. "I'm scared he did it."

"He who?"

"I'm scared my dad did it, Uncle Beau. I'm afraid he's the one who killed her."

There it was, out on the table. The admission was shocking enough to take my breath away.

"That's crazy!" I exclaimed. "Why on earth would you even think such a thing?"

"You don't know what Dad's been like lately," she said. "It's been like living with a stranger. And you should have seen what happened the other night when that poor guy served the papers about the hearing."

"What night?"

"Friday. At dinnertime. It was like Dad went crazy or something. I've never seen him act that way. And then there's whatever's going on with him and Mom," Tracy added. "They don't even sleep in the same bedroom anymore. I'm afraid they're going to get a divorce."

I had been best man at Ron and Amy's wedding. For years, while they rented a unit here in Belltown Terrace, Ron, Amy, and the girls had paraded in and out of my place with easy familiarity. I had known about the little comings and goings in their lives, their tragedies and triumphs. I had heard about soccer games and Girl Scout cookies and bandaged knees and fingers. Once they had moved into Amy's folks' old place up on Queen Anne Hill, a lot of that close, day-to-day inter-action had fallen by the wayside. Still, hearing from Tracy that Ron and Amy's marriage might be in trouble gave me another shock. Ron certainly hadn't hinted anything about marital difficulties when he had stopped by earlier.

So I did the first thing people do under those circumstances—I hit the denial button.

"It probably just seems that way to you," I said. "Maybe things aren't as bad as you think they are."

"They are, too," Tracy sobbed. "Amy's the only real mother I've ever known. What if Dad goes to jail and Amy divorces him? What then? She'll keep Jared, but what about Heather and me? What'll hap-pen to us? Our whole family will be wiped out."

While I was doing denial, Tracy was busy conjuring up every worst-case scenario in the book. If my SHIT squad colleagues were going to be asking me questions about Ron Peters tomorrow morning, this was information I would have been far better off not knowing, but I couldn't ask Tracy to stop talking. She needed somebody to listen to her right then, and J. P. Beaumont was the only guy who was handy.

"I had no idea things were this bad," I said quietly.

"And it's all because of *her*!" Tracy said forcefully. "It's been getting worse ever since she came to live with us."

Teenagers aren't long on using proper pronoun references, and her statement confused me. "Who's living with you?" I asked.

"Amy's sister," Tracy said. "Aunt Molly."

I had met Amy's prickly older sister, Molly Wright, on only one occasion. What little I knew about her came more from published news stories rather than anything Ron and Amy had told me. Molly's now former husband, Aaron, had been a high-flying dot-com millionaire CFO before the dot-coms all became dot-gones. Molly and Aaron had been an integral part of the local society scene, with their pictures prominently featured in the press coverage of various high-profile charitable events. When the dot-coms disappeared, lots of people lost jobs and money. Aaron lost both, and his freedom as well. In the subsequent financial meltdown, someone discovered that he'd been cooking the company books. What ultimately got him locked away in a federal prison cell was tax evasion.

"I had no idea Molly was living with you," I said.

"Well, she has been," Tracy said, "for months now. And she's like, well . . . she's not a very nice person. She's always picking away at Dad behind his back and causing trouble."

My one personal interaction with Molly Wright had been at Ron and Amy's wedding. Had it been up to me, I would have upgraded Molly from Tracy's tame "not nice" to a J. P. Beaumont eighteen-carat bitch. If Molly had installed herself under Ron Peters's roof, I could see how the man might be feeling a little stressed out.

But Tracy hadn't come jogging down Queen Anne Hill in what was now a full-scale blizzard to cry on my shoulder about her evil stepauntie. She had come to talk about her father. In light of the fact that SHIT was going to be investigating the case, I knew I should stay out of it, but Ron Peters is a friend of mine—my best friend. I couldn't leave it alone.

"Tell me about your dad, Tracy," I said. "What was going on between him and . . ."

I paused, uncertain of how I should refer to the dead woman.

Tracy stepped into the breach. "Rosemary?"

"Yes."

Tracy shrugged and put down her empty mug. "I guess she started talking about the custody thing a few months ago, saying she wanted us to come live with her. I turn eighteen in just a couple of months, so I wasn't worried about it, but Heather was. She turns sixteen in three months. It would mean changing schools just before her junior year, and that sucks. Dad asked Heather what she wanted to do. She said she'd run away from home before she'd go live in Tacoma, or else she'd do something drastic, whatever that means. Dad said fine, that he'd talk to Rosemary and tell her the answer was no. And he did, but then, last Friday, when we were having dinner, there was a knock on the door, which Jared opened. This guy comes in and serves Dad with papers because Rosemary isn't taking no for an answer. She's decided to take him to court."

"What happened then?" I asked.

Tracy sighed. "Like I said, Dad went nuts. Friday is pizza night at our house. When the guy left, Dad picked up a pizza box and Frisbeed it at the door. Pieces of pizza went everywhere. I've seen Dad angry sometimes, whenever Heather and I did something bad, but I've never seen him act like that. It scared me, and it scared Mom, too. I know because I heard her talking about it with Molly later, after Dad was gone.

"Anyway, after he threw the box, he turned and wheeled himself out of the room. We all followed Dad out to the carport. Mom asked him where he thought he was going. He said Tacoma. He said he was going to talk to Rosemary and set her straight about a few things. Mom kept trying to talk him out of it, but he wouldn't listen. He just got in the car and drove away like he hadn't heard a word she said. She was crying when he left."

"How long was he gone?"

Tracy paused before speaking. "A long time," she answered finally. "Mom was upset, so I took Jared into the family room to watch *Finding Nemo*. I thought I heard Dad come home while we were still watching the movie, but I must have been mistaken. Jared and I both fell asleep on the couch. I woke up around two. I put Jared to bed in his room, and then I went to bed, too. My bedroom is right over the driveway. I had just gotten into bed and turned out the lights when I heard Dad's car."

I thought about that for a minute. "Your father said he talked to two Tacoma detectives this afternoon. Did he give you any details about how Rosemary died?"

Tracy shook her head. "It happened over the weekend. Some guy out walking his dog found her body by the water yesterday afternoon. They can't tell exactly how long she's been dead because of the cold."

I nodded. Extreme cold weather delays some of the tissue changes medical examiners rely on in approximating time of death.

Exhausted, Tracy closed her eyes. Once again she leaned back against the cold window, as though she no longer had the energy to sit up on her own. She had come to me looking for a place to unload her worst nightmare—her suspicion that her beloved father had murdered her biological mother. I understood the kind of emotional barriers that had stood in the way of her doing that.

When a loved one turns homicide suspect, family members are usually the last to tumble to the idea that their husband or son or daughter or wife could possibly be guilty of such a heinous crime. Some, no matter how convincing the evidence, never do accept a family member's guilt. The fact that Tracy had reached such a damning conclusion so early in the process was something I couldn't ignore. The guys from my office wouldn't ignore it either. No wonder Tracy was worried. So was I. Tracy was focused on her father's angry outburst with the pizza box. I was concerned about how much Ron *hadn't* mentioned when he stopped by to tell me about Rosemary's death.

"I'm sure everything will be fine," I told Tracy, trying to sound more reassuring than I felt. "No doubt your father has some perfectly reasonable explanation for where he went and what he was doing so late on Friday evening."

Tracy looked at me pleadingly. "Do you really think so, Uncle Beau?" she asked. "Or are you just saying that to make me feel better?"

For an instant a terrible thought crossed my mind. Was Tracy as innocent as she seemed, or was her trip to see me a preemptive strike designed to point suspicion in her father's direction and away from her? The thought was there, but looking into her guileless blue eyes, I banished it as quickly as it came.

"Would you believe a little of both?" I asked.

She gave me a faint smile. "I'd believe it," she said. Unfolding her legs, Tracy reached for her jacket. "I'd better be going," she said.

I glanced outside. Far below, streetlights and headlights glowed in golden halos through the falling snow. I looked down at the stoplight at First and Broad. While I watched, a vehicle stopped on the steep incline west of First began to slip backward. The first vehicle slid until it bashed into a second one that had been coming up the street behind it. The second car spun like a slow-motion top before ending up sitting astraddle the opposite lane. Just then a westbound car came through the green light. The driver slammed on his brakes and then skidded down the hill until he T-boned the passenger side of the second vehicle.

There's nothing like Seattle in the snow. It can be an incredibly entertaining spectator sport as long as you're not out in it.

"No," I declared, turning away from the window. "You're not going

anywhere in this weather. You can sleep in the spare room. We'll figure out how to get you home in the morning."

"But what about . . . ?"

"Your parents?" I asked.

Tracy nodded.

"I'll call and let them know you're here. I'll tell them you came by
because you were upset about Rosemary's death and needed to talk."

"They're still going to be pissed at me," she said.

"No, I don't think so," I told her. "They have so much on their
plates right now, I doubt they'll even notice."

I gave Tracy one of my T-shirts to sleep in and a robe to wear. After
she headed for bed, I called her house. No answer. That wasn't a big
surprise. It was late. Knowing what Ron and Amy were going
through, I should have expected they'd turn off their phone. I left a
message saying Tracy was with me and that I'd bring her home in the
morning. I hit the sack then, too, but I didn't sleep.

Ron Peters's marriage was in trouble and he had been having serious difficulties with his ex-wife. I knew nothing about any of it, and
yet I was supposedly his best friend. So what kind of friend did that
make me?

Not so hot, I concluded. *And not nearly as good a friend as I thought I was.*

CHAPTER 5

I AWAKENED THE NEXT MORNING to the unwelcome news that there were five to seven inches of snow in the Denny Regrade area of downtown Seattle where I live, with more than twice that on the Eastside and at higher elevations. What followed was a droning recitation of school closures. Many offices and businesses were suggesting that unessential workers stay home.

Which am I? I wondered. *Essential or not?*

Scrambling out of bed, I pulled on some clothing and then went to make coffee. I stood in the kitchen and looked out onto a beautiful winter wonderland where the streets were practically deserted. With the exception of a chained-up bus or two and a couple of speeding SUVs, no one else seemed to be out and about.

When the phone rang I knew it would be Ron, and I was right. "What the hell was Tracy thinking, taking off like that in the middle of the night? Where is she?"

"In the other room and still asleep, if the phone didn't wake her, that is," I said.

"Wake her up," Ron told me. "I want to talk to her."

"I told her you wouldn't be mad."

"Well, you were wrong," he grumbled. "I am mad. With everything else going to hell around here, the last thing I needed was for her to go AWOL."

"She was scared," I said.

"Of what?"

"She's afraid you did it."

"Did what?"

"She's afraid you're responsible for Rosemary's death."

This stopped Ron cold. "Tracy thinks I killed her mother?" he asked after a long pause.

"Evidently," I responded.

It was one thing for homicide detectives from Tacoma to hint around that they suspected Ron Peters of being a killer. Ron already understood that, as far as the investigation was concerned, he, as the ex-husband, was bound to be a prime suspect. I understood that, too. It was quite another thing for him to realize that his own daughter was drawing that same conclusion. The realization did nothing to improve Ron's frame of mind.

"Let her sleep then," he said finally. "She isn't going to school today anyway, but when she wakes up, tell her from me that since she got herself down to your place, she can jolly well get herself home."

"That's not going to work," I said. "The snow accumulation wasn't that bad when she got here, but she showed up dressed in a jogging suit and tennis shoes. She can't walk home in that outfit in several inches of snow. I'd be glad to give her a ride, but I put off changing to winter tires too long, which makes my 928 pretty much worthless for driving in snow."

"Okay," Ron said. "I guess you'd better wake Tracy up after all.

Amy's outside now, putting chains on the Volvo. I'll ask her to stop by your place before she goes to work."

"You're not going in today?" I asked.

"As of yesterday I'm on bereavement leave," he answered. His tone was grim.

We both knew that would change. If and when Ron became an acknowledged suspect in the homicide investigation, bereavement leave would become a thing of the past. Paid administrative leave would be more like it—if he was lucky. Unpaid if he wasn't.

"And it's just as well," he added. "I guess I need to start planning Rosemary's funeral. She's been estranged from her family for years, so there's nobody else to do it. But with no way of knowing when the body will be released . . . Wait a sec. There's another call coming in. Gotta go."

Expecting to waken Tracy, I ventured as far as the guest-room door. Before I could knock, I heard a toilet flush and the shower come on. With my houseguest already up and about, I returned to the kitchen and poured another cup of coffee.

The showers in my condo are equipped with demand heaters, which means you can shower until hell freezes over without ever running out of hot water. Tracy, being a typical teenager, was nonetheless prepared to try exhausting the inexhaustible supply of hot water. The shower was still running sometime later when the phone rang again. This time Amy Peters was calling from the security phone on the first level of the parking garage.

"Tracy's still in the shower," I told her.

"That's okay," she returned. "I wanted to talk to you. Can I come up for a minute?"

"Sure," I said and buzzed her into the elevator lobby.

After a car accident had left Ron Peters paralyzed from the waist down, he was pretty much lying in a bed of pain and wallowing in self-pity until Amy Fitzgerald walked into his hospital room and into his life. She was there to do physical therapy, but it turned out she performed mental therapy as well.

In the years I had known her, I had never seen Amy Peters upset. She has always struck me as someone with a permanently positive attitude, and she's mostly unflappable. When she stepped off the elevator that morning, though, I could see she was flapped. Clearly she'd been crying, and she wasn't over it yet. Was it possible she was this upset over Rosemary's death?

No, I reasoned silently. *More likely she and Ron have had some kind of quarrel.*

"Amy," I said aloud. "What's wrong?"

She looked around. "Where's Tracy?"

"Still in the shower."

"Thank God!" She spoke in an urgent whisper and then took a deep breath. "While I was putting the chains on my car, I got grease on my hands and needed a towel. Ron usually keeps a supply of washrags in the back of his Camry. I opened the trunk and—" Amy stopped speaking. Her face crumpled, letting loose a fresh spate of tears.

"And what?" I demanded.

"There was dried blood inside Ron's trunk, Beau. Lots of it. Like somebody or something bled out in there."

I felt like I was in free fall with no parachute. Tracy's concerns were one thing. Incriminating bloodstains were something else. "Are you sure about that?"

She nodded. "Yes, I'm sure. I've worked in hospitals all my adult life, Beau. I know dried blood when I see it. What should I do?"

"You have to report it," I said at once. "It's as simple as that."

"But I can't," she wailed. "How can I? Ron's my husband, Beau. I love him. I can't be the one to turn him in."

"Then I'll have to do it," I said. "I'm a sworn police officer—an officer of the court. I don't have a choice. Do you have an attorney? Ron should have someone there with him when the detectives arrive."

"The only attorney we have right now is the guy who was representing us in the custody case against Rosemary. It turns out he was the next best thing to useless."

Amy and I had been standing in the elevator lobby talking. Tracy came out to where we were. Her light brown hair was still damp from the shower, and she was wearing the jogging suit and tennis shoes she had worn the night before.

"Mom!" she said. "What are you doing here?"

Amy Peters wiped away her tears. Then, with extraordinary effort, she somehow marshaled a semblance of composure onto her face. "Dad sent me to pick you up," she said calmly.

No wonder men never know what to expect from women. They can change courses like that in a matter of seconds and never miss a beat. And girls can do the same thing. I couldn't tell if Tracy bought into her stepmother's "everything's okay" act. If not, she certainly pretended to.

"How mad is he?" Tracy asked.

Amy shrugged. "Medium."

Tracy stood for a moment, looking back and forth between Amy and me. I imagine Tracy was expecting a bawling-out. When one wasn't forthcoming, Tracy tackled the issue head-on. "Aren't you going to ask me why I did it?"

"I'm sure you had a good reason," Amy said. Then she added, "Come on. Let's go. I'm already late for work."

As the elevator doors closed behind them, I went back into my condo, shut the door, and went straight to the telephone. I picked up the receiver and then stood staring at it as though I'd never encountered one before—as though the telephone were some alien instrument I had no idea how to operate.

Never before in my life have I faced such a clear division between friendship and duty. What I had told Amy was true. As an officer of the court I had no alternative. I had to report what she had told me about the dried blood in the trunk of Ron's car. But as his friend, I wanted him to have some kind of qualified legal representation available the next time an investigating officer rang his doorbell, search warrant in hand.

Friendship won out. I dialed Ralph Ames's home number in West Seattle. "Glad to hear you're in town," I said when he answered.

"I'm not," he returned. "With all this snow on the ground, why aren't I down in Scottsdale playing golf?"

"There's no explaining some people," I told him.

"This doesn't sound like a social call," Ralph said. "Is something wrong?"

My words may have been normal enough, but my voice must have been off. Ralph Ames is better at reading subtext than almost anybody I know.

"I think Ron Peters may be in trouble." It was a gross understatement, and Ralph picked up on it immediately.

"What kind of trouble?" he asked.

"His former wife died over the weekend," I told him. "She was murdered. Ron found out about it yesterday. He and Rosemary had been involved in a custody dispute that had turned ugly. He admitted to having said some things that might have been interpreted as threatening."

"That's troublesome," Ralph said. "But those things happen all the time in disputed custody cases."

"But there's more," I added. "And it gets worse. Amy stopped by here just a few minutes ago. This morning she was looking for something in the trunk of Ron's car and came across what she's sure is dried blood. Lots of dried blood."

"Has anybody questioned him about this or taken him into custody?" Ralph asked.

"Not officially. He said the Tacoma PD cops who came to do the next-of-kin notification yesterday afternoon asked him a lot of questions. They'll be asking more as soon as I tell them about the blood."

"And you are going to tell them?"

"Of course I'm going to tell them," I said. "I've got to. And it's going to put me in a hell of a bind. A homicide involving officer-related domestic violence? The case will come straight to Special Homicide. It's official state law. I wouldn't be surprised if it doesn't end up being assigned to Squad B."

"Assigned to Squad B, but not to you personally, right?"

"Right," I said.

"What do you want me to do?" Ralph asked.

"Call Ron up. Tell him a little birdie suggested you stop by. Or tell him straight out that I asked you to touch bases with him. Tell him I wanted him to have an attorney waiting in the wings in case one was needed. And believe me, one will be needed. I'm guessing someone will show up at his place with a search warrant within the next couple of hours."

"You're going to call in the report right now?" Ralph asked.

"As soon as I'm off the phone with you."

And that's what I did—called my office. When Harry I. Ball answered the main number, I knew Barbara Galvin hadn't made it in.

"I suppose you're calling to tell me you're snowbound," Harry observed once he knew who was calling. "That little 'Porsh' of yours may be cute as all get-out, but it isn't worth beans in the snow. If a few more people around here had four-wheel drive, I wouldn't be here holding down the fort all by myself."

The truth is, with proper tires, the 928's weight distribution makes it an excellent vehicle in snow, but Harry wouldn't have listened. I'm used to him taking jabs at the Porsche, which he consistently calls my "little foreign jobbie" and consistently mispronounces. For a change I didn't rise to Harry's bait.

"I am snowbound," I agreed. "But I'm calling about Ron Peters."

"I heard about that a few minutes ago," Harry interjected. "Since he's second in command of Internal Affairs at Seattle PD, the case is going to be a regular hot potato. I'm assigning Mel Soames and Brad Norton to handle it. You and Peters used to be partners, right?"

"Right."

"That's what I thought. So you aren't to go anywhere near that investigation. Understood?"

"It's too late," I said.

"What the hell is that supposed to mean?" Harry roared back at me. I had to hold the phone away from my ear to keep from being deafened.

"Ron and I are still good friends. And I'm friends with his family as well. His wife, Amy, stopped by here a few minutes ago. She told me she was looking for towels in the back of Ron's vehicle this morning and found what she's sure is dried blood. She didn't want to report it. I told her I had to. And I am."

I've never known Harry I. Ball to be caught speechless, but he was right then. He was quiet for so long that I wondered if the line had gone dead. Then he cut loose with a string of colorful and politically incorrect expletives.

"When the hell did that happen?" he demanded.

"Like I said. A few minutes ago. I called as soon as she left." This wasn't quite true, but my intervening call to Ralph Ames hadn't taken very long.

"Where's the vehicle?" Harry asked.

"At their house. On Queen Anne Hill." I gave Harry the address.

"Remember, Beau. You're to keep your ass out of this. You'll have to be interviewed, but other than that . . ."

"Harry," I said. "These people are friends of mine. I can't just turn my back on them."

"The hell you can't! You can and you will. Your friend, as you call him, happens to be a homicide suspect," Harry returned. "And in case you haven't noticed, cop-related domestic violence cases are very big right now. You are not, I repeat, N-O-T to be involved in any way. Ross Connors says we can't have even the slightest appearance of conflict of interest on this case. Do I make myself clear?"

"Got it," I said.

"What about that other case?" he asked. "The one I assigned you to yesterday?"

I noticed no one, including the attorney general himself, was concerned about a possible conflict of interest when it came to doing a favor for Ross Connors's old pal from O'Dea High School, but I decided that was something I'd be better off not mentioning.

"I'm working it," I told him.

"Good," Harry said. "And you keep right on working it. Following up on a cold case will keep you out of Mel and Brad's way, which is exactly where I want you. It's where Ross Connors wants you, too."

"Okay, Harry," I told him. "Okay. I can take a hint."

Bent on following orders and hoping to keep my nose clean, I sat down and tried calling the special twenty-four-hour line at the Department of Motor Vehicles to see if I could locate licensing or vehicle information that would give me an address for either of Sister Mary Katherine's parents, Sean and Molly Dunleavy. An unusual recorded message at the DMV told me that due to weather concerns the office was currently responding to emergency requests for information only. All others should call back at a later time. So much for state-run bureaucracies.

I sat there, staring out at the unfathomable blue of Elliott Bay and wondering what I should do next. That's when I spotted the small round globe on top of the *Seattle Post-Intelligencer* building a few short downhill blocks away. Why hadn't I thought of that before? Newspapers have to put out editions every day, snow or no snow. Some of the answers I was looking for might be available in the morgue at the *P.-I.* at the bottom of the hill where I had watched cars playing crash-car derby in the snow the night before.

I had no intention of taking the 928 out on the street where it was likely to end up being run over by some SUV-wielding nutcase with too much horsepower and only the dimmest grasp of physics. I was going to have to walk. It took a while to locate my long-unused snow boots. Once I did, I realized I was hungry.

I've never been much of a cook. Marshmallows aren't the only thing I don't keep around my condo. Basic foodstuffs are also in short supply. I used to hang out at a neighborhood dive called the Doghouse, but that went away years ago. Since then, I've tried various other joints, none of which have had quite the same fit as the Doghouse. When I choose restaurants, I ignore menu and atmosphere in favor of proximity. The *P.-I.* office is located on Elliott. So is the Shanty, which may have been a little out of the way, but food is food. It also gave me an excuse for taking a longer but much flatter route to the newspaper.

As I said, the good news about the Shanty is that it's close to the *P.-I.* The bad news about the Shanty is that it's close to the *P.-I.* It's also very small. As I stood in the open doorway knocking snow from my boots, I spotted none other than Maxwell Cole ensconced at the counter. If I could have ducked out without his seeing me, I would have, but it was already too late.

"Well, well, well," he said in a loud voice that carried throughout the restaurant. "If it isn't former Detective J. P. Beaumont. I was under the impression you worked mostly on the Eastside these days. Out slumming, I take it?"

Over the years I've occasionally had friends who, for one reason or another, dropped out of my life. Enemies tend to hang on forever. That's certainly the way it is with Maxwell Cole.

Max and I go way back—all the way back to our frat days back at the University of Washington. He was dating a cute girl named Karen Moffitt. I took one look at her, decided she was the one for me, and stole her away from him. Max has been pissed about it ever since.

Unfortunately, Max and I work different sides of the same mean streets. He started out as a cub reporter at the *Post-Intelligencer* about the same time I went to work for Seattle PD. Since he's never forgiven me for poaching Karen, he's never given me anything but journalistic hatchet jobs whenever he's had the chance. I'm a long way short of perfect. That means I've given him lots of opportunity to show me in a bad light. It wasn't so annoying when he was a simple reporter. Back then he more or less had to stick to the facts. Now that he's a seasoned, big-deal columnist, he's allowed to say whatever he damn well pleases. And does.

Everybody in the tiny restaurant sensed the underlying antagonism in his voice. They all fell silent as if waiting for the equivalent of a schoolyard fight to break out right there at the lunch counter.

"Just looking for a little grub," I said as pleasantly as I could manage.

For years the man has sported a handlebar mustache. It's an affectation that doesn't suit him. Think overfed walrus, droopy jowls and all. With a swipe of his arm, he cleared the place next to him at the counter, ceremoniously offering me a place to sit. The tiny restaurant was crowded. The only other available spot was at the far end of the counter. Ignoring Max's invitation would be an obvious insult, one I'd be delivering on his own turf. Bad idea. And so, even knowing that it might cause trouble later, I took the stool he indicated.

"Thanks, Maxey," I said. "That's mighty decent of you."

Assuming the confrontation was over, the other diners relaxed and resumed their chewing and talking. Max, who doesn't appreciate being called Maxey, glared at me.

"I hear that old partner of yours is in a lot of trouble," he said.

"Is that so?" I asked noncommittally. "Which partner would that be? I've had several over the years."

A harried waitress swooped by and took my order for ham and eggs and coffee. Max, finished with his food, was nursing a cup of coffee. The waitress dropped off his check at the same time she took my order. If delivering his bill was a subtle hint for Max to eat, pay, and go, he didn't take it.

"Peters," he replied. "Ron Peters. His ex-wife was gunned down over the weekend."

"Really," I said.

"Are you telling me you don't know anything about it?" he demanded.

I shook my head, and Max was only too happy to assume the role of the bearer of bad tidings. "Ron and his ex were involved in some kind of custody dispute. According to what I've heard, the wife's attorney is the one who got the investigation pointed in Ron's direction. Something about a threat Ron made last week."

"You don't say," I said.

"With Peters being a cop and all, that means the Special Homicide division will be handling the investigation, right?"

Those of us who work there may affectionately refer to our agency as SHIT, but outsiders had best beware. They're better off not referring to us by that moniker even if they think we are. As far as I was concerned, Maxwell Cole had made a good choice.

"I suppose so," I said. "In fact, I believe it's a state law."

"What do you think?"

"About the law?" I asked, acting dim.

"About Ron Peters."

"Come on, Max. You know I can't discuss ongoing investigations."

"So you're saying it is an ongoing investigation after all?"

The short-order cook on duty was a regular speed demon. My food came just then. I salted and peppered the hell out of it, not because the food needed the extra seasoning, but because I needed to do something with my hands besides throttling Maxwell Cole's bulging twenty-two-inch neck.

"Look," I said finally. "Ron Peters is a good friend of mine. Whatever may or may not be going on in his life, I have two words for you, Max, and they are 'No comment.' If you want official information, I suggest you contact my boss, the Squad B commander."

I grabbed a fresh napkin from the dispenser on the counter. After jotting Harry's name and office phone number on it, I passed the napkin along to Max. He studied it for a minute before his portly face broke into a grin.

"You're pulling my leg, right?" he asked.

"About what?"

"You want me to talk to somebody named Harry I. Ball? What kind of joke is that?"

That's something Harry Ignatius Ball counts on. He likes dealing with people who make the mistake of thinking he's some kind of joke. He sucks them in by playing dumb when he first meets them. Later on, when the opportunity presents itself, he revels in chewing those same people to pieces. From my point of view, it's one of Harry's most endearing qualities.

I could have warned Max to tread warily when it came to dealing with Harry, but I didn't. Max didn't deserve to be warned.

"It's no joke," I said. "Call him up and talk to him. It should be a laugh a minute."

"I'll just bet," Max returned.

Max's check was still there on the counter, halfway between my water glass and his empty coffee cup. He may have expected me to pick it up and pay for his breakfast, but I didn't.

Tiring of my company at last, Max sighed and slapped a meaty paw over the bill, then he got up and waddled over to the cash register. I didn't say good riddance, not even under my breath, but that's what I was thinking.

Good riddance, and don't let the door slam your butt on the way out.

CHAPTER 6

I HADN'T BOTHERED mentioning to Maxwell Cole that I was on my way to visit his digs at the *P.-I.,* and I carefully gave him plenty of lead time. I didn't want the two of us walking in through the front door and stamping snow off our boots at the same time.

In a post-9/11 world, my SHIT squad ID was enough to get me past the guard at the front door. It took my ID, ten minutes of wheedling, and a call from someone in the attorney general's office down in Olympia for me to gain access to the newspaper's holy of holies, the morgue.

Over the years I've done my share of griping about newfangled technology. I've fought integrated-circuit advances all the way down the line—from cell phones to computers—until I finally admitted defeat or came to my senses, depending on your point of view. If I hadn't already succumbed to the lure of computers, a day spent dealing with microfiche would have sent me plunging over the edge. Computers may be annoying, but microfiche is hell.

Because of Sister Mary Katherine's age relative to mine, I knew we were dealing with a time frame that was in or near the early 1950s. Although she wasn't sure, Mary Katherine seemed to be under the impression that her family had been living somewhere in the Seattle area.

Summer comes late in the Pacific Northwest. The rains last from late September until early July, so if Mary Katherine's recollection of the blue dress with the yellow flowers was accurate, we were dealing with summer or possibly very late spring.

People act as though the decade of the fifties was a halcyon June-and-Ward-Cleaver age when everyone knew everyone else and no one bothered locking their doors. Maybe that was true in some places. I'm certain that there weren't nearly the number of homicides back then as there are now. Bearing that in mind, I figured a stabbing death that had occurred in someone's front yard would be page-one news. Even if the murder occurred outside Seattle proper, it would have made headlines in what was then and still is considered to be a statewide newspaper.

A surprisingly helpful clerk who, it turned out, was actually a student intern aided me in locating what I wanted microfiche copies of newspapers that had been published between April and October, starting in 1949. I wasn't actually allowed to touch the microfiche—the clerk had to load it into the machine prior to my scanning through it.

Lots of people would be amazed at how blindingly boring detective work can be—especially when you're scrolling through page after page after page of blue-and-white microfiche print. My hunch had been right. Back then, homicide cases from all over the state had indeed been front-page fodder. One or two of them seemed promising, but once I read through the articles, the facts didn't seem to coincide with anything Sister Mary Katherine had told us.

By two o'clock, I had finished 1949. I also had a splitting headache, but something good had happened. Headache or no, while I was concentrating on scrolling through those old stories, I most certainly hadn't been thinking about Ron Peters and his problems. Rather than calling it a day, I asked the clerk for the next set and started in on 1950.

Halfway through May, in a newspaper dated Tuesday, May 16, 1950, I found what I was looking for: a headline that read "Seattle Woman Murdered in Her Bed." Bed wasn't quite right, but I continued reading anyway.

Seattle police detectives today released the name of a woman who was stabbed to death in her bed over the weekend while her bedridden mother lay helpless in a nearby room. When Ravenna area resident Madeline Marchbank was murdered, her mother, Abigail Marchbank, was left without food or water for several days. Mrs. Marchbank is hospitalized in fair condition at Columbus Hospital, where she is being treated for severe dehydration.

Madeline wasn't quite the right name, but wasn't Mimi a nickname for Madeline? And having the victim stabbed to death in her bed didn't square with what Mary Katherine had reported either, but I remembered that by the time Bonnie Jeanne had ventured out of her hiding place that day, the body had disappeared. I had assumed it had been loaded into a waiting vehicle and carted off for dumping elsewhere. Was it possible that the killers had simply moved the body into the house and then arranged the room to make it look as if the crime had been committed there?

Seattle coroner Randall Mathers estimated that the crime most likely happened sometime between Friday evening and Sunday morning, although it wasn't discovered until Miss Marchbank failed to report to work on Monday morning and arrangements were made for someone to go by the house to check on her.

So the time frame fit. Saturday afternoon was what Bonnie Jean had said—Saturday afternoon while she waited for her parents.

Seattle homicide detective Lieutenant William Winkler, lead investigator on the case, said that when Miss Marchbank's employer was unable to raise anyone at the family home by telephone, they contacted her brother, Seattle attorney Albert P. Marchbank, at his Smith Tower office. Mr. Marchbank immediately drove to his mother's home, where he discovered the body.

I was startled when two familiar names tumbled out at me in the same paragraph. William "Wink" Winkler had been a rough-and-tumble cop whose case-closure rates had helped him rise like a rocket through the ranks of Seattle PD. By the midfifties he had reached the exalted position of assistant chief of police. In 1950 he had been riding high and was on his way up. Five short years later he had been caught up in the web of graft and corruption that had been widespread inside the force at that time. As the pattern of payoffs and double-dealings became public, Wink Winkler had been one of the first officers forced to resign. As I remembered the story, something like twenty officers had been tried and convicted of various charges. Many of those had gone to jail. I had no idea whether or not Wink Winkler was one of them.

In a different way, Al Marchbank was also a Seattle-area legend. He was a local boy who had made good. He had been sent off to some East Coast boarding school at an early age and had just graduated from an Ivy League law school when World War II broke out. In 1943, he joined the army and spent most of the war working in Washington, D.C.

He returned to Seattle after the war. Using his well-heeled parents' contacts, he established a successful law practice. By the midfifties he and a partner, Phil Landreth, were beginning to put together a collection of small-town radio stations that would soon become Marchbank Broadcasting, a medium-size media fish that would eventually be swallowed whole by a much larger media entity. Unlike that of Wink Winkler, who seemed to have disappeared into utter obscurity, the Marchbank name still held sway in Seattle more than half a century later in the form of the Albert P. and Elvira S. Marchbank Foundation. Likewise, Phil Landreth had gone on to make a name for himself in local and statewide politics. I couldn't help thinking that as a child Bonnie Jean Dunleavy had encountered a collection of pretty heavy hitters.

The article continued:

Mr. Marchbank told reporters that he last saw his sister and mother on Friday afternoon, shortly before he and his wife left for Harrison Hot Springs in British Columbia, where they attended a wedding. He said that when he found his mother alone and untended late Monday morning, she was delirious from a lack of food and water and had no idea of her daughter's fate. All she knew was that no one had come to look after her.

In addition to caring for her invalid mother for the last several years, Miss Marchbank worked as a receptionist for Harris, Harris, and Rainy, Incorporated, a Seattle-area public accounting firm. Her supervisor there, Hal Rainy, said that Miss Marchbank had been an entirely reliable employee and had always called in to let them know if she was going to be absent.

"That's why we called her home once we realized she wasn't here," Mr. Rainy said. "That's also why, when we failed to reach her, we were alarmed enough to notify her brother. I can't imagine anyone wanting to do the poor girl harm. She was just as nice a person as can be."

Detective Winkler, when asked about a possible suspect or motive, told reporters that as of this time there is no viable suspect. Investigators are working on the theory that Miss Marchbank may have returned home unexpectedly and interrupted a burglary in progress. He said they are conferring with Mr. Marchbank and his wife, Elvira, to determine what, if anything, might be missing from his mother's residence.

The murder weapon, an ordinary kitchen knife, was recovered at the scene and is believed to have come from the victim's own kitchen.

Police are asking that anyone with information about this case contact Detective Winkler at Seattle Police Headquarters. Mr. Marchbank and his business partner, Phil Landreth, indicated that they are posting a $1,000 reward for anyone who can provide information that will lead to the arrest and conviction of Madeline Marchbank's killer. Funeral services for Miss Marchbank are pending at this time and will not be finalized until after the coroner's office releases the body sometime later this week.

That was the end of that first story. The clerk helpfully made a hard copy of that one for me. Then I scrolled through the next several weeks of newspapers, watching as the story unfolded. Madeline Marchbank's funeral at Saint Mark's Cathedral on Friday, May 19, was a well-attended affair that merited front-page attention. The microfiche record indicated the existence of a photo that could be retrieved from the photo file. When I asked the clerk to bring me a copy of that, the picture featured a grief-stricken Albert Marchbank, accompanied by his wife, Elvira, pushing a wheelchair-bound Abigail Marchbank down a rain-slick sidewalk.

Once the funeral was over, stories related to Madeline Marchbank's death gradually migrated from front page to back, growing ever smaller as they went. Despite Detective Winkler's best efforts, no suspects were ever identified. Nowhere was there any mention of a child who may have witnessed the fatal attack on Madeline Marchbank. Without testimony from that small, frightened witness, the case had gone cold—until now, until remnants from a recurring nightmare had awakened Sister Mary Katherine's haunting memories out of their sound sleep.

I sat back in the chair and rubbed my burning eyes.

"Will that be all?" the intern asked. "I was supposed to go to lunch at two. I'm not allowed to leave you alone, and no one else came in today."

She was young and not terribly attractive, but she was also bright and willing to help. She'd gone to the trouble of making her way in to work on a day when lots of other people had begged off. I hoped she'd go far.

"No," I said, gathering my sheaf of papers. "That's all for now. You've been a great help. What's your name again?"

"Linda," she said. "Linda Carter." She shrugged apologetically and added, "My father's last name is Carter. When he was young, he loved *Wonder Woman* on TV. When I was born, he just couldn't resist."

"Works for me," I said. "You've certainly worked wonders for me today. Hope I haven't made you too late for lunch."

She smiled shyly. "Thanks," she said. "And don't worry about lunch. I don't mind. It's usually so boring around here. It was fun to have something useful to do for a change."

I rode the elevator to the lobby and turned in my visitor's badge. I went outside and joined the clutch of coat-swaddled smokers who had been exiled outside in the freezing weather. Standing in a pall of secondhand smoke, I contemplated the steep climb back up to Second

Avenue and wondered if I should once again take the long way around.

The morgue had been so confined that I had turned my cell phone on "silent" while I was there. Still wavering about what route to take, I pulled my phone out of my pocket and checked it. There were three messages waiting.

The first was from Ralph Ames. "Hey, Beau," he said. "Sorry to say I struck out. I called Ron and let him know what the deal was. I offered to come over and be there to back him up, but he said thanks but no thanks. If he isn't interested in my help, there's not much I can do. I wanted to let you know that I tried."

The second call followed Ralph's by a matter of minutes. It was from my colleague, Melissa Soames. "Hey, J.P.," she said. "This is Mel. According to Harry, we need to talk. Give me a call ASAP."

The third message came from Tracy Peters. She was crying. "Uncle Beau? Mom's not here, and I can't reach her. I don't know what to do. Two people, a man and a woman, showed up a little while ago with a search warrant for Dad's car. When they left, they took him with them, and they didn't say where they were going. Now there's a big tow truck down in the driveway. Some guy is loading Dad's Camry onto it right now. Please call me back or else come by. We need you."

The call had come in a good two hours earlier.

I immediately tried calling back, but there was no answer. This was hardly a surprise. No doubt Ron Peters's home and his family were in the midst of a full media onslaught. If they were smart, they would be hunkered down inside, not answering phones or doorbells. I stuffed the phone back in my pocket, ducked my chin into my chest, and ran up the hill.

Amazingly enough, I didn't slip and fall on my butt, and I didn't have a heart attack or collapse before I hit Second Avenue, either, but it was close. I was still panting when I staggered up to the lobby at Belltown Terrace. Jerome opened the door to let me in.

"Hey, man," he said. "What's with you? You been running that four-minute mile again?"

"More like ten," I gasped. "But I need a car or a cab. With either four-wheel drive and snow tires or chains, I don't care which. And I need it now."

"A good doorman is like a Boy Scout. We're always prepared," he said with a grin. "I have a friend who drives a cab, and he and I have an arrangement. He came to work today with his cab all decked out in chains. I've got his cell number right here, and I've been calling him all day long whenever any of my people need help. I'll give him a call."

"Please," I said. "I don't know how long I'm going to need him, but tell him I'll make it worth his while."

"He's been pretty busy today," Jerome said. "As you can well imagine. So why don't you go upstairs and wait. I'll call you just as soon as Mohammad Ibrahim shows up."

"Thanks," I said. "I'll do that."

While I was upstairs waiting for the cab, I switched on the TV. On KOMO a special early edition of the evening news was dishing out wall-to-wall weather. "The Counterbalance on Queen Anne Avenue is closed to all vehicular traffic, while kids, taking advantage of their snow day, turn it into a place for sledding. Reporter Megan Forester has a live report."

Years ago, Seattle used to have a working trolley system, not just the current tourist-attraction-type outfit that runs back and forth along the waterfront without really making much of a contribution to mass transportation. Like similar trolleys in San Francisco, the old system required a counterbalance in order for cars to make it up and down the steepest part of Queen Anne Hill. The working trolleys are long gone, but on Queen Anne the word "counterbalance" persists, and it is, as the name implies, very steep. Letting kids use it for sledding seemed like a recipe for disaster. I was surprised the city hadn't put a stop to it based solely on liability concerns.

Kamikaze sledders weren't my problem. Queen Anne Hill was. If the main drag up and down the hill was closed, Mohammad Ibrahim might have a tough time getting me anywhere near Ron and Amy's place. When Jerome called upstairs to tell me the cab had arrived, I rode down in the elevator expecting that the driver would be a newly arrived immigrant from some Middle Eastern country and that communication might be difficult.

It turned out Mr. Ibrahim wasn't exactly a newly landed immigrant. He had been driving cabs in Seattle for some time, but he hadn't gotten around to changing the name on his driver's license photo ID, where he was still listed as James L. Jackson, and the old country he hailed from was actually west Texas.

"You tell me where y'all want to go," he said in a thick Texas drawl, "and I'll be getting you there."

I expected he'd drive like a madman. He didn't. Instead of tackling Queen Anne Hill straight on, he took a circuitous route that eased us up the flanks of the hill, the same way a highway zigzags back and forth climbing a mountain. When we reached Ron and Amy's street, however, we weren't the first to arrive. Not everybody in local television land was focused on the weather. Two television cam-vans were parked out front.

"Park here," I told Mr. Ibrahim. "If you don't mind, I'd like you to wait here with the meter running." I reached into my wallet and pulled out a hundred-dollar bill. "This isn't on the meter, by the way," I added. "And there's more where that came from if you're still here when I get back."

"Where y'all gonna be?" he asked.

"That house up there," I said, pointing.

"The one with all the cameras outside?"

I didn't want to think about what Harry I. Ball would do if one of the television cameras happened to catch an image of me wandering up to Ron and Amy's front door. He would be pissed. So would Ross Connors.

"That's right," I said. "And since they're out front, I'm going to try going in the back."

Mohammad took the proffered bill and stuck it in his pocket. Then he leaned back in his seat. "Well, good luck to you, mister," he said. "I don't know what you're up to, but it should be fun. I'll be right here waiting whenever y'all get done."

Lame as it may sound now, I did have a plan. I knew that Tracy had managed to sneak out of the house the night before without anyone being the wiser, and she had told me that Heather often pulled the same stunt. I took that to mean that there had to be some way for the girls to come and go without being noticed. Hoping to stumble on their secret route, I went in through the front yard two houses up the street. After leaving a very obvious trail in the snow behind me and falling once or twice, I finally clambered over the last fence and landed in Ron and Amy's snow-clad but familiar backyard.

I was standing there reconnoitering when the back patio door slid open, and Molly Wright, Amy's older sister, stepped out onto the snow-covered deck. "I don't know who the hell you think you are, pal," she said, "but you'd better get your ass out of here before I call the cops."

I was astounded at Molly Wright's appearance. The last time I saw her, the woman had been dressed to the nines. She had definitely gone downhill since then. Out of the heady atmosphere of the public limelight and dealing with financial and marital issues, Molly had put on weight—lots of it. The tight sweats she wore made her look more like an overstuffed sausage than a fashion diva. Her hair flew in all directions like a fright wig, and her puffy white face was devoid of makeup.

"I *am* a cop, Molly," I told her. "It's me, J. P. Beaumont. Tracy called and asked me to come help out."

She studied me narrowly for a moment or two. "Oh, that's right," she said. "Beaumont. I remember you. Weren't you the designated drunk at Ron and Amy's wedding?"

The wedding reception hadn't been one of my finest hours. As Molly had so kindly reminded me, I had in fact tied one on at Ron and Amy's reception. In the process I had ended up injuring three of my fingers and had come away with no recollection of how or why it had happened. That humiliating incident—of being hurt and not remembering why—had been the so-called tipping point in my beginning to sober up. It's something I talk about in the privacy of AA meetings on occasion, but I resented the hell out of having somebody outside the program feel free to bring it up. If this was Ron and Amy's star boarder's typical MO, no wonder Tracy wasn't fond of her stepauntie.

I could have said "I seem to remember you weighed about a hundred pounds less back then than you do now." But I didn't. My mother raised me to have better manners than that. Just because someone is rude first doesn't mean you have to be rude back.

"Yup," I admitted. "That was me, all right. Thank you so much for remembering. And, in case you're interested, I've been pretty much sober ever since. Now is Tracy here or not?"

At first I thought Molly Wright was going to tell me to get lost, and slam the door in my face. Finally she shrugged and emitted a resigned sigh. "Tracy's here, but Amy's not." She stood aside and reluctantly motioned me inside.

"Tracy's the one I came to see," I told her. "Where is she?"

"Upstairs in the family room with her brother, watching TV."

"Good," I said. "Don't bother showing me. I know the way."

CHAPTER 7

As soon as little Jared saw me in the doorway, he launched himself off the couch and clobbered me in the testicles. "Uncle Beau!" he exclaimed as I struggled to catch my breath. "Are you here to help my daddy? That's what Tracy said—that you'd come help."

My eyes stopped watering as I wrapped Jared in a tight bear hug and then shifted him onto my hip. "I don't know how much I can help," I said. "But I'll do what I can. How's your sister doing?"

Tracy was sitting on the couch with a box of tissues in her lap and a pile of used Kleenex on the cushion beside her. She looked at me bleakly and shook her head. "Not very well," she said.

"You should have seen it," Jared continued excitedly. "It was just like *Cops* on TV. They came and put handcuffs on him and everything. Did they take him to jail, do you think? Will they let him out so he can come back home? I want him here. I don't want him to sleep over."

Jared's five-year-old version of the unfolding family tragedy reminded me of Bonnie Jean's remembrances of that long-ago murder, and it wrenched my heart. This was far more serious than a simple sleepover. Thank God it wasn't up to me to tell him so. That tough job would fall to Amy.

Tracy cleared away the wad of used tissues so Jared and I could sit down beside her on the couch. "Where's your mom?" I asked.

"As he was leaving, Dad told me to call Mom and have her get in touch with Ralph Ames. I called her and she called back a little later to say she was meeting him. She didn't say where."

"How long ago was that?" I asked.

"A long time," Tracy said. "Hours."

I was delighted to hear that Ron had come to his senses as far as calling Ralph Ames was concerned. As for where Mel and Brad had taken him for questioning? My best guess was that they would conduct their interview in the Squad B conference room. They sure as hell couldn't question the second in command of the Seattle PD Internal Affairs Division in a cop shop interview room in downtown Seattle.

"That's good news," I said. "About your mom contacting Ralph, that is. He's about the best there is."

The front door slammed. "Tracy?" Heather called. "Where are you?"

"Up here," Tracy called down. "In the family room."

Heather was still talking as she pounded up the stairs. "Do you know the front yard is full of reporters? What are they doing out there? Why doesn't Mom make them leave?" She rounded the corner and stopped just inside the doorway. "Where's Dad? Some jerk outside told me they'd arrested him. I told him he was a stupid liar."

I looked at Heather Peters and could barely believe my eyes. Her long blond tresses had been bobbed off. Her natural golden blond had been replaced by a hideously incandescent shade of red. Her shirt ended a good six inches above the dropped waistband of a pair of faded ragtag jeans. Something brilliant winked out at me from her belly button. And she had a nose ring, an honest-to-God nose ring! For all I knew, she probably had a tattoo as well. It just wasn't visible. What the hell had happened to my sweet little Heather?

Behind her, hanging back in the doorway as if unsure of his welcome, stood a scruffy teenage boy. His hair was dyed the same appalling shade of red as Heather's, and he wore a matching nose ring. Maybe this was how kids showed the world they were going steady these days—matching hair color and nose rings. In that moment the idea of letting a girl wear a class ring or a letterman's sweater seemed incredibly old-fashioned and quaint. I was grateful the kid was wearing a knee-length T-shirt. If he had a bauble in his belly button, I didn't want to see it.

I remembered Tracy saying Heather had a steady boyfriend. And I remembered her mentioning that their parents didn't like him. No wonder. I couldn't recall the kid's name, and we hadn't yet been introduced, but I didn't like him either. His appearance didn't make for a favorable first impression. I've had plenty of sensitivity training over the years, complete with talks about not judging people by appearances. That's fine when appearance issues aren't ones that come by choice, but defacing your body by adding optional accessories changes the whole equation.

"It's possible your dad isn't actually under arrest," I said, answering in Tracy's stead. "But they did take him in for questioning."

Heather came over to the couch and gave me a hug. "Hi, Uncle Beau," she said, plopping down on the couch and snuggling up next to me. "I didn't know you were here. I didn't see your car."

I would have appreciated the hug more if it hadn't been accompanied by the distinctively sweetish odor of marijuana smoke. It clung to her clothes and hair. My heart constricted. What had become of *my* Heather Peters? Halfheartedly returning her hug, I somehow didn't mention that the reason she hadn't seen my car was that I had snuck in the back way in order to avoid the very reporters she had just brazened her way through.

"But this is, like, so stupid," Heather continued. "They think Daddy killed my mother? He wouldn't do something like that, never in a million years. Can't you make them understand that?"

If Heather was grieving about the death of her biological mother, it wasn't apparent in her demeanor. High or not, her main concern was for her father. So was mine.

"I'll do my best," I said.

Jared turned to me, his eyes wide. "They think Daddy killed Mom?"

"No, Jared," Heather answered. "Not Mom, my mother. You don't even know her."

Jared looked mystified. "We don't have the same mother?" he asked.

Obviously, all of this was unwelcome news to poor little Jared. His innocent question meant Amy Peters would have even more difficult explaining to do.

"Oh," Heather added as an afterthought. She tilted her head in the direction of the boy lingering in the doorway. "By the way, this is Dillon, my boyfriend. And this is my Uncle Beau. He's a cop, too. Like my dad."

Dillon nodded at me and shambled a few steps into the room. His hands were buried in pockets that hung so low on his hips he could barely reach them. He sank into an easy chair across from the couch. Heather immediately abandoned me in favor of perching on the arm of Dillon's chair.

"Where's Mom, still at work?"

Tracy answered. "She found an attorney for Dad. Remember Mr. Ames?"

Heather nodded.

"She and Mr. Ames went to be with Daddy while they're questioning him."

"Just like on TV," Jared marveled.

"This isn't like on TV," I corrected. "It's a lot more serious than that."

"But you and Mr. Ames will be able to get him out, won't you?" Heather asked. Her blue eyes searched my face. I tried to glimpse her pupils, to ascertain whether or not she was using. From across the room, I couldn't tell, and she certainly sounded lucid enough.

"That's the problem," I said. "Your mother's homicide is being treated as a possible case of officer-related domestic violence. By law, that has to be investigated by the attorney general's Special Homicide Investigation Team, which happens to be where I work."

Tracy brightened. "Good," she said. "That means you'll be working on Daddy's case then."

I shook my head. "No, it means exactly the opposite. Since your father and I are friends, my involvement in the investigation would constitute a conflict of interest. I've been ordered to stay out of it completely. I came by here today, against my boss's direct orders, because we're friends and because Tracy called and asked for my help. But after this—until this case is settled—I'm going to have to keep my distance."

"They seemed mean," Jared put in.

"Who seemed mean?" I asked.

"The man and woman who took Daddy away."

"They're not mean, Jared," I told him. "I know Mel Soames and Brad Norton. They're both nice people. They were just doing their job."

Molly Wright appeared in the doorway just then. "I'm about to start dinner," she said. "Who all's staying?"

"Not me," Dillon said.

"I'm not staying, either," I answered.

"And I'm not hungry," Tracy said.

Shaking her head, Molly stalked back down the stairs the way she had come. I stood up. "I have to go," I told them. "Don't talk to the reporters if you can help it."

"Not even to tell them they're stupid?" Heather asked.

"Not even. Especially not to tell them that. Their job is to find out every detail of your father's life. The more you antagonize them, the worse it's going to be."

"Are you going to talk to them?" Jared asked.

"No, I'm not, and I'm not going out the front way, either. I'm going out the back door and over your neighbors' fences, the same way I got here." I gave Heather a meaningful look. "I have it on good authority that there's a lot of that going on these days—sneaking in and out."

Heather knew I had nailed her. She had the good grace to blush slightly and to drop her gaze.

"For the time being, it might be a good idea to cut that out," I added. "Your mom has enough going on right now without having to worry about her kids coming and going at all kinds of ungodly hours."

Heather nodded. "Okay," she said. "I'll be good."

I glanced questioningly at Tracy.

"Me, too," she said.

"Good," I said, and I was on my way.

I felt a bit silly retracing my snowy backyard route. Fortunately, it gets dark early in Seattle in the winter. I don't think any of the neighbors noticed, and Mohammad was waiting in the cab right where I'd left him.

"Glad to see you," he said. "I was beginning to wonder if you were going to stay all night. Where to next, back home?"

"Let me check."

I called the number Mel had used much earlier when she had left her message. I could tell from the prefix that it was her cell. I wasn't at all surprised when she didn't answer.

"Sorry it took so long to get back to you," I told her voice mail. "I've been busy. I'm heading home now. Give me a call there later if you still want to see me tonight. Otherwise, we can talk tomorrow."

"Home, then," I told Mohammad.

Lots of people had evidently taken the day off. It was the middle of rush hour, but traffic was much lighter than usual. When we reached Belltown Terrace, I paid Mohammad what was on the meter and gave him another sizable tip. Jerome had another eager customer lined up and waiting the moment I stepped out of the cab.

I went upstairs. My body, especially my shins, were feeling a little worse for wear after my uphill run earlier in the day. I was looking forward to spending some quality clicker time in my recliner. Grateful to be rid of my boots, I tossed them into the entryway closet and pulled on a ratty but well-loved sweater. Naturally the phone rang the moment I sat down. It was Freddy Mac.

"What gives?" I asked.

"The roads are so bad up on Whidbey that Sister Mary Katherine decided to stay over last night, tonight, and maybe even tomorrow if things don't improve," he told me. "She had already checked out of her room before we had lunch yesterday. Most of the hotels were booked solid, but I was finally able to get her into a room at the Westin downtown. Since she was still around and since I had several weather-related cancellations, we went ahead and did another session today. I have one more tape to add to your collection. I think we're making real progress now, Beau. She exhibited far less resistance this time around, and she was able to uncover a few more telling details. Would you like to see the tape?"

"Absolutely."

"Where are you?"

"Belltown Terrace," I told him. "Second and Broad."

"I'm just now leaving my office up on Pill Hill. I could drop it off on my way home."

You won't find the name Pill Hill on any official map of the Seattle area, but it's what we call the area of First Hill that's full of hospitals and clinics. For all I knew, the place could have been crawling with hypnotherapists as well.

"Sure," I said. "I'll wait down in the lobby. That way you won't have to park and come in. I have some news as well."

"What's that?"

"The murder victim's full name—Madeline Marchbank. She was found stabbed to death in her bed in May of 1950."

"But Sister Mary Katherine said . . ."

"That it happened outside. I know. But she also said that the body and the blood were both gone when she came out of her hiding place. All that means is the killers moved the body and made it look like the attack happened inside the house."

"So it really did happen then!" Fred MacKinzie breathed.

He had been acting as if he believed Bonnie Jean Dunleavy's story all along, and he had convinced me to believe it as well, but right up until I told him Mimi's real name, Fred must have been hanging on to the tiniest shred of doubt.

"Yes," I said. "It really did."

"Did they ever solve it?" Fred asked.

"They may have," I said, "but there was no indication of an arrest or even a prime suspect in any of the material I read today. I'll be able to get into the official records tomorrow. My question to you is: Should I tell Sister Mary Katherine?"

There was a long pause before Fred answered. "I'm not sure what the best course of action is on that," he said. "Let me think about it on my way down the hill."

I shoved my aching feet into a pair of loafers and headed for the lobby. For the next twenty minutes or so I sat there listening to Belltown Terrace's weather wimps come and go, complaining all the way. When a sand-dollar-colored Lexus LX 470 pulled up on the street outside, I figured it had to be Freddy Mac's, and I was right.

I went out to the curb and stood under the canopy as Fred opened the passenger-side window. "When I called the Westin, Sister Mary Katherine was on her way down to the coffee shop for dinner. What say we go there now and tell her together—unless you're busy. If that's the case . . ."

"No," I said. "It's fine. Wait here while I run back upstairs and get a coat."

"Don't bother," Fred said. "The car's warm. And I'll bring you back here when we finish."

So off we went—him in his snazzy brushed camel sports coat and me in a disreputable sweater that I would have been embarrassed to donate to Goodwill. I was feeling grungy as we followed the hostess through the Westin's brightly lit Corner Café, where Sister Mary Katherine was already seated in a booth.

She smiled at Fred as he walked toward her. When she saw me trailing along in his wake, the smile faded. "You didn't say you were bringing Beau with you," she said.

"That's because I didn't know I was," Fred said. "He has some news I thought you'd want to hear from him directly."

Sister Mary Katherine looked at me gravely and then said to the hostess, "I believe I'll have that glass of wine after all. Chardonnay, please."

The hostess looked questioningly at Fred and me. He ordered coffee with cream. I shook my head. "Nothing, thank you."

"What is it?" Sister Mary Katherine asked.

There was no point in beating around the bush. "Mimi's real name was Madeline Marchbank," I said. "She was murdered—stabbed to death—in the middle of May of 1950."

"And I watched it happen," Sister Mary Katherine confirmed quietly.

"I believe so."

"Were the killers ever caught?"

"That I don't know," I said. "Tomorrow I'll be able to access some of the official records I wasn't able to get to today. The material I've located so far came from newspaper archives, and it covered the story for only the first several weeks after it happened. During that time the investigators had developed no leads in her death."

"That must mean that I didn't tell anyone what I saw. Why on earth didn't I?" Sister Mary Katherine demanded accusingly. "Not telling is inexcusable."

Fred and I exchanged glances. No one who had heard the frightened little-girl voice of Bonnie Jean Dunleavy would have wondered why she had kept quiet or blamed her for her silence. "Have you viewed the tapes of your own sessions?" I asked.

Sister Mary Katherine shook her head. Fred was the one who answered aloud. "I still want what she remembers to be what she remembers," he replied. "I didn't want to layer in what she had already related on the tapes."

"You were scared to death," I said. "The woman threatened you. She said you'd end up like Mimi if you told anyone what you had seen."

But Sister Mary Katherine wasn't satisfied. "Still," she said disapprovingly, "keeping quiet about such a thing is unforgivable."

The wine and coffee came. Sister Mary Katherine took a careful sip before asking, "What do we do now? Clearly this Marchbank woman was once my friend. I want to know whether or not her killers were ever brought to justice. Certainly I owe her that much. It's the only way to atone for my silence back then."

I wanted to tell her to give the poor little kid she had once been a break, but Fred cut me off before I had a chance.

"What do you know about forgotten memories?" he asked me.

"Not much. It usually happens with kids who have been sexually molested, right?"

Fred nodded. "Most of the time. But it can also have to do with some other early childhood trauma. Beau, you're focused on the crime aspect of all this. My job has to do with helping Sister Mary Katherine rid herself of the nightmare that's been robbing her and her nuns of their good night's sleep. You've been able to verify some of the details of what happened and where. If we can compare additional details with what's been buried in Sister Mary Katherine's subconscious all this time, we may be able to bring it back into her conscious memory as well. Hypnosis is fine as far as it goes, but in my experience, dealing with the memory consciously is what it's going to take to break the nightmare's hold."

"But how?" Sister Mary Katherine asked.

"Do you have the exact address where Madeline Marchbank was living when she was murdered?" Fred asked.

"I don't have it right this minute," I told him. "But I can get it tomorrow once I can access official case files. By then I'll be able to have vehicle licensing records as well. Why?"

"I have appointments in the morning, but it might be helpful if you could drive her through her old neighborhood—past the house where she lived—to see if there's a chance that recognizing familiar ground might be enough to cause a breakthrough in her memory barrier."

Sister Mary Katherine shook her head. "I doubt Mr. Beaumont has either the time or the inclination to drive me around my old neighborhood."

I remembered what Harry had said. Busying myself with the good sister's difficulties would keep me from interfering in Ron's situation.

"You're wrong about that," I said. "In fact, there's nothing I'd rather do. Give me a chance to get into the official records on the Marchbank case. I'll also make copies of all the material I found today. Once I have the information I need, I'll call and make arrangements to drive you to Mimi Marchbank's former residence. By the way, when are you planning to head back to Whidbey?"

"Tomorrow afternoon," she said. "Weather permitting," she added. "But believe me, if I need to stay longer, I will. I'm ready to put an end to this problem, and so is everyone else at Saint Benedict's. In fact, they may be even more ready than I am."

My cell phone rang. "Beau?" Mel Soames asked. "I thought you said you'd be home all evening. I'm at your place, but the doorman said you took off."

"Sorry. Something came up, but I'm only a few minutes away. I'll be there shortly."

I ended the call and turned back to Sister Mary Katherine. "I have to get back home. Give me until midmorning to gather information, then I'll call you and we can figure out what to do next." As I stood up, so did Fred. "You don't have to leave," I told him. "I'm sure I can catch a cab."

"No, I said I'd take you home," he insisted, "and I will."

"I didn't expect her to be so hard on herself for not telling someone what she had seen," I said to Fred as we waited for the valet to return Fred's Lexus. "She couldn't have been more than four years old when the murder happened."

"She's spent forty years as a Catholic nun," Fred said. "I suspect you don't do that without having a well-developed sense of responsibility for the state of humanity."

"I suppose you're right," I told him.

With the lift from Fred, I was back at Belltown Terrace within ten minutes of Mel Soames's phone call and found her waiting in the lobby. She was bundled in a long black leather coat complete with scarf, gloves, and boots. She surveyed my sweater and loafers with visible disdain. "You did take off in a hurry."

"As I said on the phone, something unexpected came up."

"How unexpected?" she asked. Her tone of voice was sharper than it should have been, and it put me on edge. So did the icy look on her face. I've finally learned that seeing an expression like that on a woman's face usually means bad news for any man dumb enough to remain in close proximity.

The front door opened and a group of people, sharing a laugh, tumbled into the lobby. They were all drenched in snow, having just been through some kind of killer snowball fight. All of them seemed to be having a very good time. Their high spirts and easygoing banter stood in stark contrast to Melissa Soames's dour expression.

"Maybe we should talk about this upstairs," I suggested. "In private."

She nodded. "You're right," she agreed stiffly. "Privacy is probably a very good idea."

CHAPTER 8

MOST OF THE TIME when people walk into my twenty-fifth-floor penthouse apartment, they are so agog at the wall-to-wall windows and amazing views that they're momentarily struck dumb. I doubt Mel Soames even noticed the view. Blue eyes blazing, she rounded on me the moment I shut the door.

"What the hell were you thinking?" she demanded.

Seeing Melissa Soames that angry was a daunting sight. I was pretty sure I knew what she meant, but I decided to play dumb anyway. "What are you talking about?"

"About your going to Ron Peters's place this afternoon, as if you didn't know!" she exclaimed. "Didn't Harry give you strict orders to keep your nose out of it?"

"Tracy called me," I said in my defense. "She's seventeen. Her dad had just been hauled off for questioning in handcuffs, her mother had gone to meet with a lawyer. She called me asking for help. Do you have any idea what it feels like to be a teenager in circumstances like that?"

"You'd be surprised," Mel returned.

"Well, what was I supposed to do?"

"Obey orders, for starters," Mel shot back.

"Who told you I had been there?" I asked the question more to get her off track than because I wanted an answer.

"Does it matter?"

My first guess was easy. Based on my latest meeting with Amy's sharp-tongued sister and her obvious low opinion of me, I assumed Molly Wright to be the probable squealer. "It doesn't matter at all," I said. "Now, are you going to stay awhile? Would you like me to take your coat?"

Mel seemed to consider. With a resigned shrug, she removed her gloves, stuffed them into a pocket, and then slipped out of the coat, folded it and laid it down beside her.

"Something to drink?"

This was a bluff, of course. I don't keep booze in the house and only a limited supply of sodas.

"Coffee," she said. "I'm working."

Fortunately, I do keep a supply of Seattle's Best Saturday Blend beans in my freezer. "I'll be right back," I said. "Make yourself comfortable."

Once the coffee was started, I came back into the living room. By then some of Mel's temper had worn off. Like everyone else, she had gravitated toward the expanse of western-exposure windows and had settled on the window seat.

"If you're working, where's Brad?" I asked.

"His wife called. Their pipes are frozen. She needed him to come home."

"One of the joys of home ownership," I said.

"You know how it's going to look, don't you?" she asked.

"Your being out working on your own?"

"No, your going by Ron Peters's place. It's going to look like you went there to give Ron inside information on what's going on in our investigation—information that you can then hand over to that slick attorney of his who, as I understand it, also happens to be your attorney of record."

"Look, Mel," I said patiently. "I tried to explain this to Harry this morning. Ron and I have been friends for years. Ditto Ralph Ames. The three of us have shared a lot of ups and downs over that time. It's only natural that Ron would turn to Ralph when he was in need of legal representation. Besides, how could I give Ron information I don't have? I know Rosemary Peters died over the weekend, but Ron himself told me that. I know blood was found in Ron's car. Amy told me that. And I heard there had been some kind of family altercation that caused suspicion to point at Ron."

"Where did that come from?"

Maxwell Cole was the one who had provided that last little tidbit, but I knew if I told Melissa Soames that, she'd go ballistic on me again—something I wanted to avoid if at all possible.

"Ron told me that, too," I hedged. "And so did Tracy. Ron and Rosemary were in a legal wrangle over custody of his younger daughter, Heather."

From the kitchen, I heard the last of the water burble into the pot. "I hope you don't take cream," I said. "I'm out of cream."

"No. Black is fine."

Minutes later, I returned to the living room with two mugs of coffee. I knew that meant I probably wouldn't sleep very well for the second night in a row, but I wanted to appear hospitable enough to keep Mel from lighting into me again.

"You're sure you don't know anything more than that?" she asked as I handed over her cup.

"I understand that you and Brad took Ron someplace for questioning—to the office, presumably."

Mel pursed her lips as if considering what, if anything, she should say. After a pause she said, "Rosemary Peters was the on-prem manager of a soup kitchen run by an organization called Bread of Life Mission at Fifth and Puyallup in downtown Tacoma, not far from the Tacoma Dome. The place is closed over the weekend. On Monday morning, when her two cooks came in to start breakfast, the back door was unlocked, with no sign of forced entry, but Rosemary was nowhere to be found. Tacoma PD was summoned to the scene. They found a few blood spatters in the parking lot, along with a single shoe. Nothing else. No brass. No usable footprints. And, since the area is paved, no tire tracks, either.

"Michael Lujan is on the Bread of Life board of directors. He's also an attorney. He was doing pro bono work for Rosemary Peters in regard to the custody matter. She called him late Friday evening and said that after Ron Peters was served with the papers, he came roaring down to Tacoma and bitched her out. Said he'd—"

"See her in hell before he'd hand Heather over," I supplied.

Mel looked at me questioningly. "He told you that?"

"As I said earlier, Ron and I are friends—good friends."

"When Lujan heard what had happened, that Rosemary was missing, he called Tacoma PD and reported what Rosemary had told him about the incident with her ex. On Sunday afternoon a guy out walking with his dog along the edge of the tide flats stumbled across the body of a dead female. She was found at the bottom of the steep bank that runs along Commencement Bay just south of Brown's Point. Tacoma PD responded to that incident as well. Sometime late Monday morning someone put two and two together and realized that the missing woman and the dead woman were one and the same. The unidentified gunshot victim was barefoot and wearing nothing but a T-shirt, panties, and robe in frigid weather. From the looks of it, she was forced into the trunk of the vehicle, probably at gunpoint, and then shot while the vehicle was still in the soup kitchen parking lot. The killer then transported the victim to a pullout along Highway 509, where he removed her from the vehicle and rolled her down a steep embankment. Fortunately she didn't get hung up in a blackberry bramble. If she had, it might have been years before we found the body."

I thought about the muscles in Ron's arms and the upper-body strength that came from years of pushing his own wheelchair and lifting himself in and out of vehicles. Unfortunately, none of this sounded as if it were beyond his physical capabilities.

"No tire tracks there, either?" I asked.

Mel shook her head. "Blacktop," she said. "But we do have something."

"What's that?"

"There's a restaurant just up the road—at Brown's Point. We checked their security camera. We've got a grainy but identifiable video of Ron's very distinctive vehicle going past the restaurant northbound at eleven fifty-nine P.M. Friday."

"His clamshell wheelchair topper is pretty distinctive, all right." That's what I said, but it wasn't what I was thinking.

What time did Tracy say she heard Ron's car return to the carport? I wondered. *Two A.M. or so? That would be just about time enough to make it home to Queen Anne Hill from Brown's Point, which is between Tacoma and Federal Way.*

"Yes, it is," Mel continued. "So based on the security tape and your report that someone had found dried blood in Ron's car, Brad and I showed up armed with a search warrant. We also impounded his car. We found the blood, lots of it . . ." She paused, her eyes trained on my face. "And something else. Wedged into the wheel well, where he wouldn't have seen it in the dark, was a single shoe—a shoe that matches the one found in the parking lot outside the Bread of Life Mission."

I felt like all the air had been sucked out of my lungs. For lack of something to say, I took Mel's cup and mine and headed for the kitchen. My hands shook as I poured coffee. I stayed in the kitchen until my breathing and shaking hands were back under control.

By the time I returned to the living room, Mel had kicked off her boots and had wrapped an afghan around her shoulders.

"Did your wife make this?" she asked. "It's lovely."

"Neither one of my wives were into crocheting," I said. "My grandmother made that for me."

"Oh," Mel said.

I sat back down beside her. I had no idea what to say. Neither did she, evidently. For a time we both sipped our respective coffees in silence.

"I knew you and Ron Peters had been partners," she said finally. "But I guess I didn't realize how tight you were and still are."

"Yes," I agreed. "We're tight, all right." For a while I thought I was going to let it go at that, but then I surprised myself and told Melissa Soames the rest of it.

"When Ron and I first started working together, I thought he was a prissy jerk. He was a vegan, and that pissed the hell out of me. I mean, how many vegan cops do you know? I gave him a hard time about it every chance I got. Then, in the course of the case we were working on, I met this woman, an amazing woman, and fell in love with her. Anne was her name, Anne Corley. I realized eventually that she was . . . well, let's say troubled . . . but I was in love and figured it wasn't anything I couldn't handle. Except she was more than troubled, so troubled she suckered me into shooting her on the afternoon of our wedding day. They didn't call her death suicide by cop back then, but that's what it was."

"I had no idea," Mel said after a long pause. "I'm sorry."

I nodded. "It happened a long time ago. I got winged by a bullet in the shoot-out. Once the doctors got through with me, Ron Peters was the one who dragged me home from Harborview Hospital. Not here—but to my old apartment. This is the one I bought after Anne died, and soon after I found out how well off she had left me as far as money is concerned."

Mel looked around the room as if taking it in for the first time. "She left you all this?"

I nodded. "And more." I was silent for a long time. I didn't resume the story until Mel shifted restlessly on the window seat.

"But to go back to Ron. When we came home from the ER, he helped me up to my room in the Royal Crest. There, right in plain sight on the kitchen counter, was what was left of our wedding cake. Ron never said a word. He just picked it up and stuffed it down the garbage disposal. We've been friends ever since. Later on, Ralph Ames, who was Anne's attorney originally, helped Ron get his kids back from a drug-dealing commune in eastern Oregon, where Rosemary had taken up residence."

"So the three of you have a history."

"You could say that," I agreed. "Just call us the three musketeers."

I talked about Ron then, telling Mel everything I knew about him. She took notes and asked occasional questions. I probably sounded pretty lame. Maybe I was hoping that if I could convince Mel that Ron Peters was a good guy, I could also get her to disregard the mounting evidence against him. The unchanging expression on her face told me I wasn't making any progress.

"So that's it, then?" she asked when I finally ran out of steam.

"Pretty much."

She closed her notebook, stuffed it in her purse, and retrieved one of her boots from the floor.

"Where is he?" I asked, expecting her to say the King County Jail in downtown Seattle, or else the Justice Center out in Kent.

"He's back home for now," Mel answered. "At least until the preliminary hearing. We were going to arrest him, but none of the local jails would take him."

"Because he's a cop?"

"That's part of it," Mel conceded. "But also because of his physical situation. Mrs. Peters and your friend, Ralph Ames, made it quite clear that wherever he ended up, the facility needed to be prepared to handle his ongoing medical needs."

"As in elimination issues?" I asked, stating what I knew about Ron's physical challenges as diplomatically as possible.

Mel simply nodded. "That and the possibility of his developing bedsores—or maybe they call them chair sores. If the AG's office had its own detention facility, it might be different, but none of the jail commanders we talked to were willing to accept the liability. We had to take him back home for now."

"Doesn't that leave Ross Connors open to charges of playing favorites?"

Finished zipping up her second boot, Mel gave me a wan smile. "Maybe. But even Ross Connors doesn't carry much weight when it comes to local officials worrying about possible liability claims. Besides, realistically speaking, Ron Peters doesn't seem like much of a flight risk. His kids and his wife are here. We've confiscated his Camry and his weapons. What's he going to do?"

I thought of Jared not wanting his daddy to sleep over anywhere else. For tonight, at least, that was true. "Sounds like it's handled," I said.

Mel gathered up her purse and coat and started for the door. She paused in the entryway with her fingers on the doorknob. She turned back to me. Once again, her blue eyes were ablaze, but this time her anger wasn't directed at me.

"I was eleven the first time the cops carted my dad off to jail for beating the crap out of my mother," she said. "And all the while they were putting the cuffs on him, she kept screaming that it was an accident, that he never meant to hurt her. As soon as they let him out, it started all over again. I moved out when I was seventeen, when I couldn't stand to be around it a minute longer. Five years later and three years after she divorced him, he came after her again. That time he killed her."

"I'm sorry," I said. What else was there to say?

She nodded. "Me, too. And I'm sorry that Ron Peters is your friend, Beau. Because it looks like he murdered his ex-wife."

With that she opened the door and walked out. The Rosemary Peters homicide was a case Melissa Soames was taking personally. And so was I—for entirely different reasons.

Mel's motivation was simple. If she could nail Ron with his ex-wife's murder, Mel would be reclaiming a measure of justice not only for Rosemary but also for Mel's long-deceased mother. If she succeeded and Ron went to prison, I would be losing a good friend and three wonderful kids would be losing their father.

Mounting evidence to the contrary, I hoped to hell that wouldn't happen.

Looking back at what I had told Mel about Ron, I was struck by my sins of omission, by what I'd left out of the story—the web of cracks that seemed to be appearing in his ostensibly happy marriage to Amy; the constant and unwelcome presence of a difficult sister-in-law; a rebellious and possibly drug-using daughter. Had all of those, combined with new demands from his ex-wife, turned into a volatile mix that had pushed Ron over the edge?

After drinking so much coffee, I didn't expect to fall asleep in my chair, but I should have known better. I did, only to awake, stiff and sore, at four o'clock in the morning. I dragged my butt off to bed, but then I tossed and turned and went right back to worrying about what would happen to Ron and Amy and the kids. Finally, conceding there was no hope of going back to sleep, I went out to the kitchen and made more coffee.

My old SPD shrink, Dr. Baxter, always said that the best cure for insomnia is to work on something other than what you're worrying about. With that in mind I hauled out the tape Freddy Mac had brought me and stuck it into the VCR. I saw at once what he had meant about there being a breakthrough. This time when he put Sister Mary Katherine under, there was far less resistance to going back to that Saturday afternoon. In her little-girl voice, Bonnie Jean Dunleavy was able to talk about what was going on outside the kitchen window without having to interpose a make-believe camera between herself and the action.

This time Fred focused Bonnie Jean's attention on the vehicle that the killers had driven into Bonnie's neighbor's driveway.

"What's it like?" he asked.

"Big," Bonnie Jean answered. "It's a big car."

"What color?"

"Red," she answered. "Sort of red. And the nose is empty."

"Empty?" Fred asked.

"It's just round. There's nothing on it—nothing shiny."

"You mean there's no hood ornament?"

Bonnie Jean shrugged her shoulders. "I guess," she said.

I put the VCR on pause and reached for the file folder of material I had collected from the *P.-I.* And there it was parked in the background of the photo taken after Madeline Marchbank's funeral. Behind Madeline's brother, Albert, and his wheelchair-bound mother was the naked-nosed hood of an automobile—a 1949 or 1950 Frazer Deluxe.

I'm far from being a car nut who knows the make, model, cubic inches, and horsepower of every vehicle ever made. What I had instead was direct personal experience with a very similar car.

One of my high school buddies, Sonny Sondegaard, was another Ballard kid who went salmon fishing with his dad's commercial fishing crew. The year we all turned sixteen he came back to school at the end of the summer with a pocketful of money. He spent two hundred bucks of his hard-earned cash buying himself a teal-blue 1949 Frazer.

During our junior year we had some great times in Sonny's car. Back then hood ornaments were all the rage, but the Frazer didn't have one. We teased Sonny endlessly about it, even threatening to steal an ornament off someone else's car and graft it onto his. Sonny took the teasing in stride. The Frazer was a fun car to fool around in right up until the beginning of our senior year. On Sunday of Labor Day weekend, coming back from a kegger on Camano Island, Sonny ran off Highway 99 and wrapped the front end of the Frazer around a telephone pole. He was dead before they ever removed him from the wreckage. My whole senior year was colored by the fact that the first day of school started with classes in the morning and ended with Sonny's funeral later that afternoon.

And here, all these years later, I was dealing with another Frazer and another death. Leaving the VCR on pause, I once again dialed law enforcement's special twenty-four-hour number at the Department of Motor Vehicles. This time I went straight to a human being, as opposed to a recorded message. When I told the clerk who I was and that I was looking for licensing information from 1950, I expected her to laugh her head off, but she didn't. "One moment, please," she said.

I heard the clatter of computer keystrokes in the background. Then, within seconds, I had my answer. Albert and Elvira Marchbank had indeed owned a 1950 Frazer—a Caribbean coral Deluxe. I had no doubt that in the eyes of an unsophisticated not-quite-five-year-old girl, coral would indeed be "sort of " red.

I sat for some time, studying the freeze-frame likeness of Sister Mary Katherine staring back at me from the television screen. Bonnie Jean Dunleavy had been an eyewitness to Mimi Marchbank's murder. Given that circumstance, surely the killers must have been caught, right? So I called the Records department at Seattle PD to see if Madeline Marchbank's killer had ever been apprehended. Once again, after a surprisingly few keystrokes, I had my answer, and it wasn't one I liked. Madeline Marchbank's 1950 murder, perpetrated by person or persons unknown, was still listed as an open case of homicide—fifty-four years after the fact.

After checking in and letting Barbara Galvin know I'd be working outside the office all day, I spent the next hour or so researching the Marchbank Foundation. It had been created in 1972 on the occasion of Albert's death from colon cancer. The financial arrangements weren't spelled out in the material available to the general public through the foundation's Web site. I had a feeling, though, that some provision had probably been made for Albert's widow throughout her lifetime and that, upon Elvira's subsequent death, any residual assets would revert to the trust. Creating a charitable foundation had no doubt been a way of dodging state and federal estate taxes while still allowing the family to maintain some degree of control over the disposition of assets. The Marchbank Foundation was into the fine arts in a big way. The Seattle Opera, the Seattle Symphony, and the Seattle Art Museum were all major beneficiaries of Marchbank Foundation grants, but other smaller organizations were listed as well.

Each time I went back to the Web site's home page, I looked at the formally staged portrait of the founders taken on their twenty-fifth wedding anniversary and only a short time before Albert's death. He couldn't have been much older than his early sixties, but he already had a gaunt and fading look about him while his wife looked robust— and immensely pleased with herself. In the photo they looked like the fine upstanding citizens the Marchbank Foundation PR flacks claimed them to be. Could these two people, smiling broadly into the camera's lens, actually be a pair of cold-blooded killers?

I wondered about whether or not I should print a copy of the photo to take with me when I went to see Sister Mary Katherine. I had gone off to the Westin in such a hurry the night before that I hadn't taken my copy of the *Post-Intelligencer* photo along with me. Finally, when it was late enough to be halfway civilized, I called Freddy Mac at home.

"What's up?" he asked. "Did you find a record of the car?"

I said, "Albert Marchbank owned a 1949 Caribbean coral Frazer—a vehicle with no hood ornament, just like Bonnie Jean said. I've also located photos of Mimi Marchbank's brother and sister-in-law. One is contemporary, taken the day of Mimi's funeral. The other is from the early seventies, almost twenty years later."

"And?" Fred asked.

"I'm wondering if it's a good idea to show them to her."

Fred took his time before answering. "Well," he said finally, "it'll go one of two ways—either she'll remember or she won't."

"Do you want to be there when I show them to her?"

"Can't," he said. "I'm backed up with appointments all morning long, and I know Sister Mary Katherine is hoping to head back to Whidbey sometime this afternoon."

"But you don't think seeing the pictures will hurt her?" I pressed.

"In my personal opinion, not remembering is what's hurting her,"

Fred countered. "If seeing the photos happens to jar her to conscious memory of what went on back then, that should be all to the good."

With Fred MacKinzie's Good Housekeeping seal of approval, I printed a copy of Albert and Elvira's official Web-site photograph as well as a photo of the Marchbank Foundation corporate headquarters, an imposing-looking two-story Georgian with an address that put the place just north of the University of Washington on Twelfth Avenue NE.

At 10:00 A.M., I stuffed everything I'd gleaned through my research efforts into my briefcase and headed for the Westin for my meeting with Sister Mary Katherine. It was raining hard when I drove the 928 out onto the street from the Belltown Terrace. Rain, especially a warm rain like this one, was good news. It meant the snow would melt that much faster and life in Seattle would soon return to normal. As I waited for the light at Second and Wall, I realized that I hadn't heard a word from Ron or Amy Peters.

Oh, well, I told myself. *Maybe no news is good news.*

That was wrong, of course, but I wouldn't find that out until much, much later.

CHAPTER 9

SISTER MARY KATHERINE WAS WAITING for me as I walked into the hotel café. "We've got to stop meeting like this," I said. "People will talk."

She smiled and shook her head. "People aren't interested in nuns," she said. "They're a lot more interested in what some priests have been up to—and with good reason. Compared with misbehaving priests, nuns are a pretty boring lot."

Considering what I'd learned about Sister Mary Katherine herself in the course of the last several days, I could have argued the point, but I didn't.

"Would you like some breakfast?"

"Sure," I said, "but only if it's my treat."

Sister Mary Katherine waited while I negotiated with the waitress for eggs and bacon. Once the server departed, I reached for my briefcase. "I brought along few things for show-and-tell," I told her.

"Tell me this first," she said. "I need to know. Were Mimi's killers ever caught?"

"No," I said. "They never were."

Disappointment shrouded her face. "They probably would have been had I told the authorities what I had seen at the time."

"Maybe," I said. "But you need to know that it's possible the perpetrators were very influential people in Seattle at the time of the murder."

Her eyes widened. "You've actually identified suspects?"

I nodded. "Have you ever heard of the Marchbank Foundation?" I asked.

Sister Mary Katherine nodded. "I believe it was started by Madeline's brother and his wife."

Now it was my turn to be surprised. "You know about Albert and Elvira Marchbank then?"

Sister Mary Katherine laughed and shrugged. "I live on Whidbey Island, not on the moon," she said. Then she grew serious. "After you and Fred left last night, I called home. Sister Therese got on the computer and tracked down some information for me on Madeline Marchbank. In the process I learned something about her brother and sister-in-law as well."

"Have you seen pictures of them?" I asked. "There are photos posted on the Web site."

Sister Mary Katherine shook her head. "I won't have a chance to do that until later on this evening, when I get home."

"You don't have to wait that long," I said, pulling out my file of photos. "I brought them with me. Take a look at these."

Sister Mary Katherine's hand shook slightly as she opened the file. The topmost photo was of the Marchbank Foundation headquarters. Frowning, she studied it for some time. "This one looks familiar somehow, but I don't know why," she said. "I've had dealings with many of the local charitable foundations, but not this one. I never remember going there."

She put that paper down and picked up my copy of the newspaper photo taken after Madeline Marchbank's funeral. Sister Mary Katherine stared at it in utter silence for the better part of a minute. As she did so, all color drained from her face. At last she opened her fingers and the photo drifted away like a leaf caught in a breeze. I reached out and caught it in midair.

"You recognize them?"

Sister Mary Katherine nodded. "The man and woman in the picture are the ones I saw that day," she said in a voice that was barely audible. "The woman in the wheelchair was Mimi's mother. I remember all of them now. I remember everything. The looks, the smells, the colors." She shuddered.

Freddy Mac had suggested that seeing the photos might finally unleash the memories Sister Mary Katherine had kept buried for more than fifty years, but I guess I hadn't really expected it to happen. Alternating waves of shock and horror registered on Mary Katherine's face. Watching her, I realized she was once again reliving that terrible Saturday afternoon. This time, though, she was doing so without the emotional buffer that had vividly preserved the awful memories, all the while keeping them safely out of conscious reach.

I'm a cop, not a counselor, so while Sister Mary Katherine grappled with this new reality, I sat there feeling like a dolt and fervently wishing Fred MacKinzie were on hand to do and say the right things. For several long minutes she sat with her head bowed and with one hand covering her eyes. I wondered if she was crying or praying. At last she seemed to get a grip.

"It was so awful," she said at last. "No wonder I suppressed it."

"Are you going to be all right?" I asked.

"I think so," she said.

For the next hour or so, over the comforting everyday background noises of clinking glassware and cutlery, we went over everything Sister Mary Katherine was now able to recall from that terrible afternoon— the gory details her conscious mind had concealed for so many years. I took careful notes, but it turned out there was little an adult Sister Mary Katherine could add to the hypnotically induced revelations Bonnie Jean Dunleavy had already made. A lesser woman might have fallen apart during that stressful interview, but once Sister Mary Katherine had regained her composure, she kept it.

At last, exhausted, she leaned back in her chair. "Why?" she asked. "What made them decide to kill her? What could possibly have been so bad or so important that murder was their only option?"

"At least the only option they could see," I countered. "And the answer to your question is that I have no idea. Desperate people seldom see the world in the same terms you and I do. On the tapes you mentioned several times that the man, Albert, seemed angry when he was talking to Mimi. You said you thought he was asking Mimi for something and that she kept telling him no."

"Maybe his business was in some kind of trouble," Sister Mary Katherine speculated. "Maybe he needed money."

"That could be," I told her. "Money woes often translate into motives for murder, but as I said before, Albert Marchbank was a big deal in Seattle back then. If he was in any kind of financial difficulty at the time, I should be able to find some record of it. But then again sometimes murders grow out of nothing more than a bad case of sibling rivalry."

"Like Cain and Abel," Sister Mary Katherine murmured.

"That's right," I said. "So maybe sometimes it's not such a bad thing to be an only child."

She shook her head. "The whole idea is awful."

"Murder is always awful," I returned. "For everyone involved. No exceptions. Now, if you're up to it, let's go back to the murder scene again. Can you tell me anything at all about the weapon?"

"About the knife?" Sister Mary Katherine frowned in concentration before she answered, as though trying to peer at the scene through the fog of time. "It was just a regular knife—an ordinary kitchen knife—but it came from Elvira's purse. I saw her open the purse and take it out."

"But the newspaper article said that police thought the knife was most likely taken from Mimi's own kitchen."

"Then the article and the police were both wrong," Mary Katherine declared. "Or if it was Mimi's knife, it was taken from her kitchen at some time other than on that day. I saw Elvira take it from her purse after she got out of the car. And if they brought the knife along with them when they came to Mimi's house, wouldn't that mean premeditation?"

"Yes, it would," I agreed. "You mentioned Elvira getting out of the car. Let's talk about that vehicle for a moment." I returned to the file folder and pulled out a stock photo of a 1949 Caribbean coral Frazer Deluxe, one I had downloaded from the Internet. "Does this look familiar?"

Sister Mary Katherine studied the photo for only a matter of seconds before she nodded. "This is the one," she said. "Or one just like it."

"The officer in charge of the investigation was a Seattle Police Department detective named William Winkler. Do you ever remember talking to him about what you had seen?"

"No."

"And you never spoke to any other police officer about what happened that day?"

"As far as I know, no one ever asked me about any of it," Mary Katherine said. "They may have talked to my parents, but not to me. They should have, shouldn't they?"

"If they'd been doing their jobs," I responded.

Bonnie Jean may have been scared by what she had witnessed and by being threatened by one of the killers, but I couldn't believe she would have kept quiet if any of the detectives on the case had actually bothered asking her about it.

"What about Mimi's funeral?" I continued. "Did you go?"

Sister Mary Katherine shook her head. "Not that I remember. My parents probably thought I was too young to understand what was going on."

"Did your parents attend?"

"I don't believe so, but I don't know for sure."

"But the woman was your friend," I objected. "It seems to me they would have gone if for no other reason than to pay their respects."

"It's strange," Sister Mary Katherine said. "It's as though seeing the pictures has reopened that whole chapter in my life. Now I remember it all—not only Mimi's death, but the rest of it, too. I thought we were friends, but Mother didn't agree. She said Mimi felt sorry for us because she was rich and we were poor. Mother said that whatever Mimi did for me she was doing out of pity or charity, not out of friendship. But regardless, Mimi was nice to me. She seemed magical, almost like a fairy godmother. She taught me to play hopscotch and jacks. Sometimes she'd read to me from books she brought home from the library. A few times, we even walked up the street to the drugstore and she bought me strawberry sodas."

Mary Katherine reached across the table and picked up the picture of the Marchbank Foundation headquarters. This time she nodded in recognition. "Now I remember. That's her house—the one where Mimi used to live. The house we lived in, Mrs. Ridder's house, was right over here—to the right of this driveway."

On the tapes, Bonnie Jean couldn't remember the landlady's name. Now the name emerged effortlessly.

"How long did you live there?"

"Not very long—a few months maybe. We must have moved out within weeks of when Mimi was killed, but I could be mistaken about that."

"Any idea where you went?"

Sister Mary Katherine shook her head. "We moved so many times over the years, I'm really not sure."

The waitress stopped by to refill our cups. "Is Elvira Marchbank still alive?" Sister Mary Katherine asked.

"I don't know," I told her. "She could be. Nothing I found this morning indicated otherwise. Albert died in the early seventies, but as far as I know, Elvira's still around."

"That doesn't seem fair," Sister Mary Katherine said. "How is it possible that Mimi died so young and yet Elvira is still walking around free as a bird after all these years? If she's still alive, she must be in her eighties. I can't imagine living with that kind of guilt for so many years. I wonder if she ever feels any remorse about what she did."

"I doubt it," I said. "Most of the killers I've met come up short in the remorse department."

"After such a long time, could she still be convicted and go to jail?"

"There's no statute of limitations on murder," I said. "And I'm sure they have some sort of geriatric wing in the women's prison down at Purdy, but I wouldn't count on a conviction if I were you."

"Why not?"

"Time, for one thing. As you said, the crime happened years ago. I'm going to do my best to send her there, but you'll have to be patient. It won't be easy."

"Why not? There's a witness," Sister Mary Katherine objected, "an eyewitness who saw the whole thing."

"Yes, but we're talking about an eyewitness who took half a century to speak up. A good defense attorney will tear your testimony to shreds. And a jury is going to wonder what caused you to suddenly recall those events now. There are a lot of people out there who don't go along with the idea of repressed memories, so I can't base my entire case on your word alone. I'm going to have to dig up enough corroborating evidence that a prosecutor and a jury will be willing to go with it."

"Can you find that kind of evidence?" she asked.

"I'll do my best," I told her. "Finding evidence is what I do. It's what I've done all my life."

"While all I've been doing is praying and sewing," she said. I heard the self-reproach in her voice and knew Sister Mary Katherine was still holding Bonnie Jean Dunleavy's silence against her.

"Sometimes," I told her, "praying is the only thing that works."

"It seems to me I should be the one telling you about the wonders of prayer," Sister Mary Katherine said with a tight smile.

"That's all right," I told her. "No extra charge."

She raised her hand, flagged down the waitress, and asked for her bill. She turned down my offer to pick up the check. "I like to pay my own way," she said. "And I need to be heading out. I have some shopping to do before I leave town, but Sister Therese expects to have the road cleared by early this afternoon, and I want to be home well before dark."

"I hadn't realized the highway on Whidbey was closed."

"Not the highway," she said. "That's open. The problem is our road—the private one that goes from the highway to the convent. There's snow and several downed trees as well. But I've been away for days now, and I'm ready to be home, even if I have to get out and walk."

                       ·

Sister Mary Katherine struck me as the kind of woman who wouldn't be above hiking through snow and ice to get where she wanted to go, but I wondered if she was strong-willed enough to deal with all the emotional fallout from that long-ago Saturday afternoon.

I helped her retrieve her bags from the bellman, then we stood together under the covered portico waiting for our vehicles to be brought around. A steady downpour was falling on the street outside. Compared with the previous days of bitter cold, the forty-degree weather felt downright balmy.

"Are you sure you're going to be all right?" I asked again.

Sister Mary Katherine nodded. "Yes," she said. "But it's not easy. I just never thought I'd be involved in something like this. These kinds of things aren't supposed to happen to people in my line of work."

"You'd be surprised," I said.

The parking valet drove up in a white Odyssey minivan. Once Sister Mary Katherine's bags had been loaded, she turned back to me and held out her hand. "Thank you, Beau," she said. "I'm sure working with you and Freddy—with people I know and trust—has made this far less traumatic than it would have been otherwise."

"You're welcome," I said. I handed her one of my cards. "Call me if you remember anything more."

She studied the card for a moment before slipping it into the pocket of her coat. "All right," she said. "And you'll let me know what's going on?"

"Yes, but remember, this is going to take time."

"I'll keep that in mind," she said.

I watched her drive away. By then my 928 was there as well. I got into the Porsche and headed for SPD. Melting snow and the warm driving rain combined to turn Seattle's downtown streets into rivers. I felt sorry for hapless pedestrians trying to stay out of the way of rooster tails of oily, dirty spray kicked up in the wake of passing cars.

Even though the department is now in its new digs up the hill from the old Public Safety Building, out of habit I drove to the old parking garage on James where I used to be a regular customer. No one there recognized me or the 928. And the same thing was true for the new Seattle Police Department Headquarters building on Fifth Avenue. None of the officers on duty in the classy lobby had any idea of who I was. After being issued a visitor's pass, I went upstairs to Records.

When I told the woman in charge what I wanted, she shook her head. "Oh, honey," she said. "All cold case stuff that old is still down in the vault at the old Public Safety Building. You know where that is?"

"I'm pretty sure I can find it," I assured her.

"Good. You go right on down there then. I'll call ahead and let them know you're coming."

Being a typical Seattle native, I have a natural aversion to umbrellas. By the time I walked first up the hill and then back down again, I was wet through. And once I reached the building that had been my place of employment for so many years, I found out you really can't go home again. The Public Safety Building, soon scheduled to meet the wrecking ball, was a pale shadow of its former self. One side of the once busy lobby was stacked with the cots used by a men's homeless shelter that temporarily occupies that space overnight. A janitor was haphazardly mopping the granite floor. He nodded at me as I made my way to the bored security guard stationed near the elevator bank.

"Basement, right?" he asked, putting down his worn paperback.

That meant someone had called ahead to say I was coming. "Yes," I said.

"Downstairs," he said. "Take a right when you exit the elevators and go to the end of the corridor."

Here no pass was necessary. The lobby may have been a cot ware-house, but the basement corridor was worse. It was stacked floor to ceiling with a collection of decrepit gray metal desks, shelving units and cubicle dividers, along with dozens of broken-down desk chairs missing backs and casters. I suspect my old fifth-floor desk was there in that collection of wreckage that looked more like a gigantic garage sale than a corridor.

I dodged my way through the maze of furniture and into what's called the vault. The clerk in charge of the evidence room was a middle-aged lady whom I didn't recognize. "This is from a long time ago," she said, examining my request form complete with the specifics of the Mimi Marchbank murder. "It may take a while for me to dig this out," she added. "Why don't you have a seat?"

The only place to sit was at a battered wooden study carrel that looked as though it predated the junk in the corridor by several de-cades and made me wonder if it wasn't a displaced refugee from an early version of the U. Dub Library.

Convinced I had come into the building entirely under everybody's radar, I was taking a load off when, two minutes later, the door slammed open. A fighting-mad, rain-drenched Paul Kramer marched into the room.

That would be Captain Paul Kramer. At the time I left Seattle PD, it may have looked to the world as though I was bailing because of Sue Danielson's death. Sue, my partner at the time, had been gunned down by her ex-husband, and I admit it—her murder was a contribut-ing factor to my leaving when I did. Sue's senseless slaughter was one more than I could stand. But the other part of it was the fact that the departmental hierarchy had seen fit to promote a backstabbing worm like Paul Kramer to the rank of captain.

Sure, he had aced the test. I don't question the fact that he had the scores to justify a promotion. What Kramer didn't have were people skills. He was an ambitious, brownnosing jerk who flimflammed his superiors by being utterly scrupulous about his paperwork, but he wasn't above hanging his fellow detectives out to dry whenever it suited him. He and I had been on a collision course from the first day he turned up in Homicide. Back then it was all I could do to tolerate being in the same room with him. In the aftermath of Sue's death, the idea of having to report to the guy was more than I could handle.

Now, years later, someone had gone to the trouble of sounding an alarm and letting him know I was in the building. Territorial as any dog, he had hurried down the hill and down to the basement to lift his leg metaphorically and pee in my shoe.

"Hello there, Beaumont," he said, sounding as obnoxiously official as ever. "Long time no see. Imagine meeting you here."

"Yes," I agreed. "Imagine that."

He meandered over to the counter and looked around for a piece of paper that might give him a clue as to why I was there. Fortunately, the clerk had taken my request with her when she had wandered off through the towering maze of sagging metal shelving. If Captain Kramer wanted to find out what I was doing in the evidence room, he was going to have to come straight out and ask—which he did with as much hail-fellow-well-met phoniness as he could muster.

"What brings you back to the old stamping ground?"

"Working a case," I said.

"Really," he said. "For SHIT?"

"Yup," I told him. "That's where I hang my hat these days."

Kramer leaned back against the counter and folded his arms across his chest. "Your being here wouldn't have anything to do with what's going on with Ron Peters, would it?"

I could have answered the question straight out, but Kramer has always brought out the worst in me. This was no exception. "Since Ron and I are good friends, wouldn't that be a clear conflict of interest?" I asked.

Kramer made a sour face. "When has that ever stopped you?" he asked.

"It might not have stopped me, but I happen to work for the Washington State Attorney General's office. Ross Connors doesn't tolerate that kind of thing."

"That must mean you're working one of our old cases then? Did you clear it with anyone upstairs before you came down here?"

When he said "upstairs," he wasn't talking about the sleepy security guard up in the lobby. He meant upstairs upstairs—back on the top floors of the new building where the brass hang out.

"Paul," I told him patiently, "I have a badge, and I have an assignment. Special Homicide means just exactly that—special. I don't have to clear what I'm doing with you or with anyone else."

"It seems to me that as a simple matter of interdepartmental courtesy, you would have stopped by . . ."

"Look, Kramer," I interrupted. "Can it. I don't work for you. I don't answer to you. If you have any questions about what I'm doing here, you're more than welcome to contact my boss and find out."

"And your boss would be?"

Before I could reply, the clerk returned to the counter carrying a document box. She looked from me to Kramer.

"Oh, Captain Kramer," she said. "I didn't hear you come in. Is there something I can do for you?"

"Sure," he said, staring pointedly at the box she was carrying. "I'll sign for that, Sandy. Mr. Beaumont and I can take it back to my office where we can go through it together."

In the bad old days, I probably would have punched him out, but I like to think I'm older and wiser now. Besides, there was no point. Eager to be of help, the clerk produced the proper form, which Kramer signed with all due ceremony. Then, picking up the box—my evidence box—he turned back to me. "Shall we?" he asked.

Kramer had the box in his hands—a box that contained all the surviving evidence as well as the musty case books to Madeline Marchbank's murder, a homicide that was more than fifty years old. Kramer had the box, but he didn't have access to the information I had recently unearthed—eyewitness accounts to that murder from both Bonnie Jean Dunleavy's and Sister Mary Katherine's separate points of view. Without those bits of the puzzle or the information I had managed to pull together, the box was just that—a useless thousand-piece jigsaw puzzle with all the critical pieces missing. Kramer could study whatever was in the box until hell froze over. Without my help, he wouldn't learn a thing.

"No, thanks, Paul," I said after a moment. "That's all right. Be my guest. Go through it on your own." I reached into my pocket and pulled out one of my business cards. "Here's my number," I added, dropping the card on the dust-laden lid to the box. "Give me a call a little later. I'll be very interested to hear what you find out."

With that, I opened the door to the evidence room and stepped back into the cluttered basement corridor. I left Paul Kramer standing there with his mouth open, holding on to the box and holding on to all his unanswered questions as well. It wasn't a very dramatic exit. It wasn't one of those high-testosterone departures where you go out in a blaze of gun-firing glory, but from my point of view, it still felt damned good.

Even if Harry I. Ball or Ross Connors ended up calling me on the carpet later, it was still worth doing. And given half a chance, I'd do it again.

CHAPTER 10

I COULD HAVE BAILED RIGHT THEN. I could have called Harry and dropped the case along with the dust-covered evidence box right in Kramer's lap, but I wasn't ready to do that. I guess what I really wanted to know was where all this was going. Was the attorney general's office's involvement really as benign as I'd been told, or was there more to it than the simple fact that Ross Connors and Father Andrew had played football together back in high school? I wouldn't know what Paul Harvey and his much younger successor continue to call "the rest of the story" until I had followed the Marchbank murder trail all the way to the end.

I spent more than twenty years at Seattle PD, most of it in Homicide. I've forgotten the details of most of the killers we caught and sent to prison, but every day of my life I carry around a complete catalog of the ones who got away. I can tell you the names and ages of the victims along with where, when, and how they died. Those ugly memories sit lodged in my heart, but unlike grains of sand trapped inside oyster shells, my remembered victims don't turn into iridescent pearls. Instead, they show up in the middle of the night, waking or sleeping, as an ugly Greek chorus of accusatory ghosts demanding to know why I allowed their unnatural deaths to pass into oblivion and their killers to go free.

I can also list by name all the grieving relatives—parents, sisters, brothers, and occasionally even children—who called me each year, usually on or near the anniversary of their loved ones' deaths. The family members called looking for closure. They called wondering if anything new had turned up. They called asking if anyone was still looking for their loved one's killer and seeking reassurance that someone else—anyone else—still cared.

Yes, William Winkler may have run off the rails when he got moved upstairs in Seattle PD, and yes, he may have been drummed out of the corps along with a lot of other dirty cops back in the mid- to late fifties, but once a homicide detective, always a homicide detective. Mimi Marchbank's murder had happened on his watch, and her killer was one of Wink's loose ends. I didn't know whether or not the man was still alive, but if he was—and if he was still in possession of his faculties—I guessed he'd remember everything that was in Paul Kramer's dusty evidence box—everything to be found in the box and possibly more besides.

While I stood in the garage lobby waiting for the attendant to return the 928, I called directory assistance. There were five Winklers listed. Two of them were listed as William and one was initial W only. Rather than dialing the three at random, I tried a different tack.

The International Order of Footprinters is a service organization made up of some still active but mostly retired law enforcement folks. The Seattle area chapter includes people who once served and protected in King, Pierce, Snohomish, and Thurston counties, and in various municipal jurisdictions as well—Seattle, Renton, Tacoma, Bellevue, and Everett. Some of the retired officers served in local branches of the FBI, the DEA, and the INS or in local port-policing agencies. There may be some ongoing competition and sibling rivalry among those branches, but once you graduate into Footprinters, it's time to get over it and let bygones be bygones.

Martin Woodman, a long-retired FBI special-agent-in-charge, is the grand old man of the Seattle area chapter. Widowed for at least twenty years now, he lives alone in the Wall Street Tower, which used to be called the Grosvenor House, and spends his long afternoons and relatively short evenings hanging out at the Five-Spot Café. Marty is too old and arthritic to carry on as part of the Keystone Kops anymore, and he's served in all the organization's various elective offices, both local and national, on numerous occasions. Now that he's slowing down, he limits his Footprinters involvement to that of self-appointed goodwill ambassador.

Whenever former or retired cops from this side of the mountains run into difficulties, Marty is on hand to look out for them regardless of where or when they served. He makes it a point to visit and collect get-well cards for whoever ends up in a hospital, and when somebody dies, Marty is on hand to make sure the deceased officer is laid to rest with all due ceremony and respect. It's his personal mission in life to make sure those old cops and their families aren't forgotten. You have to respect a guy like that. Marty Wood was the one man in Seattle who would know for sure whether or not Wink Winkler was still alive. He'd also probably know where I could find him.

I called Wall Street Tower. When no one answered the phone in Marty's room, I drove straight to the Five-Spot and parked on the street at a parking meter that had an astonishing thirty-nine minutes still left on it. Darting inside out of the rain, I spotted Marty sitting alone in a booth at the far end of the room, absently stirring a cup of coffee while staring down at the black-and-white-tiled floor.

"Hey, Marty," I said. "How's it going?"

"Who is it?" he asked, holding out a tremulous hand. "Can't see the way I used to, you know. This damned macular degeneration."

"Beaumont," I said. "J. P. Beaumont."

Martin Woodman's hand may have trembled when he offered it to me, but his grip was as bone-crushingly firm as ever.

"Oh, yes," he said. "I remember you. From Seattle PD. You're with that new outfit now, aren't you, the one from the AG's office? What's its name again?"

"Special Homicide Investigation Team."

He nodded sagely. "That's right. SHIT. Hell of a name, if you ask me. Wouldn't have gotten away with calling it that back in the old days, never in a million years. Have a seat, J.P. What can I do for you?"

Marty's vision may have been going, but his mental faculties were as sharp as ever.

"I'm looking for William Winkler," I said without preamble. "I was wondering if he's still around."

"Wink? Oh, sure. Lives at a retirement home over in West Seattle. It's not that good a place, but it's the best he could afford. Wink's cantankerous as hell, but then he always has been. I'm guessing his son put him there when he and his wife couldn't take care of him anymore or when they couldn't stand being around him."

"Health's no good?" I asked.

"Hell," Marty replied. "At our age, if you're still alive, you shouldn't complain. Doesn't do any good, anyway. What do you want him for?"

"I'm following up on a case of his from a long time ago. I wanted to see if he could shed any light on it."

Marty Woodman frowned. "You know he left the department . . ."

"Under a cloud?" I supplied. "Yes, but all this went on quite a while before that. You wouldn't happen to have his address or telephone number, would you?"

"I do, but it's back at my apartment. If you wouldn't mind walking me over there. They keep trying to get me to use this." He picked up a white cane and tapped it impatiently on the floor. "But it's hard teaching an old dog new tricks. So usually, when I'm ready to go back home, I call the reception desk and they send someone over to walk me there."

As we walked through the rain across the plaza and into the lobby of Wall Street Tower, I wondered how someone as blind as Marty Woodman would be able to find and decipher an address or phone number, but I shouldn't have worried. Marty's one-bedroom apartment was tiny and immaculate. Most of the living room was occupied by an enormous dining-room table, the surface of which was almost completely covered with an array of complicated computer equipment and a snarl of cables.

Standing next to the CRT, Marty clapped his hands once and the familiar start-up screen appeared. "Works just like one of those clickers," Marty said with a grin. "One clap turns it on, two turn it off. When I told Footprinters I was going blind, some of them came over and jury-rigged this sound-and-voice-activated outfit together for me. They didn't want me to quit working, especially since nobody else wants to do what I do. Have a chair," he added. "This shouldn't take too long. I call her Joyce, by the way."

And it didn't take long at all. In order to access his database, he spoke into some unseen microphone. His voice-recognition software responded in the form of a computer-generated female voice. Marty's "Joyce" sounded just like the woman who has spent years annoying everyone unfortunate enough to venture into the phone company's version of voice-mail hell. Before long Joyce was reeling off Wink Winkler's telephone number along with an address on Thirty-fifth in West Seattle. I jotted them down as she delivered them.

"You get all that?" Marty asked.

"Yes, I did. Thanks. But you were wrong."

Marty frowned. "About what?"

"You said you were too old to learn new tricks. Obviously you have."

The frown disappeared. Marty gave the top of his CRT an affectionate pat. "Modern science is a miracle, isn't it? Without her I'd be just plain useless."

I had to agree with him there. Modern science was a miracle. "You're right," I said. "It's downright amazing, but you might think about giving that cane of yours a try, too."

"Why?" he asked. "So I can walk in front of a bus?"

"Never mind," I said.

When I left, Marty walked me as far as the door. "I don't know what kind of a case you're working," he said, "but don't be too hard on poor old Wink. He did all right when he first left the department—had a lot of helpful connections and made some good investments, but then things started falling apart. Drank too much, gambled too much, his marriage broke up. You know the drill."

I nodded. It was an end-of-career path for far too many of the cops I knew.

"He and his son wound up owning a place called Emerald City Security, a moderately successful rent-a-cop company," Marty continued. "That went on until a few years ago. I'm not sure of all the details, but when the dust settled, the kid had the company and Wink ended up with next to nothing."

"I'll bear all that in mind," I said.

As I rode down in the elevator, I realized that the very existence of Marty Woodman's computer setup was one of those things where what goes around comes around. For a change it had happened the right way. After all the years Marty had spent making sure Footprint-ers weren't forgotten, it was nice to know that they had returned the favor.

People who live in Seattle have two constant sources of complaint. We're forever whining about either the weather or the traffic, or both. It seems to me that people who don't like the weather should leave. That by itself would probably go a long way toward fixing the traffic woes. And then, the next time our elected officials ask for money to fix the roads, the complainers who stay on should all belly up to the bar and offer to pay their fair share.

All this is to say that the drive to West Seattle, which should have taken about twenty minutes in the middle of the day, ended up taking an hour and twenty minutes. I hadn't called ahead to say I was drop-ping by because I didn't want to give Wink Winkler an opportunity to tell me not to. Besides, I didn't want to give him too much time in ad-vance to wonder about why I was paying him a visit.

Even from the street, Home Sweet Home Retirement Center looked depressing. Someone had carved a steep wheelchair ramp up the bank between the street and a tiny front yard that was a sea of melt-ing snow and mud and punctuated with cigarette butts. A second ramp, a makeshift plywood travesty covered with frayed indoor-outdoor car-peting, went from yard level to a rickety front porch. A hand-stenciled sign on the door casing announced "All Visitors Check with Front Desk," but of course there was no one manning the dingy front desk. The place smelled of mold and mildew and years of bad cooking, but a current health inspection certificate was prominently displayed behind the desk as if defying anyone to question the center's good reputation.

Home Sweet Home made Marty Woodman's digs at Wall Street Tower and Lars and Beverly Jenssen's cozy apartment at the Queen Anne Gardens seem downright palatial.

There was a bell on the desk. I rang it three times before anyone appeared, then a door opened and a tiny Asian woman stepped through a swinging door. She looked old enough and frail enough to be one of the residents, but she was wearing a baggy flowered uniform and carried a broom with a handle that was a foot taller than she was.

"Yes?" she asked.

"I'd like to see William Winkler."

"One moment," she said and disappeared.

I cooled my heels for the better part of five minutes before the door opened again. This time a heavyset, bulldog-faced black woman stepped into the office alcove. "What do you want?" she demanded.

"I'm here to see William Winkler."

"Is Mr. Winkler expecting you?"

"No," I said. "It's a surprise."

"Our guests don't like no surprises," she said. "Can I tell him what this is about?"

I have a problem with gatekeepers. I've *always* had a problem with gatekeepers. If and when I get to heaven, I'll probably end up arguing with Saint Peter himself.

"It's a private matter," I said, handing her one of my cards. "If you don't mind, I'd rather discuss it with Mr. Winkler directly."

The woman held the card at arm's length to read it. "All right," she said with a sigh as she stuffed the card into her pocket. "This way."

I followed her down a narrow corridor to the back of the house. Along the way we went past a series of rooms, all of them with their doors propped open. A television game show blared from one. In others I caught sad glimpses of aged residents sitting quietly in chairs positioned next to grimy windows. There were no bars on the windows, but the inmates of Home Sweet Home were as much prisoners in their individual rooms as if they were incarcerated felons sentenced to solitary confinement. And William Winkler's existence was no different from that of any of his fellows.

Because his room was at the very back of the house, he had two dirty windows instead of the usual one. His view consisted of a dilapidated garage and a moss-encrusted block wall, so having those two windows didn't offer much of a benefit. And since his chair was positioned with its back to both windows, I doubt Wink spent much time savoring the view. He sat dozing in a vinyl-covered recliner that resembled the leather one back home in my condo, but stuffing poking through holes on the arms testified to years of very hard use. A walker with traction-enhancing tennis balls on the feet was parked within easy reach next to his chair.

"Mr. Winkler," my escort said. "Someone's here to see you."

Startled awake, he gave me a sour look. "Who are you?" he demanded querulously. "I suppose you're some lawyer that jerk of a son of mine has sent around to hassle me some more, right? He can't wait for me to die. Cheated me out of my own company. Now he wants to declare me incompetent so he can have control of whatever pittance I have left. How's that for gratitude?"

Having been warned that Wink was somewhat cantankerous, I wasn't surprised by his initial tirade. "My name's Beaumont," I said. "J. P. Beaumont. Marty Woodman said I could find you here."

"Oh," Wink said, softening a little. "Marty sent you? That's different then. Have a chair."

The black woman had lingered in the room during this exchange. Now, evidently satisfied that I was an approved visitor, she left Wink and me alone. Next to the bed sat a single chair. I picked it up and dragged it over closer to Wink's.

"What do you want?" he asked once I was seated.

"I work for the Washington State Attorney General's office with the Special Homicide Investigation Team. I'm looking into one of your cold cases from years ago."

Wink's countenance brightened with a hint of interest. "One of mine," he muttered. "Which one?"

"From May of 1950," I said. "Madeline Marchbank. Her friends called her Mimi."

That brief flicker of interest went away, not because it burned itself out but because Wink Winkler slammed the door shut on it. "Don't recall it at all," he said firmly.

There's a new technology out these days, a new kind of lie detector—or rather truth detector. It measures the way a subject's brain waves react to familiar information. Lie detectors measure respiration, blood pressure, and galvanic skin responses when the interviewee gives untruthful answers to questions. The problem with that is that experienced lie-detector subjects can sometimes train themselves to outwit the old machines. With this new equipment measuring involuntary brain waves, it's impossible to trick the brain into reacting to familiar information as though it were unfamiliar.

I may not be new technology, but I operate on a similar system. I could see from that initial involuntary reaction that Wink Winkler remembered exactly who Madeline Marchbank was as well as what had happened to her. If he was prepared to lie about it more than fifty years later, I wondered why.

"Madeline was a young woman who was supposedly murdered by an intruder in her home with her mother confined to a bed in a nearby room," I explained smoothly, going along with the program that Wink remembered nothing. "But now a new witness has surfaced," I added. "An eyewitness who saw the whole thing and says the initial attack occurred outside the house, near the back porch. It's possible the victim was still alive when she was carried into the house, where she died."

"You say all this happened way back in 1950?" Wink asked, still playing dumb. "Where's the supposed eyewitness been all this time? If she knew about this, why didn't she come forward years ago?"

She! I caught the slip almost as soon as it was out of Wink's mouth. I had made no mention that the newly discovered witness was female, but Winkler already knew that. That meant that regardless of whether or not he had questioned Bonnie Jean Dunleavy, he had known about her existence all along. Not wanting to reveal that he had tipped his hand, I glossed it over as well as I could.

"Let's just say she's been out of touch," I said.

He stared at me for some time without speaking. "Well, like I said, I don't remember anything about it, so you're barking up the wrong tree asking me."

"You had a pretty good closure rate back in those days, didn't you?" I asked.

"So what if I did?"

"It just seems odd to me that you don't remember one you didn't close."

"Are you calling me a liar?" he demanded.

"No," I returned. "Just surprisingly forgetful."

"Wait till you're my age," he said. "See how much you remember."

I took my leave then. There was no sense arguing with the man. No matter how much I didn't want to, it looked as though I was going to have to go back to Paul Kramer with my hat in my hand and beg him for a look at the Mimi Marchbank evidence box. And since there's no sense in putting off the inevitable, I headed straight for police head-quarters. Once again I went through the whole check-in procedure. This time, though, rather than stopping off at Records, I went on up to Homicide on the seventh floor.

And was astonished. This was my first visit to Homicide since the move to the new building. And it wasn't just the building that was new. No wonder all the old broken-down furniture had been abandoned in the basement of the Public Safety Building. All the furniture here was new. Somewhere a high-tech company had disappeared and some City of Seattle budget genius had used the resulting bankruptcy proceedings to furnish the new building—in cherry. Cherry cubicle dividers! Cherry desks! Cherry shelves! I felt like I'd landed in a cabinetry warehouse instead of a homicide squad.

I wandered through a sea of unfamiliar faces before someone called my name. "Hey, Beau," Clarence Holly said, coming forward to shake my hand. "I thought you gave this stuff up."

Clarence, who had been coming into Homicide from Patrol just as I was leaving, seemed happy to see me.

"Stopped by for old times' sake," I said. "Which way is Kramer's office?"

"That way," he said, pointing toward a wall of windows. "A room with a view. Don't be such a stranger. Stop by later to visit."

"I will," I said.

Following Clarence's nod, I headed toward the windows, ones that looked out on the wet expanse of Fifth Avenue, seven stories below. Kramer's old office, the one we had called the Fishbowl, had been a glass enclosure that looked out on Homicide. This one, with Captain Kramer's name on a nameplate beside it, had its back to the unit and its face—including a door and another interior window—looking toward the view. Kramer himself was nowhere to be seen, but the Marchbank evidence box was sitting in plain sight on the desk. So much for maintaining the chain of evidence.

I was standing outside the office, cooling my heels and looking down at the rain pelting the melting snow on Fifth Avenue, when my phone rang. It was Ralph.

"What's up?" I asked. "You sound upset."

"I *am* upset," he growled back at me. "Ron just fired me."

"He what?"

"Fired me. He told me he wants to plead guilty at the preliminary hearing, for God's sake! When I told him that was a perfectly stupid idea, he told me to hit the road. You've got to talk to him, Beau. See if you can pound some sense into his head."

I could barely believe my ears. "Ron is going to plead guilty? How can he do that?"

"Beats me. The only thing that makes sense is that he's protecting someone," Ralph said. "Or trying to."

"Who?"

"I think maybe it's Heather. I gather she's been quite the handful lately—boy troubles, playing hooky from school, really, really didn't want to be dragged down to Tacoma to live with her mother."

Ralph didn't say anything about possible drug use, and neither did I.

"So much so that she'd shoot her own mother to keep from going?"

"It's the only thing I can think of," Ralph continued. "By copping a plea, Ron probably hopes to forestall a more thorough investigation, one that would point suspicion in Heather's direction. You've got to talk him out of this, Beau. Heather's a juvenile. The worst she would end up with is a couple of years in Juvie. If Ron goes down for Rosemary's murder, he'll go away for good. A plea deal might take the death penalty off the table, but for an officer-related domestic-violence homicide, life without parole would be the next most likely possibility."

The thought of Jared Peters growing up without his father made a hole in the pit of my stomach.

"I'll go see him right away," I said.

I started for the elevators only to run headfirst into Kramer. "You wanted to see me?" he asked.

"I did," I replied. "Can't now."

But he followed me through the squad room and out into the elevator lobby. "I've been doing some checking," he said. "Everyone I've talked to says they think reopening the Marchbank case is a very bad idea."

I rounded on him. "Bad, why?" I demanded. "Bad because the Marchbank name still carries a whole lot of weight in this town? Has it occurred to anyone that maybe that's precisely why the case was never solved in the first place?"

Kramer's face darkened. His promotion didn't seem to be agreeing with him. I suspected the man's blood pressure had gone through the roof about the same time he put on his captain's uniform.

"We're not reopening this case on your say-so alone," he muttered. "I've gone through the box. Whoever broke into Madeline Marchbank's house and murdered her in her bed is long gone."

"I think you're wrong about that," I said. "And I think Ross Connors will most likely have the final word on whether or not the case is reopened. In the meantime, I'd be mighty careful about how you handle that evidence box. If anything that should be in it turns up missing, I'll make sure that the AG has your ears."

Kramer bristled. "Are you threatening me?" he demanded.

"You can take it however you want, but I think the answer is probably yes. No, it's definitely a yes. And believe me, Captain Kramer, it couldn't happen to a nicer guy."

CHAPTER 11

I DROVE STRAIGHT FROM KRAMER'S OFFICE to Amy and Ron's place on Queen Anne Hill. I did not pass Go. I did not collect two hundred dollars. What Ralph Ames had surmised made perfect sense. Ron Peters was going to sacrifice himself in an effort to save his daughter.

And had Heather done it? Not the Heather I had known—not the sweet little girl who had sold me Girl Scout cookies and wrapped my heart around her little finger. But the Heather I had seen the other night? That teenager with all her piercings and her bare midriff, with her hennaed hair and pouty lips covered with black lipstick had been another Heather entirely—a stranger. And with the possibility of drug use involved? There was no way for me to fathom what she might do or how far she might have gone in order to have her own way.

There were two clearly marked media vehicles parked on the street outside Ron and Amy's house. A bright red two-year-old Cadillac Escalade was parked directly behind Amy's Volvo wagon. Yes, Harry I. Ball had told me to stay the hell out of the Peters situation, but at that point in the proceedings his prohibition had fallen completely out of my head. I parked directly behind the Escalade, jumped out, hurried up to the front door, and rang the bell. I was relieved when Amy herself, rather than her grump of a sister, answered the door.

"Oh, Beau," she said. "Thank God you're here!"

"What's wrong?" I asked.

"In there." She motioned toward a pair of French doors that opened into the living room. Through them, I heard Ron's voice raised in anger.

"I don't care if you're the damned Second Coming himself!" Ron was saying. "The memorial service is for my girls, and I'm the one making the arrangements. As far as I'm concerned, Bread of Life Mission is having nothing to do with it!"

When I stopped in the doorway I saw that Ron was seated in his chair. A well-dressed but immense Hispanic man—six-six or six-seven at least and as broad as a wall—stood next to the fireplace.

"I don't think you understand what a mainstay Rosemary was to our church and to the mission," the man was saying.

"And I don't *care!*" Ron retorted. "You've got a lot of nerve coming here, Mr. Lujan, a hell of a lot of nerve! None of this would have happened if you hadn't started messing around in the child-custody situation. We were all doing fine until you stuck your nose into it. And now you think you should have a hand in the memorial service? Not on your life! Have your own memorial service if you want to, but the one we're having tomorrow is strictly private. Now, I think it's time you showed yourself out."

When Michael Lujan made no move to leave, I decided it was time for me to interject the voice of sweet reason into the conversation.

"Hi, Ron," I said. Approaching the man by the fireplace, I held out my hand. "How do you do. I'm Ron and Amy's friend, J. P. Beaumont."

Michael Lujan looked straight through me as though I didn't exist.

"Trying to regain custody of her children was no reason for Rosemary Peters to die," he said tightly. "Being a mother and wanting to have your child with you isn't a capital offense, Mr. Peters, but Rosemary is dead nonetheless. You and I both know that you deserve to be in jail awaiting trial right now instead of sitting here in the comfort of your own home. If you weren't a cop, you would be."

"Whether or not I'm in jail is up to the agency investigating the case," Ron answered. "It isn't up to me, Mr. Lujan, and it isn't up to you, either." His voice was tense. White knuckles showed in the fingers that held a death grip on the armrests of his chair. In all the years I had known him, I had never seen Ron Peters so angry. Fortunately, there were no pizza boxes within easy reach.

"Perhaps not," Michael Lujan agreed. "But the investigating agency is answerable to the court of public opinion. Ross Connors may be the Washington State attorney general now, but he was a politician before that, and he'll be a politician long after he leaves office."

"Fine," Ron said. "Do your worst. Now get the hell out of my house before I call the cops."

Without another word, Lujan stalked from the room. Leaving the house, he slammed the front door hard enough to make the windows rattle. I should have realized what was coming, but I didn't, not until it was too late. He fired up the Escalade and slammed it into reverse—directly into the front end of my poor little 928, which was parked behind him. I heard the crunch of sheet metal and the tinkling of falling glass and knew at once that my beloved Porsche, which had been totaled and rebuilt once before, would never be the same.

By the time I got outside, Michael Lujan was standing beside the wreckage, surveying the damage and cussing under his breath. When Lujan had hit the gas pedal, his Cadillac had simply run up and over my Porsche's Guards' Red hood, flattening the aluminum body as it went. The Escalade came to rest with the ball of a trailer hitch and much of its rear bumper protruding into the 928's shattered windshield. The force of the collision had been enough to move the Porsche backward, and the vehicles had come to rest in the middle of the street.

"Where the hell did this piece of junk come from?" he demanded. "I didn't even see it."

Piece of junk? My 928's connection to Anne Corley was a little like George Washington's ax—a new head and three new handles, but George Washington's ax in spirit. This wasn't the exact same 928 Anne had given me originally, but it was one just like it, and in my mind the two were one and the same. Seeing the crumpled remains, I felt as though a final and mystical connection had been severed. Had Lujan been even a little apologetic, it might have been different, but having him blame me for his accident definitely rubbed me the wrong way. And it didn't help that other than a smashed rear bumper, the Escalade was fine, while my poor Porsche looked like a squashed bug.

"And who the hell issued you a driver's license?" I demanded in return. "It's not my fault you're obviously blind. Ever hear of using your rearview mirror?" So much for the voice of sweet reason.

Lujan was already reaching for his wallet. He was probably under the assumption that we'd simply exchange insurance information and settle the situation later. Even then, though, I knew from the amount of damage inflicted on the Porsche that a police report would be necessary. Besides, the media guys, bored silly with being parked outside Ron Peters's house while nothing much seemed to be happening, had already called 911. Seconds later, a blue-and-white Seattle PD patrol car with two baby-faced uniformed officers in it—a man and a woman—appeared on the scene, along with a small crowd of neighborhood onlookers.

As the two uniforms approached, clipboards at the ready, I could already tell how this was going to play out with Harry I. Ball. To say nothing of Mel Soames. The next time I had nerve enough to appear in person at SHIT's east side office I could expect the atmosphere to be more than a little frosty.

While the patrol officers began gathering necessary information, Jared somehow escaped his mother's grasp. He shot out to where I was standing and wrapped himself around my leg. I picked him up and held him on one hip while I answered questions. I was focused on the questions—and on what I was sure would turn out to be my totaled Porsche. I wasn't focused on the fact that the guys in the media vans were busy the whole time snapping photos and videos of Jared Peters and me. I didn't notice the cameras at the time, but I've been around the news media long enough to know that I should have.

The rain let up for a while, but by the time the police reports had been taken and a tow truck had come to haul off the shattered remains of my Porsche, it was pouring again. Jared and I were both soaked when we finally went into the house. Amy took Jared off my hands and then handed me a towel. Ron sat with his chair parked in the entry into the living room, watching me dry off.

"Sorry about that," he said. "I know how much that car means to you."

"Meant," I said. "I think it's a goner now, but don't apologize. It wasn't your fault."

"Oh? Seems to me everything is my fault these days," Ron said in a ragged voice. He turned his chair and wheeled himself back into the living room, with me right behind him.

"Stop feeling sorry for yourself, Ron," I ordered. "And get off your cross. A little while ago, when you were dealing with Mr. Lujan, you were all pissed off. Great. I can handle pissed off, but when you're busy feeling sorry for yourself and drowning in self-pity, you can be down-right pathetic. I have a hard time with pathetic."

Ron swung his chair around and faced me from the far side of the room. "Screw you," he said.

"Good," I told him. "That's more like it."

"What are you doing here?" he demanded. "You work for SHIT. I should think you'd be giving me a wide berth about now."

"I'm supposed to be giving you a wide berth, but at the moment maybe I'm a better friend than I am a cop. Why did you fire Ralph? What the hell got into you?"

Ron paused for a moment before he replied. "None of your business," he snapped back finally. "And if Ralph told you that about me, he may have violated my attorney/client privilege. I should probably sue him."

"Sure you should," I retorted. "And maybe you're dumb enough to represent yourself while you're suing him just like you're planning to represent yourself at that preliminary hearing. How come, Ron? Tell me."

Ron shook his head. "No," he said. "I don't owe you an explanation."

"Well, then, let me take a crack at explaining it myself," I said. "I think you're going to cop a plea in hopes of protecting Heather."

The color drained from Ron's face. I might as well have slapped him. Instead of answering, he turned his chair away so he was facing the empty fireplace instead of me.

"If Heather did this and you let her get away with it," I continued, "you're going against everything you've ever stood for, worked for, or believed in."

"Nobody gave you the right to judge me," he said.

"No," I agreed. "But I think I've earned the right to be your friend."

We were silent for a long time. Finally, his shoulders heaved. "If you repeat any of this, I'll say you're lying, that it's my word against yours."

"Repeat what?"

Ron turned to face me at last. His eyes were red-rimmed and desolate. "The ballistics tests came back this morning, Beau," he said quietly. "That's why I fired Ralph. Rosemary was shot to death with one of my weapons—with my very own Glock. I let your friends from SHIT, Mel Soames and Brad Norton, think I kept the Glock in my car, but I didn't. The last I knew, it was locked in my desk in the den. Somebody had to have access to both the desk and my Camry. Rosemary's missing shoe was found in the trunk, and so was her blood."

"But why would Heather do such a thing?" I asked.

Ron shook his head. "She's been a handful lately," Ron admitted. "Missing school, hanging out with the wrong crowd. In a way—if I could have been rational about the whole thing—it might have been easier for Amy and me if she had gone to Tacoma to live with her mother. But after everything Rosemary had done, I couldn't stomach it, and Heather hated the idea. She must be the one who did it," he added bleakly after a pause. "Who else would there be?"

Had I been dealing with anyone else, it would have been natural to bring up the possibility of Heather's being involved in drugs, but friendship trumped my being a cop right then, and so I didn't mention it. The burden on Ron Peters already seemed to be more than his wide shoulders could bear. Still, I didn't fold entirely.

"Look, Ron," I argued, "you can't just let her off the hook. If she did this—if she committed a murder—she has to pay for it. Admittedly, Heather's your daughter and not mine, but I love her, too. No matter what, you and I both have to make her accountable for her actions."

"But she's just a kid," Ron returned. "She has her whole life in front of her."

"Yes," I said. "Precisely. What's the worst that can happen to her— Juvie until she turns twenty-one? If you take the rap for this, you're probably looking at nothing less than life in prison."

"I'm already serving life in prison," he said bitterly. "I'm in prison every damned day I'm stuck in this chair. What's the point? What difference does it make if I'm in a cell or out of it?"

"It'll make a hell of a difference to Amy and Tracy," I said. "And what about Jared?"

I had told Ron I could handle anger, but what he delivered surprised me.

"What about Jared?" he demanded in return. "He's a little boy. Who's going to take him on his father-son camp-out when it comes time for Cub Scouts? Who's going to teach him to swim or ski or hit a baseball or even drive a car, for that matter? Oh, sure, I can do what I've done with the girls and teach him to drive whatever handicapped conversion vehicle I happen to be driving at the moment, but what about a regular car or one with a stick shift? That'll all be up to Amy, won't it. Just like everything else is up to Amy. When does she get a break?"

"When did I ever ask for a break?" Amy Peters asked.

Ron and I had been so locked in our nose-to-nose confrontation that neither of us had heard her enter the room. I have no idea how long she had been standing there or how much she had overheard. For the longest time after Amy asked her question, no one moved or even breathed. In the aftermath of the Escalade's crashing into the 928, I had distinctly heard the tinkle of shattering glass. Now, in the stark silence that followed, I was convinced I could hear the shattering of broken hearts.

"Amy," Ron began. "I didn't mean . . ."

But it was too late. Amy didn't hang around long enough to listen.

Instead, she fled back the way she had come. Her departure left me with absolutely nothing to say. I hadn't walked a mile in Amy's moccasins—or in Ron's, either, for that matter.

"Just go," Ron said at last. "That's enough damage for one day."

I stopped in the doorway. "What about the memorial service?" I asked.

"What about it?"

"You told Lujan it was private. Is it family only or am I invited?"

"Of course you're invited," Ron said. "Whatever made you think you weren't? Two o'clock tomorrow afternoon. The Bleitz Funeral Chapel over by the Fremont Bridge."

"Okay," I said. "See you there."

It wasn't until I was back outside and standing in the rain that I remembered my car had been towed. I was about to call for a cab when a battered Ford Focus with British Columbia plates pulled into the driveway. The passenger door opened and Heather charged out of the car. She raced past me with her head bowed, without a glance or a word of greeting. The mascara running down her face had nothing to do with falling rain. I was standing looking after her when a voice asked, "Need a lift?"

"Yes," I said. "As a matter of fact, I do."

"Where to?" Dillon asked as I climbed into the cramped front seat. It was pulled so far forward I had to readjust it before I could fit my knees past the glove box.

"Belltown Terrace," I said. "It's at the corner of Second and Broad."

The interior of Dillon's Focus was littered with a layer of fast-food wrappers and crushed soft-drink containers. When Heather and Tracy were little, Ron had tried his level best to turn them into vegans and to keep them safe from the evils of Coca-Cola. The strategy hadn't taken—at least not as far as Heather was concerned. If, as I suspected, she was experimenting with drug use, eating right wasn't the only lesson she had failed to learn at her father's knee.

I sniffed the air for telltale odors and glanced around for drug paraphernalia—a stray roach clip or a visible hypodermic needle—that would tend to confirm my suspicions, but nothing jumped out at me. All that really indicated, though, was that whatever was going on probably wasn't going on in the Focus.

As we started down Queen Anne Hill, I caught a glimpse of Queen Anne Gardens and realized that I hadn't talked to Lars in several days, not since he had told me my grandmother was a little under the weather. When my phone rang halfway down Queen Anne Hill, I thought it might be Lars and Beverly, even though they seldom try calling my cell. When I saw the SHIT office number in the caller ID window, I slipped the phone back into my pocket without answering. Whoever was calling to chew me out—Harry I. Ball or Mel Soames—I wasn't about to endure what would most likely be a severe dressing-down within earshot of a young punk like Dillon.

"What's going to happen?" Dillon asked as he drove. "To Heather's dad, I mean. Do you think he'll go to prison?"

"Not if he didn't do it," I said grimly.

"Heather's real upset about all this, you know," Dillon continued. "I mean, like, she's upset about her mother being dead and everything, too, but her dad . . . It's like he's her hero or something."

He ought to be her hero, I thought grimly. *He's willing to give up everything in order to save her hide.*

"Heather says you're a cop," Dillon continued. "Do you think he did it?"

On the surface, it could have been an innocent comment from someone just making conversation. On the other hand, it could have been someone fishing for inside information. I decided to turn the question right back on the questioner.

"What do you think?" I asked.

"Me?" Dillon stammered.

"Yes, you. You're evidently close to Heather. You're around the house a lot. Do you think Heather's dad is capable of doing such a thing?"

Dillon concentrated on his driving for a time before he answered. "You mean, like, do I think he'd kill somebody?"

I nodded.

"He seems like a regular guy to me," Dillon answered at last.

"And Heather?"

"What do you mean?"

"Is she capable of murder?"

This time his answer was as explosive as it was immediate. "Of course not! No way!"

"Were the two of you together Friday night?"

"Sort of," he said.

"What does that mean?"

"We were, but we weren't supposed to be. Heather told her parents she was going to a friend's house, but she came over to my place instead. We planned on going to a movie, but she was too upset. There was some big hassle with her family at dinner."

"Her father got served papers in the custody dispute."

Dillon nodded. "That's right," he said.

"What did you think about that?" I asked.

"About Heather maybe moving to Tacoma?"

I nodded and Dillon shrugged his shoulders. "It wasn't that big a deal," he said. "I've got wheels. I can go where I need to go."

"So you would have kept on seeing Heather even if she had gone to live with her mother?"

"Sure," he said. "Why wouldn't I?"

"And when did you bring her home on Friday?"

"I don't know."

"Early or late?"

"Late, I guess."

"How late?"

"Five-thirty," he said. "Or maybe six."

That stopped me. "In the morning? She spent the night?"

"We fell asleep," he said. "No big deal. Nothing happened."

Right, I thought. *And the pope ain't Catholic!*

"So how do you get along with Heather's folks?" I asked.

"Fine," he said. "We get along just fine."

That was the first straight-out lie I had caught him in. I might have caught him in more, but we pulled up to Belltown Terrace right then. "Thanks for the lift."

"Don't you worry about Heather," he said as I got out and started to close the door. "Whatever happens, I'll be there for her because that's the kind of guy I am."

"Good," I said. "Glad to hear it." But of course that was a lie on my part, too, because I didn't think for a minute that this little weasel was a stand-up kind of guy.

As Dillon drove away, I realized that I had no idea what his last name was or where he lived, but I'm a cop. Years of habit came into play. I noted the number of his license plate and jotted it down.

When I turned to enter the building, Jerome was there to open the door. "Where's your pretty little Porsche, Mr. Beaumont?" he asked. "I thought for sure I saw you drive it out of the garage this morning."

"Somebody wrecked it," I said. "A guy put a big old SUV in reverse and drove right over the top of it."

"You're kidding," Jerome said.

"I only wish I were."

"I'm real sorry to hear it," he said. "It's a crying shame."

"Yes, it is," I agreed. "In fact, I'm going upstairs right now to see if my insurance company will set me up with a rental."

Except I didn't. Instead, I went up to my apartment and paced back and forth, trying to sort things out. Who had killed Rosemary Peters? I knew for sure that Ron hadn't done it. He was convinced Heather had done it. And maybe Dillon was, too. No wonder he had given me that phony and most likely unverifiable alibi for Heather's whereabouts on the night in question.

But what if everyone was wrong? What if, in focusing on the complicated family aspects of the murder, we were missing someone else—someone who was using the custody dispute as camouflage for getting away with murder? Michael Lujan, for example? What was his relationship with Rosemary Peters? Involvement on Lujan's part might explain why the body had been moved from the Bread of Life parking lot. Or maybe she had been killed by one of her coworkers at the mission. Had anyone looked into that? Of course, the problem with all of those possibilities came back to the use of Ron's gun as well as his vehicle.

Whom did that leave as possible suspects then? Ron or Amy or maybe, God forbid, Heather's big sister, Tracy. That was another thought that was too awful to consider. The point was, if Mel and Brad could be suckered into accepting Ron's claim of responsibility, then the real killer—maybe Heather or maybe someone else entirely— might well get away with murder.

The big question for me was whether or not I was going to go along with the program—and the cover-up. Ron was thinking of Heather. I was thinking of everyone else—of Ron and Amy, of Tracy and Jared.

Four to one, Heather, I told myself finally. *You lose.*

Cops make judgment calls all the time. So do friends. I picked up the phone and called Mel Soames's cell number.

"Well, I'll be damned," she muttered when she answered. "If you aren't about the last person in the universe I expected to hear from about now."

"Why would that be?" I asked.

"Because I just saw a picture of you on the evening news, holding Ron Peters's little boy, Jared. Looked like a really cozy photo op. I'm guessing Harry will be livid when he hears about it, and so will Ross Connors. I'm not too happy about it myself."

"Want to talk about it?" I asked.

"Is there something to talk about?" I heard the stir of interest in her voice.

"Possibly," I said. "We could have dinner somewhere."

"Not out in public," she returned. "You were on the evening news tonight, and so was I. Seattle's not that big a town. If we're seen having dinner together, someone's bound to report it. Do you have any food in that penthouse bachelor pad of yours?"

"Not really," I admitted.

"That's what I thought. I'll pick up something on the way. What about wine?"

"I don't drink."

"Well, I do," she said. "Do you mind if I bring some along, too?"

"Suit yourself," I said. "I'll see you when you get here."

CHAPTER 12

WHILE WAITING FOR MEL TO ARRIVE, I finally got on the phone to my insurance guy, who told me he'd make arrangements to have a car delivered to Belltown Terrace for me in the morning. I also tried calling Lars and Beverly. When there was no answer at their place, I left a message on their machine saying I was thinking about them. Then I took a shower and put on clean clothes.

A little over an hour later, when I opened the door in answer to Mel's ring, she walked into my apartment in a pungent cloud of garlic.

"Hope you don't mind chicken or garlic," she said. "It's shish tawouk from the Mediterranean Kitchen. They're right next door to where I live."

"I didn't know you lived on Queen Anne Hill," I said.

She looked at me and rolled her eyes. "I don't," she said. "I mean the one in downtown Bellevue. I live in the Parkvue Apartments, just down from Bel-Square." She set the bags of food on the kitchen counter, along with a bottle of chardonnay. "And I brought along an opener in case you didn't have one."

"I have openers," I said. "And glasses. I just don't keep wine around anymore. Or booze."

"In AA?" The offhand way she asked the question made it sound as though she knew something about the subject. I nodded.

"My ex sobered up after we got a divorce," Mel said with a shrug. "Pissed the hell out of me, too. I guess I thought he should have done it for me, but of course he had to do it for himself in order for it to take. We're on reasonably good terms now," she added, "as long as he stays on his side of the country and I stay on mine."

"That what caused the divorce?" I asked. "Drinking?"

"Booze was only a part of the problem," she said. "He's a liberal and I'm not. I think I thought I could fix that, too, but I couldn't. We called it irreconcilable differences. Fortunately, we didn't have any kids, so there wasn't anyone else for us to screw up."

In a matter of a few minutes I learned more about Mel Soames than I had picked up in months of working with her, and her light-hearted way of chatting about things put me at ease in a way I hadn't expected. While I busied myself with uncorking the wine she made herself at home, searching through cupboards and drawers until she found enough dishes and silverware to set the table. She had transferred the food to serving dishes and was surveying her handiwork when I handed her a glass of wine.

"Thanks," she said. "Now what are you going to drink?"

"Coffee," I answered. "I made a new pot just before you got here."

"You can drink coffee at night and it doesn't bother you?"

"I can drink coffee round the clock," I said. That wasn't entirely true, but I thought the comment hit the right notes of casual macho-dudeness.

"You're lucky," she said. "The other night I hardly slept at all after you filled me full of caffeine."

"Sorry about that," I told her.

"Don't apologize. Staying awake late at night is good for me some-times. Gives me a chance to think about stuff I usually manage to ig-nore during the day."

I like to think of the Mediterranean Kitchen's shish tawouk as gar-lic squared. The fluffy saffron rice is infused with garlic and then the grilled hunks of chicken are covered with a milky crushed-garlic sauce and it comes with lentil soup and salad. The first savory bites were nothing short of glorious.

"You like it?" she asked.

"Love it," I returned.

She grinned. "My ex didn't like garlic, either. Now maybe you'd bet-ter tell me how come you called. I have a feeling something happened."

There it was again, that sudden switching of topics and moods that women do so effortlessly and, in the process, drive men nuts. Because I knew I was about to breach Ron's confidence, it took me a moment to answer.

"Ron Peters fired his attorney today," I said for starters.

Mel nodded. "I know. I met him—Ralph Ames. Didn't expect to like him, but he seems like a pretty squared-away guy."

"Ralph is squared away," I told her. "And he would have done a good job for Ron. The problem is, I believe Ron is getting ready to plead guilty to a murder he didn't commit."

"I think you're right," Mel Soames said.

That stopped me. I hadn't expected the two of us to be on the same side of this question. "But the other night I thought you said . . ."

"I wouldn't be much of a cop if I let my personal experience get in the way of an investigation, would I?" she asked.

"No, but what changed your mind?"

"Facts, mostly," she said. "Like the fact that someone had wiped down Ron's Camry for fingerprints, but they left all the blood in the trunk. Brad and I think someone's trying to frame Ron Peters for his ex-wife's murder, and we're thinking whoever did it is likely one of his own family members."

"Heather," I said at once.

"The younger daughter," Mel confirmed with a nod. "The one who was the subject of the custody battle and who didn't want to go live with her mother."

I felt a sudden wave of relief. If Mel and Brad had already reached many of the same conclusions, that let me off the hook.

"Have you spoken to her directly?"

"No. For the moment, it's easier for us to play along and act like Ron's the only game in town. In the meantime, we're talking to everyone else and gathering what additional information we can. We're hoping to have what we need so we can question Heather either before tomorrow's funeral or after it."

"Ron isn't going to want you anywhere near her."

"What Ron Peters wants and what he gets are two entirely different things," Mel said.

"Are you looking at anyone else for this?"

Mel looked at me sharply. "Any suggestions?"

"What about Michael Lujan? He was at Ron and Amy's this afternoon, raising hell about the funeral tomorrow, throwing his considerable weight around, and insisting Bread of Life be part of it."

"Ah," Mel said. "Rosemary's attorney. Now there's a guy who's completely convinced Ron did it no matter what the evidence may say. What happened?"

"Ron told him to take a hike, and he did, running his Escalade over my 928 in the process."

"Ouch," Mel said. "Hope he didn't hurt it."

"Smashed it flat is more like it, but getting back to Rosemary, I'm worried about having tunnel vision here. Lujan is certainly more involved than I'd expect. And what about the clients who show up at Bread of Life? Did any of them have some kind of beef with the victim?"

"You don't want us to look at Heather any more than her father does," Mel observed with a smile.

"I suppose you're right about that."

"But think about it. She lives there. She'd have access to her father's car keys, and my guess is that she also knows how to gain access to his weapons. According to Tracy, Heather went to her room right after dinner that night and stayed there."

"That's not what I heard," I told her. "That may be the story she and Tracy told Ron and Amy, but I have it on good authority that Tracy and Heather let themselves in and out of the house overnight with complete impunity."

"That's pretty typical," Mel said. "When I was in junior high and high school, I pulled that same stunt."

"Maybe not quite," I said. "According to a kid named Dillon, Heather Peters spent most of Friday night at his house."

"Dillon would be Dillon Middleton," Mel said. "Tracy told us about him. He's the boyfriend, isn't he?"

I nodded.

"How do you know him?"

"I never heard his last name, but the little creep gave me a ride down the hill in his garbage-heap Ford Focus." I retrieved my notebook from the entryway table, tore out the page with Dillon's plate number written on it, and handed the paper over to Mel.

"He's Canadian, then?" Mel asked after studying it for a moment.

"Maybe," I said. "But whatever nationality he is, he's also a worm who ought to be brought up on charges of statutory rape. Heather's still not sixteen."

"Not old enough to screw around," Mel said, "but she's old enough to be a homicide suspect. There's something wrong with that picture."

"What about the security video?" I asked. "Can you tell whether or not she's the one driving the car?"

"It's grainy. You can see the vehicle but not the driver. We've sent it off to the FBI in hopes their people can enhance it. And Brad has been collecting security tapes from Friday night and early Saturday morning on every route we can think of from here to Tacoma and back in hopes of coming up with a video that might give us a clearer shot of the Camry and its occupant or maybe even occupants."

"As in more than one?"

"Rosemary wasn't a tiny person," Mel said. "If Heather actually did it, she might have needed help."

"Heather and Dillon together?" I suggested.

"Maybe. The crime lab folks are going over the car looking for anything and everything. One way or the other, we will find out who was driving the car."

"And break Ron Peters's heart," I said.

"That, too," she agreed.

When dinner was over, we cleared away the dishes and then adjourned to the living room. I turned on the gas log fire while she settled in the window seat. "So tell me about the case you're working on," she said.

I did. Mel listened, making occasional comments and suggestions as I told her about Sister Mary Katherine and her long-suppressed memory of a brutal murder. The easy give-and-take between us was almost like . . . having a partner again, and that worried me. Over the years I've been very hard on partners.

"Fifty-plus years later, you work on a cold case for what—two days—and it's solved already? How could the detectives have missed it the first time around?"

"Wink Winkler missed it because he wanted to miss it," I said. "Why else would he have lied about it today? And how else would he have known that the eyewitness was female?"

"What's your plan?" Mel asked.

"Since Elvira is evidently still alive, I'm going to track her down and see what, if anything, she has to say."

"You've already identified her as a suspect. Are you going to read her her rights?"

"Absolutely. I'm not going to do anything that might screw up this case. Would you mind taking a look at the Sister Mary Katherine videos? You might notice something I've missed."

"I'd love to," Mel Soames said, and we did. For the next two hours or so, we sat side by side—with me in my recliner and Mel cross-legged on the floor—and watched the videos, starting, stopping, and replaying them as we went. I was about to put the last one into the VCR when my phone rang.

It was late by then, almost ten. I checked the number on caller ID. When the name Lars Jenssen appeared, I picked up.

"Beau?" Lars said, sounding relieved. "I'm glad you're there."

"Why? Is something wrong?"

"Ya, sure," he said. "I yust got back from the hospital. They took Beverly over to Swedish in Ballard."

I felt my heart constrict. "What's wrong? Do you need me to go there?"

"No. Not now. She's sleeping. Has a touch of pneumonia, is all. They're keeping her for a day or two."

I wasn't reassured. At age ninety-one, "a touch" of pneumonia can be very serious. And I was also more than a little annoyed that no one had bothered to let me know that Beverly's condition had changed from being a little "under the weather" to something potentially fatal.

"Are you sure there's nothing I can do?" I asked. "What about taking you back to the hospital in the morning? Will you need a ride?"

"No. I talked to the lady at the front desk. Queen Anne Gardens has a van that takes residents where they need to go. I've already lined up a ride. Now I yust want to go to bed."

"You'll call if you need anything?"

"You bet," he said and hung up.

Mel was watching me closely. "Is someone ill?" she asked.

I nodded. "My grandmother. She's ninety-one, and they've slapped her in the hospital with pneumonia."

"She's the one who made the afghan?" Mel asked.

I nodded again. "Beverly Jenssen. My mother was pregnant with me and unmarried when my father died in a motorcycle accident. My grandfather—my biological grandfather—disapproved of unwed mothers and threw Mother out of the house. She raised me on her own and remained estranged from her parents for as long as she lived. In fact, I never met them until I stumbled across them by accident a few years ago. By then my grandfather had suffered a stroke and was ready to let bygones be bygones. After my grandfather died, Beverly met and married an old friend of mine, Lars Jenssen. He's the one who just called. He's also an independent old cuss who won't even let me give him a ride to the hospital."

I didn't add that, other than my kids, Lars and Beverly were all the family I had left in the world, but I think Mel picked up on that anyway. "You're sure there's nothing we should do?"

"Lars as good as told me to mind my own business."

There was a knock on the door, and it startled me. Belltown

Terrace is a secure building. People inside the building usually don't go knocking on doors at that hour of the night, and if it was someone from outside, either the doorman should have let me know a visitor was coming up or that person should have announced himself over the security phone at the front door or in the elevator lobby.

"Who is it?" I asked without opening the door.

"It's me," Paul Kramer growled from the far side of the door. "Now let me in before I break the damned door down!"

I opened the door to find him, bristling with rage, standing in the corridor.

"Who let you up here?" I demanded.

"My badge let me up here," he returned. "What the hell do you think you're doing, Beaumont?"

"Until you knocked on the door, I was sitting in my own living room and minding my own business. Why?"

"I want to know what you're up to. If you had told me what the deal was instead of going off and leaving me with that evidence box and nothing to go on, maybe she wouldn't be dead."

"Who's dead?" I asked, sure his answer would be Sister Mary Katherine. It wasn't.

"Elvira Marchbank was found dead this evening at the bottom of her basement stairs," he said. "And I don't believe it's a coincidence that she would die under suspicious circumstances on the very same day I catch you prowling around the cold case file of her sister-in-law, who was murdered some fifty-plus years ago. So now that you've managed to get my name instead of yours on the checkout sheet for that evidence box, you're going to tell me what the hell is going on."

"Wait a minute," I said. "Don't blame me because your name is on the sheet. I seem to remember your insisting on taking charge of that cold case box all on your own."

Kramer looked as though he was going to explode. "I asked you straight out what this was all about and you—"

"Is something the matter?" Mel asked, stepping into view behind me.

Kramer was taken aback. Clearly he hadn't expected me to have a visitor at this hour of the night. If Elvira was dead and the captain was worried about a public relations problem, the last thing he needed was a witness to this little tirade. I, on the other hand, was worried about Sister Mary Katherine for fear she could be next on someone's list.

"This is police business," Kramer snapped. "Tell your girlfriend it's got nothing to do with her and to stay the hell out of it."

I was about to explain that Mel Soames was a colleague of mine and not a girlfriend, but Mel handled that on her own.

"Would you like to see my badge?" she asked sweetly. "Or should I do us all a favor and start out by shoving it up your ass?"

I could have kissed her—probably should have, especially considering the fact that her comment left Kramer utterly speechless for the better part of a minute. Finally, with blood throbbing in his temples, he turned his fury on me.

"If Mrs. Marchbank's death could have been prevented by my knowing what was going on—"

"Wait a minute, Kramer," I interrupted. "I told you if you wanted that information, you should call my boss. I even gave you his number. Did you call him?"

"Well, no, but—"

"Sorry. No buts allowed," I returned. "If you had gone by the book, you would have had the info. Aren't you the guy who's always such a stickler for going through channels and across desks? As I told you before, I don't work for you or Seattle PD anymore. If you've got questions about my case, talk to Harry I. Ball or, better yet, talk to Ross Connors himself. Once they give the okay, I'll be glad to talk to you or your investigators about this. Just have them drop by. Obviously you know where I live."

Kramer turned and stalked back down the hallway. "Why didn't you tell him about Sister Mary Katherine?" Mel asked, once the elevator door shut behind him.

"He's a jerk," I replied.

"That's true," she said, "and readily apparent. But I still don't know why you shut him down like that."

"Because Paul Kramer and I have a history," I replied.

I expected her to argue the point or to ask for more details, but she didn't.

"Okay," Mel said. "Makes sense to me."

With that she went back over to the window seat, plugged her feet back into her shoes, and picked up her coat. "It's late," she said. "I need to be going." She paused by the door. "See you tomorrow. At the office?"

"Probably."

She left then. As I took the last of the Sister Katherine tapes out of the VCR, I asked myself Mel Soames's question. Why hadn't I told Kramer? Wasn't I being as territorial as he had been in the evidence room? And I would be talking to him or at least to the detectives assigned to investigate Elvira Marchbank's death. All I was doing was putting him off for a few hours—until the AG's office was open for business the next morning.

But the really troubling part was a question raised by Kramer himself. Had my refusal to give him the information contributed to what had happened to Elvira? She had been found at the bottom of a flight of stairs. Had she fallen or had she been pushed? By being stubborn, I had put myself out of the loop. Paul Kramer didn't know about Sister Mary Katherine, but I didn't know about Elvira. In the game of tit for tat I was as much of a jerk as he was. That was not high praise.

So what was I going to do about it? I worried about it for a while. Finally I picked up the phone and dialed a number I knew by heart, one that brought me to the homicide desk at Seattle PD. Sergeant Angie Jerrold answered the phone. I was relieved to hear a familiar voice, and she seemed happy to hear from me as well.

"What can I do for you?"

"Who's assigned to the Marchbank case?" I asked.

"Which one?" she asked. "As of tonight, there are two of them on the board," she said. "Madeline and Elvira."

I was stunned to learn that based on Elvira's death, Kramer had reopened Madeline's long cold case. I was stunned and a little relieved.

"Either," I said. "Whoever's available."

Which is how I ended up talking to Detective Kendall Jackson. "What can I do for you, Mr. Beaumont?"

Jackson had been a uniformed officer and still working the cars when I left the department. Having him call me Mr. Beaumont made me feel slightly ancient.

"Which Marchbank belongs to you?" I asked.

"Elvira," he said. "Hank and I just got back from the crime scene."

Hank was Detective Henry Ramsdahl.

"I'm working Madeline," I said. "For the AG's office. Captain Kramer was here a little while ago. He suggested it might be a good idea if we compared notes."

"Sure thing," Jackson said. "Sounds good to me. What do you have?"

"An eyewitness."

"To Madeline's murder?" He sounded incredulous. "From 1950?"

"Yup."

"When can we talk to this witness?"

"That's a little tougher," I said. "She's a nun. Lives in a convent up on Whidbey Island."

"Can I call her up?"

That was when I realized that in all my transactions with Sister Mary Katherine, no one—not Sister Mary Katherine and not Freddy Mac—had given me her phone number. I knew the convent had to have a telephone. Hadn't she told me someone named Sister Therese had surfed the Net for information on Alfred and Elvira Marchbank?

"I don't have that number right now," I said. "Once I get it, I can have her call you. Or better yet, maybe I can convince her to come talk to you."

"If you can talk a nun out of a convent, you must be some kind of guy."

"We'll see," I said. "If I can get her to come to town, how hard will it be to meet up with you?"

"Not hard at all," Jackson returned. "You tell us when and where, and Hank and I will be there. Captain Kramer gave us our marching orders. Both cases are highest priority."

Captain Kramer! Just hearing the word *captain* used in conjunction with Kramer's name rankled, but I was going to have to get used to it.

"All right, then," I said. "Let's see what we can do."

Good to my word, I was up and on the phone to Freddy Mac bright and early the next morning, asking for Sister Mary Katherine's phone number.

"Is it too early to call?" I asked after he gave me what I needed.

"Hardly," Fred said with a laugh. "You won't be waking her. She tells me morning devotionals start at five A.M."

So I dialed Saint Benedict's and was put through to Sister Mary Katherine. "Beaumont here," I said. "I'm wondering if you can come back to Seattle today to meet with some Seattle PD detectives."

"This evening, perhaps," she said. "Sister Therese and Sister Margaret just left in the van to run some errands. They won't be back until around lunchtime. I could leave after that."

I didn't want the meeting with the Seattle PD homicide detectives to conflict with Rosemary Peters's funeral. I needed it to be earlier instead of later. "What if I came out to Whidbey and picked you up?"

"That seems dreadfully inconvenient for you. Does it really have to be today?" Sister Mary Katherine asked. "I've been away for several days, and I just got home late yesterday."

"Elvira Marchbank is dead," I told her.

"Oh, no," Mary Katherine murmured. Her regretful tone surprised me. "She was fine when I saw her. What happened?"

"When you saw her?" I repeated. "When was that?"

"Yesterday afternoon," Sister Mary Katherine said. "After our lunch. I decided to drive back to the old neighborhood just to look around. I stopped outside the foundation office and wondered what to do. Finally I worked up my courage and went inside. When I asked to see Mrs. Marchbank, the woman there told me Elvira wasn't available. But as I was leaving, a limo drove up to the house next door—the place where my parents and I used to live. It turns out that's where Elvira lives now. The limo was bringing her home from a doctor's appointment. Even after all these years, I recognized her the moment she stepped out of the car."

I was thunderstruck. "You didn't talk to her, did you?"

"Of course I did," Sister Mary Katherine said. "After all these years, it seemed like the right thing to do, and I'm glad I did, too. She was old and frail and she told me she was sorry."

"Sorry?" I asked.

"Sorry about the part she played in Mimi's death. She said she'd always known I'd come back someday and that she was finally ready to 'do the right thing.' I took that to mean that she was prepared to turn herself in and accept responsibility for her actions. What happened to her?"

"She fell down a flight of stairs. The detectives working the case seem to think she was pushed."

"That's terrible," Sister Katherine said. "I'm so sorry."

From my point of view, terrible just about covered it. Sister Mary Katherine had just gone from being a homicide eyewitness to being a possible homicide suspect.

"I'm on my way to pick you up," I said. "I'll be there as soon as I can."

CHAPTER 13

IT TOOK TIME TO MAKE Enterprise shape up and come through with the rental car the insurance company had ordered for me. Once it appeared, I headed north on I-5. After the 928, the Ford Taurus was a bit of a letdown. As the ads say about Porsches: There is no substitute. I had been told that the adjuster would be getting back to me either that day or the next with the verdict as to whether or not the 928 was totaled. In the meantime, the Taurus was my ride.

I lucked out and caught the Mukilteo Ferry and headed for Useless Bay on Whidbey Island. Useless Bay is useless because it's so shallow that at low tide it's little more than a glorified mudflat. On the way I called into the office to let people know what I was up to.

"Keeping a low profile, I see," Barbara Galvin observed.

"No, I'm working," I told her. "If you like, I'll be glad to talk to Harry."

"Wouldn't recommend it," she returned. "He's still on the warpath about your five o'clock news appearance. If I were you, I'd give him more time to cool off—unless he calls you, that is."

It seemed like a good idea to take Barbara's advice as far as Harry was concerned. "What about Mel?"

"She and Brad are in Seattle doing interviews," Barbara said.

If one of the people they were interviewing was Heather Peters, that meant I didn't want to talk to Mel, and I certainly didn't want to talk to Ron or Amy. I put my phone back in my pocket and hoped it wouldn't ring.

Once on Whidbey, I left the Clinton Ferry Dock behind and drove north, past the turnoff to Useless Bay Country Club and onto Double Bluff Road. Evidence of downed trees was everywhere. The entrance to Saint Benedict's was barred with an imposing iron gate. Alongside were a keypad and an intercom.

When the invisible gatekeeper allowed me entrance, I was amazed. The convent grounds had been lovingly landscaped into something that rivaled Victoria's famed Buchart Gardens. On this midwinter day, nothing was in bloom, but the snow was mostly gone, and the carefully tended beds were clean and empty and ready for planting. A coveralls-clad woman with a noisy leaf blower was herding the last few fallen leaves off the manicured and graveled pathways. She looked up and nodded as I drove past, but she didn't stop what she was doing.

The convent's several buildings, nestled in a slight hollow, looked old and European. Thick hay-bale walls were covered with whitewashed stucco. The roofs were covered with red clay tiles. The centerpiece of the place was a tiny chapel, no bigger than a two-car garage.

As I stopped beside what appeared to be the main building, the door to the chapel opened and Sister Mary Katherine stepped out. She was dressed in an old-fashioned flowing habit.

"I was saying prayers for Elvira Marchbank," she said. "If you'll come in and wait for a few minutes, I'll change into civilian clothing for our drive into town."

She led me into the main building and left me seated on a couch in front of a cheerfully crackling fire. The fire may have been cheerful, but I wasn't. Not telling Sister Mary Katherine to stay away from Elvira Marchbank had been a serious error on my part. I hadn't mentioned it because it hadn't seemed necessary. It never occurred to me that Sister Mary Katherine would want to have anything to do with the woman who had helped murder her friend, Mimi. I understood that my refusing to give Paul Kramer information about the cold case I was working hadn't caused Elvira's death, but it was likely that she had been killed because I was working the Mimi Marchbank case.

One way or the other, that made what had happened my fault. But even with all that free-floating guilt, somehow the warmth of the fire got to me. I was dozing in front of it when Sister Mary Katherine opened a heavy wooden door and reentered the room. She was wearing the same skirt, blouse, and cardigan she had worn the first time I saw her. "Ready?" she said.

I nodded and stood.

"It'll be a long time before the next ferry," she announced. "We could just as well drive around."

"How long will it take us to get to downtown Seattle from here?"

"Two hours or so. Maybe more, depending on traffic."

I called Detective Jackson and gave him our ETA. Then, once we were in the Taurus, I waited until we had left the convent grounds before I lit into her. "What were you thinking?" I demanded. "Why on earth did you go see Elvira?"

Sister Mary Katherine seemed totally unperturbed by my question. "I didn't do the right thing when I was a girl," she returned. "I wanted to talk to Elvira about it. I wanted to know if she was sorry for what she'd done—and she was."

I could just imagine how hearing that would go over with the

Seattle PD detectives. "So you actually spoke to her about Mimi's murder?"

"Yes, of course I did. I already told you that. I went up to the door and knocked. When she opened it and I told her who I was, she invited me in and we had tea."

"How civilized. You sip tea and talk murder."

"We sipped tea, and I prayed with her," Sister Mary Katherine corrected. "I believe Elvira was glad to see me—glad to have a way to put what she and Albert had done behind her."

This was not going to go over at all well with my fellow detectives. "When did you leave?" I asked.

"About three-thirty," Sister Mary Katherine said, "but I didn't kill her, if that's what you're thinking."

"I may not be thinking that," I grumbled back at her, "but other people will be. Like the Seattle homicide detectives working the case, for instance. I don't know about the time of death, but if you were one of the last people to see her—"

"I'm not a detective," she interrupted. "I'm a woman of God. Once I remembered what had happened, I admit, my first reaction—my very human reaction—was to want to see Elvira Marchbank punished for what she did. But after I left you at the Westin, I came to my senses. My real purpose in life is saving souls, not in seeing that the guilty go to prison. In the case of Elvira's soul, I think I may have been of some help."

"She confessed to you, then?" I asked.

"Certainly not," Sister Mary Katherine responded. "I'm a nun, not a priest. She's an Episcopalian, you know."

"So she didn't come right out and admit to you that she helped murder Madeline Marchbank, but she said she was sorry?"

"She didn't have to say she did it. I know she did it," Sister Mary

174

Katherine said, verbally underscoring the word *know*. "I saw her do it, remember?"

We rode for some time in silence. I tended to believe that Sister Mary Katherine was telling the truth, that she had gone to Elvira's house in hopes of saving the woman's soul. I doubted my former colleagues in the homicide section of Seattle PD would see things in that same light.

"I'm sorry if what I did disappointed you," she added finally. "We seem to be working at cross-purposes here. Tell me, who exactly are we meeting with once we get to town?"

"We're meeting with four Seattle PD homicide detectives. Two of them are assigned to Elvira's case. The other two are working Madeline's."

"They've reopened it?"

"Yes."

Sister Mary Katherine sighed. "But Elvira's dead. So that will finally be the end of it."

"Probably," I agreed. "For Madeline's homicide, anyway. Closing a case with a dead defendant isn't nearly as difficult as convicting a live one. Detectives don't have to develop evidence that will hold up in court, and they don't have to prove culpability 'beyond a reasonable doubt.' In Elvira's case, however, it seems likely that you may have been one of the last people to see her alive. That means you may be considered a person of interest, if not a possible suspect. You probably shouldn't go to this meeting without counsel."

"I have counsel," she said firmly.

"If you're thinking of me as counsel, you need to know I don't count. You should have an attorney present. Maybe your friend at the archbishop's office could help."

"Our Father in Heaven is my counsel," Sister Mary Katherine declared. "He's all I need."

It would have been rude of me to mention the number of vehicles I've seen hauled away from accident scenes to wrecking yards while still proudly displaying their "God is my copilot" bumper stickers. So I kept my mouth shut and kept driving.

Heavy snowfall followed by two days of warm drenching rain had brought every river in western Washington above flood stage. As we drove east toward Mount Vernon, the fields on either side of the road were inundated with water, making it seem as if we were on a causeway rather than a highway. Living in the city, it's easy to forget that out in the hinterlands people often have to resort to sandbags in order to wage hand-to-hand combat with Mother Nature.

Just north of Marysville, my cell phone rang. "We've got a problem," Kendall Jackson told me. "Captain Kramer wants to see you ASAP."

"Since Sister Mary Katherine and I are already on our way to meet with you, that should be easy to arrange."

"Not as easy as you think," Kendall responded. "It's about Wink Winkler."

"What about him?"

"He's been reported missing. From his retirement home in West Seattle. According to the person who called it in, he left in a cab shortly after talking to you—left and never came back."

I thought about the bulldog-faced woman at the nursing home to whom I had given my card. With that card and with Wink Winkler having at one time been the lead investigator in the Madeline Marchbank homicide, it hadn't taken long for Kramer to connect the dots. I was connecting the same dots. If Winkler had disappeared after talking to me, then in some way I didn't yet understand, I was probably responsible for that disappearance. No wonder Kramer was on the warpath.

"Tell him I'm on my way. I'll see him when I get there." I hung up the phone.

"Winkler," Sister Mary Katherine mused. "Isn't that the name of the detective on Mimi's case?"

"That's right. I talked to him yesterday afternoon, about the same time you were talking to Elvira. Now she's dead, and he's missing. The nursing home said he left in a cab shortly after I did."

"A cab?" Sister Mary Katherine asked suddenly. "What kind of cab?"

"I don't know. Detective Jackson didn't say. Why?"

"There was a yellow cab parked right behind my van when I left Elvira Marchbank's home. I noticed it because it was parked so close to my bumper that I had to work to get out of the parking place without hitting the cab or the car in front of me."

I picked my phone back up and dialed Detective Jackson. "Check with Yellow Cab," I told him. "Find out whether or not they're the ones who picked Wink Winkler up. If they did, find out where and when they took him."

"Will do," Jackson said.

When I glanced back in Sister Mary Katherine's direction, I found that my phone call had left her shaken. "What if he's dead, too?" she asked.

Sister Mary Katherine had dealt with the news of Elvira's death with far more equanimity than she showed at hearing that Wink Winkler had gone missing. Where Elvira was concerned, Sister Mary Katherine was operating with the firm conviction that the woman had gone to her death with her soul saved. If Wink was dead now, too, she couldn't be so certain.

"He may have just wandered off," I suggested, trying to make us both feel better.

"No," Sister Mary Katherine insisted. "All of this is happening because of me—because I turned up after all these years and brought Mimi's death back to the forefront."

"That may be true," I agreed. "But the real problem is that there are still people around here who, even after all this time, don't want Mimi's homicide solved."

"But why?" Sister Mary Katherine asked.

"Once we know that," I told her, "we may know everything."

When we reached Seattle PD we had to go through the routine of collecting our visitor's badges before we were met by Detective Jackson and escorted upstairs. I thought we'd be going into one of the interview rooms. Wrong. We were taken directly to Homicide and crammed, cheek by jowl, into Kramer's new glass-lined office. In the old building, we'd have been inside the glass-lined Fishbowl with everything done there coming under the scrutiny of the entire squad room. In his new office with glass walls opening on a window-lined corridor, only passing seagulls and pigeons had a bird's-eye view. Dealing with Paul Kramer in relative privacy didn't make it any easier.

Kramer is one of those negative people who go through life spreading ill will and divisiveness in their wake. I had been hoping to establish a good working relationship with Detective Jackson and the other investigators assigned to the two Marchbank cases, but Kramer's MO was to lop cooperation off at the knees. He's also one of the enforcers of that old saw "No good deed goes unpunished." Most homicide cops would have been happy to have a leg up in an investigation. Not Kramer. His opening question to me, asked without benefit of introductions, made his lack of gratitude perfectly clear.

"How is it you happen to know that Wink Winkler left Home Sweet Home yesterday afternoon in a yellow cab?" he demanded.

"I didn't actually *know* anything of the kind," I said. "I merely asked the question. Are you saying that checked out?"

I glanced at Detective Jackson. He nodded slightly in my direction but said nothing while Captain Kramer glowered at both of us.

"Yes, it did," he answered. "According to Yellow Cab's log, they dropped him off—"

"In front of the Marchbank Foundation," Sister Mary Katherine interjected.

I shot her a look that was meant to say "Stifle," but my warning came too late. It was as though everyone and everything in that seventh-floor room went into a state of suspended animation. No one spoke or moved except for the hands on the clock on the credenza behind Kramer's desk.

"And who exactly are you?" Kramer demanded.

I answered first. "This is Sister Mary Katherine, mother superior of Saint Benedict's Convent on Whidbey Island."

"All right. Fine. Glad to make your acquaintance." Then he turned back to me. "But what the hell is she doing here?"

"Excuse me, Captain Kramer, is it?" Sister Mary Katherine asked. "I'm perfectly capable of answering questions on my own without requiring Mr. Beaumont's help. Years ago I was an eyewitness to Mimi Marchbank's murder. It's been suggested that you or someone like you might want to talk to me about it."

Kramer's eyes narrowed. His forehead bulged. "An eyewitness?" he asked. "To a homicide that happened more than half a century ago?"

"I was quite young at the time."

"And where have you been since then? What kept you from coming forward until now?" Kramer asked.

I had Freddy Mac's videotapes in my briefcase and was prepared to show them. I started to say as much, but Sister Mary Katherine silenced me with a wave of her hand.

"It was a brutal murder," she said evenly. "Seeing it was traumatic enough that I repressed the memories completely. Only recently, with the help of a hypnotherapist, have I been able to bring them to the surface."

Kramer looked shocked—like a little old lady who has suddenly encountered the unexpected use of the *F*-word in public. "A hypnotherapist?" he repeated, but he was looking at me. "You set up this meeting with four of my top homicide detectives—pulled them off the streets—to discuss the findings of a hypnotherapist!"

It was a statement, not a question. I simply nodded.

Kramer stood up. "I always knew you were a crackpot, Beaumont. If this is where your yellow cab information came from, it just about takes the cake. Good-bye. Get out of here, and don't be wasting any more of my detectives' and my valuable time."

I was more than ready to take the man at his word. I stood up to go. Sister Mary Katherine didn't budge.

"I understand Elvira Marchbank died yesterday," the nun said. "I believe I was one of the last people to see her alive. I should think you would want your detectives to speak with me even if you're too busy."

"My dear lady," Kramer said in his most condescending fashion, "you being a nun and all, you might not be aware of this, but whenever news of an unexpected death happens, there are always plenty of people who line up outside waiting to tell us what they know." He used his fingers to create imaginary quotation marks around the word "know." "If what you have to tell us is what some quack was able to dredge up while you were under his suggestive spell, I doubt it's going to be of much help. Now, if you don't mind, we have work to do."

I had sidled over to the door. Now Sister Mary Katherine stood, but she leveled a reproving look at Captain Kramer through her wire-framed glasses. "There are people in this world, Mr. Kramer . . ." His use of the word "lady" may have deprived Sister Mary Katherine of her rightful title, but at least none of her subordinates had been in the room to hear it. Kramer wasn't so lucky. His demotion from captain to mister fell on the ears of four of his top detectives. Sister Mary Katherine knew it, he knew it, and so did everyone else in the room. None of his rapt detectives cracked a smile. Neither did I.

". . . people," Sister Mary Katherine continued firmly, "who pray to God for help in their hour of need and then refuse to accept that help when it's offered. If the answer doesn't arrive in exactly the guise they expect, they assume no answer was given. I regret to say, Mr. Kramer, that you may very well be one of those unfortunate people. For a man in your position, that's not only surprising, it's also quite unfortunate. Good day to you, Mr. Kramer. And good luck. You'll most likely need it."

As we walked down the corridor, I glanced back at Kramer. His face was beet red. He looked ready to explode. I was glad I would be out of earshot when it happened. His quartet of detectives wouldn't be that lucky.

"What a disagreeable man!" Sister Mary Katherine exclaimed as we walked unescorted toward the elevator. "Are all police captains that incredibly rude?"

I laughed. "Don't judge everybody by Paul Kramer. He's in a class by himself."

We were handing in our visitor's badges downstairs when my cell phone rang. It was Detective Jackson. "We'd still like to talk to you and Sister Mary Katherine, only not officially. If you happened to be going to lunch somewhere where we just might run into you . . ."

"I'm feeling a lot like a turkey sandwich," I said.

In the world of Seattle PD the words "turkey sandwich" and a place called Bakeman's on Cherry west of Second Avenue are synonymous. It was close enough to police headquarters to make the idea of "running into one another" a lot more believable. It was also right next door to the place where I'd parked my rented Taurus.

Bakeman's is a deli—a joint that's open for lunch and that's it. Every weekday they roast nine turkeys, make thirty pounds of meat loaf, and bake eighty loaves of bread, and the food is good enough that it's all gone by the time they close at three in the afternoon. Knowing the head cook's propensity for yelling at indecisive customers, I handled the ordering.

Sister Mary Katherine and I split a huge turkey sandwich on fluffy white bread and waited for Detective Jackson and his cohorts to show up. We were done with our sandwiches and still waiting when Sister Mary Katherine reached into her purse and pulled out a small manila envelope, which she handed to me.

"I thought you might want to see these," she said. "It's what I saved from the box of mementos my foster mother kept for me all those years."

The words "Bonnie Jean" were written on the envelope in the spidery, old-fashioned Spencerian style of penmanship that had gone out of vogue before I ever sat down to learn the dreaded Palmer method in second grade.

When I opened the envelope, out fell a few black-and-white photos with their deckle Kodak print edges. Someone had printed names and dates on the backs of the photos, but I didn't need to read the caption to recognize the subject of the first one: Little Bonnie Jean, her smiling face framed by a mass of perpendicular curls, was dressed in a frilly white dress.

"Your First Communion?" I asked.

Sister Mary Katherine nodded.

The second showed a young couple, probably in their late twenties, holding hands and laughing while sitting side by side on a porch swing. The resemblance between the woman in the photo and Sister Mary Katherine was striking.

"Your folks?"

"Yes."

I remembered what Sister Mary Katherine had told me about her parents defying their respective families and eloping. Judging from that particular photo, I would have to say the families had been wrong. "They look happy."

"I think they were," Sister Mary Katherine said. "They didn't have it easy, but they always seemed to enjoy being together. I didn't understand it at the time, but now I believe it's a blessing the two of them died together. I think whoever was left behind would have been lost without the other."

Next came a picture of an older man wearing a clerical collar. "That's Father Mark," Sister Mary Katherine said. "He's the one who looked out for me after my parents died."

The last photo was one of Sister Mary Katherine as a little girl standing beside her father. Barefoot and wearing a sundress, Bonnie Jean posed for the camera, squinting into the lens from a perch on the hood of a vehicle. Her father wore jeans and a white T-shirt with a pack of cigarettes rolled into one sleeve. He stood with his arms folded across his chest, grinning proudly.

"New car?" I asked.

Back when I was growing up and even earlier, photographing young men with their new cars was a rite of passage. Guys bought new cars. Then, as soon as they had them home, they posed with their new prize and had their pictures taken.

"It's the only new car my father ever owned," Sister Mary Katherine said.

I took out my reading glasses and studied the photo up close. The hood ornament and the bumper details told me I was looking at a 1950 Ford Custom Deluxe. Sister Mary Katherine said the car was new. She had also said that her parents had struggled to make ends meet. The sundress and glaring sunlight told me it was summer in Seattle, the summer of 1950, a month or two after Mimi Marchbank's murder.

"Did your father ever say how he came to have this car?" I asked.

Sister Mary Katherine shrugged. "I always assumed he bought it. Why?"

I collected the photos and returned them to the envelope as a way of avoiding answering her question, but I suddenly had a much better idea of why the Dunleavy family might have moved to a new home within days or weeks of Mimi's death. And I thought I also had a better idea of why Wink Winkler hadn't interviewed Bonnie Jean in the course of his homicide investigation.

"I'm not sure," I said. "But as soon as I figure it out, I'll let you know."

CHAPTER 14

IT WAS AFTER ONE when I finally gave up on what was supposed to be an "accidental" rendezvous with Detective Jackson.

"I hate to leave," I told Sister Mary Katherine. "But there's a memorial service starting at two, and I need to be there."

"I could stay here and wait for him," she suggested.

"No," I told her. "Once this place shuts down, where would you go? Why don't you ride along with me? Maybe we can hook up with Detective Jackson later."

I knew that Ron had specified that Rosemary's memorial service would be private. I wondered how upset he'd be if I showed up with a stranger in tow, but the truth was, by then it was so late that there wasn't enough time for me to stop by Belltown Terrace and drop Sister Mary Katherine off.

"Fine," she said.

While we waited in the garage entrance for the attendant to return my rental car, I checked my phone and was annoyed to see that I had missed two calls, both of them from Jackson. In all the hubbub of Bakeman's, I hadn't heard the ringer. I returned his call immediately.

"We've been called out on something else," he said guardedly. "I'll have to get back to you later."

From the way he said it, I guessed he was replying under the watchful eyes and ears of Captain Kramer—another very good reason to be working for Harry I. Ball and the SHIT squad rather than for Seattle PD. Better Ken Jackson than me.

"Who died?" Sister Mary Katherine asked, once we had settled into the Taurus.

"The former wife of a good friend," I said. "She was murdered last weekend down in Tacoma." I could have said a lot more than that, but I didn't. There was no need to burden Sister Mary Katherine with the gory details of yet another homicide investigation. She was already dealing with two as it was.

"I'm sorry," Sister Mary Katherine said.

"So am I."

"Are you sure the family members won't mind if I tag along?"

"Ron Peters, the ex-husband, is a police officer," I said. "He'll understand."

We drove to Bleitz Funeral Chapel, which is west of the Fremont Bridge and only a few blocks from where my former partner, Sue Danielson, died. I had managed to avoid that neighborhood ever since her death. Returning to it now on the occasion of another murder made me uneasy—right up until I saw the gang of reporters massed outside the front door. That made me mad.

"Damn!" I muttered under my breath.

"What are all those reporters doing here?" Sister Mary Katherine asked, observing the crush of people gathered near the entryway into the chapel.

"Because they're vultures," I said. "And the idea that a police officer may have done something wrong sends them into a feeding frenzy."

"Your friend is a suspect?" Sister Mary Katherine asked.

"As far as the press is concerned, he is," I answered.

As we walked toward the chapel, I heard footsteps hurrying behind me. I turned to see Mel Soames rushing to catch up. "Are we late?" she asked.

"Not yet," I said. "But close. Come on."

Introductions happened as we walked while the gaggle of reporters turned their attention and lenses on us. I did my best to shield the two women from the cameras as we made our way through the crush to the door, but my efforts weren't entirely successful.

Inside the funeral home's vestibule, we were approached by a man in a dark suit. "You're here for the Peters service?" he asked in a hushed voice.

I nodded, and he handed each of us a program. "Down the hall and to the right," he said. "And you'd best hurry. They're about to start."

By the time we reached the room and slipped into the back row of folding chairs, the service, such as it was, had indeed started. The room was small. Since Rosemary had been cremated, there was no coffin, only a photo of her that looked as if it might have been taken from a high school yearbook. She was a sweet-faced girl back then, before she had succumbed to the ravages of substance abuse.

The media may have been milling around outside, but the service itself was sparsely attended. Even counting Mel, Sister Mary Katherine, the minister, and me, there couldn't have been more than a dozen or so people in the room. Besides Ron and Amy and the kids, Ron's parents and Amy's were there as well. So was an older couple I later learned were Rosemary's grandparents.

It was telling that, despite the fact that Ron had worked for Seattle

PD most of his adult life, only one current police officer from that jurisdiction was in attendance. To me that meant that word had filtered down from on high that Ron Peters was to be hung out to dry and that everybody in the department, if they knew what was good for them, should distance themselves from him. The only exception to that ostensibly unofficial order was Commander Anthony Freeman, head of Internal Affairs and Ron Peters's boss.

Even as head of IA—an unenviable job if ever there was one—Tony had maintained his reputation as a straight shooter. He was the one who had plucked Ron from his long exile in Media Relations and had given him an avenue back into what Ron regarded as active police work. It didn't surprise me that Tony alone would defy the brass and come to the memorial service.

Molly Wright, Amy's sister, was also there. I thought it odd that she was sitting by herself toward the back of the room rather than with her parents, who were up front, just behind Ron and Amy. And then, a minute or so after we arrived, Dillon Middleton showed up. Instead of joining Heather, he slipped into an empty chair next to Molly. She reached over, greeted him with a hug, and then whispered something in his ear. When we stood up for the opening prayer, I noticed she was holding his hand.

It wasn't out of character that Dillon wouldn't attempt to sit near Heather. In fact, considering what he and Heather were most likely doing behind her parents' backs, I would have expected him to make himself scarce whenever Ron or Amy was around, but Molly's apparent closeness to Dillon surprised me and I wondered what exactly was going on, but by then the memorial service was well under way.

I'm sure Ron had arranged the affair in order to give Tracy and Heather some kind of closure in the aftermath of their mother's death. I don't know how much the service did for them, but it didn't do much for me. I've attended funerals and memorials that moved me. This one didn't. The man who officiated seemed to have almost no knowledge about Rosemary Peters and her many demons and struggles. He seemed to know even less about the broken and grieving people who were left behind or the forces that had splintered Ron and Rosemary's marriage and family. By the time the minister segued into a lame benediction, the only person in the room who was actually weeping was Rosemary's grandmother.

When it was time to go, Dillon was the first to leave and Mel shot after him. Shoving his wheelchair into high gear, Ron Peters dodged away from his family and made straight for me. "What's she doing here?" he demanded.

At first I thought he was talking about Sister Mary Katherine. Then I realized he meant Mel. "She's only doing her job," I said. "She needs to talk to Dillon."

"That little creep?" Ron asked. "You mean he was here, too?" He rounded on Molly. "I suppose you told him it was all right for him to come, didn't you!" he said accusingly. Shaking his head in disgust, Ron turned his back on Molly and rolled away.

Watching him go, Molly's face flushed deep red. Whether the color came from anger or embarrassment I couldn't tell. Maybe it was both. An uncomfortable silence settled over the room.

"Just because I have to stay with you at the moment doesn't give you the right to talk to me that way," Molly called after him. "I'm not your wife, you know, and I'm not one of your daughters, either. You can't tell me what to do."

Ron stopped, turned, and came back. "And you don't have the right to undermine my authority over my own children," he retorted. "Dillon's too old for Heather. I told her that, and I told him, too. And I meant it. Just because he's your friend's son . . ."

189

"There's nothing wrong with Dillon Middleton," Molly interrupted. "If you'd give him a chance, you might find out what a nice boy he is. As for Heather, one of these days you're going to have to let her grow up and make her own decisions."

"Maybe when she's grown up," Ron returned, "she'll be capable of making better decisions than she's making right now."

Amy's mother, Carol, attempted to intervene. "Come on, Molly," she said. "Everyone's upset right now. Let it be."

"I won't let it be!" Molly stormed. "He seems to think I'm some kind of charity case and it's okay for him to treat me like dirt. I look after his kids when he and Amy are off at work, I cook the meals, and this is the thanks I get."

"Enough, both of you," Amy interjected, leveling searing looks at both her husband and her sister. Then, to everyone else, she announced, "Come on up to the house. We'll have refreshments there."

With Sister Mary Katherine in tow, I hadn't planned to accept that invitation, but Amy changed my mind. "Please stop by," she said as I was holding the door for my passenger. "It would be a huge help to me."

I looked questioningly at Sister Mary Katherine. "It's fine," she said. "I don't mind. I can wait in the car."

When we stopped in front of the Peterses' place, the media horde was once again on our heels. "You'd better come on in," I said, changing my mind about leaving Sister Mary Katherine in the car. "I don't want you to be at their mercy. They're going to want to know who you are and why you're here. Until we talk to Detective Jackson, it's probably best if you don't talk to any reporters at all."

I parked on the street and then ushered Sister Mary Katherine up to Ron and Amy's front door. When I rang the bell, Tracy opened the door and let us in. She reached up and hugged me. "Are you okay?"

Biting her lip, she nodded. "Dad's downstairs," she said. "He's the one who needs help."

I looked back at Sister Mary Katherine. "Go ahead," she said. "I'll wait right here."

She settled into a chair near the door while I went looking for Ron. He was in the daylit basement apartment staring up at the crowd of reporters milling outside. "I wanted it to be private," he said.

"It was private," I said.

"The parking lot wasn't private, not with those yahoos chasing people to and from their cars. And it's not private here, either. And then I had to go and make an ass of myself and jump all over you about that Soames woman. I'm sorry," he added. "I thought you had brought her."

"Mel's perfectly capable of taking herself anywhere she wants to go," I said.

"She wants to talk to Heather."

"She needs to talk to Heather," I corrected. "It's her job."

"Not without a parent and an attorney present," he said. "I've called Ralph. We've made an appointment for tomorrow morning.

"And then I had to make an ass of myself about Molly. I'm tired of having her underfoot. At the time we bought the house from Amy and Molly's folks, Molly and her husband were flying high and they said it was fine—they wanted no part of it. But now that Molly's broke, she seems to think she can stay here forever. That we owe her a place to live for however long she cares to hang around. I married Amy," he added miserably. "I sure as hell didn't marry her sister. The woman despises me, and the feeling's pretty much mutual."

"Look, Ron," I said reasonably, "there's a whole lot on your plate right now. No one could blame you for being depressed, but—"

He rounded on me. "Depressed? Who the hell said I was depressed?"

he demanded. "Here I am about to lose my daughter, and you say I'm depressed? Next you'll be telling me I need to drag my butt off to see the nearest doc and get myself a prescription for antidepressants."

"Ron," Amy called from upstairs. "Are you coming up or not? Tony's here, but he's going to have to leave in a few minutes."

"Time for my command performance," Ron said grimly, pushing the elevator button; then, to me, he added, "Going up?"

I crowded into the tiny elevator with him and rode up to the living-room level. Amy was watching the elevator from across the room, but as soon as the door opened, she turned away and resumed a quiet conversation with her parents. The look on her face as she looked away told me she wasn't any happier than her husband was.

Someone waylaid Ron the moment he rolled out of the elevator. I caught sight of Anthony Freeman, who was standing near a food-laden table on the far side of the room, thoughtfully sipping a cup of coffee. I made my way over to him. His face brightened as I approached. He put down his coffee cup and held out a hand.

"Beaumont," he exclaimed. "It's good to see you again, even if it isn't under the best of circumstances. How's your new job working out?"

"Fine," I said. "Given the choice between working for Harry I. Ball or working for Paul Kramer, I'll take Harry every time."

"Understandable," Tony Freeman said. "What are you working on these days? Not this, I assume."

As soon as he asked the question, it dawned on me that Anthony Freeman was one of the few people still inside Seattle PD who might be able to help me in my search for Mimi Marchbank's killer.

"I'm tracking down a cold case from 1950. The investigating officer was William Winkler. Ever heard of him?"

"Wink Winkler?" Tony replied. "I've heard of him all right, just today. It was on the radio as I came from the funeral home."

"What was on the radio?"

"He's dead," Tony Freeman said. "A tugboat captain spotted his body this morning. He was snagged on a pier over by Harbor Island."

"Wink Winkler is dead!" I repeated in disbelief.

Tony shrugged. "What I heard made it sound like a self-inflicted gunshot wound. I believe he had already been reported missing, and they must have contacted next of kin, since they've already announced it on the air."

"Damn!" I said.

"What's wrong?"

"I went to see him yesterday in reference to that old case. He wasn't exactly thrilled to hear that I now had an eyewitness. How much do you know about him?"

"Not that much. I know he was brought down in the bribery and corruption scandals that went on in the midfifties. But I could take a look at what's in his file to see if there's anything that might apply." Tony reached in his pocket and pulled out a notebook. "What's the name of the case you're working?"

"Marchbank," I said. "Madeline Marchbank. She was stabbed to death in May of 1950."

Tony Freeman gave me a searching look. "Marchbank. The name sounds familiar. Wait a minute. Isn't Marchbank the name of the woman who was found at the bottom of a flight of stairs last night?"

"That's right. Elvira Marchbank, not Madeline. And Elvira was one of two perpetrators identified by the eyewitness in that other case."

"And Wink Winkler was the investigating officer."

I nodded. "You're sure he committed suicide?"

"Nothing's for sure. If he didn't and with this Elvira woman dead as well, that eyewitness of yours could be a whole lot more than what she claims to be," Tony Freeman observed.

193

It was a fair conjecture. If Paul Kramer and his detectives weren't making the same connection themselves, they soon would be.

"Is there money involved?" Tony asked.

I thought about the Marchbank Foundation. "Probably," I said.

"Well, then," Tony said. "Do what I do. Follow the money."

He finished writing his note and stuffed the notepad back in his pocket. "I'll take a look at the file," he said. "If anything jumps out at me, I'll let you know."

Tony excused himself to go talk to Ron while I went looking for Sister Mary Katherine. She was sitting in the same place where I had left her, but someone—Tracy, presumably—had brought her a cup of coffee and a plate of tiny sandwiches and cookies.

"Time to go home?" she asked.

"Home," I agreed. "But mine, not yours."

"We're going to your place?" Sister Mary Katherine asked. "Why?"

"Wink Winkler is dead."

"What happened?"

"First reports suggest a possible suicide."

"Is he dead because of me?" Sister Mary Katherine asked.

It seemed to me that was probably true, but I chose not to say so.

"Is that why I can't go home?" she added.

"Kramer may have blown us off this morning, and we didn't see Detective Jackson at lunch, but you can bet they're going to want to talk to you this evening. If I take you home, you'll just have to turn around and come straight back."

"Why are you so sure they're going to want to talk to me?" she asked.

"Because I'm going to call them up and tell them to," I said.

And I did. Some telephone numbers never fall out of your head. Captain Larry Powell's number was still there in my dialing finger even though his desk was now in another building and belonged to someone else. Kramer answered his phone on the second ring.

"Oh, it's you," he said dismissively once I identified myself. "That little lady of yours is something else. Everywhere she goes, people are dropping like flies."

I bristled at that. Sister Mary Katherine was nobody's "little lady" and she most especially wasn't mine.

"This is a courtesy call," I said civilly. "Sister Mary Katherine was about to head home for Whidbey Island when we heard about Wink Winkler's death. I thought you might want to speak with her about the Madeline Marchbank situation after all."

"I doubt that will be necessary," Kramer replied brusquely. "That whole situation is under control."

I could hardly believe my ears. "You're not interested in interviewing her?"

"Not at this time. I told you earlier that we're not going to do any kind of investigation based on the faulty premise of forgotten memories. Maybe the AG's office can afford to squander resources like that, but I can't. We've reopened Madeline Marchbank's homicide, and we'll be following up on it through conventional methods and with conventional detective work."

"I don't think you're paying attention, Paul. Sister Mary Katherine says Elvira Marchbank was one of the perpetrators in that case—"

"One of the alleged perpetrators," Kramer corrected.

"And Winkler was the lead investigating officer," I continued. "Both of them died within hours of learning about Sister Mary Katherine's potentially damaging allegations. Doesn't that tell you something?"

"It tells me people are messing around where they shouldn't be messing," Kramer replied. "Wink Winkler blew his brains out. Lots of ex-cops do that. Would he have done it if Sister Mary Katherine hadn't been stirring up those old pots? Who knows? We'll be investigating that, of course, and trying to find out what else was going on in his life that might have pushed him over the edge. As for Elvira Marchbank? I suspect her death will end up being ruled accidental. There was a stack of magazines near the top of the stairs where she took that fall. One of them—one that was found near her body at the bottom of the stairs—showed evidence of a partial shoe print. I'm guessing she stepped on it and went flying—sort of like stepping on a banana peel."

Earlier in the day Kramer had referred to Elvira's death as being unexpected. He hadn't said a word about it being a possible homicide. Now that previous statement made sense. The good captain was playing the closure game. Ruling a homicide an accidental death and conveniently labeling something suicide when it maybe wasn't suicide at all helps skew the statistics. It keeps those pesky unsolved cases from showing up on your squad's track record.

Captain Paul Kramer was definitely a bottom-line kind of guy. If he couldn't solve a particular case—or if he didn't want to be bothered—he simply made it disappear. As for Mimi Marchbank? Her death hadn't happened on his watch, so he could afford to reopen that one and leave it open indefinitely. Regardless of whether or not the case was solved, it wouldn't count against Kramer's closure stats.

I put the phone down and found Sister Mary Katherine staring at me. "What's wrong?" she asked. "You look upset."

"I'll take you back to Whidbey," I said. "It turns out I was wrong. We won't be paying another visit to Homicide after all."

"Why not? Because the captain thinks I made the whole thing up?"

I simply nodded. Explaining the reality of Seattle PD internal politics was beyond my ability right then.

"I'll call Sister Therese and have her meet us in Mount Vernon,"

Sister Mary Katherine offered. "There's no sense in your having to drive me all the way home."

Dealing with Kramer had taken the edge off my ability to argue. "All right," I agreed, and handed her my cell phone so she could make the call.

We started north on I-5 in rush-hour traffic. Sister Mary Katherine was quiet for a long time. Finally she sighed. "There's something else I should tell you," she said. "I should have mentioned it right away."

"What's that?" I asked, assuming it was some other fragment of memory she had dredged up about Mimi Marchbank's murder.

"The people from the memorial service, Ron and Amy, they're good friends of yours, aren't they?"

"Yes, why?"

"None of this is any of my business, but I couldn't help overhearing the unpleasantness after the service. The daughter they were talking about, the girl . . ."

"Heather?" I asked.

Sister Mary Katherine nodded. "How old is she?"

"Fifteen. Why?"

"I was just sitting there near the entryway door when the boy from the funeral home . . ."

"Dillon Middleton," I supplied.

"Yes, if that's his name. He came to the front door and rang the bell. Heather came down from upstairs. Neither one of them realized I was right there, but I heard what they were saying. Dillon asked Heather to come away with him, and she went straight upstairs to pack a bag."

I pulled out my phone and dialed Ron and Amy's number. Tracy answered. "Trace," I said, using a pet name I alone am allowed. "Do me a favor. Put your sister on the phone."

The receiver clattered onto some hard surface. That sound was followed by a very long silence. Finally Tracy came back on the line. "I can't find her. She's not here."

"That's what I was afraid of," I said. "You'd better let me talk to your father."

CHAPTER 15

I DIDN'T WANT TO BE the one to tell Ron Peters that Heather had run away, but I did. Once he heard what I had to say, Ron was every bit as upset as I thought he'd be. "Running away makes it look pretty bad," he said glumly.

"Depends on how far she ran," I said. "And which direction. Tell me about the guy she's with."

"Until today I thought Heather had broken up with that little creep," he growled. "He's from Vancouver. His parents are divorced. His father still lives in Canada along with his second wife. His mother went to college with Molly, and they've been great pals ever since. The mother is a complete ditz who has married and divorced several times. One of her husbands lived here in Seattle, and she brought Dillon along for the ride. When she left that guy and moved to greener pastures in San Francisco, she more or less abandoned the kid. Rather than sending him home to his father where he belonged, she set him up with an apartment of his own. The idea was that he would stay here and go to school, but school doesn't seem to be very high on his list of priorities. He was lonesome and needing company, so Molly took pity on him. She invited him over for dinner. That's how Heather first met him."

"So Dillon is Molly's doing?" I asked.

"He is as far as I'm concerned."

That went a long way toward explaining what had gone on at the end of the memorial service.

"Mel Soames was supposed to interview Heather tomorrow morning. Are you going to tell her about Heather taking off, or am I?"

"Maybe she's just over at Dillon's place," Ron said. "I'm sure Molly knows where he lives. Let me try to find her. If I can't . . ."

"Okay," I said. "I'm on my way to Mount Vernon right now. I'll give you until I get back to see if you can find her. If you haven't located her by then . . ."

"All right," Ron said. "I'll see what I can do."

Timing was everything, and I probably shouldn't have given Ron that much leeway. At the very least, Heather was a person of interest in her mother's homicide. At worst, she was a prime suspect. Her boyfriend was from Canada, which, depending on traffic, is only two and a half hours north of Seattle—about the same amount of time it would take me to drive to Mount Vernon and back.

If Canada was where Heather and Dillon were heading, Ron was right. It always looks bad if you attempt to flee across an international border. With Canada in particular, bringing homicide suspects back across the U.S.-Canadian border to face charges is never a slam dunk. I tried looking on the bright side. Maybe Ron and Amy would go to Dillon's apartment and find their fifteen-year-old daughter in bed with her boyfriend. The fact that such an eventuality would be good news left me feeling sick to my stomach.

"I should have kept quiet," Sister Mary Katherine said in response to my long, brooding silence. "I should have minded my own business, but I just didn't think that a girl that young should be running off with a boy like that."

"No," I said. "You did exactly the right thing."

"You really care about this girl, don't you?"

"Yes," I said. "I've known her since she was tiny."

"Is she in trouble?" Sister Mary Katherine asked.

I didn't know if she meant "in trouble" in the way it was used in our day, when "in trouble" and "pregnant" were used interchangeably. Or if Sister Mary Katherine meant something else entirely.

"It's possible Heather shot her own mother," I answered at last. "Which sounds like trouble to me."

"Yes," Sister Mary Katherine breathed. "I suppose it is. As soon as I get back to the convent, I'll put her name on our prayer list," she said. "The sisters and I will pray for her, morning, noon, and night. That's what we do best."

"Thank you," I said. "I really appreciate it."

We met up with Sister Therese and the Odyssey van in the parking lot of the Burger King north of town. I was headed back to Seattle when Ron called.

"I can't find her," he said.

"Are you going to call Mel, or should I?"

"You go ahead," Ron said.

And I did. "What do you mean, she took off?" Mel Soames asked.

"Just that. She and her boyfriend disappeared."

"The boyfriend is from Canada," Mel responded. "Do you think they went there?"

"That would be my first guess."

"Damn," Mel said. "How much of a head start do they have?"

"Probably a couple of hours." I didn't specify how much of that head start was due to my delay in sending out an alarm.

"That's long enough for them to have made it across the border."

"I know," I said. I wasn't even sorry. No matter what I said, a part of me wanted Heather to walk. It was the reason I shouldn't have been involved in the case to begin with—I cared too much. It's the same reason doctors shouldn't treat themselves—or their loved ones.

"Thanks for the heads-up, Beau," Mel said. "I'll get right on it."

I might not have felt so guilty if she hadn't thanked me. But there you are. I always have been a magnet for guilt.

The long solitary drive back to Seattle gave me plenty of time to think. In order to avoid thinking about Heather Peters, I focused on Kramer. Once you reach a certain level in the police hierarchy, newspaper headlines, not necessarily the articles themselves, become far more important to you. "Local Philanthropist Dies in Fall" was less of a hot potato than "Local Socialite Found Murdered." And "Former Officer Commits Suicide" would be far less inflammatory than something like "Disgraced Cop Slain." And if Kramer could convince the media to say those things long enough and loud enough, he might convince the general public they were true.

But I wasn't the general public, and I wasn't convinced. Wink Winkler had carried his wrongdoing around with him for fifty-plus years. Why would having it revealed now push him far enough to put a bullet through his own head? And Elvira Marchbank had fallen to her death due to stepping on a magazine? How lame was that? But if Kramer was on track for quick closures in both those cases, details on them were going to be hard to come by—especially for a Seattle PD outsider like me.

One of the good things about the attorney general's Special Homicide Investigation Team is that it's relatively new—so new that it hasn't had time to develop the kind of entrenched bureaucracy that exists in many law enforcement agencies. As a result, there's less emphasis on paperwork and more emphasis on fieldwork; less emphasis on punching the clock and more emphasis on getting the job done. That calls for people who are self-starters. Ross Connors decides on who works for him and who doesn't. Harry I. Ball is in charge of the Bellevue branch, but Connors is the one calling the shots, and every investigator has access to the attorney general himself. We have his phone numbers, and we're encouraged to call if necessary without being hassled about going through channels and across desks. This was one of those instances where I thought a call was in order.

Months earlier, Ross Connors's wife had committed suicide when a witness protection scandal in Ross's office had come to light. Instead of covering up what had happened, Ross had faced up to it in public, and voters reelected him in a statewide landslide.

I know what it feels like to lose a spouse to suicide. It hurts like hell. And I know that burying yourself in work is sometimes a substitute for dealing with the empty spot in your heart, so I wasn't surprised to find the attorney general still in his office at eight o'clock at night.

"Hey, Beau," Ross Connor said cordially when he heard my voice on the phone. "How's it going with Sister Mary Katherine? Are you making progress?"

"Some progress," I said. "And some new developments as well." Over the next several minutes I brought him up to speed on everything that had happened.

"You'll write all this up for me?" Connors asked when I finished.

"Yes," I said. "I'll have a report in Harry's hands in the morning."

"And you think Kramer's going to deep-six both of the new cases?" Connors continued.

"He's going to try. He'll most likely do a cursory job on Wink Winkler and come up with some kind of plausible excuse for the suicide. With Elvira he'll go for an accidental death. By ignoring Sister Mary

Katherine's allegations, he's most likely giving Elvira and Albert a pass on their involvement in Mimi Marchbank's homicide, which, according to him, he intends to solve by 'traditional' methods."

"Meaning, of course," Connors said, "that he's really going to let it disappear once again. What do you think the chances are that Kramer's conclusions are being suggested from the top down? Doing it Kramer's way avoids the awkward possibility of besmirching the beloved memory of a local and recently departed arts patroness."

"Are you suggesting the possibility of more police corruption?" I asked. I didn't want to hear an affirmative answer. I didn't want to think that some of the people I had worked with for so many years had gone over to the dark side.

"Not necessarily," Connors said. "More like wanting to avoid bad PR. The Marchbank Foundation was and is an influential arts institution in Seattle. But you know what? I work in Olympia, and I don't give a rat's ass about what goes on in Seattle. So what do you need from me?"

"Access to official information," I said at once. "If Paul Kramer's being pressured to close these two cases as quickly and quietly as possible, he's going to stonewall me at every turn. To do the job right I'm going to need to see the crime scenes and autopsy reports and to have a look at any and all witness interviews that have been done so far."

Connors paused. "I'm not sure how much good seeing that material will do. After all, street cops can tell which way the wind is blowing. What they write down may have more to do with what's expected as opposed to what is. If I were you, I'd rely on whatever information you're able to turn up on your own."

"Still," I said, "it'll be easier to have the names, addresses, and phone numbers of who has been interviewed and who hasn't. I don't mind going back over the same territory, but I shouldn't have to reinvent the wheel to do it."

"Yes," Ross Connors agreed. "You're right. Fortunately for you, I can apply a certain amount of pressure in all the right places."

As the call ended, I was coming up on the Northgate Exit on I-5. In all the hubbub of the last day or two, I realized, I had barely thought about my grandmother, much less called or stopped by since Lars told me she was in the hospital. Maybe, if I hurried, I could get to Swedish in Ballard before visiting hours ended. Abruptly crossing three lanes of traffic, I exited the freeway and headed straight there.

But I was too late. "Beverly Jenssen?" the receptionist said, typing in the name and then frowning at the answer that appeared on her computer screen. For a moment I held my breath.

"I'm afraid she's not here," the receptionist said. "She was released earlier this afternoon."

Hearing the word "released" allowed my breathing to resume. I hurried back outside and stood in the haze of secondhand cigarette smoke that surrounds the entrances to most of Seattle's public buildings. When I called Lars and Beverly's apartment, he was the one who answered.

"Oh, ja," Lars said. "The doctor sent her home today. Shouldn't have, if you ask me. Beverly's still weak as a kitten, but she wanted to be home with me. Doesn't t'ink I can take care of myself."

"I'm sorry," I apologized. "I should have come by the hospital long before this."

"You're busy," Lars said, excusing me. "Beverly and I don't expect you to drop everyt'ing and come running every time one or the other of us ends up in the hospital. That's why we have each other."

"Can I speak to her now?" I asked.

"She's already asleep, and I don't want to wake her up. Coming back from the hospital pretty well wore her out," Lars said. "Why don't you give her a call in the morning. She'll be glad to hear from you."

I was on my way home from the hospital when my phone rang again. It was Ross Connors. "I've been in touch with Seattle PD," he said. "If you'll drop by the main lobby in the next little while and ask for Denise, she'll have a care package waiting for you."

It seems to me I spent most of my Seattle PD career at odds with one superior or another. Having Ross Connors go to the mat for me like this was an entirely new experience. Not sure what to expect, I drove straight to Seattle PD.

Denise was a uniformed officer womaning the Seattle PD reception desk. I gave her my name along with my ID. When she returned my ID, she also handed me a thick manila envelope. Standing off to one side of the nearly deserted lobby, I tore open the envelope and sorted through its contents. Inside I found copies of the official police reports on Elvira Marchbank and Wink Winkler. And at the very bottom of the envelope was a laminated special visitor's pass that, for the next thirty days, allowed me unlimited access to come and go as I pleased in and around Seattle PD without the need of an escort.

In other words, Ross Connors was nothing short of a miracle worker.

Just to see if it would work, I left police headquarters and went downhill to the old Public Safety Building. The pass worked like a charm on both the outside entrance as well as for controlling the elevators. I went straight downstairs to the evidence room. There I filled out the proper form requesting access to the Madeline Marchbank evidence box. In Kramer's eagerness to sign off on the other two cases, I guessed that he would have returned the box to where it belonged, and I was right.

Through some quirk in scheduling, the clerk behind the counter— the same one who had sicced Kramer on me two days earlier—found the box and handed it to me with no sign of recognition and without so much as a raised eyebrow.

"Is there someplace I can sit to look this over?" I asked.

She pointed wordlessly at the old wooden library carrel, and I didn't bother to argue. The scarred surface at least offered a flat place for me to work.

When I opened the box, I discovered that, after three days of handling, the cardboard cover wasn't nearly as dusty as it had been earlier. The first item I removed from inside—a bloodstained apron—sent a shiver of recognition down my spine. I wasn't sure in which tape Sister Mary Katherine had mentioned the apron, but I remembered her saying in one of them that Mimi Marchbank had been wearing a flower-covered apron on the day she was murdered, but subsequent newspaper accounts of the crime had indicated that Mimi had been found stabbed to death in her bed. In my experience, not that many people wear aprons in bed. In addition to the apron I found a bagged and still-bloody knife, along with several more items of bloodstained clothing and bedding.

None of that surprised me. The contents all seemed perfectly normal. What wasn't normal was what wasn't there—the case log. With that missing, there was no official written account of Mimi Marchbank's murder investigation—no record of where and when the physical evidence had been gathered and no list of who had been interviewed by detectives or why. Without that background information, the physical evidence itself was virtually useless.

So where did the case log go? I asked myself.

How long had it been missing? Had it been gone for decades—say, from the time Wink Winkler had left the department in disgrace—or was its disappearance as recent as this last Tuesday morning?

I replaced the items I had removed, and returned the box to the counter. "Did you find everything you needed?" the clerk asked.

"Absolutely," I told her with what I hoped sounded like a hint of a swagger. "Everything I needed and more." I walked out the door hoping that conversation, too, would be reported back to Captain Kramer.

I went home, dragged out my computer, and used my notes to type up the report I had promised to deliver to SHIT in the morning. Next I tackled the police reports I had collected on the deaths of Elvira Marchbank and Wink Winkler. It made for slow going.

Elvira had been found at the bottom of the stairs. A partial shoe print had been found on the glossy cover of a magazine that had landed close to the body. There had been no sign of forced entry; no sign of an altercation. Hair and fiber trace evidence had been collected for analysis, but that would take time. Detectives Jackson and Ramsdahl had conducted a series of interviews with people from the surrounding neighborhood, including one Raelene Landreth, executive director of the Marchbank Foundation. None of the interviewees had reported hearing or seeing anything amiss at Elvira's residence.

With Wink Winkler there was obviously a crime scene somewhere, but so far no one had found it. Dead bodies sink. They don't float back up to the surface until there's a certain amount of decomposition. Wink's body had been found snagged by a piling under a dock on Harbor Island. What that said to me was that the unknown crime scene was most likely relatively close to where the body was found and that the fact that he had come to the surface had more to do with currents and flood and ebb tide than with anything else.

Wink's son, William Winkler III—Bill—had been interviewed twice, both times at corporate offices of Emerald City Security, the firm Wink had founded but which was now being run by his son. The first interview had occurred on Wednesday morning, when a uniformed officer had been dispatched to speak to him in regard to the missing person report called in by Wink's assisted-living facility. The second interview had been conducted late that afternoon by Detectives

Jackson and Ramsdahl. By then Wink's body had been found and identified. Bill Winkler told them that his father had been unhappy about living in the "home" but that he hadn't seemed either despondent or suicidal.

My spirit was willing, but the flesh is weak. Halfway through Detective Jackson's interview with Wink's son, I fell sound asleep. I woke up sometime later to find the loose pages of the reports scattered around the legs of my recliner. I took that as a sign that it was time to toddle off to bed.

The next morning my back was killing me. I lay in bed for a long time, drifting and dozing and waiting for the kinks to straighten out.

When I had first heard Sister Mary Katherine's account of what had happened on that glorious day in May so long ago, I had thought Elvira Marchbank would be the only surviving person who would know whether or not the story was true. Then Wink Winkler had been added into the mix. Now, with both of them dead, I had too many years of homicide work behind me to buy into Kramer's notion that the two deaths—an accident and a suicide—were purely coincidental.

I happened to believe that Elvira Marchbank had been alive when Sister Mary Katherine left the old woman's home. I also believed that, as Sister Mary Katherine left, Wink Winkler had arrived. That meant that Wink was, if not the last, then certainly among the last to see Elvira Marchbank alive. Had he killed her and then rearranged the evidence so her death would appear to be an accident rather than a homicide? And what was the point of killing Elvira in the first place? What in Sister Mary Katherine's account of Mimi Marchbank's death was so damaging that Wink Winkler would be willing to commit yet another murder in order to avoid having that story revealed more than half a century later?

Presumably Elvira, determined to make things right, would have identified the long-silent witness who had effected Elvira's remarkable change in attitude. And if Wink's sole purpose had been to suppress the story, wouldn't he have attempted to silence not only Elvira but Sister Mary Katherine as well? And what was the point in his killing himself?

Or had he? Was there another person involved in all this—another person who knew all the particulars and who was smart enough to manipulate evidence? What if Elvira had been murdered and the evidence had been doctored to make it look as though she had died of an accidental fall? And if that was the case, could the same be true of Wink Winkler's supposed suicide? What if someone other than Wink held the gun to his head and pulled the trigger? Suicide can be successfully faked, but only if the killer is smart enough to take bullet trajectories, blood spatter, and gunpowder residue into consideration.

Half awake and half asleep, I tried to catalog everything I had learned in the last several days. I was jolted out of my half-sleep by the recollection of the photograph Sister Mary Katherine had shown me in Bakeman's at lunch the day before—the one of her and her father posing together, with her perched on the hood of his spanking-new car.

Hurrying into the living room, I found the phone book and tracked down the number for the Department of Licensing.

After passing through the required verbal identification process, I gave the clerk the year I was interested in and the name—William Winkler.

"Which one?" she asked. "Senior or junior?"

"I don't know," I said. "Give me both."

And that's when I hit pay dirt. In 1950, William Winkler Sr., the man who was evidently Wink's father, was still making do with a two-year-old 1948 Oldsmobile Futuramic 98. William Winkler Jr., on the other hand, began the year driving a 1946 Ford Super Deluxe, but in June of 1950, he must have landed in tall cotton. Suddenly he was listed as the proud owner of a Ford Custom Deluxe two-door convertible.

Was it my imagination, or had Sister Mary Katherine's father's new Ford arrived at almost the same time as Wink Winkler's? So I checked the DOL records for Sean Dunleavy as well. Sure enough, his new Ford had arrived on the same day as Wink Winkler's. And the Dunleavys' new address was listed as an apartment on Market Street in Ballard.

The same day? Two brand-new Fords for two guys who both were probably having a hard time making ends meet? This had all the trappings of a classic payoff and cover-up. Between them, Wink Winkler and Sean Dunleavy had managed to keep Bonnie Jean from coming forward to reveal what she had seen.

Was that the first time Wink had stepped outside the bounds? I wondered. Maybe, but it certainly wasn't the last. I suspected he had gone on to bigger and better scores, right up until he was drummed out of Seattle PD and maybe even beyond that. Sean Dunleavy, on the other hand, had hit it big just that one time before he'd had to swallow his pride and go back to buying used cars.

I dialed the number for Saint Benedict's Convent. It was still relatively early in the morning, but long after 5:00 A.M. prayers. I identified myself and was put through to Sister Mary Katherine.

"What is it?" she asked. "Has something else happened?"

"Do you remember that picture you showed me yesterday, the one with you sitting on the hood of your father's new car?"

"Of course I remember."

"Who else do you think got a new Ford about the same time your father got his?" I asked.

"Who?" she asked.

"William Winkler," I answered. "Wink's vehicle was a slightly different and more expensive model than your dad's, but he got his car on the exact same day."

"Are you telling me that somebody bribed my father?" Sister Mary Katherine asked. "You're saying they bought him a car on the condition that he keep me from telling what I knew?"

"And they bought Wink a car to ensure that whatever you said, he wouldn't hear it."

"So I must have told somebody," Sister Mary Katherine breathed after a long pause. "At least I must have tried to tell someone."

"Yes," I agreed. "I believe you did."

"Thank you, Beau," she managed, stifling a sob. "Thank you for telling me."

With that she hung up. I didn't blame her for crying. Bonnie Jean Dunleavy's silence hadn't wronged her murdered friend. The five-year-old girl had tried her best to help Mimi Marchbank and to tell what she knew, but the system had betrayed her. It had betrayed them both, and I was the one tasked with setting it right.

CHAPTER 16

ONCE I GOT OFF THE PHONE with Sister Mary Katherine, I headed to Bellevue to deliver the written report I had promised Ross Connors. When I arrived at the building, Mel and I rode up in the elevator together. "Any sign of Dillon and Heather?" I asked.

She shook her head. "We've been in touch with Dillon's father in White Rock and with his mother in San Francisco. Both claim they haven't heard a word. What do you know about the sister?"

"Whose sister?"

"Amy Peters's sister, the one who lives with them."

"Oh, Molly," I said. "Molly Wright. Not exactly my cup of tea. Why?"

"Brad and I got a search warrant for Dillon's apartment. We found an empty packet of birth control pills with Molly Wright's name on the prescription."

"You think she got them for Heather?" I asked.

"That would be my guess," Mel said. "And Molly is the person Dillon sat with at the funeral. Considering how much Ron and Amy disapprove of Dillon, why would Molly be so chummy with him?"

"Causing trouble?" I asked.

"But why?"

"Jealousy, maybe?" I suggested. "Molly and her husband used to be big deals here in Seattle, then her life went to hell. They lost everything. Her husband went to jail and she was forced to file for bankruptcy. From what I can tell, Ron and Amy took her in because she had nowhere else to go. She's got nothing—no home, no husband, no kids. From where she's standing, it must look like her sister has everything."

"So she repays Ron's and Amy's kindness by undermining their authority with their own kids?" Mel asked.

Suddenly I was in the odd position of defending Molly Wright. Compared with her, Melissa Soames was a newcomer. "I guess she helps out with the kids," I said lamely. "Makes meals, that kind of thing."

Mel was not appeased. "She also helps by arranging for their fifteen-year-old to get birth control pills," she returned. "If I were them, I'd throw her out."

"Wait a minute," I said. "I thought you were a compassionate conservative."

"Conservative, yes," she responded. "Compassionate? Not necessarily, and certainly not when it comes to dealing with someone like her."

Harry, coffee cup in hand, was standing near Barbara Galvin's desk when Mel and I came in. "Someone like who?" he asked.

"Ron Peters's freeloading sister-in-law," Mel said and then stalked off to her office. Moments later the sounds of morning talk radio drifted down the hall.

"What's wrong with her?" Harry asked.

"Beats me," I said.

"And what have you been up to?" he asked slyly. "I haven't seen you in several days, but I hear tell you're going around town rattling chains and pushing buttons. And a little bird told me that you're supposed to have a report on my desk first thing this morning."

"It's in my laptop," I told him. "You'll have it as soon as it's printed and signed."

"So stop standing around jawing about it and get it done," Harry said.

I went into my own office and shut the door. I booted up my laptop, located the document, and revised it enough to add in what I had learned about the apparent payoffs to both Wink Winkler and Sean Dunleavy. I was about to press "print" when my phone rang.

"So you went back to the evidence room again," Paul Kramer said. "What the hell do you think you're up to?"

Obviously the evidence-room tattletale was still in Kramer's corner. "Just doing my job," I said.

"I won't have you messing around in my cases or second-guessing my decisions."

"Kramer," I said. "What you will or won't have is irrelevant to me. I don't answer to you. I've got a mandate from the attorney general to look into a cold case, and I'm going to do just that."

"I already told you. We've reopened that old Marchbank case."

"Where's the case log, then?" I interrupted. "Was it there the other day when you grabbed the evidence box out from under me?"

"Are you implying that I removed it?"

"I'm not implying anything. I'm straight-out asking."

"The log wasn't there," he said. "I have no idea what happened to it, but whatever did happen is none of your business, Beaumont."

"Ross Connors is making it my business, Kramer. And the same holds true for the Elvira Marchbank and Wink Winkler cases. You want to write 'em off? So be it, but I'm not going to. Timely case closures may count for something when it comes to promotions at Seattle PD, but Ross takes a longer view of things. He's interested in solving cases right however long it takes rather than solving them fast and wrong."

For a moment Kramer said nothing. I couldn't see his face, but I could imagine it. Once again I was thankful I wouldn't be anywhere near his office when he started cutting loose.

"You stay out of my way and out of my people's way, understand?" he said at last.

"I hear you, Kramer," I told him. "But I'm not listening." I put the phone down and finished printing my document. When I delivered it to Harry's office, he was just hanging up his telephone.

"Paul Kramer?" I asked.

"How did you know?" Harry returned with a grin. "He wants me to take you off the Marchbank case. He feels your presence is disruptive to the investigation."

"What investigation?" I demanded. "He refuses to interview Sister Mary Katherine about what happened to Mimi Marchbank, and he's as good as washed his hands of both Elvira Marchbank and Wink Winkler."

"Well, then," Harry said, leaning back in his chair. "I guess you'd better see what you can do about it."

"I guess I'd better."

I went back to my office and sat there for a time, thinking. My early-morning revelation about the payoff Fords had convinced me that someone else was involved in this mess, someone who was well aware of everything that had gone on in May of 1950. The challenge was finding out that person's identity.

And then I remembered. Once, when I was a boy, my mother lost her purse. In those pre-credit-card days, losing your purse or wallet was a serious crisis, especially for someone of my mother's limited means. She finally found it—in the refrigerator, tucked in with the vegetables in what used to be called a humidrawer. She told me afterward, "I found it in the very last place I looked." And that was true on any number of levels. Of course it was the last place she looked, because as soon as she found it, she stopped looking. But the refrigerator was also the very last place she would have thought to look.

In this case, I decided to take a page from my mother's book and to go looking in the least likely of places—somewhere most cops, including Paul Kramer, would be loath to look. My reasoning was simple. Whatever had happened to Wink Winkler and Elvira Marchbank had its genesis in what had happened to Madeline Marchbank. The answer, if it actually existed, might well be found in old newspaper files. Paul Kramer wouldn't go through those on a bet, and he wouldn't let his people do so, either.

I drove straight to the offices of the *Post-Intelligencer*, sweet-talked my way down to the morgue, and threw myself on the mercy of Linda Carter, the same helpful intern who had worked with me days earlier.

"Good to see you again, Mr. Beaumont," she said with a cordial smile. "How can I help you?"

"I need you to take me back to the fifties one more time," I told her. "The big difference now is, I know more or less what I'm looking for. The files are indexed, aren't they?"

"Pretty much," Linda agreed. "Why?"

"I want to see all references to people named Marchbank—Elvira, Abigail, Albert, and Madeline—along with anybody else named Marchbank that I may not happen to know about. I'd also like to see anything on Albert's partner, Phil Landreth."

"Starting when?"

"Let's say the late forties and early fifties."

Soon I was again scrolling through the blue-and-white pages. Once I located the articles, I went ahead and printed them without necessarily reading them all the way through. More from sheer boredom than anything else, Linda joined me in tracking down articles.

"I'm not sure this is something you want," she said. "It's a wedding announcement from the society section."

"Go ahead and print it," I said. "I'll read it later." I didn't add, "When I'm wearing my reading glasses so I can see the damned print," but that's what I meant.

Two hours later, after thanking Linda profusely, I left the *P.-I.* morgue with a stack of reading material. It was noon by then, so I picked up a sandwich on the way and went back up the hill to Belltown Terrace to read the articles.

The first batch from the archives I had brought home—the ones on Madeline Marchbank's murder—had been relatively interesting. As expected, the articles in this one were incredibly boring. Most of them concerned Albert Marchbank's business dealings. Each time he and his partner, Phil Landreth, added another radio station or two to their growing media empire, the purchase was duly reported in the newspaper. The first time I saw the name Landreth, it leaped out at me. I remembered seeing that name on one of the police reports I hadn't gotten around to reading completely before I fell asleep. So I stopped right then and dug the report in question out of my briefcase.

There wasn't much to it. After giving her name, address, and phone numbers to investigating officers, Raelene Landreth had reported that she was the executive director of the Marchbank Foundation. She had last seen Elvira Marchbank about noon on the day in question, when she went from her office to Elvira's next-door residence with some papers to be signed. She heard and saw nothing more until late that evening, when a police officer came to her home in Medina to tell Raelene and her husband that Elvira was dead. End of story.

Having learned little, I turned back to the unstintingly boring articles that recorded the growth of the Marchbank-Landreth media empire. In their enthusiasm to tell the local-boys-make-good saga, the writers took the position that bigger was better without ever once mentioning how the local radio stations—the small outlets in Bellingham and Chehalis and Ellensburg—regarded being swallowed up by Seattle's neophyte media moguls.

One story in particular struck me as significant. On June 16, 1950, Phil and Albert had closed on the purchase of a total of five separate stations. This particular transaction, the largest one so far, was the only one that listed Abigail Marchbank as a partner. Was that why Albert had come to see his mother that day? Had he come to Mimi's house in order to ask his mother for funds to complete this purchase? If so, Mimi's standing on her back porch and telling him no might have been what sealed her fate.

The last article I picked up happened to be the one Linda Carter had found for me, a wedding announcement from the June 4 issue of the paper. It was something less than a paragraph in a column called "Comings and Goings."

On May 13, Seattle residents Faye Darlene Downs and Thomas Kincade Landreth were united in marriage at a small private ceremony in Harrison Hot Springs, B.C. Faye is the daughter of Mr. and Mrs. Acton Downs. Thomas is the son of Mr. and Mrs. Philip Landreth.

The day leaped out at me—May 13, the Saturday Mimi Marchbank was murdered. Hadn't there been some mention of a wedding in one of the previous articles I had read? I retrieved my first set of duplicated

P.-I. articles and rummaged through it. It didn't take long to find what I was looking for:

> Mr. Marchbank told reporters that he last saw his sister and mother on Friday afternoon, shortly before he and his wife left for Harrison Hot Springs in British Columbia, where they attended a wedding.

Attending that wedding had provided Albert and Elvira Marchbank with an airtight alibi at the time of Mimi's murder. I wondered if Wink Winkler had ever bothered to check to see if they'd actually been there.

I went back to the paltry announcement. Usually the weddings of offspring of local luminaries are given the full journalistic treatment. Mr. and Mrs. Downs may have been social nobodies, but Mr. and Mrs. Landreth certainly weren't. I recognized at once what most likely wasn't being said about this "small private ceremony."

How small and how private? I wondered. *And is there anyone around who would still remember the guest list of a shotgun wedding that happened back in 1950?*

I put down the papers and reached for my phone book. In the Ls, I found no listing for Thomas Landreth, but there was one for F. D. Landreth. It came with a downtown Seattle telephone prefix but no printed address. I picked up the phone and dialed.

"Hello." The woman's voice sounded as if she was probably the right age—a bit more mature than mature.

"Is this Faye Landreth?" I asked.

"Who's calling, please?"

"My name's Beaumont," I said. "J. P. Beaumont. I'm an investigator for the attorney general's Special Homicide Investigation Team. It's about—"

"Mimi Marchbank's murder," she interrupted. "I was wondering if anyone would ever get around to talking to me about that."

I felt a rush of excitement. Elvira Marchbank's death had probably garnered front-page treatment in today's newspapers, but Faye Landreth was more concerned about Mimi's murder—an unsolved homicide from fifty-plus years earlier.

"Would it be possible to meet with you?" I asked. "Today, maybe?"

"Today would be fine," she said. "What time and where?"

"Where do you live?" I countered.

"In a condo downtown," she said. "Cedar Heights on Second Avenue."

She had no idea that I was calling from only a block away at Belltown Terrace.

"I can be there in ten minutes," I said.

"Should I put the coffeepot on?"

"That would be great."

Ten minutes later, she buzzed me into the building, and I made my way up to the ninth floor. The woman who opened the door looked to be in her early seventies. She was relatively tall and unbent. She wore her hair in a short pixie cut, but there was nothing pixielike in her firm handshake.

"Mr. Beaumont?" she said cordially. "Won't you come in?"

She ushered me into a well-kept room. Her unit was much lower than mine and smaller, but the territorial view of the Space Needle and the bottom of Lake Union was similar to what I see from my penthouse bedroom. The furnishings were simple and not particularly elegant. Large, colorful pieces of inexpensively framed artwork filled the walls. I walked close enough to one of them that I could decipher the signature scrawled in the lower right-hand corner: F. D. Landreth.

"Yours?" I asked.

She nodded.

"They're very good," I told her. She flushed slightly at the compliment.

"Thank you," she replied. "Painting is the only thing that keeps me from running the streets. Help yourself to a chair. How do you take your coffee—cream and sugar?"

"Black, please," I told her.

Faye Landreth ducked into the tiny galley kitchen while I made my way to a comfortable leather couch at the far end of the combination living/dining room. On the end table next to where I took a seat stood a gilt-framed eight-by-ten photo of a handsome young man wearing his United States Marine Corps dress uniform.

"Your son?" I asked as she handed me a mug of coffee.

Faye nodded. "Timothy," she said. "Timothy Acton Landreth. He's been gone for a long time now—ten years. It's the old story," she added. "Drugs and booze. He went through treatment a couple of times, but he just couldn't get his act together. That's why I keep this particular photo—because he looks so good in it. Being a marine was the best thing that ever happened to him. After that, life was all downhill."

"I'm sorry," I said.

She smiled. "I know. So am I. I wanted to help him, but I just couldn't. He's why I'm talking to you now, though. I wouldn't do it while Timmy was still alive. Things were tough enough between him and his father. I didn't want to do anything that would make their relationship worse, but now . . ."

I was impatient. I wanted Faye Landreth to move on to the subject of Mimi Marchbank and how she had known I would be asking questions about that long-ago murder, but good sense won out. Like Sister Mary Katherine, Faye had kept whatever she was going to reveal secret for a very long time. I'd be better off waiting for her to relay the information in her own fashion and in her own good time rather than trying to rush her into it.

"You're a widow, then?" I asked finally.

"A widow?" she repeated, then laughed outright. "Hardly. I've been divorced for years. In fact, Tom announced he was leaving the night before our thirtieth anniversary. He left the house that night and married his secretary, Raelene Jarvis, the day the divorce was final. His second wife, Raelene, happened to be two years younger than Timmy."

"Which probably didn't do much to improve father-son relations," I suggested.

"No, it didn't," Faye agreed. "Tim stopped speaking to his father then and there. I always hoped they'd reconcile, but they never did. And I kept quiet because . . ." She paused and gave a self-deprecating laugh. "Well, I had been quiet for so long by then that it didn't seem to make much difference. After Tim died, though, I told myself that if anyone ever did get around to asking me about what happened, I was going to tell what I knew."

"Which is?"

Faye sighed. "Tom and I had to get married," she admitted.

I'd already figured that out on my own. "I know," I said. "May 13, 1950. Harrison Hot Springs, British Columbia."

She gave me a searching look, then continued. "I was sixteen. He was nineteen. Tom's father was furious."

"That would be Phil Landreth, Albert Marchbank's partner?"

"Yes. Tom's dad wanted him to go to college and then on to law school, but that wasn't possible, not with a wife and baby to support. Against his parents' wishes, Tom dropped out of college and went to work for his grandfather—his mother's father—as a manager in his car dealership."

My ears pricked up. "Car dealership? Which one?"

"Crosby Motors," she said. "It was a Ford agency up on Aurora Boulevard."

I thought about those two brand-new Fords—the one that had gone to Sean Dunleavy and the other that had gone to Wink Winkler. Was that where they had come from—Crosby Motors?

"The dealership's been gone for years now," Faye went on. "Grandpa Crosby made a nice piece of change for himself, first when he sold the agency, and then later, when he sold the land itself. By then, Tom had enough management experience that Phil and Albert hired him to work in their company."

"With the radio stations?"

Faye Landreth nodded. "Tom worked for Albert, who managed the overall holding company. Other people managed the stations themselves, but it wasn't just radio. Albert Marchbank saw the coming boom in television very early on. He moved from radio broadcasting to television without ever missing a beat. Everybody connected to the company made money, Tom and me included."

"Sounds like Tom was in the right place at the right time," I suggested.

"It wasn't all luck," Faye Landreth said. For the first time I heard the bitterness in her voice.

"What was it?" I asked.

"They weren't there," she said.

Faye's sudden segue caught me off guard. "Who wasn't there?" I asked.

"Albert and Elvira," Faye answered. "In Harrison Hot Springs. I know the newspaper notice said they came to our wedding, but that wasn't true."

"And what about your folks, Faye?" I said. "Did they suddenly become the proud owners of a brand-new 1950 Ford? It seems like someone was passing them out for free right about then."

She ducked her head. Finally she raised it defiantly and looked me full in the eye. "Yes," she admitted. "Yes, they did."

"From Crosby Motors?"

She nodded.

"Who bought it?"

"I don't even know. Does it matter? My folks needed a car. All I had to do for them to have one was keep my mouth shut."

"Which happened to give Albert and Elvira Marchbank an unbreakable alibi for murder," I added.

"I'm not proud of what I did, but yes." Her voice was very small.

"And you never told. Why not?"

"For one thing, I was scared to death of Albert. I think Tom was, too. If the man was willing to stab his own sister to death right there in broad daylight, what kind of person was he? And I don't think Elvira was much better than Albert. They were both ruthless people. The problem was, Tom told me that keeping quiet about what happened made us all accessories after the fact to what they had done—my parents, too. He said we'd all be held responsible for Mimi's murder, every bit as much as the people who actually stabbed her."

"Why are you telling me this now?"

"Because Timmy's dead," Faye Landreth said. "Tom's parents are both gone now, and so are mine. If somebody wants to arrest me for my part in the cover-up, so be it, but it would have been wonderful if they had put Elvira on trial for murder, convicted her, and hauled her off to prison."

"But she's dead now, too," I said.

Faye nodded. "I know," she said. "I saw it in the paper this morning."

"And so is a man named William Winkler. Wink Winkler was the detective who investigated Madeline Marchbank's murder back in 1950," I added. "Investigators think he committed suicide within hours of Elvira Marchbank's fatal fall. According to my count, that doesn't leave behind very many people from back then. If the people are gone, so are all the witnesses."

"Except for me," Faye volunteered. "I would be one; Tom's the other."

"You're suggesting that your former husband might be involved in all this?"

"He was involved in 1950," Faye said. "Why wouldn't he be involved now?"

"And if he were to go to jail because of his involvement? What then?"

Faye Landreth smiled. "That would be his problem, now wouldn't it. His problem and Raelene's."

I don't remember who it was who said "Hell hath no fury like a woman scorned," and all that jazz, but he must have had someone like Faye Landreth in mind. She had waited almost a quarter of a century to lower the boom on her philandering ex-husband and his new wife. Now she was doing it—in spades.

"Any idea where I could find Tom Landreth about now?"

"He's retired. He still lives in our old house over in Medina, but I hear he likes to hang out at the clubhouse at Overlake Golf and Country Club, even when it's too cold to play golf."

"And Raelene?"

"She's the breadwinner now. Still works full-time."

"For the Marchbank Foundation," I said.

Faye nodded. "Interesting that she'd manage to fall into a job like that, wouldn't you say?"

I didn't know Tom Landreth, but I felt a twinge of sympathy for the man. He had walked away from his marriage vows all those years ago thinking that he was getting off easy. He must have thought all the divorce would cost him would be whatever the presiding judge decided he owed his ex-wife in terms of property settlement and alimony. He was about to find out those were small sums in comparison to the price Faye Landreth prepared to extract from him now. She was going for his jugular. If what she said was true, he deserved it, but right at that moment, the poor unsuspecting bastard had no idea it was coming.

Woman scorned, indeed!

CHAPTER 17

WHEN I LEFT FAYE LANDRETH'S CONDO, I was floating on air. Suddenly I had a legitimate suspect—someone who had been involved in the aftermath of Mimi Marchbank's murder back in 1950. Considering the part Tom Landreth had played in the cover-up, it seemed reasonable to assume that he might have some compelling motive for keeping the names of the real perpetrators in that case from surfacing.

For one thing, Faye had told me that with Tom retired, Raelene's job as executive director of the Marchbank Foundation now provided a major portion of the family's income. Elvira Marchbank and, to a lesser extent, Tom Landreth, had participated in Mimi's murder. Once that news leaked out, the Marchbank Foundation and Raelene's plush little job would both be doomed. Bad publicity and nonprofits do not go together. People don't like giving money to organizations whose founders or current managers are caught doing bad things—and murder is a pretty bad thing.

Before I interviewed Tom Landreth, I needed to interview his wife. Detectives Jackson and Ramsdahl had asked Raelene about what she had seen and heard on the day Elvira Marchbank died. I wanted to ask about Tom Landreth. I also needed to collect a Kevlar vest. My current one had been hauled off in the trunk of the 928 when the tow truck took it away, but there was an old one still gathering dust in my hall closet. When I tried to put the damned thing on, I was sure it had shrunk. I was struggling to fasten it when the phone rang.

"Jonas?" Beverly Jenssen asked.

I was instantly awash in guilt. I had promised to call this morning and had neglected to do so. "Beverly," I said. "It's good to hear your voice. How are you?"

"Weak," she said. "Still sleeping a lot of the time."

"I'm sorry I didn't get by the hospital to see you . . ." I began.

She cut me off. "Don't worry about it," she said. "I was asleep there, too. I probably wouldn't have noticed if you'd been there."

Just because Beverly seemed to be giving me a free pass didn't mean I deserved one. And it turned out it wasn't free after all.

"I was hoping, though, that I could talk you into coming up to our place for dinner tonight."

"Are you sure you're up to having company?" I asked. "I mean, if you just got out of the hospital . . ."

"Oh, for goodness' sakes, Jonas. It's no trouble. I'm certainly not going to cook. We have to go down to the dining room to eat. Besides, I have something to show you—a surprise."

Having been remiss in not stopping by the hospital, I knuckled under immediately. "Of course," I said. "What time?"

"The dining room starts serving at five-thirty. We usually go early, but anytime between then and eight o'clock will work, so whenever you can make it will be fine."

"I'll see you as close to six as I can."

"Good," she said. "We'll be expecting you."

I left Belltown Terrace hoping like hell I wouldn't forget.

I drove to the University District and pulled up in front of the two neighboring houses. Several other large houses in the neighborhood had all been carved up and converted into low-cost student-style apartments. Only these two buildings seemed to have retained some of their single-family-dwelling identity and elegance.

Of the two houses, then, I supposed that Mimi Marchbank's would have been in far better shape, but considering what had happened in the driveway of that house on that May afternoon, why had the Marchbank family kept it? And why had they purchased the house next door? That was a puzzle.

On this particular morning, the front door of Elvira's house was barred by a band of yellow crime scene tape. Next door the Marchbank Foundation was a beehive of activity. A noisy carpet-cleaning van was parked outside and two people were hard at work washing windows.

I made my way up the paved brick walkway, past the black-ribboned wreath hanging on a porch post, and through the front entrance, where I was instantly headed off by a young receptionist.

"I'm sorry," she said. "We're closed today. There's been a death . . ."

I pulled out my ID and badge. "I'm looking for Mrs. Landreth," I said. "Is she in?"

"Well, yes, but she's very busy. The funeral is tomorrow afternoon and we're going to host the reception here after the services. Ms. Landreth is making all the arrangements."

"I still need to talk to her," I said. "Would you please let her know I'm here."

"One moment," the receptionist said and disappeared into an inner office.

From the looks of the name-brand artwork and lavish furnishings, it was clear no one at the Marchbank Foundation was concerned about pinching pennies. Raelene Landreth, when she appeared, was a petite, well-preserved babe in her early fifties who looked as though she'd never been forced to pinch personal pennies, either. She wore what I calculated to be a size 3 dress tastefully accessorized with several size 10 diamonds. The circumstances of the second Mrs. Tom Landreth appeared to be quite a step up from those of her predecessor.

"I hope this won't take long, Mr. Beaumont," she said. "I've already spoken to two other detectives. Since I'm working on funeral arrangements today, I'm really quite pressed. And losing her is such a shock. Elvira was one of those people you thought would be around forever."

"What I need shouldn't take long," I said.

Sighing and pursing her lips, Raelene showed me into a plush office that was as ultramodern as the lobby was. She directed me to take a seat in a low leather chair that may have been ergonomically correct but was hard as hell to get in and out of.

"What can I do for you?" she asked.

"You mentioned that the foundation is making Mrs. Marchbank's funeral arrangements?" I asked.

"I'm making all the arrangements," she corrected. "Elvira had no remaining family. She and Albert never had any children. The foundation itself is their real legacy. So the funeral will be at Saint Mark's Cathedral at two o'clock in the afternoon. We'll be hosting a post-funeral reception here."

"I see," I said, putting the chitchat aside. "Now, would you mind telling me what you remember about Wednesday afternoon?"

Raelene's facial expression didn't change. "I already told the other officers," she said. "Nothing much went on Wednesday afternoon. The last time I saw Elvira was around noontime, when I went next door with some papers for her to sign. I didn't find out what had happened to her until much later that night, after I got home."

"Was there anyone here with you that day?"

"No. I was here by myself. Mindy was gone, too. Mindy's the receptionist you saw outside. Her son had an appointment with the dentist."

"And you saw and heard nothing unusual?" I asked.

"No. Not really." Raelene paused. "Well, that nun was here. Sister Mary something. I don't remember her exact name."

"Sister Mary Katherine," I supplied.

"Yes. That's the one. She showed up in the middle of the afternoon. She gave me her business card from some convent up on Whidbey Island and said she wanted to see Elvira. Lots of people think that just because we're a charitable foundation they can waltz in here, say 'pretty please,' and walk away with a fistful of money. The fact that we're a charitable *arts* foundation goes right over their heads. I explained to Sister Mary Katherine that we have an official application procedure for giving grants and that, for the most part, churches don't qualify. She said she didn't want our money. When I tried to inquire what she was really after, she went back to insisting she needed to speak to Elvira in person."

"What happened then?" I asked.

"Nothing. She left. She did seem . . . well . . . agitated, somehow. Upset. I worried about whether or not she was some kind of nutcase, but then she left on her own."

"Did you see her go next door?"

"To Elvira's place?" Raelene asked. "No. Certainly not. Did she?"

"Yes. She saw Elvira being driven up to her door, so she went over and rang the bell."

"She had no business doing that. Elvira should have called me," Raelene said stoutly. "Nun or not, I would have come over and sent the woman packing."

"What happened after Sister Mary Katherine left here?" I asked.

"I finished up what I was working on. When five o'clock came, I went out to the spa for a massage and my regular mani-pedi. It was when I got home from there that the cops showed up with the news that Elvira was dead. As I said, it was a terrible shock. She had been perfectly fine when I saw her earlier in the day."

"But no one else came by—a man named Wink Winkler, for example?"

Momentary confusion washed across Raelene Landreth's face. "I know Mr. Winkler, of course," she said. "But he didn't stop by here."

"He was seen across the street," I said. "He could have come here or he could have come to Elvira's."

"He didn't come here!" Raelene was surprisingly adamant about that.

"And how exactly do you know him?"

"His company, Emerald City Security, has handled burglar- and fire-alarm equipment and security monitoring for the Marchbanks and their companies for as long as I can remember," Raelene said. "Since before I went to work here, certainly."

Makes sense, I thought. *First he gets that Ford convertible, followed by half a century's worth of employment. Not bad for hush money, but if Wink did that well, how did Tom Landreth score?*

"You're aware, then, that shortly after being seen exiting a taxi out in front of this building, Mr. Winkler senior committed suicide?"

"Yes. I heard about it from his son, Bill. He called to let me know. Bill and his father were estranged, you see. Still, it was a shock, especially coming on the heels of what had happened to Elvira."

"Did it occur to you that maybe Mr. Winkler was responsible for what happened to Elvira?"

Raelene looked startled. "What are you saying? I talked to the other detectives. They indicated that it looked like Elvira slipped on a magazine, that her death was entirely accidental."

"What if it wasn't?" I asked. "What if Mr. Winkler pushed her and made it look like an accident? Then he went out and blew his brains out?"

"That's crazy," Raelene said. "Why would he do such a thing?"

"I'm not sure," I said. "That's what I'm trying to find out. So why don't you tell me about your husband."

Raelene's expression hardened slightly. "What about him?"

"Was he close to Elvira?" I asked.

"Very," she said. "Tom was the son Elvira and Albert never had, and he worked in the business his whole life—up until he retired a few years ago."

"And how long have you worked here?"

"Just over ten years. Elvira finally reached a point where she didn't want to work so hard. Sifting through the grant applications and working on fund-raising got to be too much for her. She was glad to relinquish some of the responsibilities, and I was here to pick up the slack."

"Did Elvira ever mention her sister-in-law, Mimi, the one who was murdered out here in your driveway in May of 1950?"

The abrupt change of subject was calculated. I wanted to see Raelene's reaction. My use of the word "driveway" was also deliberate. The official story had always claimed that Madeline Marchbank had died in her bedroom. Given the layout of the building, that room could well have been the one where we were sitting now—Raelene's ultramodern office.

Raelene took a deep breath. "Madeline," she corrected. "Her name was Madeline, not Mimi."

Not as far as Bonnie Jean Dunleavy was concerned, I thought.

"Her death at such a young age was a tragedy that never went away," Raelene declared. "She was several years older than Tom, so my husband knew of her rather than knowing her directly. From what I've been told, Madeline was a kind, thoughtful, hardworking girl. Devoted to her invalid mother. Just an all-around nice person."

If Raelene knew the truth about Mimi's death, her coolly measured response was nothing short of an Emmy Award–winning performance. On the other hand, her lack of reaction could have come from her never having been apprised of the real story to begin with.

"If Madeline's death was so hard on everyone, why didn't the Marchbanks ever sell this place?" I asked. "It seems to me they would have unloaded it at the first opportunity."

"Because they wouldn't have gotten what it was worth," Raelene said promptly. "Once prospective buyers know something bad has happened in a house, property values drop like a rock. Their strategy was to keep this one. They also bought up the house next door. Albert and Elvira remodeled that one and lived there, then they turned this place—the old family home—into company offices for Marchbank Broadcasting. When company growth necessitated a move downtown, the foundation took over this space."

"Thus keeping it all in the family," I said.

If Raelene heard the snide undercurrent in my statement, she ignored it. "I suppose," she said.

"I'd like to speak to your husband," I said, once again changing the subject. "Is he available?"

"He's certainly not here," she said defensively. "As I told you, he's retired. Besides, why do you need to talk to him? He wasn't here. He didn't even see Elvira on Wednesday."

"You said Tom was like a son to Elvira—the son she never had. Does that mean he's a beneficiary under her will?"

That provoked a reaction. Raelene's dark eyes flashed fire. "What are you implying?" she demanded.

"I'm asking the usual questions," I said. "When someone dies unexpectedly and under somewhat mysterious circumstances . . ."

"The detectives said she *fell!*" Raelene insisted. "There's nothing *mysterious* about it." She stood up. "Now I think it's time you left," she said. "I have nothing more to say to you."

"Thank you," I said, allowing myself to be booted out of her office. "I appreciate your taking the time to talk to me."

"You're welcome," she said, but I could tell she didn't mean it.

I went back outside feeling as though I had landed in a nest of vipers. In 1950 a brutal murder had occurred right there, within mere feet of where I was standing. A conspiracy of silence surrounding that murder had held for more than fifty years. Now, due to Sister Mary Katherine's revelations, that silence was crumbling under its own weight—and yet another person had died in the house next door.

Walking the length of the driveway, I saw that both houses sported new siding. The basement window through which Bonnie Jean Dunleavy had watched the unfolding drama had been covered over, but behind the house, the garden shed Sister Mary Katherine had described as a tumbledown wreck had been rebuilt and turned into a genuine greenhouse. Seeing the place where Bonnie Jean had hidden from her pursuers struck me. The hair rose on the back of my neck the same way it had when I found Mimi's bloodied apron in the cold case evidence box.

The perpetrators of Madeline Marchbank's murder were both dead, but obviously there was more to the story than that. I wanted all the answers. Only that would help redress Mimi's awful death and Sister Mary Katherine's years of silent suffering.

I walked back to the Taurus and sat in it for a while, thinking. For more than fifty years Elvira Marchbank thought she and her husband had gotten away with murder. Having an eyewitness show up on her doorstep to say otherwise must have come as a terrible shock. I tried to put myself in Elvira's position. What would I do? Once I showed Sister Mary Katherine out, would I sit there and keep my own counsel, or would I turn to someone else? Raelene claimed there had been nothing out of the ordinary about that afternoon. If that was the case, it seemed likely Elvira hadn't turned to the younger Mrs. Landreth for help. And why would she? It was far more likely that she would look to one of her fellow conspirators.

Yes, Wink Winkler had turned up in his cab before Sister Mary Katherine had a chance to drive away. Was Elvira the one who had summoned him? And if Wink had arrived in a cab, how had he left? Had another taxi been dispatched to take him somewhere else?

I took out my phone and called Sister Mary Katherine. "How are you?" I asked, knowing that the news that her father had succumbed to bribery had hit her hard.

"Better," she said. "I'm feeling much better."

"Good, so maybe you can help me. I need to ask you about your visit with Elvira on Tuesday. Did she make any phone calls while you were there?"

"Not that I remember," Sister Mary Katherine said.

"Did she leave the room at any time, or did you?"

"She went into the kitchen to bring us tea," Sister Mary Katherine said. "She was gone several minutes, heating the water and so forth. I suppose she could have made a call then."

"And what was her demeanor like when you introduced yourself and told her who you were?"

"She was surprised."

"Did she cry, break down, or anything?" I asked. "Was she afraid or upset?"

237

"I'd say she was emotional but not upset—relieved more than anything. I think what she and Albert did has been on her conscience for a very long time. She was ready to unburden herself."

"Did she happen to mention how that unburdening might affect any other people?" I asked.

"What other people?" Sister Mary Katherine said. "I saw it. Albert and Elvira Marchbank were the only ones there."

"They may have been the only ones at the scene," I told her. "But they weren't the only ones involved. There were other people who profited from maintaining their silence."

"Other people besides my parents?" Sister Mary Katherine asked.

"Yes."

"So they weren't the only ones who were bribed?"

"No."

"I suppose that should make me feel better," she added after a pause. "But it doesn't. And no, Elvira didn't say anything about her actions impacting anyone else."

"I don't suppose she would have. Thanks for your help."

"Just a minute," Sister Mary Katherine said. "Before you hang up, have you heard any more about that little girl who ran away, about Heather?"

"Not yet," I said. "We're working on it."

I wasn't actually working on Heather's disappearance right then—wasn't even allowed to be working on it, but I figured I could be forgiven for the use of the royal "we" in that instance. Not only did it keep me from telling Sister Mary Katherine the absolute truth, it kept the truth from me as well.

Determined to do some follow-up work, I headed back to the office. While I was crossing the 520 Bridge, my phone rang. The caller was Andy Howard, my insurance agent.

"Just finished talking with our adjuster," he said. "He says your Porsche is totaled. It would cost more to repair it than it's worth. If you want to go ahead and fix it . . ."

I thought about it. Hanging on to the 928, even though it wasn't the original one Anne had given me, had been a way of hanging on to her. Maybe it was time I stepped away from her and moved on. That momentous decision—one I had avoided making for years—came after only a moment of reflection and before I hit the end of the bridge.

"I guess I'll take the check," I said. "What about all the personal effects that were still in the vehicle?"

"The check will come in the mail," Andy replied. "I can bring everything else by your place, if you like. Just tell me when."

Andy was all business. To him a wrecked car is a wrecked car. He had no idea what saying good-bye to that piece of my life meant to me.

"Whenever," I said, swallowing a lump that had suddenly lodged in my throat. "If I'm not home, you can leave it with the doorman. What about the rented Taurus?"

"The rental is authorized for another week," he told me. "If you keep it beyond that, it'll be on your nickel."

Owning the Porsche had been a permanent way of avoiding buying a new car. Now I'd have to deal with it. The Taurus just wasn't doing it for me. The sooner I was out of it, the better.

I drove back to the office. Mel wasn't anywhere in sight, but I knew she hadn't gone far, since Rush Limbaugh's voice blared from her radio. I slipped into my own office, shut the door, and picked up the telephone.

In the days before easy access to computers, getting a look at someone's telephone records took time. And getting permission to look at them took even longer, especially if you happened to be working for a jurisdiction or on a case that didn't have a lot of impact. I had learned that having Ross Connors for a boss made accessing those numbers far easier, but first I had to work my way through the telephone company's version of voice-mail hell. When I finally reached the right person and told her what I was looking for, she said she'd need time to check out my credentials as well as to gather the information. Fair enough.

While I waited for her to get back to me, I let my fingers do the walking to check out cab companies. Wink Winkler had definitely taken a cab to the University District. How had he left? As soon as I tried talking with dispatchers, I ran into a stumbling block. They needed an exact address in order to check their records, but I still didn't know where Wink had been going when he exited the cab. Had he been on his way to see Elvira or had he been headed for the foundation offices instead?

In order to get a handle on that, I called the Washington State Patrol Crime Lab and asked to speak to Wendy Dryer. I had known her from the time she had walked into the crime lab as a lowly evidence clerk. Now she was the state's lead fiber analyst. Wendy sounded genuinely glad to hear from me.

"Hey, Beau," she said. "Long time no see. What are you doing these days?"

"Working for the AG's office."

"The SHIT squad?" she asked with a barely suppressed giggle.

"That's the one, and don't give me any grief about it," I grumbled. "I only work here. I'm not the numbskull who dreamed up the name."

"What do you need?"

"Are you the one who's handling the Elvira Marchbank case?"

"Holding rather than handling," she said. "Captain Kramer told me it's most likely an accidental death with no particular rush."

"Captain Kramer could be wrong about its being an accident," I countered. "And I seem to be working the same case."

Wendy's tone turned serious. "A homicide, then," she said. "What exactly are you looking for?"

"I'm trying to learn who all might have been at the house before Elvira died."

"You should check with latent fingerprints for that."

"I will," I said, "but in the meantime, I'd like you to check for tennis-ball fibers on the carpet."

Wendy laughed outright at that. "Tennis-ball fibers? Are you kidding? The woman was in her eighties. It doesn't seem like she'd be whacking tennis balls around."

"Humor me," I said. "And let me know if you find any."

"Give me your number, then," she said. "I'll call you when I know something."

An hour after I originally got off the phone with the telephone company rep, Barbara Galvin knocked on my door and handed over a multipage fax. With my reading glasses plastered on my face, I read down the column of computer-generated records. And there, at 3:45 P.M. on Tuesday—right in the middle of the time when Sister Mary Katherine had said she was there—was the last phone call Elvira Marchbank ever made—a call from Seattle's 206 area code to a 425 number on the east side of Lake Washington.

As soon I saw the number, it looked familiar. I pulled out my notebook and thumbed through it to the last few pages and the things I had jotted down in the course of my conversation with Raelene Landreth. The 425 number was the same one Raelene had given me as her home number in Medina, so I was right. When things started to go bad, Elvira had gone looking for help, all right, but not to Wink Winkler. No, she had gone straight to Tom Landreth, the guy whose first wedding had given Elvira and Albert Marchbank their unassailable alibi for murder.

Phone calls work like daisy chains—one phone number leads to another. If Elvira had called Tom, whom had he called in turn? While I still had the phone company numbers in order, I called back to trace Landreth's recent telephone history. And while that process was under way, it seemed like a good idea to go see the man.

Telephone calls are fine as far as they go, but for getting usable information and real answers to tough questions, there's nothing like an old-fashioned eyeball-to-eyeball visit.

CHAPTER 18

WHEN YOU HEAR ABOUT "Lone Ranger cops," you're usually hearing about young cops—ambitious ones. By the time cops get to be my age, Lone Ranger cops have either wised up or are dead. There's not much middle ground.

With my unfortunate track record with partners, when I joined SHIT, the ability to work solo had been high on my list of require ments, but working solo is fine only up to a point, and working without backup is downright stupid. Needing to enlist some help, I went prowling through the office.

A glance at the duty roster at midafternoon on this January Friday told me that Mel Soames and I were the only Special Homicide inves tigators still in the office. Mel wasn't my first choice for this little ride-along, and not because she isn't a good cop. My reluctance had nothing to do with her and everything to do with me.

I'm still carrying a lot of emotional baggage from losing Sue Daniel-son in her tiny Fremont apartment. Her death may not have been my fault but, in my book, it was still my responsibility. Her ex-husband was the one who actually pulled the trigger. Rationally I know I didn't cause Sue's death. The problem is, I didn't prevent it either. If only I had arrived on the scene a few minutes earlier . . . If only I had been smart enough to figure out what was going on . . . An endless supply of woulda, coulda, shoulda litanies plague my late-night hours. I drag out of bed the next morning groggy and sleep-deprived, but the outcome is always the same: I'm alive, and Sue Danielson is dead.

Heading out to interview a possible homicide suspect, I was reluctant to put Mel Soames into a life-or-death situation. What if some blunder on my part put Mel at risk? Still, I didn't have much choice. When I tapped on her door, she turned down her radio. "Come in," she said. "What's up?"

"Care to take a trip?"

"What kind of trip?"

"The bulletproof vest kind," I told her.

"You bet," she said with a grin, and reached for her small-of-back holster, which was hanging on the back of her chair. "Sounds like the best offer I've had all day."

By the time we pulled up in front of Tom and Raelene Landreth's place in Medina, I had briefed Mel on everything I knew.

"So you suspect Elvira's death wasn't accidental after all and you think Landreth may have had something to do with it?"

"That's one possible scenario," I said. "Raelene said Elvira treated Tom like a long-lost son, so maybe he's in line to inherit."

"Sounds possible," Mel agreed. "Even sounds like motive."

"We'll see," I said. "Once we talk to him."

If you live in the Seattle area, the word "Medina" conjures an image of palatial mansions spilling over steep lakeside bluffs and wandering down to the water. It's where many of Seattle's elite meet and greet.

It's also where Bill and Melinda Gates have their sprawling family compound.

I may live in a downtown penthouse condo now, but in my heart I'm still a poor kid from the wrong side of the tracks in Ballard. My mother struggled every day to keep things together. She stretched our meager budget by sewing her own clothing and mine as well. All my classmates' shirts came from places like JCPenney or Monkey Ward. Mine were homemade, a telling difference that made me the butt of countless schoolyard jokes. The sense of inadequacy that grew out of those years is still a visible chip on my shoulder.

When I pulled up in front of Raelene and Tom Landreth's place in Medina, I was prepared to be intimidated. The house, a large two-story affair with faded cedar-shingle siding and two separate wings, was set in the middle of a huge hedge-lined lot. A big Dodge Ram Diesel hauling a trailer full of lawn equipment was parked outside. One guy was raking fallen leaves and branches while another gave the hedge a dead-level flattop. A third was blowing debris off the front porch and sidewalk. He nodded in acknowledgment as Mel and I stepped onto the porch and rang the bell.

Although the yard swarmed with landscape workers, the house itself seemed almost deserted. Drapes were still drawn and no interior lights were visible. For a long time after the bell sounded, no one answered. Mel and I were about to leave when I heard a muttering from inside.

"I'm coming. I'm coming. Hold your horses." Seconds later the door was flung open by an unkempt man wearing a frayed woolen bathrobe and a pair of worn Romeos. "Who are you?" he demanded. "Whatever you're selling, I don't want any."

I produced my wallet and ID and handed it over. "I'm J. P. Beaumont," I explained as he peered at it through bleary, bloodshot eyes.

"This is my associate, Melissa Soames. We're with the attorney general's Special Homicide Investigation Team. We're looking for Tom Landreth."

"That's me," he mumbled. "Did you say homicide? Whaddya want?"

I had known Tom Landreth was about three years older than his first wife, but compared with the quiet-spoken, dignified Faye, this guy appeared to be a loudmouthed, doddering old man. He was also a drunk.

They say it takes one to know one. I knew Tom Landreth was a drunk the moment he opened the door. I knew it even before I saw the beaker-sized glass of scotch—scotch with no ice—that he held in one hand. There was booze in his hand, booze on his breath, and booze leaking out of his pores. When people in AA meetings talk about "drinking and stinking," they aren't kidding. Poor Tom Landreth was a textbook case.

"We'd like to talk to you about Madeline Marchbank," I said.

Tom staggered back on his heels. He might have fallen over backward if Mel hadn't reached out, grabbed his elbow, and steadied him. Once he regained his balance he shook off her hand and then glowered at me.

"Madeline? Whaddya want to know about her for?" he asked. "Been dead a long damned time. Who cares anymore?"

"That's what we were wondering," I said. "Who does care? Someone must. Mind if we come in?"

Reluctantly, Tom stepped aside and allowed us into what should have been a gracious living room. It wasn't. The place was a wreck. A disorderly jumble of old newspapers, stacks of magazines, loose mail, and dirty dishes covered every flat surface. The dirty carpet was mostly invisible beneath heaps and mounds of unwashed clothing.

Someone was willing to pay to maintain the outside appearance of the place and make it look as though it still belonged in this neighborhood. Inside, they didn't bother to keep up the pretense.

Seemingly unaffected by the filth, Tom led us through the debris. He halfheartedly swiped some of the mess off a grimy couch, clearing a place for us to sit. I couldn't help thinking about Faye Landreth in her tiny but immaculate downtown condo. And I thought about Raelene Landreth wearing her designer outfit and sitting behind her polished desk in the Marchbank Foundation office. There was nothing in the mess that looked as if it belonged to Raelene, making me wonder if she didn't hole up in some other part of the house, as far away from her drunken husband as she could get.

Faye Landreth may have thought she had gotten the short end of the stick when Raelene moved in on her marriage, but right then— sitting on a dirty couch in that filthy living room—I knew that, no matter what the financial arrangements, Faye was better off than she would have been had she stuck it out.

Tom Landreth cleared off a nearby chair and dropped heavily onto it. Despite his inebriation, he managed this maneuver without spilling any of his scotch. Not only was he a drunk, he was a practiced drunk.

"Sorry about that—the mess, I mean," he said after taking a long drink. "Cleaning lady quit, you know. Wife can't seem to find another." He slurred his words despite an obvious effort on his part to enunciate clearly. "What was it you want again?"

"To talk about Madeline Marchbank," I said.

"That's right, that's right," he muttered. "My father's partner's sister. Died young. Murdered. Tragic loss—tragic." He took another drink. He tapped his foot. "Never solved, either," he added.

"You're right," I agreed. "It was never solved."

"So why're you talking to me about it?"

"I believe the murder took place on your wedding day—the day you married your first wife."

"Yes," he said, nodding. "I guess it did."

"Two people involved in that case, Albert and Elvira Marchbank, were dropped from the list of suspects because detectives were told they had been in Canada attending your wedding."

Tom Landreth frowned in wary concentration, the way drunks do when they know the conversation has gone too far but they're too smashed to do anything but answer. "Right," he said at last. "They were there all right, Albert and Elvira."

"Who else was there?"

He stared at me dumbly.

"At the wedding," I prodded. "Who else attended?"

"Well, Faye, of course," he said. "And her parents."

The bride and her parents. I gave the man credit for going for the obvious. "What about your grandparents?" I asked. "The Crosbys. Were they there?"

"My mother's parents?" He looked puzzled. "I don't remember. It was a long time ago, for chrissakes. More than fifty years."

"You can't remember if your grandparents were there, but you're sure Albert and Elvira Marchbank were?"

Landreth stood up, swayed slightly, got his bearings, then lurched across the room. On the far side of the living room was a wet bar, the granite countertop littered with countless dead-soldier Dewar's bottles standing at attention. He refilled his glass, took a drink, and then stared at me belligerently.

"They were there," he declared. "That I do remember!"

"Good," I said reassuringly. "Fine. I'm glad to hear it. Now, about Wednesday."

"What about Wednesday?"

"Did you hear from Elvira that day?"

He blinked once before he answered as if sensing a trap. "No," he said then. "Of course not."

"Why 'of course not'?" I asked. "You and Elvira were close, weren't you? You're sure she didn't call you on Wednesday afternoon to tell you about her unexpected visitor?"

"No," he repeated. "I don't know anything about a visitor. No idea what you're talking about."

Had it been up to me, I probably would have left right then, but that was when Mel turned on the charm and went into action.

"Come on, Mr. Landreth," she said. "You see, we already know about the phone call. We know that an eyewitness from that old case came to visit Elvira. I'm guessing she called to tell you—to warn you—that she had decided to do the right thing and turn herself in."

Landreth stared at Mel. His mouth dropped open. "You've got no right to tap my phone. I've done nothing wrong."

In his effort to be cagey, Landreth had tripped himself up. We had the phone records, but he had made the assumption that we had somehow heard what Elvira had said to him.

"So that is what she said?" Mel probed.

"I couldn't believe she'd do such a thing," Tom declared. "I asked her that—why after all these years? And do you know what she said? That she was going to dissolve the Marchbank Foundation and sell off all the assets—just like that. After all the work Raelene and I have done. Elvira said there was no point. That once people heard about what happened to Madeline, it would all be over anyway. We wouldn't be able to raise another dime."

"How would she go about doing that?" Mel asked. "Dissolving the foundation, I mean."

"The board of directors would have to agree."

"And they are?"

"Elvira, of course, myself, and a longtime friend of the family."

"This longtime friend wouldn't happen to be named William Winkler, would he?" I asked.

Tom looked at me balefully. "As a matter of fact, yes," he said. "But no one calls him William. Dad always called him Wink. My father didn't mind when the Marchbank name was the one that went on the foundation. Even though he and Albert were partners, that was the name of the company as well—Marchbank Broadcasting. But Dad was the one who insisted that Wink be on the board of directors. He said it was important to have someone impartial on it, someone who wasn't directly involved."

There was a television set in the room, but it wasn't on, and the screen was half obscured by the junk piled high on a chair in front of it. And some of the newspapers scattered about were old enough to be turning yellow. I realized suddenly that Tom Landreth probably had no inkling that Wink Winkler was dead. It was possible he didn't even know about Elvira.

"You know they're dead, then, don't you?" I asked.

"Who's dead?" he asked. "I thought we were talking about Madeline. Of course I know she's dead."

"What about Elvira?"

"Elvira's fine."

"And Wink?"

"He's fine, too." Tom paused and frowned at me. "As far as I know. He is fine, isn't he?"

"Mr. Landreth," Mel said sympathetically. "I'm sorry to have to tell you this. Elvira Marchbank died in her home a short time after speaking to you on the phone on Wednesday. Not long after that, Mr. Winkler committed suicide."

"No!" Tom exclaimed. "That can't be right. Raelene would have said something. She would have told me."

"What time does your wife come home?" Mel asked.

Tom looked at his watch and then shrugged. "Late," he said.

"But you don't know what time?"

"It depends." He was wavering now—covering. Given the state of her home and husband, it seemed likely Raelene Landreth didn't come home anymore at all.

"We'd like to speak to her again," Mel said kindly. "It would help to clear up a few things. If you think she'll be here soon, we could just wait until she arrives."

"No," Tom said. "That's not a good idea. Wait a minute. What day is it?"

"Day?" Mel asked.

"What day of the week?"

"Friday," Mel replied. "Why?"

"Friday is when she has her hair and nails done," Tom declared, as if proud to be able to dredge up this little item of domestic trivia. "Three o'clock," he added. "Gene Juarez, downtown." He squinted at his watch—a Rolex. "If you hurry," he said, "you might be able to catch her there."

I stood up. "We'll be going then, Mr. Landreth." He started to lurch to his feet. "Don't bother," I told him. "We can find our way out."

As we walked back to the car, something nagged at me, something Raelene had said. Back in the Taurus, I opened my notebook and scanned through it. And there it was. Raelene had told me about going for her "regular mani-pedi" after work. I glanced over at Mel, noticing for the first time that her nails gleamed with scarlet polish.

"What?" she asked when she caught me staring at her.

"If someone had a manicure and pedicure on Wednesday, would they need another one on Friday?" I asked.

"I wouldn't," Mel responded.

"Raelene Landreth told me she left work on Wednesday, the day Elvira died, and went to have her regular mani-pedi, as she put it. So either poor old Tom is out of the loop when it comes to Raelene's schedule or she was lying through her teeth about what she did that day."

Raelene [Mel] pulled out her phone. "I have an idea," she said. "Why don't I call down to Gene Juarez and ask them?"

"Good idea."

Mel was smooth as glass. Claiming to be an old chum, Mel confirmed that Raelene was finished with her pedicure and was having her manicure. "No," Mel said, "don't bother giving her a message. I want this to be a surprise." Turning off her phone, Mel looked at me. "So chances are she did lie about Wednesday. Are we going to go talk to her or not?"

"I thought I was taking you back to your car."

"Don't be silly," she said. "We're almost to the 520 Bridge. If we leave from here right now, maybe we can catch her."

The Landreth house was just off Eighty-fourth and close to the bridge. From there I knew it couldn't be more than fifteen miles to downtown Seattle, but it was a rainy Friday afternoon with a Sonics game scheduled at KeyArena. In other words, traffic was a mess. As we worked our way toward the freeway entrance, Mel was silent for some time.

"How come he could remember the phone call but didn't know Elvira and Wink were dead?" Mel asked. "Or was he lying about that?"

"I don't think he was lying," I said. "I think what Elvira told him pushed the man so far over the edge that he drank himself into a stupor. I know from the Seattle PD reports that the officers who came to the Landreth house that evening stated that they spoke to both Raelene and Tom."

"They remember, but he doesn't?" Mel asked.

"Blackout, maybe?" I suggested.

"Oh," Mel said, nodding. "Of course."

That was all she said, but I read in her acknowledgment that she and I both knew what we were talking about.

"Will Tom Landreth remember our talking to him today?"

"Considering how much scotch he was stowing away, he may not."

"So why would Raelene Landreth stay with such a loser?" Mel asked. "When you first told me about Raelene Landreth, it sounded like she had something on the ball. Now I'm not so sure."

"Raelene told me Tom and Elvira were close," I explained. "That Tom was like a son to her. It's possible that if Raelene had booted Tom out of the house, Elvira might have sent her packing from her job at the foundation. That would have left Raelene with no husband—however lame—no job, and no status in the community."

"Just like someone else I know," Mel muttered. I wondered what she meant, but before I could ask she continued. "Were Tom and Elvira close enough that he might be a beneficiary under her will?"

"I don't know," I said.

"If he is, and as long as they're still married, then Raelene benefits as well. So we'll need to check that."

"We?" I asked.

"You did ask me along, didn't you?" she demanded.

"Well, yes, but . . ."

"No buts," she said. "You may be allergic to having a partner, but I'm here and I'm not a silent partner, so get used to it."

"Yes, ma'am," I said. And then we both laughed.

We were inching our way across the bridge when my phone rang. I tossed it to Mel so she could answer. "Hi, Barbara," she said. "He's driving. And since he's a man, it's probably just as well that he doesn't try doing two things at once. What do you have for him?"

When Barbara Galvin finished speaking, Mel held the phone away from her ear. "The phone company info on Tom Landreth's number just came in. She wants to know if you need it right now or if it can wait until Monday?"

"Have her look at Wednesday," I told her. "We need a list of any numbers Tom Landreth may have called after three forty-five that afternoon."

There was silence in the car for several minutes while I drove and Mel scribbled telephone numbers into the notebook I handed her.

"Now," I said, "check those numbers against the ones listed on the page with Raelene Landreth's number on it."

"Bingo," Mel said. "At four-ten there's a call from the Landreth residence to the one you have down as Raelene's cell phone."

"There you go," I said. "Lie number two. By four-ten Raelene knows Elvira is about to pull the plug on the foundation. She told me nothing out of the ordinary happened on Wednesday afternoon, but finding out your job is about to disappear can't be counted as nothing."

I had barely put the phone away when it rang again. Mel answered, spoke briefly, and then handed it over to me. "Wendy Dryer," she said. "From the crime lab. Says she'll speak only to you."

Wendy Dryer wasn't nearly as cordial as she had been earlier. "I don't like it when people play games with me," she snarled.

"Games," I repeated innocently. "I'm not playing any games."

"But I'll bet you've seen Elvira Marchbank's autopsy report."

"No," I said. "As a matter of fact, I haven't. It wasn't in yet when I went by Seattle PD to pick up my material last night. Why?"

"Because there was an unexplained bruise in the middle of her back, right between her shoulder blades," Wendy said. "They thought maybe she had landed on the newel at the bottom of the banister, but you already knew better than that, didn't you, Beau. You just had to be cute."

"I'm anything but cute. What are you talking about?"

"So I checked the back of the dress Elvira was wearing when she died, and what did I find? Tennis-ball fibers. What a surprise. So if the murder weapon was a tennis ball, maybe you'd like to speculate if she was killed by a forehand stroke or a backhand."

"It was a walker," I said. "The tennis balls were on the bottom of Wink Winkler's walker. I thought he had been to the house, but I wasn't sure and I had no idea he might be the one who killed her."

"Sure you didn't," Wendy said. "It was just a lucky guess. Captain Kramer wasn't in when I called his office to pass along this information, but I'm sure you'll be hearing from him once he's aware of the situation. He'll be as interested in your pet theories as I am."

And then she hung up.

"That sounded bad," Mel said when I got off the phone.

"It is. Kramer's detectives are working the Marchbank and Winkler cases. He'll go ballistic once he finds out I'm still nosing around in them, and now the crime lab is mad at me, too."

"That's no problem," Mel replied. "All we have to do is find out what happened before he does."

It was almost five-thirty by the time we hit Sixth Avenue. Heading northbound, I crossed Pine and pulled into the valet parking line beside Nordstrom. I gave the attendant twenty bucks for him to keep the car on the street, then Mel and I walked over to Gene Juarez. When we stepped off the elevator, the lady at the check-in desk gave us the bad news.

"Oh," she said to Mel when we asked about Raelene Landreth. "I'll bet you're the one who was looking for her earlier. I'm sorry to say you just missed her."

My phone rang again. I expected it to be Kramer, ready to tear me to pieces, but it wasn't. It was Beverly.

"Oh, good," she said when I answered. "Where are you? Will you be here soon? Lars and I are down in the lobby waiting, so you won't have to come all the way up to the room."

Damn! I had forgotten the dinner arrangement. Traffic was a mess. Taking Mel back to the office in Bellevue and returning to Queen Anne Gardens before dinner was over just wasn't an option. "Can I get back to you in a minute?"

"You're not planning on standing us up, are you?" she warned.

"No, Beverly," I reassured her. "I'll call you right back."

"When the desk answers, tell them we're waiting over by the piano."

"What's that all about?" Mel asked.

"Dinner," I answered. "I'm supposed to be having dinner with my grandparents tonight, at their assisted-living place up on Queen Anne Hill. The problem is, I forgot about it."

"Is this the same grandmother who crocheted your afghan?" Mel asked.

"Yes."

"Sounds like a neat lady."

"Beverly and Lars eat in the dining room," I said. "So it probably wouldn't be a problem if you came along. But if you'd rather go straight home, I understand. I'll be glad to call you a cab."

"Are you kidding? I'd love to meet your grandparents," Mel said. "It'll be fun."

I called Beverly right back. "I have someone with me at the moment," I said. "Would you mind if I brought her along—to dinner, I mean?"

"Heavens no," Beverly said. "You'd better warn her, though. We're just plain folks here. The food won't be anything fancy."

The food was fine. Dinner was one of those life-changing events that sneak up on you when you least expect it. Beverly may have been one day out of the hospital and stuck in a wheelchair, but she was in rare form. The surprise she had promised was a small wedding photo album that Scott and Cherisse had put together and sent off via FedEx from their honeymoon in Hawaii. Going through the photos gave Beverly a chance to tell Mel everything she knew about the whole family— about Scott and Cherisse as well as Kelly, Jeremy, and Kayla, my only grandchild. She also did a comic routine about how Dave Livingston was my first wife's second husband. All Lars and I could do was sit on the sidelines and listen.

For her part, Mel was a good sport. She listened politely, laughed when appropriate, and asked interested questions. When Beverly's dissertation ended, she snapped the album shut and then beamed at Melissa Soames.

"Well, now," she asked us, "how long have you two been dating? Don't waste too much time. Men aren't very good at being alone," she added. "I understand they live a lot longer if they're married."

I was flabbergasted! Floored! I had no idea what to say. Mel looked at me and grinned that impossible grin of hers. "Sometime after he gets around to asking me, I suppose," she said.

With that, she leaned over, gave Beverly a grazing kiss on the cheek, and then added, "Thanks so much for dinner. We'd better be going."

Lars followed us out to the car. I was seething. I didn't say a word until after I had let Mel into the Taurus and closed the door.

"What in the world was Beverly thinking?" I wondered.

Lars simply shrugged his shoulders. "Sometimes," he said philosophically, "it's better if you yust give in and do as she says."

CHAPTER 19

"YOU'RE UPSET," Mel said as we started back down Queen Anne Hill.

"I'm sorry Beverly did that," I said. "It was completely out of line."

"It was cute," Mel returned. "Your grandmother has your best interests at heart."

"Maybe so, but if I were ever going to marry again, I'm perfectly capable of wife-hunting on my own."

"So you've ruled out remarrying?" Mel asked.

Without seeing it coming, I had suddenly been maneuvered into one of those hopeless trick questions—the old "Do I look fat in this?" ploy. It was time to tread very gingerly.

"Pretty much," I said. "My life is fine the way it is."

After an unbearably pregnant pause, Mel said, "Oh." And then later she added, "In that case you should probably take me back to the office so I can get my car."

As the silence between us lengthened, I could see that one way or the other I had screwed up. Mel's feelings seemed to be hurt. Obviously, and as usual, I was at fault. Had I somehow led her on? On previous occasions I had spoken to her with an uncharacteristic candor. Now I could think of nothing to say. Or do. Were her feelings hurt because she *was* interested in me? That seemed unlikely. She had always been friendly enough, but I hadn't seen anything that bordered on romantic interest. Yes, she had readily agreed to come along when I invited her to accompany me on my questioning excursion with Tom Landreth, but I thought that was because she was interested in helping me with my case, just as I would be in helping with one of hers. After all, we are on the same team.

That's the funny thing about women. You say one thing—at least you think that's what you've done—and it turns out they've turned it into a whole different conversation.

Mel remained silent until I pulled up next to her Beemer in the parking garage. "What time is Elvira's service tomorrow?" she asked.

"In the afternoon—two P.M., I believe. Saint Mark's Cathedral. Why?"

"Are you going?"

"Yes."

"Do you want company?" she asked. "If you get a chance to talk to Raelene after the funeral and want someone along, I suppose I could help out."

That's another thing that's so baffling about women. You don't know where you stand with them. If Mel was mad at me—if I had hurt her feelings—why would she be willing to help me out?

"That would be nice," I said. "Would you like me to come pick you up?"

"No. I think I can locate Saint Mark's Cathedral on my own," she said. "I am a detective, after all."

She got out of my car and walked to her own. I was going to drive away, but then, at the last minute, I decided to go upstairs and pick up the remainder of the phone company information. Barbara had said she'd leave it in my in-box. The office was empty, but the lights were on. I grabbed the envelope and headed back out. To my surprise, Mel's car was still in the parking lot, next to mine. She got out of the car as soon as I walked up.

"I guess I owe you an apology," Mel said. "For making a fool of myself. Just because I'm interested in you doesn't mean the reverse is true. I'm sorry."

"It doesn't mean that it isn't true, either," I said. "Let's just say having my grandmother initiate the proceedings left me more than slightly speechless."

"Oh," she said again. "Okay then. See you tomorrow." And off she went, leaving me to drive home in a state of complete mystification.

In Belltown Terrace, the P-1 parking level is public parking. The gate for that is open daytime hours on weekdays but closed evenings and weekends. Residents have clickers that allow them to open that gate as well as the one at the far end of the P-1 level, which gives access to the lower parking levels that contain the reserved spots for residents.

I pulled into my spot, shut off the lights, and opened the door. As soon as I did, a figure emerged from behind a car two spots away.

"Uncle Beau?"

"Heather!" I exclaimed. "What are you doing here?"

"Waiting for you," she said. "I need to talk."

It was cold in the garage. When I got close enough to her, I could see she was shivering. She looked disheveled. And scared. I stifled all the things I wanted to say to her, like: "Where the hell have you been?" "What were you thinking?" and "Do you realize your parents are worried sick?" I didn't have to ask how she had gotten into the building. Obviously she had dodged inside before the gate closed behind some entering or departing vehicle. Once in and by staying hidden behind a parked vehicle, she had remained out of range of Belltown Terrace's scanning security cameras and the watchful eyes of the doorman.

"Come on," I said wearily. "Let's go upstairs and get you warm."

It wasn't until we were inside the elevator lobby that I saw the bruising on her face. "What happened?" I asked.

She bit her swollen lip. Tears welled in her eyes. "I ran away," she said.

This was hardly news. "I know," I said.

She shook her head. Her hennaed hair was knotted and bedraggled. "No," she said. "You don't understand. I ran away from Dillon."

"Is he the one who hit you?"

Heather nodded. "He wanted me to go with him," she said. "To Canada. He said we had to leave right then, and that as soon as we crossed the border, no one would be able to put me in jail. I asked him why I would go to jail. I didn't do anything. And I told him I didn't want to go. It's all right for Dillon. He's got family there—well, his father anyway. But my family is here in Seattle—Dad and Mom, Tracy and Jared."

We reached my floor and stepped off the elevator. I was so full of righteous indignation that I could barely speak. In fact, it took all the self-control I could muster to manage the key and unlock the door. I held the door open for her and turned on the lights. She bolted for the window seat and wrapped herself in Beverly's afghan. It enveloped her completely, like a gigantic, comforting cape.

A note had been slipped under my door saying there was a package waiting for me at the doorman's desk. Tossing the note aside, I settled into my recliner and gave Heather plenty of space.

"How did it happen?" I asked. In the state I was in, that was all I trusted myself to say, but I was pretty sure I knew the answer. It's been my experience that domestic-violence victims always assume that whatever befalls them is somehow their fault. Heather was only fifteen, but she was no exception to that rule.

"I shouldn't have made him so mad," Heather said.

"How did you do that?" I asked.

She shrugged. "We argued," she said. "As soon as we left the house and he told me where we were going, I told him I didn't want to go. Dillon told me he had just talked to one of the detectives, a female detective . . ."

"Mel Soames," I interjected.

Heather nodded. "That's the one. Dillon said that she was planning on talking to me next, and I said I'd be glad to talk to her. But he wouldn't bring me back, Uncle Beau. And he wouldn't stop the car so I could get out. We argued all the way to Bellingham. When Dillon stopped for gas, I started to open the door and leave. That's when he hit me."

She touched her bruised lip tentatively as though still unable to believe what had happened. I remembered Dillon Middleton puffing out his chest and saying he'd be there for Heather no matter what—the arrogant little shit!

"So he backhanded you," I said.

Heather nodded again. "And I stayed in the car the whole time he was getting gas. I couldn't believe it had happened. But it had. I was seeing stars. My lip was bleeding. I was so . . . so shocked . . . that I couldn't even move. I just sat there like I was frozen or something."

"Did anybody see what happened or try to help you?"

"It was dark," Heather said. "And there weren't many cars at the gas station. I don't think anyone noticed."

"What happened then?"

"I was scared. I mean, Dillon's been jealous sometimes—especially if I talked to another guy or something—but never anything like that. I knew I had to get away from him. I thought that maybe when he went inside to pay for the gas, I'd be able to jump out of the car and run for it, but he never went inside. Instead, he used one of those pay-at-pump things."

"He used a credit card?" I asked.

"His mother's," Heather said with a nod. "She's got plenty of money, and she doesn't seem to mind how much he charges."

Right, I thought. *Give the kid everything he wants. As long as he stays out of her way and life, she can ship him money from a distance. That's a surefire way to create a relatively useless human being. But credit-card trails are excellent when it comes to tracking down someone on the run.*

"What gas station?" I asked.

"A Chevron, I think," Heather replied. "But I don't remember for sure."

It took conscious effort on my part to keep from reaching for my notebook. "What happened after that?" I asked.

"We drove on up to Blaine. I sat as far away from him as I could. There was a long line at the border, waiting to get through customs. While we were stopped in line, I opened the door, jumped out, and ran away. He got out of line to come after me, but I managed to make it into one of the rest rooms in the park. I heard him calling for me, but I didn't come out. When they came around to lock up the rest room for the night, I climbed up on one of the toilets so they didn't see me. I stayed there the rest of the night and most of today. I didn't start hitchhiking home until it was dark enough that people wouldn't notice my face."

The thought of Heather hitchhiking alone in the dark down the I-5 corridor made my blood run cold. She's much too young to have lived through the era of a handsome psycho named Ted Bundy and to remember the awful things he did to the unfortunate young women who happened to cross his path. I remember Bundy's crimes all too well.

"But is it true that detective is looking for me?" Heather was asking. "Does she really think I shot Rosemary?"

"She needs to talk to you," I hedged. "But just because she wants to interview you doesn't automatically mean you're a suspect."

"But I could be."

"Whether you are or aren't a suspect is really beside the point here, Heather," I said. "What we need to do is call your folks and let them know you're safe. They're both worried sick."

"No," Heather said. "I don't want to call them."

"Why not?"

"Because they'll just tell me they told me so. Especially Dad. About Dillon, I mean. Dad told me Dillon was trouble the first time he met him. I thought he was just being . . . well . . . Dad. I mean, isn't that what fathers usually do?"

"Just because your father was right is no reason not to call him," I said. "Your parents need to know where you are. Come on. I'll take you home."

"No," she said. "I don't want to go home. There's that place down on First Avenue, the one that's a shelter for homeless teenagers."

"Heather," I said, "you're not homeless. You have two wonderful parents. They both love you. They want the best for you. That's why they took such an instant dislike to Dillon. They didn't think he had your best interests at heart. From where I'm standing, I'd say they were right to be concerned. But you can't cut them out of your life. Parents are bound to be right some of the time."

Heather began to cry. "But I'm embarrassed," she said. "I don't want to talk to them."

"Because Dillon beat you up?" I asked. "Or is there some other reason?"

"You mean like am I pregnant or something?" she asked.

The thought had crossed my mind. "Yes," I said.

"Well, I'm not!" Heather declared defiantly. "I'm on the pill, if you must know."

Pill or no pill, I was relieved to hear she wasn't pregnant.

"I'm guessing Amy didn't get them for you," I said.

"You're right," Heather said. "Molly got them for me. She said she didn't want anything bad to happen."

"How very thoughtful of her," I said.

"I couldn't talk to Dad about it," Heather said. "He wouldn't have understood."

Neither did I.

"Well," I said. "No matter what, we still have to call your parents. Whether or not you go home is up to you and them, but you have to let them know you're safe. You owe them that much."

"All right," Heather conceded at last. "Go ahead and call."

So I did. Ron picked up the phone on the first ring. That was hardly surprising. Had I been in his position, I would have been sitting by the telephone, too. I didn't waste time on pleasantries.

"Heather's here with me," I said. "She showed up a little while ago, and she's fine."

Ron's answer took me aback. "No," he said. "We still haven't heard from her. We're pretty worried."

I thought maybe I hadn't spoken clearly enough. Or maybe the call had broken up.

"I said, Heather's here," I repeated, speaking a little louder this time. "She's fine. Do you want me to bring her home or do you or Amy want to come get her?"

"No," he said. "That isn't necessary. I appreciate the offer, but we've had about all the company we can stand."

I felt like I was watching a movie where the soundtrack is a minute or two out of sync with the visual images. Ron's disjointed responses seemed to have nothing at all to do with what I was saying. I was about to repeat myself for a third time when it finally dawned on me that the problem wasn't my hearing or his. Something was wrong at Ron and Amy's house. Ron was trying to warn me by speaking in a form of code.

When Ron Peters and I worked as partners for Seattle PD, we knew each other so well that we could almost read each other's mind. It happens that way when you're chasing bad guys and your life depends on knowing in advance what your partner is likely to say or do. But Ron and I hadn't worked together that way for years, and I wasn't sure what he was telling me.

"I'll keep her here with me then," I said. "She'll be safe."

"Good," Ron responded. "That'll be great."

There was no code-breaking technology necessary to translate that last statement. The relief in his voice was readily apparent. Whatever was going on at Ron and Amy's house, Ron wanted Heather kept as far away from the action as possible.

I put the phone down. Heather was staring at me from across the room. "What's going on?" she asked. "Dad's so mad at me that he doesn't want me to come home, right?"

I didn't answer immediately. I was trying to make sense of Ron's seemingly disconnected answers and to formulate some reasonable course of action.

"Is there a chance that Dillon went back to your house looking for you?" I asked.

Heather stopped short. "You think he's there? With Mom and Dad, waiting for me to show up?"

"It's possible," I said, but the wariness in Ron's voice and his intentionally misleading statements spoke to something more ominous than simply having an unwelcome boyfriend hanging around the house.

"Does Dillon have access to any weapons?" I asked.

"He has a gun, if that's what you mean," Heather said. "I've seen it in his apartment sometimes, but I don't know if he had it along with him yesterday in the car."

"What kind of gun?" I asked.

"I don't know exactly. It looked sort of like Dad's."

"A thirty-eight?" I asked. "A Glock, maybe?"

Heather shrugged. "I never really looked at it. Guns don't interest me very much."

That made Ron's answers far more understandable. If Dillon was there, not only was the boyfriend violent, he was also possibly armed and dangerous. So what were my possible courses of action? Call 911 and tell the Seattle PD dispatcher that there was a potential hostage situation on Queen Anne Hill? They'd send in an Emergency Response Team, with sirens blaring and lights flashing. And if that happened, what were the chances that Jared or Tracy or Amy might end up caught in some kind of cross fire? That didn't seem like a good option, but neither did sitting around doing nothing, not when my showing up even a few minutes earlier might have saved Sue Danielson's life.

Lost in thought, I almost didn't hear Heather's question. "You don't think he'd hurt them, do you?" she asked.

"You didn't think he'd hurt you," I returned.

She turned away from me and didn't answer. A moment later she turned back. "Maybe I should call there," she said. "That way I could find out if Dillon really is there, find out what he wants."

It was a sensible suggestion. I picked up the handset, dialed the code to block caller ID, switched on the speaker option, and handed it over. "Be my guest," I said.

"Dad!" Heather exclaimed when Ron came on the line. "It's me, Heather. I'm fine."

"This isn't a good time right now," Ron said brusquely. "If you'd call back later—"

"Is Dillon there, Dad? What does he want? Can I speak to him?"

The telephone clicked in Heather's ear as Ron ended the call.

"He hung up on me!" a dismayed Heather said. "He wouldn't even talk to me."

"Couldn't," I corrected. "But calling again was the right thing to do. Things must be pretty tough at the house for him to drop your call like that."

I was now more convinced than ever that Dillon was there. The trick was going to be getting him out of the house and away from the family. Only when Ron, Amy, and the kids were safe would it be time to bring Dillon Middleton to ground.

How well is he armed? I wondered. *Does he have more than one weapon?*

Heather had seen only the one handgun. If Mel Soames and Brad Norton had been doing their jobs, all of Ron's weapons would have been confiscated and hauled away until the investigation into Rosemary's homicide was concluded. That was a good thing. Facing down a deranged kid with one handgun at his disposal was bad enough. Dealing with one armed with a whole arsenal was out of the question.

Suddenly I had an idea. "Where exactly is the door you and Tracy use to sneak in and out of the house?"

"It's on the north side of the house," Heather answered. "On that side we're close to the house next door, but there's a trellis with a huge vine on it that covers that whole wall. If we stay behind that, we can get almost all the way out to the street without being seen."

"Does Dillon know about it—the door, I mean?"

"I guess so."

"And do you still keep it locked?"

Heather nodded. "Yes, but there's a space right above the door. We keep the key in that. Why do you want to know? Are you going there? Can I come with you?"

"No," I said. "You're going to stay right here, out of the line of fire."

"You're not going to hurt him, are you?" Heather demanded. "I mean, he hit me, but it was really an accident. I don't want anything bad to happen to him."

That, too, was textbook domestic-violence-victim behavior. They're often the abuser's first line of defense.

"Look, Heather, if Dillon is at your house, causing trouble for your parents, then it's no accident and it's my job to see to it that he doesn't hurt anyone else."

She turned away from me and stared out the window at the lighted ships and ferries moving slowly on the darkened waters.

"I'll try not to hurt him," I added. "But if he has a gun and tries using it, I can't make any promises. Does he have a cell phone?"

"Of course."

"I need the number."

"Why?" Heather asked.

"Because if we're going to negotiate with Dillon, we need a way to reach him."

Heather gave me the number. When I reached for the telephone, her face sprang to life. "Are you going to call him?" she asked.

"Not right now," I said. "I'm calling for reinforcements."

I had made the decision that I wasn't going to call Seattle PD, but I was enough of a realist to know I couldn't pull this off on my own. Knowing the girls' secret entryway into the house gave me a possible edge, but I needed help. And so, for the second time that day, I turned to Mel Soames. We weren't officially partners, but we could just as well have been.

When she heard my voice on the phone, however, she wasn't exactly overjoyed. "What's up?" she asked, sounding as though I had awakened her.

"I need your help with something," I said.

"What?" Mel was all business. Maybe I had made up the idea that her feelings had been hurt earlier.

"Heather Peters is here—at my apartment."

That got her undivided attention. "You mean she and Dillon didn't go to Canada after all?"

"They tried," I said. "But on the way they got into an argument. He claimed he was taking Heather there to protect her and keep her out of your reach. Heather said she hadn't done anything wrong and had no reason to hide out in Canada. Things escalated and Dillon ended up slapping Heather around. She took off and came back here. When Heather said she didn't want to go, Dillon was prepared to take her there by force. I believe he still is."

"What do you mean?"

"Something's wrong up at Ron and Amy's," I explained. "When I called Ron to tell him Heather was safe, he brushed me off. A few minutes later when Heather tried calling, Ron hung up on her."

"Maybe he's upset with her for running away," Mel suggested.

"You didn't hear his voice, Mel. I know Ron Peters. He was upset—really upset. I'm thinking Dillon Middleton may be holed up at their house, waiting for Heather to come home so he can drag her along on another run for Canada."

"You mean take her by force. As in kidnapping?"

"Exactly."

"Is he armed?"

"I think so. Heather tells me Dillon owns a gun, although she didn't see it with him in the Focus yesterday when they were driving north."

"If he's armed, dangerous, and possibly holding hostages, why haven't you called Seattle PD?"

Good question, I thought. I said, "Because an Emergency Response Team is likely to turn Lower Queen Anne into a war zone. I have an idea how to handle this, but as I said, I need your help."

"Just the two of us?"

"Yes, the two of us and the added element of surprise," I said.

"How do you plan on pulling it off?" she asked.

"I'm working on the logistics right now."

There was a long pause, then Mel sighed. "Beaumont," she said, "has anyone ever told you that you're a grandstanding jerk? If this goes wrong, you'll be run out of Dodge."

"Yes," I returned. "I know. Now, are you coming or not?"

Another pause. "I guess I'm coming," she said at last.

"Good," I told her. "Bring your vest. You're probably going to need it."

CHAPTER 20

I WAS STARTING TO SQUEEZE my body back into my old vest when I remembered the note that had been pushed under my door. I called downstairs to the lobby. "It's Beaumont," I said. "On 25. I understand you have a package for me?"

"Yup," Fred Tompkins, the night-shift doorman, replied. "A cardboard box. Want me to bring it up?"

"Is there a name on it?"

"It says 'Andrew Howard, Insurance Associates.'"

"Yes, please," I said. "Bring it up."

"That person on the phone," Heather said when I hung up. "The one you were talking to before . . ."

"Mel Soames?"

"She's the one who caused all this," Heather said bitterly. "If she hadn't been talking to Dillon after the funeral, none of this would have happened."

"Talking to Dillon is Mel's job," I said. "She's one of the investigators charged with finding out what happened to your mother. The person who started all this is the one who murdered Rosemary Peters."

Heather shook her head and looked unconvinced.

"Let me ask you a question, Heather. Have you given any thought as to why Dillon was so frantic to get you to Canada?"

"Dillon loves me," she said. "He wanted to protect me."

"Isn't it possible he wanted to protect himself?"

"What do you mean?"

"You told me before that Dillon was jealous of other guys. Rosemary wanted you to move to Tacoma to live with her. What did Dillon think about that?"

The doorbell rang as Fred arrived to deliver the box that contained years of accumulated miscellaneous car debris. I dug through it, extracted my Kevlar vest, and began strapping it on.

"Are you saying you think Dillon had something to do with Rosemary's death?"

"I don't know. You tell me. Mel Soames and her partner have been looking at suspects who had access to your house and, as a consequence, access to your father's very distinctive vehicle. You just told me that Dillon knew all about the secret entrance in and out of your furnace room. You also told me he has a handgun. That means he also most likely knows how to use it, which means he'd also know how to use a similar one that belongs to your father."

"But why?" Heather asked. "Why would he?"

"Because getting rid of Rosemary would mean you wouldn't be moving to Tacoma. And you've told me yourself that your father didn't approve of Dillon. In trying to frame your father for Rosemary's death, Dillon might have expected to unload two inconvenient people at once rather than just one. Kill two birds with one stone, as they say."

"No," Heather said. "I'm sure that's not true. He could never kill anybody."

"By fleeing to Canada he knew he'd be delaying extradition, if not avoiding it altogether. Has it occurred to you that maybe the whole idea of taking you along was to implicate you, rather than protect you? What if he wants to turn you into a patsy so you share the blame?"

Heather was shaking her head in firm denial when my phone rang.

"I'm on the Mercer exit," Mel said. "And I asked Brad to meet us at your place. It sounded to me like calling for reinforcements was a good idea."

She was right. "Three-to-one odds are better than two to one," I said.

"He's about ten minutes out," Mel said. "I'm five. Do you have a game plan yet?"

I looked at Heather. She was still so adamantly convinced of Dillon's innocence that I was afraid she might try to alert him to what was going on. The rough outline of my plan called for me to gain access to the house through Heather and Tracy's secret door while others lured Dillon outside. Success in my getting inside depended on maintaining the element of surprise. Success in bringing Dillon out depended on Heather.

"Not yet," I said. "I'm working on it."

I put down the phone and turned to Heather. "Will you help us?" I asked.

"No," she said. "No way! What if he gets hurt? What if something bad happens?"

"Heather, think about what might happen if we have to call in Seattle PD. It's possible lots of people could get hurt. The guys on the Emergency Response Team are great, and they'll do the best job they can. They'll be focused on saving your family—your parents and brother and sister—far more than they will be focused on saving Dillon."

"Would they shoot him?"

"If he's holding your family hostage? Absolutely. Believe me, Heather, you and Mel Soames and I are Dillon's best shot. The best thing that could happen would be for us to persuade him to come out of the house and surrender. We need to do that without jeopardizing his life or anyone else's."

I could see my words had made an impact. At least Heather was thinking about it rather than dismissing the idea entirely.

"How would you do that?" she asked at last. "Get him out of the house, I mean."

"Why do you think he went there?" I asked in return.

Heather shrugged. "Looking for me, I guess."

"Exactly. And he's waiting there, hoping you'll return."

"Maybe he just wants to talk to me," Heather said hopefully.

"Maybe so," I agreed, although I didn't think that was all Dillon wanted. "And in that case, you're our best bet for getting him out of the house. When everyone is in position, I want you to call him on his cell phone and ask him to come outside. Once your family is safe, we'll deal with getting him to surrender."

"For what?"

For kidnapping you, for starters, I thought. *And for beating you up.* But those weren't things I could say to Heather Peters, not right then.

"Dillon is unstable," I said. "He needs help."

"You think he's crazy?"

"It's possible," I said.

Again there was a long silence. Finally Heather looked up at me. Behind the garish hair and the body piercings I caught a glimpse of the little blue-eyed heartbreaker who had sold me cases of Girl Scout cookies and charmed me into helping her dog-sit.

"What do you need me to do?" she asked.

I handed her my old vest. "Put this on," I said.

"You want me to come along?" Heather asked in disbelief.

I didn't answer because I hardly believed it myself. Taking her with us was incredibly risky. There was always a chance that she could be hurt or even killed in what was likely to be an ugly confrontation. But leaving her alone wasn't an option, either. That would give her far too much time to reconsider. It would give her time to decide to warn Dillon that we were on our way. Keeping a close eye on her would be far safer for Mel, Brad, and me than leaving Heather to her own devices.

"Yes," I said. "You'll be in one of the cars. You'll be relatively safe as long as you stay in the vehicle. When we're ready, we'll need you to call Dillon and get him to come outside."

"What should I say?"

"I don't know. How about telling him you've changed your mind and that you're ready to go to Canada?"

"But I haven't changed my mind," Heather objected.

"Tell him whatever you like, then. Just get him out of the house. We'll take it from there."

Naturally the vest was way too big. Rather than having it hang loose, I had Heather stuff two pillows in under her shirt, which she then tucked into her pants. Once the vest was cinched up tight, the pillows helped it stay in place. She looked like a henna-haired version of the Michelin Man. Under other circumstances, it might have been comical, but this was serious—a matter of life or death. I dragged one of my old jackets out of the entryway closet to cover the bulging mess so she wouldn't look quite so ridiculous.

"Come on," I said. "Let's go downstairs and meet up with the others."

Mel was appalled when she saw Heather and realized I expected to bring the girl along.

"Are you nuts?" Mel demanded.

"She'll be staying in one of the vehicles," I said with more confidence than I felt. "She should be perfectly safe, but we need her there."

"Why?" Mel asked.

"To entice Dillon out of the house once we're all in place."

"In other words, you're planning to use her as bait?" Mel asked. "What have you been smoking, Beau? I can't condone this."

"It's all right," Heather said. "I want to help."

"You're a fifteen-year-old civilian," Mel countered. "Involving you in this is totally irresponsible. You could get hurt."

"I already am hurt," Heather said. "But I love Dillon, and I know I can talk him into coming outside."

I didn't want to explain in front of Heather that my biggest concern was the possibility that she'd warn Dillon of our intentions the minute we were out of sight.

"It's what we have to do," I said. "And it's what we're going to do. If you don't want any part of it, fine. I'll do it myself. If something goes wrong, then it's on my head, not yours."

Mel was unconvinced. "Right," she said. "And I've got some great oceanfront property in Arizona." Brad Norton pulled up and stopped behind Mel's Beemer. "Okay then," Mel added. "I suppose she's with me?"

I nodded. She escorted Heather to the car, let her into the passenger seat, and then came back and joined Brad and me on the sidewalk. "So what's the deal?"

After summarizing all I had learned in the course of the evening, I went on to explain my game plan. "I want you and Brad to take up defensive positions in the front yard," I told Mel. "There's a little-used back entrance that leads into the furnace room. The kids use that door to come and go when they don't want their parents to know what they're up to. I'll go in that way. I'll try to sort out where Ron and Amy and the kids are. If I can get some of them out of the house to safety before we make our move, I will. If not, I'll phone Heather and let her know it's time for her to make her call."

"Will she?" Mel asked. "What if she doesn't? I know more than a little about situations like this. If she and Dillon have been involved in an abusive relationship, she may well cave when it comes time to make that critical call."

I remembered what Mel had told me about her own tumultuous home life, how she had grown up in a family where domestic violence had been a daily part of her existence. Much as I didn't want to admit it, I knew she was right. It was more than possible that Heather would let us down at the last minute.

"Then we'll flex," I said. "It's the best we can do."

Mel was studying me intently. "Are you sure about this?" she asked. "These are good friends of yours. Are you sure that isn't clouding your judgment?"

"Maybe so," I admitted, "but this seems like a better idea than sending the ERT guys in with guns blazing and tear gas flying. Ron and Amy and their kids still need a place to live when all this is over. I'm thinking the three of us can do a surgical extraction. Seattle PD will end up using the law enforcement equivalent of carpet bombing."

"All right," Mel said at last. "Show us what you've got."

We caravanned our three vehicles up Queen Anne Hill to Ron and Amy's neighborhood on West Highland. I parked several houses away and made my circuitous way to their yard by the same route I had used days before, when Tracy had called me to come help out. There was no snow on the ground this time, and it wasn't particularly cold, but it was raining. That made for treacherous going in the steep spots. I was glad when I was able to duck into the relatively dry space behind the protective layer of vines that sheltered Tracy and Heather's hidden door.

No lights from above shed any kind of illumination into that ivy-shrouded cave. I stumbled forward blindly in the darkness, found the doorknob, and tried turning it, only to find it was locked. Longing for a flashlight, I felt along the upper side of the doorframe until my searching fingers encountered the key Heather had said was concealed there.

It took a long time to locate the keyhole. The scratching of metal on metal as I struggled to insert the key sounded as loud to my ears as cracks of summer lightning. Once I finally succeeded in unlocking the door, I stepped inside. Slipping off my shoes, I tied the shoelaces together and then let the shoes dangle around the back of my neck while I moved forward in my stockinged feet. Again, I had to feel my way around the room until I located a doorknob. I blessed the silence of the well-oiled hinges as the door swung open.

I was in a corner of the house I had never seen before. This was a decommissioned laundry room that seemed to be directly under the kitchen. Here a glow of outside streetlights entering the dank basement offered some relief from the oppressive darkness of the furnace room and revealed a flight of rough plank stairs that ended at another closed door.

I tiptoed up the stairs and stood with my ear pressed against the door, listening. There was no sound from the other side, but I knew if anyone happened to be in the kitchen when this door opened, all hope of surprise would be lost. This was my last chance to use my cell phone. I pressed the return call number that would take me back to Mel's phone. We'd made arrangements for Heather to answer, so I'd know the call went through, which it did.

"Okay, Uncle Beau," she said. "I'll call Dillon now."

I wanted to tell her good luck, but I didn't dare speak. Instead, I ended the call and turned the knob on the door that led into the kitchen. After the darkness in the basement, the kitchen seemed incredibly light. Standing there, I couldn't help but be grateful that Amy was allergic to pet dander. Otherwise, there might have been a barking dog on the premises to announce my arrival.

I stopped just inside the door and stood dead-still once more, listening. At first I heard nothing but the slow drip of a leaky kitchen faucet. Behind me, on the counter, sat two open and empty pizza boxes. I had to remind myself that it was only a week ago when the Peters family's Friday-night dinner tradition had been derailed by the arrival of Rosemary's custody-battle summons. So much had happened since then, I felt as though years had passed rather than a single week.

I heard no sounds. *What if they're all dead?* I asked myself. *What if I'm too late—again?*

Just then a telephone screeched on the kitchen wall behind me. I almost jumped out of my skin. The call was answered after only one ring, followed by the rumble of a single male voice—Ron's voice—speaking into the phone.

This can't be Heather calling? I told myself. *She's supposed to call on Dillon's cell phone.*

Using the noise of the call as audio cover against any possible floorboard squeaks, I crept through the swinging door that separated the kitchen from the dining room. Moving slowly, I inched forward past the dining-room table until I had a partial view of the living room. Tracy and Amy sat like bookends at opposite ends of the couch. Jared, stretched out between them, was sound asleep with his head in Amy's lap. Ron's chair was parked close enough to the couch so he could, if needed, reach out and touch his wife's hand, but right now he was busy speaking into the phone. Molly Wright was nowhere to be seen, but it was possible she, like Dillon, was sitting just outside my range of vision.

"No," Ron was saying firmly. "We have absolutely no interest in buying a vacation time share. Please remove us from your list." And then he hung up.

A thick fog of cigarette smoke filled the room. Since neither Amy nor Ron smokes, I knew the stench had to come from whoever was with them. I was still standing there like an idiot, waiting for the sound of a ringing cell phone when the front door slammed open and a Kevlar-vest-covered Heather stormed into the living room.

My stomach lurched. My plan had called for her to stay safely in the car. Instead, she had now blundered into a room where the tension was so thick it was difficult to breathe.

"Heather!" Ron exclaimed.

What the hell is she doing here? I wondered. *And how did she get past Mel?*

At the sight of her stepdaughter, Amy made as if to rise to her feet. Jared whimpered and half awakened. "Don't move." I recognized Dillon's voice at once. "Stay where you are," he commanded. Saying nothing, Amy subsided back into her seat and patted Jared's shoulder until he settled again.

Without a glance in her parents' direction, Heather walked as far as the middle of the room and stopped. Yes, it was stupid for her to be there. It was also terribly dangerous, but even as I feared for Heather's life, I couldn't help but applaud her courage as she stepped into the no-man's-land between her family and her troubled boyfriend. Standing deathly still, she fixed her unseen boyfriend in an unwavering gaze.

"I tried to call you," she said. "You didn't answer the phone."

"I lost my charger," Dillon said. "The battery ran down."

Both Mel and I had been afraid Heather would fall apart when it came time for her to confront Dillon. At the sound of his voice, Heather's cheeks, flushed from being outside in the cool air, paled suddenly, but she didn't back off.

"What's going on?" she asked. "What are you doing here? And what are you doing with that knife?"

A knife! I felt a surge of panic. Kevlar can protect someone's chest from flying bullets, but the soft armor would do little to protect Heather if Dillon came after her wielding a knife.

"Why did you run away?" Dillon asked in return and without answering any of Heather's questions. "Why did you leave me?"

"Because you hit me," Heather replied matter-of-factly. "Don't you remember?"

Ron must have missed the bruising on Heather's face as she hurried past him. Hearing the news that his daughter had been assaulted hit Ron hard. His hands darted reflexively toward the wheels on his chair. I had little doubt that his first fatherly instinct was to charge across the room and smash Dillon Middleton's face into a million pieces. Had I been in Ron's place, I'm not sure I wouldn't have, but with amazing self-control Ron forced his hands back into his lap and left his chair parked next to the couch. Only fear for his daughter's life could have forced him to stay where he was.

"I didn't mean to," Dillon replied. "Hitting you was an accident, but that's why I'm here. I came back to get you. I need you with me, so I came back."

"All right," Heather said. "I'm here. Let's go."

"No," Ron said. "Heather, you can't do this. You can't go with him. If he's already hit you, what do you think he'll do with that knife?"

"I have to go, Dad," Heather said. "Leave me alone. Come on, Dillon."

I realized then that Heather was still trying to keep to our original game plan. When Dillon's cell phone hadn't worked, she had somehow eluded Mel and Brad and come inside to carry out her part of the deal. And she was absolutely right in doing so. Whatever was going to happen next couldn't take place in a living room full of people.

Before Ron could raise another objection, I moved into the doorway far enough that he could see me. I mimed that he should zip his lip and then mouthed the words, "Let them go!"

Turning away from Dillon, Heather walked as far as the front door and held it open. Then she turned back to Dillon. "Well," she said. "Are you coming or not?"

Dillon moved forward. When he reached Heather, he grabbed her with one arm. Then with his other arm, the knife arm, wrapped around her shoulders, they stepped outside.

My part of the job was to usher Amy, Ron, and the kids to safety. Hurriedly I ducked back out of sight behind the dining-room wall.

As soon as the front door slammed shut behind then, I heard someone shout, "Freeze!"

I didn't wait to hear more. I charged out of the dining room. "Come on, come on," I yelled at Amy and Tracy, who both seemed astonished to see me. "Into the kitchen, quick!"

I grabbed the startled Jared from his mother's arms and carried him to safety. Amy and Tracy were right behind me, with Ron in his wheelchair bringing up the rear. I handed my now-wailing namesake, Jared Beaumont Peters, over to his father and then raced back to the front door. I shut off the interior lights before I opened it. Just as Heather and Dillon must have done, I had to pause on the porch for a moment before my eyes adjusted to the sudden change in light.

When I could see again, there was Dillon's Focus parked in the middle of the drive. Brad stood on the driver's side of the vehicle, and Mel Soames stood on the other. Both had their weapons drawn and were pointing toward the Ford's interior. "Drop the knife!" Mel ordered.

As I moved closer, there was some illumination from a nearby streetlight, enough that I could glimpse a single occupant in the front seat of the vehicle. If Dillon was holding Heather down on the far side of the seat, if he was threatening her with the knife, he was probably too preoccupied with the weapon to turn the key in the ignition. That explained why the Focus wasn't running.

Taking in the chilling scene, I lost all hope. With two .38s trained on the vehicle from the outside and with a drawn knife inside, Heather Peters didn't stand a chance. And if she got hurt or died, it really would be all my fault.

"Put down the knife." This time Brad issued the order. "Put it down and step out of the vehicle."

But nothing happened. The car door didn't open. The knife didn't tumble onto the driveway. Determined to help, I charged off the porch, only to be knocked off balance by someone coming toward me at breakneck speed.

"Help him, Uncle Beau," Heather pleaded as I righted myself. "Stop them before they shoot him. Please."

Overwhelmed to realize Heather wasn't being held at knifepoint, I clutched her in a quick but heartfelt bear hug. "All right," I said. "I will, but you have to go inside. Don't come back out until we say you can."

Without waiting to see whether or not Heather did as she was told, I sprinted forward.

"Come on, Dillon, we don't want to hurt you," Mel was saying. "You're not going anywhere. Now put down that knife."

"We shouldn't have done it," I heard Dillon say as I reached the back bumper of the car. "I'm sorry."

There was a sudden flurry of movement from the driver's seat.

"Shit!" Mel Soames exclaimed, and she wasn't talking about the Special Homicide Investigation Team. Brad leaned inside and retrieved the knife. He emerged with both his hand and the knife dripping with blood. By then I could see what Mel had meant. Dillon Middleton sat slumped sideways in the driver's seat with blood gushing from a self-inflicted wound to his gut.

"No!" Heather shrieked from behind me as she darted toward the car.

Seattle's award-winning EMTs arrived within two minutes of receiving my 911 call, but I suspected long before they got there that no matter what medical magic they brought with them, it would be too little too late to save Dillon Middleton.

CHAPTER 21

ALL HELL BROKE LOOSE after that. By the time the aid car took off for Harborview Hospital with Heather and Dillon on board followed by the rest of the Peters family, West Highland had filled up with cop cars and media vans. Queen Anne Hill was no longer my turf. In this instance, it wasn't Brad's or Mel's, either. Temporarily relegated to the sidelines, we stood in the rain watching the proceedings just like the other neighborhood onlookers.

"I guess you heard what Dillon said." Mel's comment was a quiet one, but it packed a gut-wrenching wallop, because I had indeed heard what he said. "We shouldn't have done it."

It was pretty apparent that the "we" in question had to be Dillon and Heather. And as for the "it"? That had to be the murder of Rosemary Peters. All three of us—three sworn police officers—had heard what might well turn out to be Dillon Middleton's deathbed confession. Dillon was on his way to a hospital and maybe a funeral home. As for Heather? If what Dillon had said was true, Heather Peters might well be headed for prison. The idea that she had played a part in her mother's murder had been a possibility all along. I simply hadn't accepted it. Now it was unavoidable.

"She told me she didn't do it," I muttered. It was difficult to speak. My heart was breaking for Ron and Amy—and for me. I was glad it was raining. With water coursing down my cheeks, I hoped people wouldn't notice some of it was tears.

"She lied to you, Beau," Mel said. "Kids lie all the time."

"Are you going to arrest her tonight?"

"Probably not," Mel said. "Tomorrow will be plenty of time. It'll take that long to get an arrest warrant. Here." She held out her hand.

"What's this?"

"A present for you," she said and handed me a spark-plug wire.

"That's how you kept him from leaving?" I asked.

"Yes."

"Good thinking," I said, slipping the wire into my pocket. "And good work. How did you get her away from him?"

Mel shrugged. "We didn't dare make a move as long as Dillon was holding the knife to her throat. But when they got close to the car, he let her loose. I think he really believed she was running away with him. That's when we made our move."

"She probably was running away with him," I said. "And all the time I thought she was doing what she was doing to help her parents."

"She was helping herself," Mel said.

Sick at heart, I couldn't argue the point.

A tow truck picked its way through the assortment of parked cars and came to collect the Focus. I was walking over to hand the spark-plug wire over to the tow-truck driver just as a uniformed officer popped the trunk. He lurched back several paces, and I heard him gasp, "Oh my God!"

When I turned to look, I saw that a bloodied corpse had been jammed into the tiny trunk. As soon as I saw the face, I knew who it was—Molly Wright.

A pair of homicide detectives had already been summoned to the scene of Dillon's attempted suicide. Now Captain Kramer appeared as if on cue. He didn't bother glancing at the car or at the open trunk. Instead he made straight for me.

"What the hell is going on here, Beaumont? I thought I told you to stop screwing around in my cases."

Mel Soames stepped out from behind me before I had a chance to respond. "Like it or not, it happens to be our case, too," she said reasonably enough.

"My associates," I interjected. "Melissa Soames and Brad Norton. And this is a former associate of mine," I added. "Captain Paul Kramer, Seattle PD Homicide, but then I believe you two have already met."

Kramer leered at Mel. "Oh, it's you," he said sarcastically. "So the SHIT squad is out in force—the attorney general *über alles*."

I didn't like his tone. And even though Mel Soames's figure was definitely worthy of leers, I sure as hell didn't like the way he looked at her, either. For her part, Mel seemed singularly unimpressed.

"One of the suspects in the Rosemary Peters homicide just tried to off himself here in his vehicle," Mel told him. "But it turns out he left a little something behind for you to work on, too."

For the first time Kramer looked inside the trunk. One glance was enough to leave him stricken. Kramer always talked a good game, but he was never all that solid when it came to crime scenes and dead bodies. I figured that was one of the main reasons he had majored in paperwork—and butt kissing.

He turned on his detectives, who had caught their first glimpse of Molly Wright's body seconds after Kramer. "Has anybody here gotten around to calling the ME yet?" he groused. "What the hell's the matter with you guys? And get this crime scene roped off. I don't want anyone walking around in here. That goes for you and your pals there, Beaumont. Get the hell out and stop messing up our evidence."

I would have said something, but Mel laid a restraining hand on my arm. "Come on," she said. "Let's go."

Walking away from Kramer, I headed for my car, which was parked several houses down the street. As I wove my way through the haphazardly parked phalanx of vehicles, Mel came trailing after me. She caught up with me when I stopped to unlock the car door. "Where are you going?" she asked.

"You notice Kramer didn't ask if we knew who the victim was," I said.

Mel nodded. "And I noticed none of us volunteered that information, either."

"It's going to take time for him to figure it out. In the meantime, I'm on my way to Harborview to let Amy know what's happened. I'd rather she heard the news from a friend rather than from Paul Kramer or the ME's office. What about you?"

She patted her cell phone. "I'm going to get on the horn to Harry I. Ball and Ross Connors—for the same reason. They need to hear about all this from us, and it can't wait until we get around to doing our paperwork. From the looks of those satellite vans, the story will be all over the eleven o'clock news."

"Want a lift back to your car?" I asked.

"No, thanks," she said. "I'm already wet." She started to walk away. "Mel?"

She turned and looked at me. "What?"

"Thanks for what you did tonight," I said. "No matter what happens to Heather now, at least we gave her a chance. She'll be able to plead her case in front of a judge and jury. If she'd gone off with Dillon, there's no telling . . ."

"So when Brad and I get around to arresting her, there'll be no hard feelings?"

"Right," I said. "None."

She walked away, disappearing into the haze of rain and flashing lights, while I headed for the hospital. It wasn't a trip I relished. The last time I had sat in the Trauma Center waiting room, I had been there with Sue Danielson's two boys, sitting with them when the doctor came to give us the bad news that she wasn't going to make it. I had known that Sue was gravely wounded, so I guess I had been prepared.

Tonight, though, for Amy, news of Molly's unexpected death would come with no warning at all, and at a time when the Peters family was already operating deep in crisis mode. Was it better to have such an emotional blow delivered by a friend? I hoped so.

The room where life-changing news was delivered daily—the place where loved ones waited and worried, wept, hoped, and despaired— was impossibly ordinary and not particularly comfortable, either. Three separate family groupings huddled miserably in various corners of the room.

The Peters family was divided into two separate camps. Tracy and an anguished, ashen-faced Heather sat at a table in the middle of the room. Amy, with the sleeping Jared's head once again cradled in her lap, sat on a sagging couch. A uniformed officer, perched on a nearby chair, was interviewing Ron.

Nodding at Ron, I made my way over to Amy. "How's it going?"

She looked up at me, shook her head, and smiled wanly. "I don't know what to hope for," she said. "If Dillon dies, it'll break Heather's heart. If he lives, he'll still break her heart. The truth is, though, he held us all at knifepoint, Heather included. In my heart of hearts, I hope he dies and goes straight to hell. Is that wrong?"

"Not wrong," I said. "And I don't blame you."

"You don't?"

"Especially not now," I told her. "Now that I know the rest of it."

"The rest of what?" Amy asked.

"I'm sorry to have to tell you this, Amy. Molly is dead. Her body was found in the trunk of Dillon's vehicle a little while ago. There's no official cause of death right now. It's too soon. When I left, the ME had yet to arrive on the scene, but I believe she was stabbed to death."

Amy's hand went to her throat. Her face blanched. "No," she said. "That's not possible!"

Ron, catching sight of Amy's stricken expression, pushed away from the officer and rolled over to his wife's side. "What is it?" he asked. "What's wrong?"

"It's Molly," Amy said. "Dillon's killed her."

Ron looked at me for confirmation. "Is that true?" he asked.

"We don't know for sure," I said. "Not this soon, but Molly's body was found in Dillon's trunk. From the amount of blood, I'd say he stabbed her repeatedly."

"But why?" Ron demanded. "I thought Molly was Dillon's friend. When he showed up at the house with his knife last night and threatened us if we didn't tell him where to find Heather, I never doubted for a moment that he'd use it on me, but I don't understand why he'd go after Molly."

Amy roused the sleeping Jared and handed him over to his father. "I've gotta go," she said. "I have to go tell the folks."

Without a word, Ron took the child into his arms. I would have expected him to say something conciliatory, but he didn't. There was no word of comfort or condolence from Ron as Amy stood up and smoothed her skirt. That surprised me.

"If you'd like some company, I'll be glad to drive you," I offered.

"Thank you," she murmured. Seemingly struck by some kind of indecision, she stood staring at Tracy and Heather, who were sitting halfway across the room. "Would you please tell Heather, Beau?" Amy asked. "I can't do it. I just can't."

I didn't want to tell Heather any more than Amy did, but not for the same reason. Dillon's damning "we" had placed Heather firmly in the enemy camp. And if she had been a part of her own mother's murder, it didn't seem likely that Molly's death would come as a surprise to her, either. But I didn't say any of that to Ron and Amy. I simply got up and walked over to the table where Heather and Tracy were sitting, their heads bent together in quiet conversation. When I got there, I could see that Heather was crying.

"What do the doctors say?" I asked.

Heather raised her teary face. "Nothing," she said. "They haven't told us anything at all. He could be dead by now for all I know."

"What do you know about your aunt Molly?" I asked.

"Molly?" Heather repeated. "Nothing. I've tried calling her. I left messages on her machine. I thought she'd be here. She's the only one who knows Dillon's mother's cell phone number. His dad's on his way down from White Rock right now, but he doesn't know the cell number either."

"There's a reason Molly isn't here." I said the words deliberately, examining Heather's every expression as I spoke.

"What is it?" Heather asked. "Is something wrong?"

"We found Molly's body a little while ago," I said. "She was . . . crammed into the trunk of Dillon's Focus."

"No!" Heather breathed. "That's not possible. It can't be true."

Heather's histrionics didn't impress me, and I was in no mood to pull punches. "Well, it is true," I shot back. "I was standing right there when the trunk was opened. And don't try to pretend you know nothing about it."

Heather's outburst quieted as quickly as it had begun. "But I don't know anything about it," she declared. "And I didn't kill her. I didn't kill anybody. You believe me, don't you?" When I didn't answer, Heather turned beseechingly to Amy. "Mom?"

"We have to go," Amy said. And we left.

We rode down in the elevator and went out through the lobby without exchanging a word.

I had met Amy's parents, Carol and Arthur Fitzgerald, but I didn't really know them. I knew that after selling their Queen Anne home to Ron and Amy, Carol and Art had moved into a water-view condominium project in Madison Park.

Art, an old-fashioned wheeler-dealer, had made a small fortune as a building contractor. It was his loving care and expertise that had transformed what had once been a derelict Queen Anne mansion into the spacious home where Ron and Amy now lived. Art had figured out a way to install the tiny but effective elevator that made several levels of the home accessible to Ron's wheelchair. Art was easygoing and garrulous—a guy who got things done. Carol struck me as quiet, ladylike, and dignified. I hated to be going to their home late at night on a mission to deliver such devastating news.

"You'll need to give me directions," I said when we were both belted into the Taurus.

"Up and over the hill on Madison," she said. "I'll tell you where to go. Sorry it was so frosty back there," she added once we were under way. "It's been like that around our house lately."

I had noticed, but I hadn't planned on mentioning it.

"What did he expect me to do," Amy continued, "throw her out into the street?"

"Who?" I asked. "Heather?"

"No, Molly, of course. She burned her bridges with our parents long ago, and when she had nowhere else to go, I agreed to let her stay with us. It was the least I could do. I mean, we had the house. She had nothing, but I had no idea how bad it would be."

"What do you mean, she burned her bridges?"

"Molly and Aaron went through money like it was water. That happens when people insist on putting every dollar they can lay hands on up their noses."

"As in coke?" I asked.

Amy nodded. "My parents bailed them out time and time again. The last time, when they wouldn't, is when Aaron started embezzling company funds. By selling Ron and me the house at less than market value, the folks thought they were simply keeping things fair. But Molly didn't see it that way. To her way of thinking, the house should have been half hers. That being the case, she automatically thought we owed her a place to stay."

"Was she still using?" I asked.

"She said she wasn't," Amy answered. "But I don't know for sure. Ron told her that he wouldn't allow the stuff in his house. She knew he meant it, but being told what to do galled her, especially considering the way she felt about Ron."

"What's wrong with Ron?"

"I think she thought that with Aaron gone, she and I would go back to being big and little sister, the way things were before. Meaning, of course, that she was the big sister and I was supposed to do things her way. It's been hell. She and Ron were at loggerheads from the moment she moved in, but I just didn't have the heart to throw her out. She's the only sister I have."

"But she was undermining you and Ron when it came to the kids."

"That's right," Amy said bitterly. "Enter Dillon Middleton."

"Dillon didn't look like such great shakes to me," I said. "So what's the big attraction as far as Molly was concerned?"

"I have no idea," Amy returned. "Maybe the fact that Ron couldn't stand him made him that much more interesting as far as Molly was concerned." She broke off. "Turn left here," she added. "It's the building down there at the end of the street."

I found a visitor parking spot. "Do you want me to come in with you?" I asked as Amy reached for the door handle.

"No," she said. "This is something I'm better off doing on my own."

She got out of the car and walked stiffly through the now-misty rain as far as the building, where she soon disappeared from sight in the small lobby. I sat there and considered what could possibly have been Molly's purpose in doing all she could to wreck Ron and Amy's relationship. What had she hoped to gain by driving a wedge between these two people, or between Ron and Amy and their children? Was she so embittered by her own unhappiness that she wanted everyone else to share in her misery? That seemed unlikely, and yet what other explanation was there? And what could be the reason behind Molly's strange obsession with a hopeless gangbanger wannabe like Dillon Middleton? None of it made any sense at all.

Eventually Amy returned. "How'd it go?" I asked.

Her chest heaved. "About how you'd expect," she returned, brushing tears from her eyes. "Mom, especially, is brokenhearted. She and Molly hadn't spoken for years. Mom always thought they'd mend the rift eventually. Now they never will."

I started the car and put it in gear. "Back to the hospital?" I asked.

"Please."

We drove back to Harborview. Upstairs in the trauma waiting room, Tracy had stretched out on a couch with one arm flung over her eyes. Jared was asleep in his father's lap. A dry-eyed and distant Heather sat across the room in self-imposed isolation from the rest of her family.

"Now that you're here, we should probably try to get some rest," Ron said to Amy. His face was ashen with weariness; his voice strained. Ron Peters had aged ten years in the past week, and he looked as though he was on the edge of despair. "We can't go to the house. It's full of detectives. I booked us a pair of rooms down here at the Sheraton."

"Is Heather coming, too?" Amy asked.

Ron shook his head. "I asked her, but she won't budge."

"It's all right," I told them. "Take Tracy and Jared and try to get some sleep. I'll stay with Heather."

"Are you sure?" Ron asked.

"I'm sure," I said. "It's no problem."

After Ron and Amy left, I went out into the hallway, grabbed a soda from the vending machine, and set it on the table beside Heather. "You look like you could use a little caffeine," I said.

She looked up at me gratefully and nodded. "Thanks," she said.

While she popped open the can and took a sip, I sat down next to her. "Any word?"

"He's still in surgery."

"What about his father?" I asked, glancing around the room. "Is he here?"

"Not yet."

We sat in silence for some time while I puzzled about how this young woman, a child who was as close to me as my own children, could possibly be a suspect in a double homicide. No wonder Ron was looking gray and drawn. I probably looked the same way myself.

"I didn't do it, Uncle Beau," Heather said finally, meeting my gaze with an intense blue-eyed stare of her own. "I heard what Dillon said. I heard him say we did it—like he and I did it together—but it's not true. I never killed anybody, I swear."

"What did Dillon have against your aunt Molly?" I asked. "Why would he hurt her? I thought Molly was his friend."

Heather shrugged. "So did I," she said.

A pair of doors swung open on the far side of the room and a man in surgical scrubs strode into the room. He glanced briefly around the room and then settled on Heather and me. The doctor came forward, holding out his hand. "Mr. Middleton?" he asked.

"No," I told him. "Sorry. I'm a friend of the family. This is Heather Peters, Dillon's girlfriend."

"Oh," the doctor replied and then looked around the room, scanning the other two sets of family members still lingering there. "I was given to understand the father was on his way."

"He is," Heather said. "He's coming down from White Rock, but he isn't here yet. How's Dillon? Is he going to be all right?"

The doctor looked at Heather and shook his head. "I'm sorry, miss. With the new federal privacy rules in effect, I'm unable to release patient information to anyone other than an authorized relative."

"But . . ." Heather objected. "Can't you . . ."

"Sorry," the doctor told her. "That's just the way it is." With that he turned and walked away.

"That's not fair," Heather called after him. "Just because I'm only a girlfriend . . ."

But the doors had already swung shut behind the retreating doctor, cutting her protestation off in midsentence.

"Maybe we should go," I suggested. "You must be tired. Let me take you home."

"No," Heather insisted. "I'm staying."

Which automatically meant that I was staying, too. Lamar Middleton, Dillon's father, arrived an hour later. He was a man in his mid-fifties, balding, heavyset, and clearly distraught. Heather recognized him as soon as he came through the door, and she hurried forward to greet him.

"I'm Heather," she said. "I recognized you from your picture. I'm so glad you're here. Dillon's doctor came out a little while ago, but since I'm only a girlfriend, he wouldn't tell me anything."

Lamar ventured behind the swinging doors and came out a few minutes later. "Dillon survived surgery," he said. "But he's in intensive care. He's stable right now, but they don't know whether or not he'll make it. What on earth happened? What's this all about?"

Heather began relating some of what had happened. It was when she reached the part about Molly Wright that Lamar slumped in his chair and covered his eyes with his hands.

"My God!" he exclaimed. "I should have known!"

"Should have known what?"

"That Molly would be involved in this. Living a lie is always a bad idea. I tried to tell Annette that years ago, but she wouldn't listen."

"Who's Annette?" I asked.

"My ex-wife," Lamar answered.

"Dillon's mother?"

"Not exactly," he said.

"What does that mean?"

"Annette and I adopted Dillon," he said. "But Molly Wright—she was Molly Fitzgerald then—was his birth mother."

For me, that was when a whole lot of what had happened finally clicked into focus. No wonder Molly had been so determined to bring Dillon into the Peters family circle. She knew he was her son even if no one else did. Using Heather as bait, she had been able to keep him close to her. If Heather had moved to Tacoma, taking Dillon with her, that connection would have been disrupted; but still, did a distance of forty miles or so justify committing murder?

Heather's eyes widened. "Did you say Aunt Molly was Dillon's mom?" she demanded.

Lamar nodded. "Molly had broken up with her long-term boyfriend when she found out she was pregnant. At first she planned to keep the baby. Then she started to date a guy named Aaron Wright. Aaron made it clear from the beginning that he didn't want to have kids. Not ever. By then Annette and I were already married. Molly came to see us, trying to figure out what to do. For one thing, it was too late to get an easy abortion. When Molly mentioned having the baby and putting it up for adoption, Annette talked her into giving him to us."

"Just like that?" I asked.

Lamar nodded ruefully. "Annette's always been like that. She tends to get her way—with everybody. I told her I thought it was a bad idea, especially since Molly was such a good friend, but Annette was adamant, and eventually I went along with the program. Molly stayed with us until Dillon was born, then she went back home and pretended nothing had happened. She and Aaron got married eventually, and we kept the baby.

"The problem is, Annette was a whole lot better at the idea of motherhood than she was at the reality of it. Ditto for being married. She likes the concept, but not the actual commitment part. So she took off and pretty much left Dillon's raising up to me. I did the best I could.

"I have to hand it to Annette. Once she left me, she's managed to marry up every time, so money isn't a problem—not for her, anyway. So here I was, trying to raise Dillon to be a decent human being, but periodically Annette would show up—often with Molly in tow. The two of them would do the whole noncustodial parent program. You know how it works. They spoiled the kid—gave him whatever he wanted. They told him that my rules didn't apply whenever they were around, and what kid isn't going to go for that? Eventually it worked."

"Dillon came here?"

Lamar nodded. "Got into trouble, dropped out of school, and came here to be with Annette—until she took off again. She rented an apartment for him while she headed for the Bay Area with her latest fling. By then, Molly's life had turned to crap. Having lost everything else, I think she saw one last chance to get Dillon back—and keep him close."

"Except he was going to come to Tacoma with me," Heather said in a small voice. "He told Molly that on the phone that night. I heard him. He said that if I had to go live with Rosemary in Tacoma, he was going to go there, too. He said he'd find a different apartment. Molly didn't want him to go. She freaked out on the phone and started screaming and yelling. I could hear her from all the way across the room. It was totally weird."

"Maybe," I said, "since she had already lost her son once, she didn't want to risk losing him again. Still, having him move to Tacoma isn't like sending him off to the ends of the earth. I still don't understand."

After that, the three of us were quiet for a very long time. There wasn't much to say, and I don't think anyone else understood any better than I did.

An hour passed and then two. It was after three in the morning when the swinging doors opened again and once more the same doctor entered the room. This time he went straight to Lamar Middleton.

"I'm sorry to have to tell you this, Mr. Middleton," he began. "I'm afraid your son didn't make it."

CHAPTER 22

WITHOUT A WORD, Heather bolted from the room. I charged after her. When I finally caught up with her, she was outside the front entrance, standing bare-armed and bareheaded in the pouring rain.

"Heather," I urged. "Come back inside."

She shrugged off my hand. "I don't want to," she said. "Leave me alone."

"It's cold and wet out here."

"Who cares? If Dillon's dead, I should be dead, too. Maybe I'll catch pneumonia and die."

Then, to my surprise, she stopped talking and fell sobbing against my chest. Comforting her as best I could, I led her to my car and helped her inside. I turned on the engine, the heater, and the defroster as well, then I waited for her to stop crying.

"Your parents are staying at a hotel downtown," I told her when she had finally cried herself out. "Do you want to go there?"

Heather shook her head. "I want to go home," she said.

"You can't. The last I heard, your house was full of cops, so I guess you're stuck with me."

"But . . ." Heather began. Then she fell quiet. "Okay," she said finally.

Once again I took Heather up to my condo in Belltown Terrace. I expected her to head straight for bed. God knows I was ready.

"Can I use your computer?" she asked.

"My computer? At this hour?"

"I need to check my e-mail." She paused. "Dillon told me in the ambulance that he sent me a message in case he didn't find me. I need to see what he said. Please."

So I led Heather into the den and helped her log on to my clunky old desktop. Then I went out into the living room to give her some privacy. I settled back in my old recliner and kicked off my shoes. My shirt and trousers were still damp, and they stuck to the leather, but I didn't bother to change. Then I called down to the Sheraton. Not wanting to awaken Ron and Amy in case they had managed to fall asleep, I left a message letting them know that Dillon had died and that I had taken Heather home with me.

A few minutes after I hung up the phone, I heard Heather crying again. I stayed where I was, figuring that if she needed consolation she'd come looking for it. Then I heard the sound of the printer coming on-line. Finally Heather emerged from the den, wiping a trail of tears from her face. Wordlessly she handed me a single sheet of paper:

Baby, Molly Wright is a evil woman. Why did I ever think she was
my friend? I don't know why, but she really really hated your dad.
She called him a stupid cripple and said he had turned Amy and her
parents against her. She told me that night that getting rid of Rosemary would get rid of him, too, because he'd be in jail and that way

Molly and Amy would be friends again and we could all live in your house together, since it was half hers, too. I didn't want to help her, but she told me that if I didn't help, she would turn me in for selling drugs which, sorry to say, I have been doing because it's a very good way for me to earn money and I knew if your dad ever found out he would send me to jail. And so I did help her and I'm sorry and scared. I really wanted to go back home yesterday because Canada doesn't have the death penalty for murder like the US does. When you wouldn't come with me, I got so mad but I didn't mean to hit you, I really really didn't. Molly's coming over to see me in a little while. She says we should go to Canada together right now, tonight. I told her I would, but that is a lie. If I don't see you tonight, I hope you have a good life. I'm sorry for everything and I love you. You are the best thing that ever happened to me in my whole life. Dillon.

When I finished reading, I looked up to see Heather watching me closely. I couldn't speak, but I was saying a small prayer of gratitude to Dillon Middleton. Suicide is said to be the most selfish of acts, yet in writing this note he had clearly exonerated Heather. Yes, her heart was broken—just as Amy had said it would be—but Dillon had gone out of his way to lift the cloud of suspicion that would otherwise have settled around her.

"That's who he meant when he said 'we,'" Heather said. "He meant Molly and him."

I nodded. "And he was right," I said when I was once again capable of speech. "Molly Wright was an evil woman."

"I don't understand. Why did she hate my dad so?" Heather asked.

I remembered what Amy had said earlier, about how much Molly had liked being Amy's older sister and how much Amy hadn't appreciated being bossed around.

"Because she was jealous," I answered. "Because your father's a good man—a good husband and father. From Molly's point of view, it must have seemed as though her sister had everything Molly's own life was lacking. In some twisted way, she thought pushing your father out of the picture would somehow even the score."

Heather thought about that for a time. "Do you think she told Dillon the truth?" Heather asked finally. Her intense eyes were focused on my face. "When he stabbed her, do you think he had any idea that she was really his mother?"

"I don't know," I said. "She certainly hadn't told him when he wrote this, and the e-mail is time-dated at five twenty-nine. If she did tell him, it would have been later than this."

Heather reached for the paper, took it back, and then held it against her chest as if by holding tight to that precious piece of paper she could somehow reach across time and space and touch Dillon as well. "Will you have to give this to the detectives?"

"Yes," I said. "They'll need to have it—a copy of it, anyway. It's what they'll use to clear the two cases."

I thought about Heather in one of the interview rooms on the homicide floor at Seattle PD. Maybe the interview rooms in the new building weren't quite as grim as the gritty old ones in the Public Safety Building. Still, I didn't like to think about her being interviewed by detectives with Paul Kramer hanging around on the sidelines.

"I could call Mel Soames," I said. "She'd come over to talk to you."

"Right now?" Heather asked.

"If I asked her." I thought that was true, but I wasn't one hundred percent sure. Regardless, it was worth a try.

"I could just as well talk to her now," Heather said. "I won't be able to sleep."

"Go get out of those wet clothes, then," I said. "There's a robe and a pair of sweats in the guest room. I'll call Mel and see what she says."

And even though it was four o'clock in the morning as I dialed her number, and even though I again awakened her out of a sound sleep, Mel Soames didn't blow me out of the water. "I'll be there in half an hour," she said. "But on two hours of sleep, this better include breakfast."

I was snoozing in the recliner when the doorman called to let me know Mel was on her way up. I tapped on the guest-room door to summon Heather. Contrary to what she had said, she was sprawled across the bed, dead to the world. I eased the hard copy of Dillon's last e-mail out from under her hand and left her sleeping. Armed with a freshly poured cup of coffee, I opened the door and met Mel in the corridor before she had a chance to ring the bell.

Considering the hour and the time she'd had available to get up and dressed, Mel looked surprisingly well put together in a dove-gray suit and a cream-colored blouse. "It's going to be a long day," she said. "I decided to wear what I'm going to wear to Elvira Marchbank's funeral later on rather than having to run back and forth across the lake. By the way," she added, "you look like hell."

"Gee, thanks. This happens to be how I look when I don't get any sleep," I told her. "Obviously lack of sleep has no effect on you whatsoever."

"Is that a compliment?" she asked.

"I think so."

"Good. Now what's up?"

"Heather's asleep in the other room, but take a look at this."

I handed her Dillon's final e-mail. She read it with pursed lips. "Five twenty-nine," she mused. "That would be consistent with what we found out."

"Which is?"

"After we left Ron and Amy's, Brad and I went back over to Dillon's apartment on the back side of Queen Anne Hill. All we had to do was look in the window to know we'd found ourselves a crime scene. There was blood spatter everywhere. We immediately called it in to Seattle PD. Your friend Kramer—who's a complete jackass, by the way . . ."

"I know," I said. "I'm well aware of that."

". . . took his damned time about sending someone over. By the time he and his detectives showed up—search warrant in hand because ours was out of date—Brad and I had already located three different people who had heard the sounds of an altercation between a man and a woman coming from Dillon's apartment around six P.M."

"Heard it but didn't report it," I interjected.

Mel nodded. "That's right. Lots of student-style apartments around there, so maybe noisy arguments are a regular occurrence. When Kramer showed up and realized Brad and I were the ones on the scene, I thought he was going to have a coronary on the spot. He ordered us to leave. Ordered!" Mel repeated derisively. "On the grounds that we were operating outside our jurisdiction! Who the hell does he think he is?"

"He's someone who's used to throwing his weight around."

"In that case, Dillon's e-mail may sound good enough for us to believe Heather wasn't involved, and it's probably good enough for the prosecutor's office, but I doubt it'll convince Kramer. He knows that you and Ron are good friends, and he's going to go after this like a pit bull. All that means is we're going to have to find proof. Or Heather's attorney will."

I liked the fact that having met Paul Kramer only once or twice, Mel already had his number.

"Any ideas?" I asked.

"Brad picked up a bunch of security videotapes. There's a company

307

down in Olympia that owns several dozen convenience stores. We need to go through those. If Molly and Dillon both had cell phones, we need to check those out. If there were calls made during the time in question, we may be able to get a physical location."

Heather appeared at the end of the hallway. "You need Dillon's phone?" she asked. "If you do, I have it. One of the medics gave it to me when we were in the ambulance. He said it was in the way."

She turned and went back down the hallway. When she returned with the phone, she handed it over to me. The phone wasn't the least bit like mine. I had to put on my reading glasses in hopes of sorting out how it worked, but the phone was as dead as could be. I remembered then that Dillon had told Heather it had lost its charge. Until we found a cord that fit it, the phone would stay dead.

"I'm so sorry to hear about Dillon," Mel said to Heather. "Please accept my condolences."

Mel's words were uttered with such sincerity that Heather was taken aback. I don't think she had expected sympathy from Mel. Nothing she said discounted the supposed "puppy love" aspects of the loss Heather was feeling. Grief was grief, and Heather nodded gratefully. "Thank you," she said.

"I know you're going through a very difficult time," Mel continued, "and you may be too tired to go into any of this right now, but Beau asked me over so I could get a jump on the interview process. Lots of people and jurisdictions are involved in these cases. In order to close them, all the investigators are going to need answers to questions— answers that you alone may be able to provide."

"I know," Heather said.

"I'm hoping that, if we do a good enough job initially, you may not have to go through this ordeal over and over, but in order to make it official, I'll need to record it."

"Yes," Heather said. "I understand."

While Mel set up her recording equipment, I refreshed our coffees and brought some for Heather as well.

Because of my close association with the Peters family and with Heather in particular, I kept my mouth shut during the interview process. I couldn't have added anything. Mel asked her probing questions in a way that was firm but not at all patronizing. She asked about Molly and about Molly's relationship to Heather and to Dillon as well. She went over everything about the day of Rosemary's murder in minute detail, pulling out every smidgen of Heather's remembrance of that day and the days since.

I stuck with it for a long time, but I have to confess as we neared the two-hour mark and the third tape, I was fading. I had drifted off in the recliner when the phone awakened me.

"Sorry about this, Mr. Beaumont," Fred Tomkins said, "but I've got me three men down here in the lobby—three policemen—who say they need to come see you right away. I tried to tell 'em it was way too early for them to go up, but . . ."

I hadn't a doubt in the world that Kramer would be one of the three. "That's okay," I told Fred. "Send them up."

Mel looked at me questioningly. "Kramer?" she asked.

"The doorman didn't say, but he'd be my first guess. This should be interesting."

I opened the door as Kramer reached for the bell. "Imagine meeting you here," I said. "You're turning into a regular."

"I'm looking for a witness named Heather Peters," he said. "I understand she left Harborview Hospital with you last night."

"She's here," I said. "But she's busy at the moment. Mel Soames is in the process of interviewing her."

Kramer practically levitated off the floor. "I told that bitch last night. This is the city of Seattle. She's got no jurisdiction here, and neither do you. What happened last night was clearly inside the city limits. I demand that you turn her over to me immediately."

Calling Mel Soames a bitch didn't go over well with me, but I managed to keep my voice steady and my temper under control.

"You can demand until the cows come home, Kramer, but it's not going to do any good. What happened on Queen Anne Hill last night is tied in with the Rosemary Peters homicide in Tacoma last week. Because of the possibility that it was an officer-involved domestic-violence case, state law makes SHIT the lead investigative agency. I'm sure Mel Soames will be happy to share a transcript of the Heather Peters interview with you once it's available. She'll share any other information she's gathered as well, but in the meantime I'm afraid you'll have to wait."

"I don't want a transcript," Kramer growled. "And I don't want to wait. We want to talk to the girl now. As a friend of the family, you should know better than to have any involvement in the interview process. It's a clear conflict of interest."

"I'm not involved," I returned. "In fact, I haven't said a word. You'll be able to tell that as soon as you see the transcript."

Kramer's complexion had gone from red to purple. "You're interfering with my investigation, Beaumont, and I won't stand for it."

"And you're interfering with ours," I returned.

"I intend to lodge a formal complaint."

"Be my guest," I said. "I'm sure Ross Connors will be more than happy to discuss the situation with you on Monday once he gets to his office, but until then I'd say you're out of luck."

With that, I closed the door in Kramer's face. Slammed it is more likely. Had he ever had the good fortune to support himself by selling goods door-to-door, Captain Kramer might have had the foresight to stick his toe in the door. But he didn't. When I turned back into the room, Mel Soames was standing behind me in the hallway, grinning. Heather, on the other hand, was wide-eyed and ashen.

Mel went back over to her. "How are you?" she asked, trying to take Heather's focus off Kramer.

"Tired," Heather admitted.

"Hungry?"

"That, too, I guess."

"Well," Mel said, "that makes two of us, and since Beau here just had the time of his life tormenting poor Captain Kramer, I'm guessing he'll be more than happy to take us to breakfast. Right?"

She was right, of course. I had tormented Kramer for no other reason than the fact that I could. And I had enjoyed the hell out of it. "As soon as I know for sure they're gone," I said.

I called downstairs a few minutes later to be sure Kramer and the two detectives had taken themselves away. Heather had forgotten her coat—my old jacket—when she bolted out of the hospital waiting room. Once again, she left my apartment wearing another of my jackets, one that came almost to her knees.

The three of us had breakfast at the Five-Spot. I was grateful we didn't run into Marty Woodman. The old man had been kind enough to put me in touch with Wink Winkler. I didn't want to have to try to explain to him how that connection had resulted in Wink's death. As we finished breakfast, Amy came by to pick up Heather.

The girl looked up warily as the door swung open. Amy hurried into the room, scanning the restaurant before she caught sight of where we were sitting. She stopped next to her stepdaughter.

"Oh, Heather," Amy said. "I'm so, so sorry."

Heather leaped up and threw herself into Amy's arms. "Me, too," she said.

And it really didn't matter what they were sorry about—whether it was Dillon or Molly or Rosemary or all of the above. What mattered most was that they were together holding and comforting each other. The night before, Heather hadn't been ready to accept comfort from anyone, most especially from her family. But this morning, whatever stresses had been eating away at the fabric of Ron and Amy's family had melted into the background and were no longer strong enough to keep the family estranged. I could only hope that I had played some small part in making that happen.

"What now?" Mel asked me a few minutes later, after Amy and Heather had taken their leave. "Did you ever talk to Wink Winkler's son?"

The way she asked the question made me feel defensive. After all, I hadn't exactly been lying around on the job. I was also smart enough to realize that general crankiness is a natural outgrowth of being too tired.

"Ran out of time," I said.

"If you want to track him down this morning, I'd be glad to go along."

I really wanted to go back to Belltown Terrace and put in a few hours in the sack instead of the recliner, but manly pride wouldn't allow me to admit such a thing, not with Mel Soames, bright as a new penny, sitting there smiling at me.

"I don't have his address info," I said, more than half hoping that would dissuade her, but it didn't. Within seconds she pulled her phone out of her purse and was jotting down Bill Winkler's home address over on Magnolia as well as the corporate address for Emerald City Security on the far side of Boeing Field.

We drove to the address on Magnolia and found ourselves in front of a neat brick bungalow. A more than middle-aged woman answered the door. "Bill's not here," Mrs. William Winkler III told us in answer to our inquiry. "He doesn't usually go in to work on Saturdays, but today something came up."

"That would be at the Columbia City address?" Mel asked.

"Yes," Mrs. Winkler said. "It's an old warehouse. Not much to look at, but when it comes to rent, the price is right."

"Have you set a time for Wink's services?" I asked.

"There won't be any. Once the body is released, we'll have it cremated and then Bill will scatter the ashes. It's Bill's father, after all," she added after a pause, "so it's his decision."

We left the Winklers' house and returned to Mel's Beemer. I would have been happier being driven around in leather-interior luxury had it not been for Mel's unfortunate tendency to drive like a bat out of hell. No wonder she could make it from Bellevue to Belltown Terrace in nothing flat, but I know better than to backseat drive. I just held on for dear life and kept my mouth shut.

"She sounded a little defensive about the 'no services' bit," Mel said once we were inside the 740.

"We know Wink and his son have been estranged for years," I replied. "If you're pissed as hell at the guy, I don't suppose you're interested in forking over big bucks for a major send-off to plant him."

"No," Mel agreed, "I suppose not."

We wheeled across the Magnolia Bridge and through downtown Seattle at a speed that should have required flashing lights and sirens. Fortunately it was still early enough on Saturday morning that there wasn't a lot of traffic. I was glad when we turned off onto South Myrtle, a short street nestled between Boeing Field and the Duwamish Waterway.

Surrounded by a chain-link fence, Emerald City Security sat at the far end of the dead-end street. The gate was wide open. Two vehicles sat next to the run-down, grubby-looking building. One was a white van with the Emerald City logo prominently displayed on either side. The second one was an unmarked Crown Vic that screamed Seattle PD.

"Damn!" I muttered.

"What?"

"I'd be willing to bet money that Kramer's here," I said.

"Great," Mel replied. "The more the merrier."

She parked on the far side of the van. The back gates of the van were open. As we walked past the back bumper, we saw that the vehicle was loaded almost window-high with stacks of wood.

"Laminate flooring," Mel announced. "I'd call that a pretty high-class floor covering for a dump like this."

"Especially if you're renting," I said.

The front door was standing open to allow for the passage of an extension cord. A portable saw with a pile of damp sawdust next to it stood just outside. We were stepping up to the door when we heard the sound of voices.

"You've got no right to come charging in here like this without so much as a by-your-leave," someone was saying.

"I just came by to talk to you," Paul Kramer said. "I wanted to go over some phone records with you. I knocked, but you must not have heard—" He stopped. "Wait a minute. What's that?"

"What's what?"

"There on the floor."

"Paint," Bill Winkler answered. "Red paint. One of my guys spilled it earlier this week. I decided covering it over would be easier than cleaning it up."

"It doesn't look like paint to me," Kramer said. "It looks more like blood—a lot of it. I think you'd better come with me, Mr. Winkler. I'd say we have far more to discuss than phone records."

"Like hell!" Bill Winkler responded. I heard a dull thud—the kind of noise you hear on a football field when one player crashes into another, only I doubted anyone here was wearing protective padding. I looked at Mel. She was already reaching for her phone.

Inside, the sounds of a desperate struggle continued. We both had our backup weapons—lightweight Glocks that were fine up close but would be useless from a distance. That meant for our guns to be useful we had to be inside the building, but neither of us was wearing a vest. Mel's was probably in her trunk. Mine was at home.

"Go," she told me in an urgent whisper. "Once you're inside, you go left. I'll go right as soon as I'm off the phone."

I stepped through the door and into the warehouse just as a muffled gunshot ended the struggle. Only half the cavernous room was lit by the feeble glow of hanging fluorescent shop lights. Thankful for the dim lighting, I dodged forward between ranks of mostly empty metal shelving. Finally I was close enough that I could see the outline of a man standing still, breathing heavily, and looking down. I could also see the outline of the gun in his hand.

I caught a flash of movement off to my right as Mel Soames darted through the door and then disappeared behind a tall wooden counter. "Drop it!" she shouted. "We've got the place surrounded. Put down your weapon and get down on the floor, facedown."

Surrounded? I knew she was bluffing. Mel knew she was bluffing. All we could hope was that Bill Winkler had no idea.

But he must have. "Hell, no!" he exclaimed. With that he turned and set off at a dead run for the far side of the building, where only now I could see the outline of another door. He reached it, pulled it open, and then stood behind it, using it for cover as he sprayed the interior of the building with a barrage of automatic gunfire.

For a moment, after the door banged shut, I stood where I was.

"Kramer," I shouted. "It's Beaumont. Can you hear me? Are you all right?"

His response was more groan than anything else. "Go get him. Don't let him get away."

I turned and sprinted toward the door. Mel was there waiting. "Here," she said, and thrust a set of keys into my hand.

"They're from his van," she said. "I saw them and took them when I was making the call. Without your vest, we'll be better off in vehicles."

"Right," I said. And away we went.

CHAPTER 23

As we exited the building, the first of several squad cars came streaming through the gate. Those guys had weapons and vests and they were all a hell of a lot younger than either Mel or me. While the young Turks went sprinting off toward the back of the building, Mel and I hurried back inside, with Mel redialing 911 and calling for medics as we went.

We found Paul Kramer lying faceup on the concrete floor. He looked so pallid in the yellow-tinged glow of the fluorescent lights that at first I was afraid he was already dead, but when we reached him, he was still breathing.

"Thank God!" I exclaimed.

He had been wearing a vest. Unfortunately, a single bullet had sliced through the edge at the bottom of the vest and veered into his ample gut. He was doing his best to maintain some kind of pressure on the bloody wound, but he was losing it and slipping into unconsciousness. I moved his hand aside and put my own in place of his.

Kramer was a pain in the ass, but I had never wished him this kind of ill.

"Stay with me, Kramer," I ordered. "You son of a bitch, you'd better not give up and die on me now. What in blazes were you thinking coming here alone?"

His eyes blinked open briefly and then closed again. "Hurts," he murmured. "Hurts like hell."

Mel whipped off her dove-gray blazer and put it under his head. "Stay here," she told me. "I've got a blanket in my trunk." She took off like a shot.

"I'm sorry . . ." Kramer began.

"Forget about it," I said. "Don't talk. Save your strength. The ambulance will be here soon."

Mel returned a minute or so later carrying a plaid wool blanket which she unfolded and carefully placed over Kramer's body. His eyes blinked open again as he felt the weight of the blanket. "Catch him?" he mumbled.

"Not yet," Mel said. "They're looking. He evidently had a boat of some kind moored out back. He took off in that. The uniforms have called for more help—a helicopter, a police boat, and a canine unit. Don't worry. They'll find him."

A wailing siren announced the arrival of an aid car and soon a troop of EMTs jogged through the door.

"Over here," Mel shouted, standing up and waving. "We're over here."

Within seconds, the latex-gloved EMTs took over. Now that the crisis was out of my hands, I moved to one side, feeling surprisingly shaky.

"Are you all right?" Mel asked.

I nodded.

"You should probably go wash up," she said. "You're covered with blood. The rest room's right over there."

She was right. There was lots of blood. I went into the rest room and spent the better part of five minutes letting the soap and water sluice over my hands, but the blood didn't want to let go. The water in the bowl turned pink time after time. Even when I could no longer see it, I knew it was still there—on my hands and on my clothing. When I finally exited the rest room, Mel was waiting outside. Her dove-gray outfit and white blouse were as bloodstained as mine. Clearly we were a matched pair.

"That's what you get for wearing good clothes so early in the day," I told her. "You're a mess, too."

"According to my mother, I always was," she said.

I looked around the interior of the warehouse. The place was crawling with cops, in uniform and out, but the EMTs and Kramer were nowhere in sight.

"Where'd they take him? Harborview?"

Mel nodded. "I told Detective Monroe, the lead investigator, that's where we'd be going, too. I gave her our cell-phone numbers."

I remembered Sasha Monroe's first day in uniform. Now she was a lead investigator. Feeling old as the hills didn't improve my frame of mind.

"Let's go then," Mel said.

As we drove out through the gate, the neighborhood was parked full of patrol cars, but somehow Bill Winkler had given them the slip.

"What the hell was Kramer doing there alone?" I demanded.

Mel laughed. "Are you trying to tell me you've never done anything stupid?"

"Well . . ."

"We were pushing him," she said. "I'm sure he had access to the same phone records we have. The only difference is he went through them, and we haven't. He wanted to ace us out of solving the case. Once he figured out what was up, he didn't want to wait around until any of his guys showed up."

"And besides," I added, "he's invincible."

"Exactly," Mel agreed.

The two of us were already in the ICU waiting room—the same waiting room I'd occupied the night before—when Kramer's wife, Sally, and his daughter, Sue Ann, showed up. Sue Ann was fifteen and could have been a dead ringer for Heather Peters, except Sue Ann's hair was green.

When they first saw the blood on my clothing both Sally and her daughter flinched away from me. Once we'd all been introduced, though, Sally went off to see what she could learn about her husband's condition. I could see Mel watching Sue Ann as the two Kramer women walked away.

"That's one reason I never wanted to have kids," Mel said. "They always have to rebel against their parents. Her green hair must drive her father absolutely nuts. Think about it. If I'd ever had kids, they probably would have turned out to be Democrats."

"Would that have been so bad?" I asked.

Mel scowled at me. "Of course it would have been bad," she returned as though my question were too ignorant to answer. "Only a true independent could even think such a thing." And then, after a pause, she added, "I may have to give up on you after all."

Sally Kramer returned a few minutes later. "The doctors are resectioning his bowel, so it's going to take time. Detective Monroe called while we were on our way here and told us what you'd done. Thank you, Mr. Beaumont. Thank you so very much."

"It's Beau," I said. "And you're welcome."

Reassured that Kramer might make it, Mel was impatient to leave the hospital. "Since it's going to be a while before we hear any more, let's go home and change," she suggested. "I'll drop you off."

As we rode down in the elevator and walked through the lobby, people caught sight of the blood and slunk out of our way as though we were carriers of some dreadfully contagious disease.

"Are we still on for the funeral?" Mel asked when she pulled up and stopped in front of Belltown Terrace.

"We can go," I said, "but with everything else that's going on, we probably won't have a chance to talk to Raelene today. And I think I'm going to grab some shut-eye first. I'm dead on my feet."

"Me, too," Mel said. "I'll call you at one, and I'll be here to pick you up by one-thirty."

I was too damn exhausted to argue. "Fine," I said. "See you then."

"Whooey, Mr. Beaumont!" Jerome Grimes exclaimed as he opened the door to let me into the lobby. "If you don't look like you've been in a hell of a fight."

I was too tired to venture that old joke about how bad the other guy must look. I was glad none of my fellow residents rode with me in the elevator as I went upstairs. Once in my apartment, I undressed and stood in a hot shower for the better part of twenty minutes. After that I fell into bed.

Good to her word, Mel called me at the stroke of one. "I'm just now leaving my apartment," she said. "I'll be there in twenty minutes."

I didn't bother telling her to drive carefully. It wouldn't make any difference. I was waiting in the lobby, dressed but barely conscious, when she pulled up half an hour later. "Sorry it took so long," she said.

"For most people it is a thirty-minute drive," I pointed out.

Mel gave me a look, and we headed for Saint Mark's Cathedral. "Any word on Winkler?" she asked.

I shook my head. "He gave everybody the slip. When I last talked to Detective Monroe, she was still on the scene. They found Winkler's boat, but they haven't found him. They're still looking. Detective Monroe says the crime scene folks are there examining the blood spatter. Her guess is that's where Wink Winkler bit it. She also says it wasn't a suicide."

"His son pulled the trigger?"

"Presumably. Monroe wants us to get together with Kendall Jackson and Hank Ramsdahl after the funeral. I told her that would be fine."

Mel nodded. "What about Kramer?" she asked.

"Sally says he's finally out of surgery but not out of the woods. I told her we'd come by there later, too."

"Good."

The funeral was a long-drawn-out affair, but not nearly as crowded as I would have expected. Elvira Marchbank had evidently outlived most of her contemporaries. Tom and Raelene Landreth were there, sitting together in the front row. Tom had cleaned up reasonably well for the event, although, if you got close enough, you could tell he'd had at least a nip or two of Scotch to brace himself for the ordeal. Next to him, dressed in a black designer suit, Raelene looked genuinely bereft—far more so than she had appeared the day before, when I had spoken to her in her office.

A former governor, the head of the Seattle Symphony, and the director of the Seattle Opera all took to the podium to say how much of a difference Elvira and Albert Marchbank's financial support had made to the social fabric of the city. At least that's what I assume they said. I dozed through much of the ceremony and all of the music. I roused myself, though, when Tom Landreth strode to the microphone as the last of the speakers listed on the program.

"Thank you for coming," he said. "Elvira Marchbank has always been part of my life. As you have heard today, she was an elegant, charming, witty woman. She was also one who knew her own mind and insisted on having things done her way. She set out detailed instructions for her funeral. She chose the speakers and the music. She has asked that her remains be cremated and scattered in the waters of her beloved Puget Sound. Even though she has left us, I can assure you that, through the Marchbank Foundation, the contributions she and Albert have made over the years will continue in perpetuity.

"It was Elvira's wish that this day would end with a celebration of her life. So my wife, Raelene, and I would like you all to join us for food and refreshments at the Marchbank Foundation. It's exactly what Elvira would have wanted."

As people began to file out of the church, I wondered how different Elvira's funeral would have been had Sister Mary Katherine's murder allegations been made public. How many people would have been here, too, if Elvira had carried through on her stated intention to dissolve the Marchbank Foundation? Certainly the social movers and shakers had been in attendance out of respect for Elvira, but they were also there because they were looking for continuing financial support from those left in charge of the foundation—Tom and Raelene.

Mel and I were headed for her car when someone tugged at my sleeve. "Beau?"

I turned and was surprised to find Sister Mary Katherine and another nun standing behind me. The second woman was tiny, a good ten years older than Sister Mary Katherine. The somber occasion hadn't clouded the merry twinkle in Sister Mary Katherine's eyes.

"I'd like you to meet Sister Elizabeth," she said. "She's a good friend of mine. I believe I told you something about her, Beau. Before Sister Elizabeth took her vows, she was Maribeth Hogan. Many years ago she was my camp counselor."

I remembered the story well—about how a camp counselor had looked out for Bonnie Jean Dunleavy during the terrible hours, days, and weeks after her parents died in the car accident. Somehow it came as no surprise that Maribeth, like her younger charge, had also become a nun.

"Yes," I said. "I do remember. I'm glad to meet you." The grip of Sister Elizabeth's handshake was far stronger than I would have expected. "And this is a colleague of mine, Melissa Soames."

"Are you going to the reception?" Sister Mary Katherine asked.

I nodded. "Me, too," she continued. "For closure."

I wasn't at all sure I agreed that visiting the old murder scene one last time was necessary, but I kept my mouth shut. If Sister Mary Katherine and Freddy had decided closure was called for, who was I to argue the point?

"One more thing," Sister Mary Katherine added. "I heard the terrible news about Dillon Middleton as I was driving into town this morning. That young friend of yours, Heather—is she all right?"

"She's not all right now," I said. "But she will be eventually."

"Yes," Sister Mary Katherine said. "She will. I'll keep on praying for her. So will everyone at Saint Benedict's."

Mel, impatient with the delay, waited until we were in the car before she called me on my sin of omission. "Shouldn't you have told Sister Mary Katherine about what's going on with Bill Winkler and Captain Kramer?"

"No," I said, "I don't think so. This all started when Sister Mary Katherine went to see Elvira. She's already carrying around enough guilt. Why add more right now? She'll find out soon enough."

Mel and I weren't the first to arrive at Elvira Marchbank's post-funeral reception, nor were we the last. Sister Mary Katherine parked her minivan directly behind Mel's BMW. The four of us ambled up the walkway together. Tom Landreth, a potent drink in hand, stood at the doorway, personally and expansively welcoming arriving guests. I would have expected to find the Marchbank Foundation's executive director at the door as well, but Raelene Landreth was nowhere in evidence.

Uniformed servers greeted guests as well, taking coats or orders for drinks. Mel and I gratefully accepted cups of coffee. As I took the first sip, I caught sight of Sister Mary Katherine walking the perimeter of the room with her head bowed and hands clasped as though she were treading hallowed ground and finally having a chance to honor Mimi Marchbank, the murdered woman who had once been kind to an isolated child named Bonnie Jean Dunleavy.

The room was crowded. People were talking and laughing while a string quartet played in the background. It seemed more like a high-class cocktail party than it did a postfuneral reception. Having had nothing to eat since breakfast, I started in on a plate stacked high with hors d'oeuvres when, much to my surprise, Detectives Jackson and Ramsdahl came looking for me.

"What are you guys doing here?" I asked.

"Looking for Raelene Landreth," Jackson said grimly. "Somebody finally got a look at the phone records Kramer dug up. If calling each other twenty times a day is any indication, I'd say she and Bill Winkler are going at it hot and heavy. We're thinking she may have some idea of where he's disappeared to. She may even have picked him up when we were looking for him and brought him here. Now which one is she?"

"She was at the funeral," I told them, "but I haven't seen her since."

Mel had joined us in time to hear the news. "Whoa," she said. "That puts things in a whole new light. Hold on while I go ask Tom Landreth if he's seen his wife."

I watched while Mel wove her way through the crowd. When she spoke to Landreth, I could see he was somewhat befuddled. He looked around the room and shook his head in a dazed way. In other words, he didn't know where his wife was either.

Mel was coming back toward me when Sister Elizabeth appeared at my elbow. "Excuse me, Mr. Beaumont, but have you seen Sister Mary Katherine? We were about to leave when she said she wanted to go outside. Now I can't find her."

There are times in my life when I simply know things. The sudden sinking sensation I felt in the pit of my stomach told me this was one of these times. I had seen Sister Mary Katherine walking meditatively through the house. If she had stepped outside, I had a pretty good idea of where she might have gone—back to pay a final visit to her old hiding place, the secret hidey-hole that had once saved her life. The problem was, there was a good chance Bill Winkler might be hiding there right now.

"Come on," I said. "Let's go."

"Where?" Jackson demanded. "What's going on?"

There wasn't time to explain. I turned to Mel. "Are you wearing a vest?"

"After this morning, are you kidding? I wouldn't leave home without it."

And neither would I.

By the time I made my way through the crowd to the front door, I was having second thoughts. I already knew Bill Winkler was armed. There were far too many people here for the kind of confrontation that might well ensue. I stopped on the porch outside. The sun had come out, bringing with it a brilliantly blue sky. I think I would have been happier if it had been raining.

"We need more people," I said. Nodding, Detective Jackson reached for his phone. I turned to Sister Elizabeth, who had followed us out onto the porch. "I think whatever's going down will happen behind the house next door," I said. "Back there in the greenhouse. Until we know for sure, we have to keep everyone else inside. No one comes in or goes out. Can you do that?" Nodding, Sister Elizabeth stepped back inside.

"You think Bill Winkler's back there, too?" Mel asked.

"I'd bet money on it."

Detective Jackson was on his phone. As I spoke, he relayed everything I said to Dispatch. "You want all the neighboring streets cordoned off?" he asked at last.

"ASAP," I said. "These two houses share a common backyard. I'll go up between the houses and see what I can see. Kendall, you take the far end of this house. Hank, you go to the far end of the one next door."

"What about me?" Mel asked.

For half a second I was torn. On the one hand, I didn't want to do anything that would put Melissa Soames in any more danger than she already was. On the other hand, there wasn't anyone else I wanted watching my back. I had lobbied hard against having another partner, but it seemed God had given me one anyway.

"You're with me," I said.

Sticking close to the wall of the house where the Dunleavys had once lived—the house where Elvira Marchbank had died—Mel and I made our way up the shared driveway. When I could peek around the corner, I half expected to see the run-down building and the weedy backyard Sister Mary Katherine had described. Instead I saw a state-of-the-art greenhouse and a well-tended expanse of yard.

From the greenhouse came the sound of voices. I motioned for Mel to be still in hopes we could hear what was being said.

"I'm leaving now," Bill Winkler announced. "The only question is whether or not you're coming with me."

"I'm afraid," Raelene returned. "There are too many cops."

"And they all know that I shot a cop, too," Winkler replied. "Even if they haven't already, they'll figure out the rest of it soon enough. We've got to get out of here. Now."

As Winkler spoke, he and Raelene stepped out of the greenhouse.

There they are, I thought. *But where the hell is Sister Mary Katherine?*

The words had barely crossed my mind when Sister Mary Katherine appeared, stepping like an apparition out from a sheltered spot between the greenhouse and a towering laurel hedge.

"You won't get away," she said. "I know who you are." She turned on Bill Winkler and added, "When I first saw you, I thought I was seeing a ghost. But you're his son, aren't you—Detective Winkler's son. You look just like him."

"Who the hell are you?" Bill Winkler asked.

But Raelene knew the answer. "She's the nun I told you about," Raelene said. "She's the one who started all the trouble." I heard the note of rising hysteria in Raelene's voice. By then she must have realized that things were going terribly wrong.

I knew for sure that Bill Winkler had a weapon. But the automatic wasn't in his hand right then, and he and Raelene were so mesmerized by the unexpected appearance of Sister Mary Katherine that I knew this was our only chance.

"Come on," I whispered over my shoulder to Mel. "You go for Raelene; I'll take Winkler."

Adrenaline is a wonderful thing. I was never much good at distance, but I can sprint like hell when I have to. So can Mel, I came to discover. We burst out from behind the house, screaming like banshees. I hit Bill Winkler with a full-body tackle before his hand got anywhere near his pocket. We both fell backward, and the weight of our two bodies together was enough to shatter the glass in the greenhouse wall.

I heard the sound of falling glass tinkling around us. It seemed to be falling in slow motion, reflecting back the sun as though someone had thrown out an armload of diamonds. Somehow Winkler had managed to extract the automatic from his pocket as we fell, but when he hit the ground the impact of the fall popped the weapon out of his hand. It flew up in the air and landed a good ten feet away. Winkler hit the ground hard and was immediately out cold. Looking back, I could see Raelene and Mel still struggling on the wet ground.

Kendall Jackson arrived on the scene first. He grabbed me by the shoulder, dragged me off Winkler, and hauled me to my feet. "You're hurt," he said.

That was when I realized there was blood dripping down the side of my face and running into my eye. As I was unable to see, my first instinct was to use my sleeve to wipe it away.

"Don't," Jackson admonished. "There's glass everywhere. You'll get it in your eye."

Out of my other eye I saw Detective Ramsdahl pull Raelene to her feet and snap a pair of handcuffs on her. As soon as she could, Mel hurried over to me. "Damn," she said. "Come on. I'll take you to the hospital."

"Does anyone want this?" Sister Mary Katherine asked. I looked around in time to see that she was using her thumb and forefinger and gingerly holding Bill Winkler's weapon by the barrel.

"Isn't that how you're supposed to do it?" she asked. "So you don't wreck the fingerprints on the handle?"

Having just cuffed the unconscious Bill Winkler, Kendall Jackson reached for his pocket. "That's exactly right, lady," he said. "You hang on to that thing while I find an evidence bag."

CHAPTER 24

MEL WASN'T WILLING TO WAIT around for more cops or an ambulance. She took me to the emergency room herself—in a hell of a hurry. Instead of going to Harborview, she opted for the U. Dub hospital only a mile or so away.

People who arrive at ERs puking, bleeding, screaming, or all of the above tend to get treated faster than those who have invisible ailments or who are willing to suffer in silence. I was only bleeding, and what Mel did wasn't exactly screaming, but once she got the young resident's attention and he took a good look at her, he was suddenly far more interested in my plight. It turned out that Mel Soames was handy to have around for more than one reason.

She spent the next two and a half hours sitting beside my gurney in the ER while the doctor picked glass out of my face and hands. They had to shave half my head to sew up a jagged cut that went from my hairline to just over my ear. Mel teased me that eventually it would look just like Harry Potter's scar, only in the wrong place. Then she took me home.

As we rode up in the Belltown Terrace elevator I noticed the blood—my blood this time—that was spattered on both her blouse and blazer. The knees of her slacks were grimy with grass stains. "I can't take you anywhere nice," I said.

She gave me a rueful grin. "I told you I was messy."

The doc had given me something for the pain before we left the hospital. By the time we got to my condo, I was done for. When she began stripping off my clothes, I was too out of it to object. Once I was in bed, she closed the blinds, shut off the lights, and left me drifting off to sleep.

When I awakened, it was daylight. The clock beside the bed said 10:09, which meant I had been asleep for the better part of twelve hours. My head hurt, I was still feeling groggy, and I had to pee like a racehorse. A look in the mirror was nothing short of scary. Half my head had been shaved, the stitches were ugly as hell. My face and hands were pitted with dozens of cuts that hadn't been big enough to sew up.

Showering was a painful process. I remembered the doc telling me not to get my head wet, so I did the best I could. When it came time to towel off I found out there were plenty of tiny shards of glass that he hadn't managed to locate with his tweezers.

It was when I was coming out of my bathroom that I smelled coffee and heard the sound of voices. I stood at the door long enough to pick out Beverly Piedmont's voice as well as Mel's, chatting away quite happily. Realizing I had company, I went back to the closet and found something to wear.

"There he is," Beverly said cheerfully when I finally wandered down the hall and into the dining room. "Alive," she added, "but looking a little the worse for wear." Of course, since she was still in a wheelchair, I didn't figure Beverly had much room to talk.

I was astonished to discover that my living room was full of people, including Harry I. Ball and Ross Connors in addition to both my grandparents. Sister Mary Kathcrinc was there along with Sister Elizabeth and a third nun I'd never met before. What the hell were all these people doing here? They all had coffee cups and plates loaded with food. Couldn't they all do Sunday brunch somewhere else?

Mel Soames came in from the kitchen just then carrying the coffeepot and wearing the pair of sweats that I keep on hand in the guest bedroom, which meant that she'd evidently spent the night.

"They came over to check on you and see how you're feeling," she said.

I've always considered myself something of a loner, but with all these well-wishers crammed into my apartment, maybe it was time to change my attitude.

"How are you feeling?" Mel asked.

"I've felt better," I acknowledged.

"Coffee?"

When I nodded, she gave me a smile that went all the way to the bone. For some unaccountable reason Mel Soames was actually glad to see me. Maybe I was feeling slightly better.

"You could just as well have the rest of your head shaved," Beverly observed. "You look pretty silly going around half-and-half that way."

Mel filled a mug of coffee and put it on the table in front of me "Paul Kramer's going to be fine," she said, answering my next question before I had a chance to ask.

The doorbell rang. Lars hobbled over to the door. When he opened it, Ralph and Mary Ames walked in carrying an armload of flowers and a grocery bag full of bagels and cream cheese. Mel and Mary went off to the kitchen to arrange the flowers and food. Count on Ralph to remember that my cupboard would be bare when it came to entertaining a houseful of company. That's the thing about Ralph. He knew there wouldn't be enough food to go around, so he went right ahead and did something about it.

"I hear you've been throwing yourself through greenhouse walls," Ralph said. "Don't you know any better than that? By the way, Ron and Amy were just parking as we were coming up." He moved one of the dining-room chairs out of the way so Ron would be able to roll directly up to the table.

"I'll start another pot of coffee," Mel said from the kitchen. "We're running low again."

By then, despite my best efforts, I was starting to feel a bit grumpy. It was like I was hosting a party and had forgotten to invite myself. This time when Mel returned from the kitchen she brought a glass of water and a single white pill. "Take it," she said. "It'll help."

Ron and Amy showed up, and Ron looked every bit as bad as I felt, but he was too concerned about how I was feeling to pay much attention to his own difficulties. "How's Heather?" I asked.

"She's having a tough time of it," Ron said. "She's spending a lot of time with Dillon's dad. As far as I know, his mother still hasn't shown up."

I looked at Amy. "And your folks?" I asked.

She shook her head and didn't answer. I didn't blame her. She had been betrayed by her sister and then lost her sister. Only time would tell if the difficulties and strife Molly Wright had brought into Amy and Ron's home would ever be put right. Or be forgiven.

Ross Connors got up from a perch on the window seat. "Mr. and Mrs. Peters?" he asked. "Ross Connors. Please accept my sincere condolences on everything you've been through in the last week or so. I had people working the problem all last night. They managed to find some credit-card activity on Ms. Wright's account at a Tacoma area convenience mart shortly before Rosemary Peters was murdered. We picked up the market's security camera film early this morning. After reviewing it my people tell me that both Mr. Middleton and Ms. Wright show up on the video. They're driving your vehicle, but they're clearly the only ones there. No one else is with them."

"So Heather's in the clear, then?" Ron asked.

"Yes," Ross said. "I believe she is. That, combined with Dillon's last e-mail, make for pretty convincing evidence. I can't imagine any prosecutor in the state wanting to take it on."

Ron heaved a sigh of relief. Without a word, Amy reached over, took his hand, and held it.

"As for your Camry," Ross continued, taking out one of his business cards, "I realize that it's a somewhat specialized vehicle and that you can't just go out and rent a replacement. The crime lab isn't going to be done with it for a while. You should probably have your insurance agent contact me about arranging for a replacement."

Ron took the card. "All right," he said.

"I've spoken to your boss, by the way," Ross said. "Tony Freeman and I have agreed that you're free to return to work tomorrow morning, if you want to, that is. Of course, if you'd like to take more time off . . ."

"No," Ron said. "I'm happy to go back to work. It's been rough at our house lately. I think everyone there will be thrilled to have me back on some kind of normal schedule."

"I'll be going then," Ross said, heading for the door. "See you when you're up to it, Beau. And thanks for the coffee, Mel. Are you coming, Harry, or are you going to hang around here all day?"

Harry I. Ball and Lars Jenssen had been caught up in some deep conversation. Harry got up and lumbered after Ross, giving me a half-salute on the way by. "Try to stay out of trouble," he said.

Ralph came over and deposited a plate of bagels and cream cheese in front of me. Whatever pill Mel had given me was already working. My head felt fuzzy around the edges. My mouth was as dry as toast. I couldn't imagine being able to choke down a single bite of the bagel without it getting caught in my throat.

"No, thanks, Ralph," I said. "I'm not hungry."

"Well, then," he said. "I hope you don't mind if I help myself." And he did.

Ralph dived into his bagel with all the relish of someone who's never had to worry about his weight. "How long are you going to keep this up?" he asked finally.

"Keep what up?" I asked.

"Keep on working for a living."

"What would I do instead?"

"I understand your 928 is done for. Why don't you get yourself a new one? Fly across the pond and pick one up at the factory?"

"In Germany?" I asked.

"Stuttgart, I believe. I understand the factory tour is really terrific."

"How would I get the time off?" I asked.

"There you are," Ralph said. "And I rest my case. Quit. When are you going to finally get used to the idea that you don't have to work for a living?"

"I've been a cop all my life," I said. "I don't know anything else."

"Did I ever tell you about the Last Chance, that cold case organization one of my clients bankrolled?"

"Maybe," I said. "But I'm not sure." The pill was working overtime. I was getting fuzzier and fuzzier.

"I'll talk to you about it some other time," Ralph said. "But you're getting a little old to be putting people through glass walls—although, from what I understand, Bill Winkler is in a lot worse shape than you are. He whacked his head a good one on a solid concrete floor. Gave himself a pretty nasty concussion. And his girlfriend's in the slammer, by the way. She probably wishes she were the one in the hospital."

I tried to focus on what Raelene Landreth would look like in one of King County's signature orange jail jumpsuits, but I couldn't make the picture come together in my head.

"Sorry, Ralph," I said. "I don't know what's the matter with me. I think I'd better go back to bed."

And I did. I seem to remember that I needed help making it back down the hall and into the bed. Those pills were really something!

The next thing I knew it was 6.00 P.M. A whole day had disappeared on me, and I was starving. I went to my bedroom door and listened. Not a sound, so maybe the house was empty. This time I didn't bother getting dressed. I pulled on a robe and padded out to the living room. Enough illumination comes into my unit from downtown that I didn't bother turning on the lights. It wasn't until I was halfway across the room that I realized I wasn't alone. Mel Soames, wrapped in Beverly's afghan, was curled up in my recliner, sound asleep and snoring softly.

I sat down on the window seat and watched her. Most of the women I know regard my beloved recliner with disdain. Mel looked completely at home.

I don't know how long I sat like that. Suddenly she jerked awake. "How long have you been up?" she asked when she saw me. "What are you doing?"

"Watching you," I said. "Did anyone ever tell you that you snore?"

"You're not exactly blameless on that score," she said. "But I chalked it up to your meds. How long have you been sitting there?"

"A while," I said.

"Do you want something to eat?"

"I'm hungry enough I could probably tackle one of Ralph's dead bagels."

"That won't be necessary," Mel said. "When I went home to shower and change clothes, I brought you back some lentil soup from the Mediterranean Kitchen. That should be good for what ails you."

I followed her into the kitchen and stood out of the way while she heated the food in my microwave, put it in a soup plate, and handed it over. (Had I been left to my own devices, I would probably have heated it in the styrofoam container and eaten it from same. I think I had forgotten I actually owned soup plates.)

"Thank you," I said.

"I remembered how much you liked the soup the other night."

"Not just thank you for the soup," I said. "Thanks for everything."

"You're welcome," she said. "But if you're feeling better, maybe I should go so you can get some rest."

"Rest?" I repeated. "I've been resting all day. When I fell asleep I had a houseful of company. Where'd they all go?"

"Home," she said. "And that's where I should be, too."

"Stay for a little while," I urged. "At least long enough for me to finish my soup, which is delicious, by the way."

Mel sat down beside me and watched while I ate. It made me feel self-conscious. "You're not having any?" I asked.

"I already ate," she said.

So we sat there in silence for a while, but it didn't seem that uncomfortable. In fact, it felt fine. It made me think about what Beverly had said—about my finding a life and a mate and doing something besides work. I thought about how it had been the last week—sharing work and coffee and soup and hospital waiting rooms with Mel Soames. It had been nice, far nicer than I would have thought possible.

I finished my soup and pushed the plate away. "The last thing I remember was Ralph Ames saying something about my going to Germany to pick up a new Porsche at the factory," I continued.

"Sounds like fun," Mel said. "I've always wondered what it would be like to drive on the autobahn, where there's no such thing as a speed limit."

"You'd probably be good at it," I said. "Take to it like a duck to water."

"Maybe so," she said with a smile.

The depth of that smile made me feel all warm and fuzzy. At first I thought the pill might be kicking in again, but even at the time, though, I was smart enough to wonder if it wasn't something else altogether— something that had the potential for making my grandmother a very happy woman.

Anne Corley had been gone from my life for a long time. Mel Soames wasn't.